The Family Rites

From The House Rules Series

Calvin Naraghi

First Edition: October 2025

ISBN: 979-8-9915614-4-0 (ebook)
ISBN: 979-8-9915614-5-7 (paperback)

Cover design by *miblart*

Published by Cozy Manor Publishing

This one goes out to all the rule breakers.

Contents

Chapter 1

We'll Always Have the Summer

Is this what it feels like to die?

Lonnie's muscles grew rigid against the pull of the warping water. Goosebumps spread across his bare chest, inching their way down his arms and to his wrists. He wanted to yelp, but didn't for fear that the little heat he had left would escape with his breath.

I can do this, he thought.

He braced his legs as he took one step deeper, the water now up to his knees. Above him, the sun had begun to set beyond the trees, forming orange slivers that illuminated his face. He gaped at the flickering lights, begging them to warm his chilled bones, but they disappeared as fast as they arrived, leaving him alone.

"Just get in already!" a voice yelled from the water.

The noise pulled him back from the depths of his mind. Lonnie stood in the shallow edge of a tiny pond, which was hidden amidst a grove of Eastern Redbuds. At the center, a red blur was splashing about.

"Hannah, it's too cold," Lonnie groaned as he lowered himself waist-deep into the water.

"Don't be such a baby," she snorted, sending a splash toward him.

He shuddered, raising his arm to block it. "Just hold on."

A light breeze rattled the leaves on the nearby branches, sending a shiver down his spine. Lonnie tried to ignore it, instead pressing his hands over his head into a diving stance. Arching his back, he plunged beneath the surface. The initial shock coursed through him like an electric wire. Kicking his feet off the rock bed, he emerged from the pond.

"Oh, my God!" he screamed.

The weight of the water flattened his hair, momentarily blinding him. He swiped it up, revealing Hannah giggling a couple of feet away. He let the faint current draw him to her, drifting him closer until he was only a breath's distance away. She raised her hands to his face, then, without warning, pressed her lips to his, sending a surge of heat through his body. He closed his eyes, and the world outside faded away.

"See? You're fine." She smiled, wrapping her arms around his neck.

In a daze, Lonnie stared at her. His mouth dropped open, yet no words came out. All he could manage to do was curve the edges of his lips into a smile. They both giggled, leaning backward to float as the water rocked them in a gentle cradle.

Lonnie crept his fingers over Hannah's, letting their palms slide along one another. The cold no longer bothered him. His mind drifted as he watched May transition the purple spring flowers to green summer leaves. In the corner of his eye, he could make out the Dreyaird Academy clock tower peering over the canopy of trees.

Only a few more weeks.

He couldn't believe eight years had already passed since his parents sent him away. Eight years of living at this boarding school, pretending that it was all just a big mistake. That his parents would arrive one day to return him to his old life, and that his brother would be waiting alongside them.

Did they ever want me?

The words echoed inside his hollow chest.

The feeling whisked him back to the funeral and his brother's picture propped up in front of the crowd. He remembered it so vividly. The way the people looked at him and the smell of pity wafting from their gossiping breath. He was just a child... only ten, with parents who treated him as though he was a stranger. They even acted as if the death of his brother, their firstborn *son*, was nothing more than an inconvenience, like a splinter or a stubbed toe.

Did they want either of us?

Maybe the death was what they'd been waiting for. The older boy, done in by his own recklessness and partying, while the younger one was still small enough to pack up and ship away as far as possible. A clean house, a new start for them to reclaim their life and promenade with their rich friends.

At the end of the day, they left me. The reason wasn't important.

Lonnie listened to the birds singing by the water, their tones harmonizing, forming a gentle tune. It was heavenly and peaceful. He must have sat by this pond a thousand times, each time imagining the old creek that hid in the forest behind his parent's home. The one he and his brother Ben could just swim in for hours without a single care in the world.

Why have I never been swimming here before? Lonnie wondered as a calm sensation overtook him.

Really, though, he knew why. He turned his head to see Hannah floating beside him, her eyes watching the birds fluttering between the branches. She was just like Ben. For one, she was just as strong-willed. She also knew how to quiet that voice in Lonnie's head. Both of them could get him to run wild in a forest or even swim in a freezing pond without a reason. Things he would never even fathom doing by himself.

They floated a while longer before eventually stretching out on the nearby grass to bake in the sun. Their underwear remained stuck to their skin, making it difficult to warm up. Using his jacket as a towel, Lonnie wrapped it around Hannah and pulled her close. He felt their bodies thaw on contact.

"Are you excited to leave?" Lonnie eventually muttered so quietly that even he didn't know if the words existed outside his head.

"Leave where?" Hannah asked, her wet hair tethering itself around Lonnie's neck.

"You know... graduate."

"What, you mean you don't love it here?" she chuckled sarcastically, gesturing to the boarding school up the hill.

A surprising anger took over him as he thought about all his years spent locked away here.

"I can't wait to leave," he replied. "You can't tell me you don't feel the same."

Hannah went quiet, her body stiffening from beneath his grip. She leaned upright, planting her feet beneath her. "Honestly, if I could, I would never leave."

"What?" Lonnie stumbled to his feet, giving her a perplexed glare.

Hannah faced toward the pond, her voice tightening. "I guess I'm just not ready for everything to change. It's so peaceful here."

"*You* are not ready for change? Miss queen of forcing people to try new things?"

"This is different."

Lonnie was dumbfounded by Hannah's response. He had thought they had always shared this yearning to leave the school, but maybe it had only existed in his head.

No, we had to have talked about this before... right?

Lonnie's anger simmered, now replaced with doubt and confusion. Had he really been that blind to her feelings? It wasn't until he stared closer at her face that he realized what was really going on. Hidden deep in her eyes, he saw what was driving her words.

She's afraid to go.

Lonnie quickly softened his voice. "You're right, it is different. But don't think of this as a change. It's more like an evolution. Jamie, you, me... It's still us, just somewhere new, somewhere *better*."

"What makes you so sure it will be better?"

"Because this time, we chose to go." He looked at her and smiled. "Together."

Hannah faced him, her eyes glazed over. The fear was still there, but she gave him a weak smile and pulled him tightly into a hug.

"Hey, what's wrong?" Lonnie mumbled.

"I just want to stay in this moment forever," she whispered.

Lonnie exhaled lightly. "Okay, then we will stay here forever."

From the grass, Hannah's phone began to ring, but she

made no move to grab it. Around them, the forest grew silent as the sun reached its final descent across the horizon. Her phone continued ringing, enveloping them in its sound.

"Do you want me to grab that?" he asked curiously.

She didn't respond, her hands gripping his back tighter.

"Hannah?" he whispered.

Her grip went rigid, locking tightly around his rib cage.

"Hannah, stop that. What are you—"

He managed to slide his arms between them, prying himself from her iron hold. Though as he touched her stomach, he was shocked to find a sticky liquid covering his fingers.

"What the—"

It was at that moment he noticed the shard of a wine bottle hidden in her palm. The point was dripping blood, as was the center of her abdomen. Panic drowned him as the backdrop of the pond melted away, replaced with the interior of an empty ballroom. Looking down, he was now wearing a blue three-piece suit, and his red-stained jacket was wrapped over Hannah's bare body.

"No, please not here again!"

Like a switch, memories from the Blythornes' gala flooded his mind. First came images of the horrific gauntlet he had endured beneath that mansion, then followed by Hannah jabbing a broken glass into her gut. He remembered she had sacrificed herself so he could pass the trials, yet holding this dying girl in his arms was like losing her all over again. To his surprise, the bleeding had stopped, and her skin felt frozen. Light from the ceiling illuminated them, revealing her pretty face had suddenly decayed into a withering corpse. Lonnie gasped, nearly dropping her to the floor. The sound of her phone continued, growing louder. Each ring now drove through his skull like a nail gun, making him jerk with angst.

Removing one of his hands, he hesitantly reached down and picked up the phone. Touching the screen, he raised it to his ears. His heart pounded in his chest, as sweat and tears dripped down his face.

The line was static for a second, followed by a distinct monotone voice that crept through his ear.

"Good to hear from you, Leonard. Are you ready to come home?"

Chapter 2

A Room of Memories

August 17th, 2023

Two months after the events of the Blythorne gala.

Lonnie violently sprang up. "No!"

Thud.

His head smacked against the bed's backrest, forcing a whimper from his lips.

"Ow." He bit his tongue, hoping he hadn't been too loud.

Gripping the edges of his blanket, he tried to settle his beating heart. The bed cushioned his weight. Normally, it would be comfortable, but now it felt like it was consuming him in a quicksand of fabric.

Breathe.

The night still held the room in darkness, aside from the faint gleam of the moon, something he was growing unbearably familiar with. Lifting his finger, he lightly stroked a bandage wrapped around his forearm. The scar underneath peeked out, a constant reminder of what this summer had entailed.

As if I could ever forget.

Suddenly a pillow slapped him across the face and landed on his lap.

"Again?" an annoyed voice hissed from across the room.

Parallel to Lonnie, a twin bed rested against the opposing wall. Atop it, the silhouette of a curly-haired boy lay, his face barely showing in the moonlight.

With a groan, the boy switched on the lamp on his bedside table. The room came to life, banishing the darkness and revealing a small office space. Lonnie found himself staring face to face with his friend Jamie. A light summer breeze wafted into the room from a nearby window, helping ground Lonnie and remind him where he was. He took in the space, noticing the degrees and business certificates that hung over a busy desk and the various bookcases covering the walls around him.

He was back in Rhode Island at Jamie's parents' house. From his first year attending Dreyaird Academy, he'd spent every summer living with the Harkens. It was something that Mr. and Mrs. Harken insisted on doing, just because he was friends with their son and that he had no home to go to for summer break. They were kind people like that.

That first summer, they had given him his own actual bedroom, but when Jamie's sister was born the following year, they had to improvise. This new room had once been Mrs. Harken's office, and technically, it still was during the school year. On holidays, though, she gave it up so Lonnie would have a room all his own... at least that is until Jamie moved in with him. Another twin bed had been squeezed into the office this past summer at the boys' adamant request. They told Jamie's parents they just wanted to *test drive* sharing a small room before committing to the college dorm.

However, if they were being honest, the real reason was that they were too afraid to sleep alone. Ever since surviving that gala, sleep was often replaced with night terrors and long bouts of insomnia. It seemed like a better idea to stay in Lonnie's makeshift room on the opposite side of the house than in Jamie's, right beside his parents' and sister's.

Lonnie had a feeling the Harkens didn't buy their reason. One night, he overheard them talking about how they thought the two of them might be more than just friends. After that, he noticed them going out of their way to make not-so-subtle hints that they were supportive of their *special relationship*. Lonnie wanted to correct them, but that would mean telling them the actual truth, and he knew doing so was against the *rules*.

He remembered the mysterious men who had drugged him and dragged him from the driveway of the Blythornes' manor into an empty black van. The last thing he saw as the door shut was the corpses splayed out on the front stairs and the sunrise peeking over the trees. What followed happened so fast, but the main thing he was to remember was:

They can't kill you if you follow the rules.

So, Lonnie kept his mouth shut when it came to the Harkens.

Besides, even if I could, what would I say?

That after eight years of being shunned by his parents, they randomly decided to invite him home. Except it turned out that they had never actually missed him; they had only brought him back as an offering to their rich cult society. How would he explain the underground gauntlet they drugged and put him in during their gala, or the genetic experiments they did to those poor people?

The trials themselves almost seemed like something only a dream could imagine, yet Lonnie knew they had been real. He remembered every death so vividly: Mr. Blythorne, Mrs. Blythorne, his father, Mr. Gulligan—who saved his life with that pocket watch—and, of course, Hannah. Lonnie couldn't even tell the Harkens that she was dead; that she sacrificed herself to try to save him. Instead, he'd simply said that they broke up. It was easier and had less follow-up questions.

There were a lot of lies he had to use that summer.

One being that Jamie had impulsively chosen to visit him in New York, rather than having been kidnapped from this house as a part of the cult's trials. Or that Lonnie cut his visit home short because Jamie and he had gotten beaten and mugged in the city, rather than from attending a deranged party. That was also how they justified all the scratches and scars and why Jamie had gone from light and bubbly to so sad.

It was the perfect cover.

Lonnie hated how easy it was for him to lie to the Harkens' faces. It reminded him of his parents, which made him grow sick whenever he looked in the mirror and saw pieces of them staring back.

Jamie propped himself upright, the lamp light showing the bags creeping around his eyes.

Did I wake him, or did he never fall asleep?

"Sorry," Lonnie blurted.

"It's fine." Jamie huffed, rubbing the top of his nose. "Which one was it tonight?"

"The pond by Dreyaird."

Jamie grabbed another pillow from his bed, tucking it behind his back. "Was she there?"

"Yeah..." Lonnie mumbled.

"Do you want to talk about it?"

Lonnie thought about it for a second, the dream already slipping from his mind. "Not really."

"Thank God," Jamie said bluntly, flicking off the light. "Go to bed."

Lonnie was so taken aback that he laughed. "Dick."

In the quietness of the night, he could hear Jamie chuckle as he settled beneath his blankets. These kinds of interactions were one of the few things keeping Lonnie sane. If he was left alone long enough, he didn't know the kinds of places his mind would go.

"Goodnight," Lonnie whispered.

"Night."

Neither one of them actually went to sleep. They just sat there quietly for the next few hours, until the smell of bacon wafted under the door gap, pulling them from their trance. Lonnie peered at the sun now shining through the window. Jamie had blocked it by pulling his blanket over his face, giving him an eerie resemblance to corpses in hospital morgues.

"Last day," Lonnie added, trying to be uplifting.

Jamie replied with a huff, "Yippee..."

Pulling themselves to their feet, they tiptoed down the finished wood floor, passing cream-painted walls covered in peppy family photos. In the kitchen, Mr. Harken was cooking eggs and bacon on the stove, while Mrs. Harken was spreading butter on bagels that had just popped from the toaster. This was not an unusual sight. They had synchronization and effortless synergy, always whispering words and giggling like they knew all the world's secrets.

The boys grabbed a seat on either side of Jamie's seven-year-old sister, Harriet, who was jotting something down in her spiral notebook. A pink backpack with her name stitched on in bright red cursive sat on the counter in front of her.

"Morning, boys," Mr. Harken said, carrying the pan over to the table.

"Hey," Jamie murmured.

"Morning, Mr. Harken," Lonnie said.

"Good morning!" Harriet lisped, her tongue sputtering through a mouthful of missing teeth.

"Morning, peanut." Jamie knocked his knuckle on her notebook, making her laugh.

"Do you guys want coffee?" Mrs. Harken gestured to the French press on the counter.

"Yes!" the boys answered in unison.

"So, are we thrilled?" Mr. Harken raised the spatula, spilling the egg and bacon from the pan and onto each of the plates. "One more day. Then Hopkins."

"So thrilled," Jamie sarcastically responded.

Or at least Lonnie thought so. He genuinely couldn't tell if he was being serious or not, as his tone had become quite monotone these days.

"And you, Lonnie?" Mr. Harken added, setting down the plates.

"Yeah... I'm ready for a change." He picked at his eggs before catching himself. "Not that I don't love being here! Just that—"

"We know what you mean." Mrs. Harken smiled, placing cups of coffee in front of them and sitting down at the end of the table.

"Right," Lonnie muttered, scratching at the scar on his wrist and then picking up his mug.

Mr. Harken's expression shifted as he gazed at Lonnie's

arm. "Man, those men better hope they never run into me in an empty street. I swear I will make their lives hell!"

"I'm sure you would," Jamie joked.

Lonnie laughed, but felt a twinge of guilt. He hated himself for saying some random guys mugged them in an alleyway in New York, but there was no other way to justify their injuries. They'd arrived on the Harkens' doorstep the day after the party, covered in bruises and missing all their belongings.

None of this is right.

Lonnie noticed his graduation picture up on the kitchen fridge beside Jamie's. It made his stomach drop.

They deserve so much better.

The look on Mrs. Harken's face showed that she was not amused by this conversation of muggers and alleyways. Instead she steered back to talking about school and classes.

"Going to college is going to be so much fun. My gosh, Johns Hopkins is just beautiful and the teachers..." she droned on. "My sister went to a medical conference there a couple of months ago, and she said that those professors were some of the most established colleagues she has ever worked with."

I wonder if she met Mr. Blythorne when he worked there.

Lonnie began to spiral at the thought of his future professors.

Did they know what I did? Who I am?

Mr. Blythorne was a powerful man. Certainly, he had some colleagues who knew what had happened. Were they waiting for him? Angry that his actions got their friend killed?

I can't think about that right now.

"Hey Jamie, after you finish breakfast, can you walk Harriet to school?" Mrs. Harken asked with no hint of a question in her voice. "Your father and I have to meet a new client."

Lonnie watched Jamie continue to eat his bacon. He gave Jamie a slight kick under the table, forcing him to grunt in acknowledgment.

"Thank you." Mrs. Harken looked at Lonnie.

Mr. Harken patted Jamie and Lonnie on their shoulders. "You should see the view on this showing, boys. It's almost not fair how fast your mother is going to rope in these suckers."

"Stop it, Sam!" Mrs. Harken giggled. "But it's true. Harken and Casper Realtors will have them signing papers before they even reach the pool house."

Lonnie grinned back, which they took as an acknowledgment of their humor. But in truth, he was caught by what Mr. Harken had said.

Your mother.

As much as he desperately wished it was true, she wasn't his mother. And Mr. Harken wasn't his father. His actual parents weren't generous real estate agents who made breakfast together and took cute family portraits. They were monsters.

Lonnie thought back to that underground basement, his father's corpse lying on the hard tile, done in by those creatures that he helped create. He wondered if he did the right thing, helping his mother escape the same fate. Maybe she deserved to die with his father.

Maybe she was dead by now?

Lonnie had no way to know. Once they had all managed to escape the house that morning, she was picked up by a mysterious black van. And just like before, she'd abandoned him all over again.

Why did I expect anything else?

Lonnie peeked at Jamie, who continued eating, his head practically drooping over his eggs.

Was he okay?

But just then, Harriet jumped up from the table and swung her backpack over her shoulders.

"All done. I'm ready to go now!" She pushed her empty plate to the center of the table.

Jamie tilted his head toward Lonnie, his eyes awakening enough to give a sassy cock of his chin. Lonnie smirked, a bit relieved to see some life behind his friend's eyes. They each put their half-empty plates in the sink and followed the bouncing pink backpack to the door.

Harriet's school was just a twenty-minute walk, hidden on the other side of Brown University. Soon, they were dropping her off at her lavish little primary school with its brick walls and its grand front gate.

"Bye!" She waved as she took her teacher's hand and skipped her way up the steps.

"Bye," the boys responded, half-waving in return. Lonnie caught himself scratching at his bandage again from a irritating pain that he couldn't seem to shake. The boys bought coffee and took the long way back to the house, cutting alongside the river. Lonnie watched Jamie from the corner of his eye as his friend trailed slightly behind, always putting a person between him and the water's edge.

Jamie had been weird around water ever since briefly drowning in that trial. Lonnie had been too afraid to ask, but a part of him always wondered if he remembered how it felt. That moment when his body cried for air, growing heavier as it filled with water.

My gosh, we are so messed up.

"Do you think we are ever going to be normal?" Lonnie slowed his pace.

"When have you ever been normal?" Jamie deflected.

"Shut up, I'm serious," Lonnie snapped. "I keep hoping that going to college will help, but I think I'm just kidding myself."

Jamie glared in disgust at the river. "Nothing is going to fix this."

"And you're fine just accepting that?"

Jamie took a long sip of his coffee and stopped to face him. "The only thing I accept is that I died in that house. And sometimes, I wonder if I ever really came back to life."

Lonnie gave him a frightened stare as Jamie's solemn words tightened his throat. He waited for Jamie to say he was joking, but the expression in his eyes was dead.

I have been living with a corpse.

Chapter 3

A White Rabbit in Spring

McCoy Hall

Lonnie read the inscription atop the double doors of the Johns Hopkins brick dormitory. White accents covered the front, wrapping around windows and smooth columns that supported the header at the entrance.

"Here we are!" Mr. Harken announced, nestling the car into a tight spot on the street.

The boys looked out at the crowd of people invading the staircase before them. People carrying bins and moving boxes shuffled up and down the steps, creating traffic jams among the incoming freshmen and their parents. Lonnie felt overwhelmed by it all. Blankets had fallen onto the grass, parents were chewing out their children for over-packing, and a small group of people in blue T-shirts were walking around blowing whistles and trying to create some sense of order.

Why did I choose this?

Lonnie turned over to see Jamie's reaction, but instead found Harriet passed out in the center car seat, blocking his view.

Six hours of non-stop questions and talking, and now she decides to sleep?

Quietly, he snatched his backpack from the floor by his feet and opened the door. Mr. Harken had already popped the trunk and was helping the boys empty the contents out onto the asphalt. Compared to the other kids, Lonnie realized they had not brought very much stuff. Barely three medium-sized boxes between the two of them, and most of it was Jamie's, as Lonnie had left all his belongings at his parents' house and had no plans on returning to get them.

"All right, boys, are you going to be okay from here?" Mrs. Harken propped open her passenger door. "We don't want to rush off, but it's a long drive back."

"Yes, we'll be fine, Mom!" Jamie said rudely.

"I know, I know." She spread out her arms. "All right, give me a hug, you two. My boys!"

There it was again.

My boys.

It still didn't sit right with him. This wonderful woman tried so hard to make him feel a part of their family, and all it did was remind him how much he wasn't. Lonnie's therapist used to say his fear of letting the Harkens in stemmed from a fear of abandonment. Which might have been true, but after the events of the gala, he had uncovered a new reason. His real family was a disease, and he loved the Harkens too much to infect them like he had their son. He briefly let her pull him into a hug, then quickly stepped away. Mr. Harken walked around the car, giving them each a goofy handshake while Harriet waved like a drunk princess from the comfort of her backseat throne.

"Goodbye!" she yawned, twisting her hand in a royal fashion.

Mr. Harken hopped back in the driver's seat, and before long, they had disappeared up the street.

"Thank God," Jamie sighed, clearly relieved.

Balancing the boxes between their hands, they made their way to a check-in table with a sign displayed in front that read: **Welcome New Blue Jays!**

A guy in a bright blue shirt sat behind the table. A sticker on his chest printed out the words: **Hi, My Name Is JARROD!!**

"Hello, welcome, baby Blue Jays!" Jarrod cheered.

"Hi," the boys simultaneously replied.

Lonnie tried not to frown, but he didn't have the energy to talk to anyone this naturally caffeinated. After an awkward and unnecessarily long interaction, the boys gave their names, and Jarrod handed over their IDs and dorm keys.

"Have a good year!" Jarrod cheered as they entered the building and walked to the side of the stairs.

"Right," Jamie muttered, giving a cynical smile to Lonnie.

They both laughed at how idiotic it sounded.

Have a good year... A bit too late for that.

"What's the room number?" Lonnie asked, holding open the elevator door.

"Room 204A," Jamie read from the paper propped atop the box in his hands.

The elevator opened, spilling them out into a chaotic hallway of carts and people.

"Come on." Lonnie led, pulling out the building map Jarrod had handed him. "It should be on the east end."

"210, 209, 208... here. 204."

Lonnie fumbled to get the key into the door while balancing the box in his hands.

Click.

The latch finally unlocked. Pushing the door open, the boys entered into some kind of kitchen, if they could even call it that. There was a miniature countertop with a sink, a microwave, and a series of tiny overhead cabinets. The white walls were bare, but in a way that felt refreshing, like they were innocent and full of potential. On each of the four walls, there was a door. One door had a bathroom hidden behind it, another led back out into the hallway, and the final two were the dorms that had 204A and 204B printed on tiny hanging plaques.

"Aw man, we have to share this place?" Jamie blurted.

"I guess so." Lonnie suddenly felt quite nervous about sharing this suite with strangers.

Jamie set the boxes on the ground, taking one of the keys from Lonnie's full hands. "Here we are," he said, whilst unlocking their door.

The room was nothing exceptional. A small space with twin beds, desks, and armoires all displayed in pairs around the dorm. The same white paint covered the walls, and a blue carpet made up the floor.

It'll do just fine.

Lonnie plopped down on his unmade bed, throwing his bag and box of belongings onto the mattress beside him.

"Not horrible," Jamie huffed.

He paced around, sliding his finger across the desk. A layer of dust stuck to it, making him groan. Lonnie snickered, covering his mouth.

Buzz.

His phone vibrated in his pocket, momentarily distracting

him. Raising the screen, he saw an alert slide across the top. He showed it to Jamie. "Hey, our schedules just got posted."

Jamie swatted at the phone. "Yeah, I don't want to look at that, cause if I do, then I have to actually acknowledge that I picked all those horrible pre-med classes."

"Well, at least you picked something..." Lonnie whined, ripping the tape from the top of his box. "I still have no idea why I came here. I signed up for Intro to Ethics. I don't even know what that means."

"I imagine something ethical."

"Amazing deduction," Lonnie said, rolling his eyes.

Lonnie pulled out a few notebooks and then made his way to the desk. But as he went to place them down, he was shocked to find that it wasn't empty. Propped up on the edge of the desk was a mysterious green envelope.

His mouth went dry. Clutching his chest, he leaned against the desk, his legs unsteady.

It can't be.

"Relax. You have time to figure it out." Jamie jumped onto the bed, the springs squeaking below him.

Lonnie went quiet, setting his things on the desk. He gave his full attention to the envelope. Its exterior was a menacing shade of forest green that stood out from the white wall with blinding contrast. It was the exact same envelope that had appeared in his dorm room a few months prior. It was the key that had brought the Blythornes, and all the hell that came with them, into his life. And here, it was again, taunting him with a secret hidden inside that he knew could mean nothing good.

Please no.

With his hands shaking, Lonnie lifted it from the counter.

Flipping it around, his finger traced the symbol pressed into the wax seal. He recognized it instantly: a five-man monstrosity with bodies sewn at the spine as though they were made of fabric. The whole creature was printed in thick white ink, but he could only picture the detailed statue version that stood in the Blythornes' ballroom. He remembered all five of the so-called Gods vividly.

Avarice, the collector.

Penury, the giver.

Donor, the pure.

Glory and Honor, the warriors.

The memory of them was etched into his brain.

Glory and Honor, holding their tiny blades. Donor with his cut-out eyes. Avarice, the heavyset one, and Penury with his protruding ribs. Lonnie shivered as a chill ran down his neck. He could have sworn it felt as though someone was breathing right behind him. Or perhaps five people...

I'm just imagining things.

These Gods weren't real. They couldn't be. The Blythornes said that everyone involved in the trials would be given immeasurable wealth and grandeur. Lonnie and Jamie had waited all summer, but nothing happened. Their lives didn't get better. If anything, they got worse.

What if that's why we got another letter? What if we messed it up so bad that it didn't work?

Lonnie took another short breath, finding it impossible to inhale fully.

"Hey!" Jamie said in a serious tone. "What's wrong?"

Lonnie hadn't noticed, but tears were dripping down his cheeks. His hands shook, and he was sure his face had gone pale with fear.

"Talk to me." Jamie jumped from the bed and moved to stand beside him.

"No..." Lonnie muttered, slipping into his own world. Digging his nail under the fold, he ripped off the seal, revealing a letter hidden beneath. It read:

To Leonard Grambell & Jamie Harken,

Your presence is requested at the Blythorne Annual Anniversary Gala.

Date: June 14th, 2024

Time: 9 pm

Call (304) 227-3452 to confirm your attendance.

"What is that?" Jamie pried it from his hands and began to read.

Lonnie's fingers felt atrophied in place. He was frozen, glimpses of the last party passing through his mind like film stills. He could taste the roofied champagne on his tongue and hear the fireworks cracking outside the window like bombshells. He was slipping away, the dorm room disappearing around him, replaced with the interior of that grand ballroom.

I can't do it again.

Rage grew in him, breaking him from his paralysis. Snatching the letter back from Jamie, he ripped it to pieces.

"I'm not doing this again!" he screamed.

He shoved the torn pieces into the trash bin. "We're never stepping into that house again."

Jamie watched him with a horrified expression. "Do we have a choice?" he choked.

We can't live like this.

"We need to forget about that place," Lonnie blurted. "Forget it ever existed."

"Well, they clearly haven't forgotten about us!" Jamie's eyes darted around the room, as though looking for something.

"Why would they want us? We did what they asked. We killed Hannah..." Lonnie frowned. "It's not our fault that the ritual didn't make money materialize from thin air. They're delusional. I mean, did they really think that gold was going to rain from the sky? Or that magic Gods would grant their wishes?"

"It doesn't matter what they think. We can't just ignore them," Jamie responded frantically.

"I think we can. The letter was an invitation." Lonnie's voice rose, emboldened. "We aren't breaking the rules! That's what they said, right? They can't kill you if you follow the rules?"

"So, what are you saying?"

What am I saying...?

Lonnie stared out the window, trying not to scratch at the gnawing itch on his scar. Outside on the street, there were still plenty of cars dropping freshmen off. Most of them were smiling, introducing themselves to their neighbors and taking funny videos with their parents.

That should be us.

"We deserve to experience that."

"What?" Jamie shrieked. "What are you talking about?"

Lonnie pointed out the window. "We should get to be happy... like them."

"And just what? Pretend the letter never happened? That's a reckless idea."

"You're right." Lonnie turned to face him. "But consider the alternative."

Jamie looked at the ripped-up paper in the trash can, panic

still lingering behind his eyes. After a few moments, he reached into his moving box, shuffling around for what felt like minutes until he finally pulled out a tiny matchbox.

"Okay, then." Jamie nodded, striking a match. Holding the flame over the bin, he let it fall, catching the scraps on fire. "Like it never happened."

"Like it never happened," Lonnie repeated, a sense of stability returning to his wobbly legs.

Lonnie watched the fire burn out and excused himself to take a walk outside. By the time he made it to the quad, the emotions finally burst out of him. An ugly cry escaped his lips, and he did his best to hide it from the last of the arriving students. They all looked so happy and excited. Who was he kidding? He would never be one of them. He was broken.

Reaching into his pocket, he pulled out one of the scraps he'd held onto from the letter. Two striking words filled his sight:

Your attendance

Why do they want us back?

The uncertainty was eating at him. Was this punishment for all the deaths at the party? Or for trying to break the rules?

I wish Hannah was here.

It was supposed to be the three of us.

Chapter 4

New Kid on the Block

One week later.

Welcome to Intro to Ethics

The words were written in chalk on the blackboard, followed by another line that read: **Dr. Peterson.**

A man in a tweed vest and matching pants sat on the corner of the front desk, looking out at the inclined lecture hall. His mouth was moving, but Lonnie had zoned out and couldn't hear a thing. Thoughts of that letter had woven around every fold of his brain.

"What is ethics?" Dr. Peterson shouted at the class, briefly knocking Lonnie back to his senses.

A scrawny boy sitting a few rows behind him shot his hand into the air, drawing the attention of everyone in the 200-person class. The professor gestured toward him.

"Ethics is the idea of morality. Like deciding what is right and wrong." The guy pushed up his glasses, looking quite proud of his answer, but Lonnie turned to the teacher, who gave a light smile like the boy had said exactly what he hoped he would.

"And how do you define right and wrong?" Dr. Peterson followed up.

The boy looked at him for a second as though it were a joke. "Well, obviously, wrong would be what is illegal. Something that hurts others. And right would be what helps others, you know, and makes the world a better place."

The professor's smile grew, and he had a twinkle in his eyes. "Okay, let's analyze that definition. Every decision that we make is a choice, right?"

The class mumbled in agreement. Lonnie leaned in, drawn to the conversation.

Not every choice is our decision.

He pictured Hannah and Jamie each hidden behind those giant metal doors. The sound of rushing water drowning them inside, as that speaker voice kept telling him to choose which to save. Lonnie felt an itch running down his arm.

Dr. Peterson continued, pacing around the stage at the front of the room. "When we make choices, how do we determine that they are 'right' or 'wrong'? Say we are at war and my commanding officer tells me that if I don't attack those on the opposing side, then they will hurt my friends. I agree, right? I care about my friends. But now, am I doing something wrong because I am hurting others, or is it right because I tried to save my friends?"

That's ridiculous. That just hurts everyone.

Lonnie pictured all the party guests' bodies splayed out on the floor as those creatures ripped through their nice suits and dresses like they were made of paper. He held onto the edge of his seat, the itch now rising to the back of his neck.

Dr. Peterson stopped pacing, sitting down on the edge of his desk.

"What do you think?" The professor gestured back to the boy, who now looked completely lost. He chuckled, then continued talking. "The thing to know about ethics is that something is only wrong until those with power decide it is right..."A girl just in front of Lonnie suddenly raised her hand.

"Yes?"

"I don't think that's true. I think people will always know what is morally right. They just don't act on it out of fear."

No, they don't. People are idiots, and fear just makes them make bolder decisions.

Dr. Peterson beamed at her response. "That is an interesting point!" He turned to write something on the chalkboard. "And it leads us directly into our first lesson: Societal Ethics vs Moral Obligation."

Are you kidding me? No!

The images of dead bodies and those creatures racked his brain. People don't care about good morals. They care about getting ahead, no matter who its hurt. Those guests at the party were no different. They were never afraid of power. They were hungry for it. And they were willing to do whatever horrible thing it took to get it. That's what got them all killed. *People are monsters.*

Lonnie's blood was boiling, his skin vibrating so much, he thought he might phase through the floor.

"That's a horrible point!" He heard the words slip from his tongue, faster than he could shut his mouth.

Oh no.

Dr. Peterson paused his writing and turned, looking quite curious. Their eyes met, and Lonnie wanted to scream.

"How so?" the professor asked.

Lonnie gulped, his throat dry. "Morally right is a made-up

term. There is just wrong and worse. Everyone is just trying to pick the path that benefits them the most." He took a breath, trying to manage his tone. "People don't make decisions because they are afraid. They make them because they see an opportunity and they want it, no matter how many get hurt in the process."

"Well, that's quite an opinion." The professor nodded his head. "I look forward to seeing it grow this semester."

Lonnie slumped down in his seat, completely mortified by all the faces that were now watching him and whispering between one another. The girl from earlier shot him an intense glare, then returned to her notebook.

I'm such an idiot.

His outburst did alleviate his itch, but that only lasted a second as someone poked him in the back. Turning around, he looked up to find a girl staring at him with doe eyes. She had a pair of round glasses and did her makeup in a way that gave her a hipster goth appearance.

"That was quite a bold statement."

"I didn't mean to—"

"No, it was great. A very persuasive argument." She smiled, her cheeks turning a light shade of pink. "I'm Tara, by the way."

"Lonnie," he said, uncomfortably stretching his arm over the divide to shake hers.

In the process, his bandaged scar peeked out from the end of his sleeve, and he quickly yanked his hand back down, the itch following shortly after.

The girl studied him curiously, then whispered something to her friend, who sat beside her dressed in similar attire. After a few moments, she leaned forward again.

Oh God, they are going to ask about it.

"Are you a freshman?"

Huh?

Lonnie was caught off guard by the question. "Yeah... Why, is it obvious?"

"Honestly, no." She laughed quietly. "You look very young, but you don't seem young, you know."

The friend joined in. "Yeah, you have this vibe about you. Very deep and twisted."

Lonnie rubbed his eyes and chuckled uncomfortably. "Oh, I don't know. I guess I—"

"Yeah, you definitely have a story. I can tell." The friend wagged her finger.

"I really don't."

"We are going to grab lunch after class. You should join us," Tara said.

Lonnie stared at the two. Something about this interaction just felt wrong. Like when he *accidentally* ran into Hannah that day at Dreyaird Academy. How could he trust them?

Do they know about the trials?

He scratched at his wrist, unsure what to say. They were both looking at him, causing sweat to grow under his shirt.

"I'm sorry. I can't," he blurted. With that, Lonnie turned forward, pretending the two girls never existed.

You're fine.

Resting his hand on his chest, he inhaled. Flashes of that house hit him in bursts, each one making him flinch.

You're not there. You will never be there again.

He looked around the room, trying to let himself slip back into the lecture and ignore everyone around him. A fuzziness wrapped around his brain for the rest of class, making his vision blurred. Briefly, he thought he felt those girls staring at him, but he managed to fade that out too.

Great first day.

Forty minutes later, everyone stood up, alerting him that the class had finally come to an end. Gathering his bag and papers, he jumped to his feet, accidentally locking eyes with the teacher once more. They were kind and welcoming, which, for some reason, made Lonnie's outburst earlier feel even more embarrassing. Facing the floor, he rushed out of the lecture, speed walking until he managed to make it to his dorm.

The entire rest of the week had him on edge. Each day, he would manage to pull himself out of bed and bury his mind with lectures and studying. But no matter how much he tried, his thoughts always drifted back to that letter. Something in his gut told him that it wasn't over. But what could he do about it?

Lonnie had been so in his head that he barely had time to acknowledge that Jamie had completely vanished. Every night, Jamie had been out late, and every morning, he was gone before sunrise. If he even came home at all.

I hope he's okay.

Lonnie finally texted him that Friday morning, and they planned to meet for lunch. As Lonnie entered the crowded cafeteria, he slowly settled himself into the overwhelming churn of people and noise. He often tried to go at unpopular hours to avoid everyone, but this was one of the few times when they were both free. Jamie had already arrived and was sitting at the small, exposed table in the center of the room.

Why did he have to pick somewhere so open?

After paying, Lonnie grabbed a sandwich from the display

fridge and approached him hesitantly. As soon as Jamie saw him, he stood from his seat and gave him a hug.

"Hey," Jamie greeted warmly.

"Hi," Lonnie said playfully, trying to cover up his anxious tone. "How's your week been going?"

"Pretty good, I love my biology professor, but my math TA definitely has a stick up his ass." He laughed. "How about you?"

"Um, yeah?" Lonnie tilted his head in confusion at Jamie's new chipper attitude. "Yeah, it's been fine."

They both sat down and unwrapped their lunches.

"Oh good, I'm glad!" he smiled, in between bites of a burger.

What's wrong with him?

Jamie was acting, for lack of a better word, *normal*. He was so alert and spunky. The bags under his eyes even had disappeared, meaning he was finally sleeping through the night. But where was he sleeping?

Where is the corpse that I was living with all summer?

"Hey, are you okay?" Lonnie asked bluntly.

Jamie continued eating his food, looking up at him like he had just told a funny joke. "Of course, why wouldn't I be?" He laughed again.

Seriously?

"I haven't seen you at the dorm all week."

Jamie set down his food, staring at something in the distance. Lonnie followed his gaze, noticing a tall, lanky boy with studded ears and long hair sitting a few tables down. Jamie smirked, raising his eyebrows at him. The boy laughed and whispered something to his friend.

"Who is that?" Lonnie asked, trying to regain his attention.

"It's just a guy from my biology class." He blushed. "We have been hanging out a little."

"I see," Lonnie muttered. "Is that where you've been every night?"

"No." Jamie's smile slipped. "I also joined a few social clubs and the school play."

Are you kidding me?

That was so typical of him. Diving into extracurricular activities and friendships and random people to drown out the actual problems going on in his life. It was just like at Dreyaird. Whenever a guy would break up with him, he suddenly became so obsessed with whatever new hobby he was doing. Didn't matter what; photography, running 5ks, smoking weed, it was all the same. Just a distraction.

But this... this wasn't a break up or being dumped. This was kidnapping, torture, and death. Things too dark to simply bury. Lonnie would know. He'd been trying all week. Hell, he'd been trying all summer. He stared at his friend, unsure what to say.

"That's great!" Lonnie faked a smile. "I can't wait to watch it."

Jamie seemed satisfied by this response as he went back to eating his burger in bliss. Both the boys sat there in silence, eating their food. Lonnie wanted to scream at Jamie for abandoning him in his misery.

Why does he get to block out all this pain, while I have to relive it every single day?

It wasn't fair. None of it was. But what could he say? He'd told Jamie to forget the letters. To forget it all... and that's exactly what Jamie did.

I won't drag him back into this. I can't hurt him like that.

So instead, Lonnie made stupid conversation the rest of lunch and pretended everything was fun and great. And he would keep pretending, if that was what it took not to drive Jamie away.

I can't lose anyone else.

Chapter 5

Seasons Greetings

Three months later.

Snow in November covered the traces of autumn like a fresh coat of paint. Similarly, Lonnie hoped the new upbeat facade he was putting on was having the same effect. Ever since that lunch with Jamie in the cafeteria, he realized that if he didn't start pretending to be as happy and nonchalant as his friend, then he would lose him. It was exhausting, trying to be so upbeat when all he wanted was to curl up in a ball and be consumed by the darkness.

Johns Hopkins was supposed to change his life, but it was just another Dreyaird Academy. Same weather, same people, same life...

Different me, I suppose, but not for the better.

He impulsively walked his finger over his now healed scar, but slid his hand into his pocket as soon as he realized what he was doing.

Be normal.

Lonnie strolled in pace with a group of people he somehow started calling his friends. How he made them, he had no idea.

They were simply people in a book club he attended from a ripped flier he found on a bulletin board. People he found he had a lot of stuff in common with, if you didn't count fighting evil cults and sociopathic families. No, the things he shared with his new friends were more along the lines of favorite authors and a general hatred for most of the population. They made him smile. When he was with them, he didn't have to pretend to put on a happy face; it just came naturally.

As they passed the dorms, Lonnie broke off, heading toward the front door.

"I'll see you guys later." Lonnie waved to his friends as he slipped through the dormitory entrance.

"Bye!" they chirped at him and then continued their conversation.

He unlocked his dorm room and flung his bag to the side before collapsing onto the bed. He smiled at the warm blanket forming a nest beneath him, but he found he couldn't settle in. An off sensation climbed up his spine, clicking against each vertebra until eventually reaching his throat. He waited, expecting some creature to dispel from his mouth, but nothing happened. The feeling just lingered on the tip of his tongue. Restless, Lonnie shifted onto his side, where he found himself face to face with his desk. Immediately he realized what he was feeling.

Fear.

Propped up on the table, just as another had been all those months ago, was a forest green envelope.

"No!"

Sitting up, he snatched the letter from the desk and, with a jagged rip, pulled it from the envelope. He read it to himself.

To Leonard Grambell & Jamie Harken,

Your presence is requested at the Blythorne Annual Anniversary Gala.
Date: June 14th, 2024
Time: 9 pm
Call (304) 227-3452 to confirm your attendance.

The invitation was practically the same as before, down to the font. The only difference was that something else was lodged in the envelope. He shook it, and a small picture floated down into his hand. The sight sucked the blood from his body.

The picture was of a small girl playing in a sandbox. She was smiling, showing off gaps where a few teeth had fallen out. Lying beside her in the sand was a bright pink backpack with red stitching on the front that read: *Harriet*.

No, not her.

Perspiration grew on his face, accompanied by a sloshing feeling of liquid in his stomach. This time, he couldn't hold down that rising sickness. He rushed over to the trashcan and hurled.

Beep.

Oh no.

Behind him, the door's lock clicked open. In a panic, Lonnie jammed the contents of the letter under his bed.

"What's that smell?" Jamie grabbed his nose in disgust as he entered the room. Upon spotting Lonnie hunched over the trashcan, his tone shifted. "Hey, are you okay?"

Oh God, what do I tell him?

"Food poisoning." The words toppled from his mouth, his mind unable to think of a better excuse. "I think... from the fish at lunch."

Jamie set his bag on the bed and bent down to take a closer look at Lonnie.

"Dang, I'm sorry. Do you need anything?"

I need you to leave.

"Can you get me some Gatorade? Something with elec-trolytes."

Jamie nodded and winked before bolting back out the door. Lonnie waited for it to completely shut and then leaned back against the bed frame.

This needs to end.

Reaching his hand under the bed, he snatched the letter, pulling it up to the light so he could read the number: *(304) 227-3452.*

He peeked at the door, half-expecting Jamie to rush back in at any second. Seeing that the coast was clear, he typed it into his phone and gritted his teeth as it rang.

Ring.

Ring

Then finally...

Click.

A surreal quietness blanketed him. He tapped his finger on the phone case, waiting impatiently for someone to speak.

"He–hello?" he stuttered.

Just do it.

He slowly exhaled, then spoke, enunciating every word. "We regretfully decline your invitation, thank you."

No response.

"Did you hear me?"

The silence was now deafening.

"Ow," he squealed.

A sharp pain pinched his wrist, and he realized he was picking at his scar again. He slid it under his butt, holding it in place as he waited impatiently for something, anything to happen.

Beep.

"Hello?"

He looked at his screen and saw that the call had dropped.

***

The next morning.

Lonnie sipped his coffee while watching Jamie from across the table. They were sat in the corner of the room, nestled into the shadows, though it didn't really matter. The cafeteria was nearly empty, which was ideal. He imagined everyone was still recovering from hangovers after going out drinking after the game last night.

Normal college activities.

Jamie hadn't said a word for a few minutes, which was worrying. He was just sitting there, staring at the contents of the envelope Lonnie had slid across the table upon sitting down. His eyes just kept rotating back and forth between scanning the words on the letter and staring deeply at the photograph of his little sister.

"You called them without me?" he finally mumbled.

Lonnie stared at the table in shame. "I declined the invitation."

"And?"

"They hung up."

"Did you call again?"

"It just goes straight to voicemail. Every time."

Jamie went silent again, staring closer at the picture in his hand. "This sandbox is inside her school."

"Yeah, I figured, but—"

"No, you don't understand. You can't see it from the street. It's only visible if you're *inside* the school." His eyes grew wide and glossy. "Someone went in and took this picture! Can't you see? This isn't an invitation. We don't have a choice!"

The chirpy illusion Jamie had been hiding behind this past month had cracked. First with a flicker of fear lighting up his eyes, and then followed by a worry line crinkling his forehead. It was heartbreaking, like watching someone relive a tragedy. Lonnie could see when the memories Jamie had worked so hard to block out suddenly flooded back into his mind.

He grew red, jostling in his seat. It was like his body was telling him to run, but where could he go to escape his own thoughts. For once, he couldn't live in denial, or hide himself behind partying and hookups and extracurriculars. The past had come back, and this time there would be no turning a blind eye.

He stared at Lonnie. Tears now dripping down his face as he struggled to hold himself together. "I don't know what to do. If they do anything to her, I—"

"I know."

Jamie leaned in closer, his lip quivering. "No, Lonnie, I couldn't live with myself if they did anything…"

He stopped himself, unable to finish the sentence. Instead, Jamie pressed the letter against his forehead in defeat.

Lonnie looked around the cafeteria, at the four students sitting nearby. Each was in their own world, eating waffles drenched in syrup and berries and typing away on laptops. They looked so boring and insignificant, their lives moving like molasses. He sighed, realizing now that what he feared most was true.

I can never be like them. My parents took that from me.

As much as he tried to pretend it didn't, that house had changed something in him. The real world had become mute compared to the one that hid behind the curtains. How could he sit around and listen to lectures on philosophy or read in book clubs while these monsters were out there doing whatever they wanted to whoever they pleased?

It didn't matter if he actually went back to that house or not, because in reality, he'd never left. Every second since he stepped down those blood-soaked marble steps, he had been looking over his shoulder. And that was going to be the case for the rest of his life.

So why are we hiding?

"We won't let anything happen to her," Lonnie stated boldly.

"How?" Jamie sniffled.

He exhaled as he imagined walking back through that manor's doors. All he could picture was the blood and bodies that he'd left in its halls. Dozens of guests, the creatures, the hosts... all dead. Yet, as the invitation stated, the party went on. People clearly weren't needed to keep it alive. It was much bigger than that.

No.

That five-headed statue crossed his mind, its jarring faces screaming for attention in the ballroom.

It relied on faith.

Lonnie smirked, an inkling of a plan forming in his mind.

"For now, we wait for them to send another letter."

"But what if they don't—"

"They will, trust me." His voice didn't waver. "And when they do, we'll be ready."

"Ready for what?"

Lonnie opened his mouth to speak, then stopped himself. Doubt flickered on his face as he imagined tiny security cameras hidden all around him. Setting his coffee down, Lonnie leaned over the table and whispered sharply, "To burn that house to the ground."

Six months later.

Tension lingered in the air as another month passed without receiving a letter. Lonnie was so sure he was right about them reaching out, but his confidence in the plan had begun to dwindle. Especially when the date on the invitation was now only a couple weeks away.

Maybe they really did accept our declined RSVP.

Which, if he was honest, gave him a bit of relief. Jamie, on the other hand, reacted the opposite. He had become obsessed with calling his parents, each time asking to speak to Harriet. And each time, he held his breath until she picked up the phone. He was losing it, holding himself together by spending every waking thought focused on their plan. However, even that was coming up short. The past few months had been a series of long nights at the library spent researching cults and rituals, as well as consuming terabytes of data on untraceable school computers. But no matter how much they tried, they could never find quite what they were looking for.

Lonnie couldn't believe it. He must have browsed through every theology textbook and religious body of work in the school's database, and he'd come up completely empty. There wasn't a single mention of any Gods of Grandeur or ritual commandments like the ten he had seen hung up within the manor. Jamie even managed to get access to the dark web, but that was still not enough. They looked for images of that five-headed statue and even inscriptions from the society's ritual book, but each time the results would come back blank.

How could the cult members hide it so well?

Were they truly so powerful that they could completely scrub it from the face of the Earth? The whole thing gave Lonnie goosebumps.

If they can erase a whole religion, how well could they erase me?

He shivered at the thought, but tried to stay focused on his work. While their research on *the House* and its history had come up short, Lonnie was feeling rather confident about his newfound understanding of cults.

Everyone in a cult has a purpose, and everyone serves a need.

'Everyone' was the word that had him thinking. He remembered Hannah mentioning something about all the members that hadn't been in attendance at last year's party. CEOs, politicians, even her parents.

Why weren't they required to come? What made them special?

The more he remembered the rules they set, the more he wondered about the solidity they held. Especially those ten commandments they had displayed so proudly on a plaque on their wall. Lonnie ran his finger over the notebook on his bedroom desk. The ten rules were written out in his chicken scratch, to the best he could remember.

1. A champion must be related to a current member.
2. Must do trials of mind, heart, and body.

3. Everyone who puts blood into the bowl will get rewarded.

4. The ritual is a maximum of 8 hours long.

5. The champion can be any age and any gender.

6. A loved one must die.

7. A champion cannot take their own life.

8. You die in the ritual, and everyone gets nothing.

9. Someone must die during every ritual.

10. Bad things happen if the ritual fails.

Over a hundred *special* guests were present at the last ritual, and yet his family has been forced to offer up his brother and then himself with less than a decade apart. What made them so unfortunate as to fast-track the line? And why did others get to skip it entirely? The more he thought about the pieces, the more the puzzle as a whole began to make less sense.

Their belief system is weak.

That idea gave Lonnie hope. If it had a bad foundation, all it would take was a hard enough push in just the right spot. But he was getting ahead of himself. First things first, he had to get re-invited to the party.

Where was that invitation?

He looked up from his desk to see Jamie splayed out on his bed with a new textbook he had found at the local library. It was something about the history of cults in southern America, though he clearly wasn't reading it. He was just tapping a pen to his knee, making a nervous rhythm whilst staring blankly at the text.

Lonnie tried to go back to his own books when he heard a loud thud hit the floor. He looked behind him to find the textbook now wrapped around the leg of the armoire. Jamie let out a rageful howl.

What the hell?

"I can't take this anymore. I can't read any more books." His face grew red. "I'm going insane!"

"Hey, relax, just go take a break outside—"

"Don't tell me what to do!" Jamie grew more flustered, this time tossing his pen at Lonnie's head. "You said they would have sent it by now. You were wrong. Admit it."

"There are still a couple of weeks left." Lonnie got up from the desk, carefully putting the chair between them. He kept his eyes on Jamie's hands, in case he found anything else to lob at his head.

"You declined the invitation, and now they are going to do God knows what to my sister. What if they kill her or worse, decide to put her in *there*?" Even saying it out loud made his forehead wrinkle.

"They aren't going to do anything to your sister. They don't need her, they just want to scare us!"

Jamie jumped off the bed. Pulling the chair aside, he got in Lonnie's face. He was volatile, a firework just waiting for something to light his fuse.

"Scare us? Or you mean me? 'Cause last time I checked, they only threatened my family," he spat. "But I guess that doesn't seem to bother you, cause you don't have any family for them to take."

"You think I don't care? I've known Harriet just as long as you. I love her!"

He laughed, rubbing the bridge of his nose. "Oh my gosh. That's not the same thing! She is *my* sister. And unlike you, I'm not going to just let my sibling die for me."

"You son of a bitch!"

A rush of adrenaline hit Lonnie out of nowhere, making his

skin crawl. He charged forward, slamming his shoulders into Jamie's ribs and driving him back against the bedpost. The boys sparred, their bodies flailing around the room, knocking objects into the air. Textbooks fell to the floor, but not before being used as blunt objects. Both boys were sweating, scrapes and bruises blossoming across their arms. The stress they'd been bottling up the past eleven months had finally popped.

Knock.

A light rattle came from their bedroom door, catching them off guard.

Was it our other roommates?

"Go away!" Jamie snarled.

"Come back later!" Lonnie spat.

The knocking grew louder..

Thud. Thud. Thud.

What if it was campus security responding to a noise complaint?

Lonnie had started the fight with the upper hand, but Jamie had managed to take control, pinning him flat on the ground. His knee now pressed down onto Lonnie's chest as he held his arms flat against the floor. Papers had been knocked from the desk, covering them and the floor in a blizzard of white.

Thud. Thud. Thud.

This time, each knock hit the door like a battering ram, shaking both the boys from their state.

They're relentless.

Jamie groaned, rolling off of Lonnie. He looked at the door, the rage in his eyes switching to a fearful curiosity. He stood up, reaching for the handle as Lonnie lay on the floor behind him, now struggling to catch his breath without the pressure of a knee resting on his lungs.

"They better have a good reason for this," Jamie huffed. He grabbed the handle and swung the door open in one swift motion. "What do you want!?"

Immediately, Jamie went quiet. Lonnie pulled himself up to his butt, leaning his back against the bed frame. "What is it?"

No answer. The back of Jamie's body appeared tense as he moved out into the kitchen area of the apartment.

"Who the hell?" Jamie circled back, standing in the doorway. "There's nobody here."

But just as he took another step into the doorway, the sound of paper crumpling came from below his foot. The boys looked down, and there, resting on the floor, was a green envelope with a black wax seal.

They exchanged a glance, a look of shock and bittersweet relief plastered on both of their faces. As Jamie picked up the letter, he reached into his pocket and pulled out his phone. His fingers then typed the phone number both boys had memorized by heart. He clicked call and listened as the previous instant voicemail changed to a dial.

Here we go.

Three weeks later.

Lonnie waited atop the Johns Hopkins sign, his feet dangling off the edge.

He sighed as the summer heat pressed in. He didn't feel like celebrating the school year ending. If anything, it was his only line of defense against what was to come.

I can't believe we are doing this.

A black Lexus pulled around the corner of the street.

Lonnie hopped down from the sign and approached the car apprehensively. In his pocket, he could feel the imprint of a new letter they had received just three days prior shifting with each step. This one was different than the others, a horrific twist that he should have seen coming. He pulled it out to read, this time hoping somehow that the words had magically changed.

Dear Leonard Grambell and Jamie Harken,

We are honored by your attendance at this year's annual gala. However, before an official welcome can be made, we must ask of you a favor. At the bottom of the envelope, we have included a picture of this year's guest of honor. Please make sure he has a wonderful night.

We know you won't disappoint!

Deeper into the envelope, he pulled out a picture of an older-looking muscular boy and a blister pack of white pills.

A swishing liquid rose in his gut, but he pushed it down.

Ignore it.

The car came to a stop. As the passenger window rolled down, Lonnie saw Jamie hunkered into the driver's seat. He looked duller. The beautiful man he once was had been replaced by this shadow. The features looked the same, but the glow had all but drained from his skin.

"Hey," Jamie said bleakly, unlocking the passenger door.

"You ready for this?" Lonnie asked.

"Nope."

Right. Stupid question.

Chapter 6

Bittersweet Reunions

Day turned to night as they approached the edge of the Catskills.

Here we go.

The car slid through a partition of trees whose branches beckoned them in as though they were old friends.

I'm gonna be sick.

He turned to Jamie, whose face remained as stoic as it had the last five hours.

What was he thinking?

Barely a word had been said for the entire road trip. Hell, more like for the majority of the last two weeks. Ever since their fight, some invisible force had filled the air between them. Part of it came from a shared fear of what was to happen tonight, but Lonnie could sense there was another layer to it.

He blames me. And maybe he is right too.

Lonnie couldn't help but feel that he was the reason for all this heartache. And as much as Jamie's hurtful words had made his blood boil, he couldn't deny they were true. Harriet wasn't Lonnie's family, because he had none... His mere existence had destroyed his family, killed his brother, and broke his mother. How could Jamie not look at him with disgust and blame at the horrific world he had drawn him into?

What am I going to do?

Their plan was already unraveling at the seams, and they hadn't even made it into the building. And on top of that, what about the new letter? Lonnie pulled out the photograph, staring at a young muscular man with bleached blond hair. Twisting the photo in his hand, he read the cursive writing hidden on the back:

Place one in his drink. That's all it takes.

Decision is yours.

Him or her.

Decision is yours.

That line made him want to gag. Mr. Blythorne had said the same phrase only a year prior.

Jamie on the left. Hannah on the right. Decision is yours.

Who would he save, and who would he sacrifice? The choice once again had fallen into Lonnie's lap. Sacrifice the stranger or sacrifice Harriet. The decision should be obvious. And yet, he was conflicted.

He doesn't deserve this fate any more than I did.

When Jamie saw the letter, he'd said, "I have to save my sister. It has to be him."

He'd said it so instantly and without bother. As though it were a fact. Lonnie found his response haunting, yet *he* was right. If they were to complete the plan, they needed to earn the trust of the society. But they weren't talking about just playing along and wearing costumes. This was sacrificing someone's life. Lonnie told Jamie he would do what had to be done, but even he didn't know if he truly believed it.

Rogue bits of light blasted through the car's windshield, and he saw the familiar explosion of fireworks in the distance. The sight alone gave him a headache.

"There!" He pointed at the building in the distance.

We're here.

Jamie pulled the car through the bend of trees and the fancy gates and eventually made it to a long stretch of driveway. Expensive cars lined the front yard, continuing down their private street with no end in sight. While Lonnie expected Jamie to start going down the row to find an empty spot, he instead flipped the car into reverse.

"What are you doing?" Lonnie challenged.

Jamie ignored his question and continued backing up until eventually he had plowed over a small garden centered between two parked vehicles.

"Jamie!"

After turning off the ignition, he finally turned to see Lonnie's astonished face.

"What?" He acted surprised. "They kill people, and you're worried about their azaleas?"

"I—"

"Let's just go." Jamie pulled out the key, opening the driver's door.

The boys stepped out onto the road and made their way around to the trunk. Jamie popped it, revealing two suit bags laid out. Inside them were black three-piece suits with gold embroidery on the vest and lapels.

"What are these?" Lonnie stared in confusion.

"They were all I could find last minute."

Checking that the coast was clear, the boys stripped to their underwear and then donned their new attire. Lonnie noticed their reflection in the car window, shocked to see how well they now blended with the other guests entering the party.

Here we go.

Finally standing in front of the house, it all became so real. Spotlights illuminated the manor in multi-colored lights as black and white balloon vines hung from the balconies. The whole thing was even more breathtaking than the first time around. There was more pizazz and flair, like a whole new style had encompassed the house, which begged the question...

Whose style was it?

The closer they got to the house, the more an unsteady sensation washed over Lonnie. He looked to see if Jamie felt it too, but he kept his jaw locked and his gaze fixed ahead.

"I'll start on the balconies, you take the dance floor," Jamie blurted.

Lonnie's head was growing fuzzy. "What?"

"To find the guy. It'll be faster if we split up." He reached out his hand. "Give me a pill."

Lonnie reached into his pocket and pulled out the blister pack, popping one into his hand.

"Thank you." Jamie nodded.

I can't believe we are doing this. How are we doing this?

Lonnie tried to block out the nerves as they approached the front steps, but the sight of the porch instantly took him back to before. The whole entrance looked absolutely immaculate compared to the crime scene they had left a year prior. Pure white marble steps hid any traces of blood, and fresh paint on the walls covered the previous claw marks and bullet holes.

They erased it... they erased it all like it never happened.

Lonnie made his way up the first step, looking up at the dozen or more left till the top.

Was it always so long?

Lonnie was swept up in a dizzy spell that forced him down onto the railing.

"You okay?" Jamie turned.

I can't be here.

His heart started beating so fast, he thought it might collapse. He felt the invisible weight of Hannah's corpse sink in his arms as he imagined her blood pour down the now pristine stairs. There wasn't a single trace of her left.

They erased her. Just like they will erase this guy.

He took a gulp, a new realization wiping across his mind.

Not them. No, it would be us.

It would be me...

Lonnie stared at Jamie, who looked worried beneath his tough guy exterior. He had never really noticed before, but Jamie had the same eyes as his sister. Even if hers were brown while his were blue, they still formed the same shape; both round and close set. Looking at him now, he saw her. The sweetest little girl in the world.

Oh, gosh.

No, Lonnie.

Pull yourself together. Keep her safe.

He steadied himself, stretching out his shaky legs. Straightening to his full height, he found his balance and moved carefully up the remaining steps.

"Yeah," he mumbled back to Jamie. "I'll be okay. Just got lightheaded."

Eventually, they reached the top, pausing ever so briefly at the door handle to gather themselves. The foyer inside was radiant. Black and white colored balloons covered the ceiling, making the space look like constellations. And on the far wall, there was a painting of Mr. and Mrs. Blythorne regally seated on a couch. They were posed in such a rigid and orthodox way, yet something about it seemed so haunting and incriminating.

Eerie.

But their picture reminded him of why they were here.

"See you in a few." Lonnie slipped under an archway, leaving the foyer for the crowded ballroom.

Jamie nodded. "See you soon."

Lonnie crossed the dance floor as partygoers blurred at the edges of his peripheral vision. This time, he didn't make the mistake of meeting anyone's eye. He was here on business. He couldn't afford to get sucked into the party or dragged to the dance floor again by old women in over-revealing dresses.

Where is he?

He scanned the crowd, looking for his target, but after a few laps, it became apparent that the boy wasn't here. Hope filled him. Maybe he was already too late, and someone else did it for him. But what did that mean for Harriet? His hand twisted the blister pack nervously in his pocket.

Keep going.

Lonnie performed another lap, until finally stopping at the bar at the corner of the ballroom, where he grabbed an empty stool and waited for the bartender.

"Two champagnes, please."

The man began opening a bottle as Lonnie felt the ground shift below him. On the seat adjacent, a tall, muscular boy in his early twenties plopped down. His hair was a bleach-blond and his eyes a dark hazel. A thin line of sweat covered his brow, and it was obvious from his quick inhales that he had just finished dancing.

Oh my God.

"Here you go." The bartender set down the two filled flutes. *It's him.*

Lonnie nearly fell from the chair as he plunged his hand into his pocket. Popping one of the pills from his blister pack, he held it close-fisted in his hand. Then, in a single swipe, he moved his hand over one of the glasses and dropped it in.

What do I do?

What do I—

"How's the party?" Lonnie nearly shouted, putting on an extreme smile.

The boy swiveled in his chair to face him. "This party is insane!"

"I know, right?" Lonnie parted his lips, tapping his ring finger on the fizzing glass.

Just do it. You have to.

"What's your name?" Lonnie pried.

"Oh, it's Roman." The boy held out his hand, displaying a series of metal rings. "Roman Capulto."

"Leonard." Lonnie extended his own, feeling the cool tinge of the jewelry on his skin. "Just Leonard."

Leonard?

They exchanged other pleasantries, but it was obvious the conversation was coming to an end. Lonnie had begun to perspire, as it was dawning on him that he might not be able to do it. His time window was growing smaller as Roman had already regained his stamina, the sweat on his forehead now nearly dry. In a minute, he would leave and head back to the party. It had to be now.

Now or never.

Lonnie wrapped his hand around the untampered glass, removing it from the table.

Do it!

"Would you like some?" Lonnie blurted out, directing his attention to the glass remaining in front of him.

Roman looked at it but didn't say anything. Lonnie could feel his blood pulsating in his veins.

Take it.

A smile crept over Roman's face, and he swiped the other glass from the counter. "Sure, thanks!"

Lonnie clenched his stomach, trying to play it cool.

"Cheers!" Lonnie clinked their cups together.

"Cheers!"

He raised the champagne and chugged it, hoping that Roman would follow suit, which he thankfully did. Both drained their glasses in a matter of seconds.

"Wow, that hit fast!" Roman snorted, jumping to his feet. His toes pointed back toward the dance floor. "Thanks for that."

"Are you going back out there?" Lonnie asked.

"Yeah." He walked off, catching himself in place. "You gonna dance?"

Lonnie swatted his hands. "Oh no, I'm good. Have fun."

Roman shrugged and continued off, merging back into the ball of people.

Lonnie waited until he had fully disappeared, then released his tensed abs.

I am a monster.

He gritted his teeth, trying desperately to hold back the tears. Disgust lingered on his tongue. He wanted to spit it out, but knew he couldn't. He'd made his choice. Even if it wasn't much of a choice at all.

From the corner of his eye, Lonnie saw Jamie walking along

the wall. He moved with an alertness, constantly darting his head around corners, most likely still searching for Roman. As he raised his gaze, they shared a glance through the crowd, and without words, they exchanged an entire conversation. Jamie too started tearing up, but Lonnie knew not for the same reasons as him. His tears were from relief.

Mine are not so joyful.

Making his way through the dancers, Jamie managed to get to the bar where he stole the now empty seat. Lonnie was scanning the floor, searching for Roman. He finally found him in a pit of people, jumping so high his head rose up above the rest. He was beaming.

"He looks like he is having fun." Jamie pointed at the dance floor, pity lingering in his voice.

Lambs never know they're about to be slaughtered.

"Right," Lonnie muttered.

It's over.

"Gin and tonic, please," Jamie begged the bartender.

"One for me as well," Lonnie added.

He could taste the lingering champagne on his gums, like a light burn. He thought of his last glass and the splitting headache that had followed.

"I can't stand the taste of champagne," he groaned, shoving the empty flutes across the bar stand.

The boys spun in their seats and looked out at the crowd. Roman's large frame put his head high above the other dancers like a buoy bobbing in the water. But as they watched him, they noticed him beginning to sink. Little by little, he went, until he toppled below the surface.

I'm so sorry.

His body emerged from the edge of the crowd, just in time

for him to fall to the floor. He tried to pull himself back up, but the weight of his muscular body had turned on him. Crawling on the floor, he headed toward the balcony, but eventually collapsed in front of a circle of guests.

"Oh, my heavens," a lady in a feathered hat and bangles hollered out beside him.

A crowd drew in to get a better view, but two burly men rushed out from a nearby hallway, pushing them away. They both wore all black suits with little walkie-talkie headphones extending to their ears. They looked calm, as though this was not their first time tending to a messy party guest or maybe even not their first time disposing of one. Lifting Roman's arms over their shoulders, they dragged him down a hallway, like he weighed nothing. Within five seconds, they had vanished, and the crowd returned to talking as though it were a momentary blip.

They erased him.

The bartender dropped off their drinks, and the boys nodded back graciously, raising them up. Jamie stirred his around, staring at it with what looked like newfound disgust. Lonnie could relate. This wasn't a call for celebration. They hadn't done anything heroic. They were cowards. The least they could do now was make his sacrifice not be in vain.

"Where should we start?" Jamie asked, downing his entire glass, then setting it on the counter.

The bartender bent to pick it up, revealing a faint red light hidden in the bar display behind his head. Lonnie recognized it instantly. Another one of those tiny security cameras. He raised his glass smugly at it, trying to hide his repressed loathing as best he could.

Lonnie imagined a new watch party was looking at him

right now on that big screen downstairs. A new group of cloaked figures that were laughing and drinking scotch as they sent another poor individual to their death. He wondered if they knew about last year's massacre or if that information was erased, along with Hannah.

Maybe they would be interested to know. He smiled at the thought.

Lonnie's brain was churning with ideas. "We need to make sure we are invited downstairs."

"Back to the basement... joy." Jamie scoffed. "And how do we do that?"

Lonnie stared at the hidden camera once again, tilting his head in thought. "By finding out who's running this place." He set down his untouched glass on the bar and stood from the chair.

Let's get this party started.

The ballroom decorations this year were something to be envious of. The room was a mixed blend of black and white, similar to the balloons in the foyer and entrance. Though this room was even more eccentric, as the black and white theme extended to the streamers, the furniture covers, and even the paintings. The place had been purposefully gray-scaled, which made the people in their bright dresses and suits really pop.

Jamie briefly paused to look at it all; the singer, the ballroom, and the decorations. Lonnie watched him, wondering if he had showed the same look of awe on his first visit.

This place was probably quite fun for the normal, naive guests. But that wasn't us.

"Come on." Lonnie guided him around the crowd to the double set of stairs on the other end of the dance floor.

As they approached, a familiar giant statue appeared before

them. On it, five men were sewn together at the spine, their anguished faces staring out at the crowd and their eyes shifting in their skulls as though watching over the party. Lonnie found them appalling and tried his best to stay out of reach of their outstretched hands. On either side of the sculpture, people hung on the railings, laughing and chatting among themselves. Below their feet, the oak steps Mr. and Mrs. Blythorne had walked so elegantly down in the past were now a black wood tile. That red dress Mrs. Blythorne wore last year would have really been something opposite to this party's muted tones.

The new host must be up there somewhere.

Making his way up the steps, Lonnie tried to squeeze around the other guests, but it was taking forever. Jamie, on the other hand, was shoving himself past anyone who blocked his path.

When did he become so reckless?

Lonnie couldn't keep up with all these mood changes. It was as if even Jamie didn't know what he wanted to be. Was he afraid, angry, reckless, or brave? Whatever he was, he couldn't be picking fights and mowing down flower patches. He had to be calm and cunning, which didn't seem to be in the cards tonight.

Where did he go?

Finally reaching the top, Lonnie discovered that Jamie was nowhere to be found. Lonnie searched, but it was impossible to see past the guests. All he could make out was a single set of double doors a couple of meters down the upstairs hallway.

God damn it Jamie...

He looked around once more, but with no sight of him, Lonnie decided he would have to reunite with him later. The crowd of people thinned out the further he got from the stairs, until eventually stopping entirely at the foot of the doorway. The frame was a solid redwood, with beautiful carvings on it that curled out like tree branches. To his surprise, the whole upstairs floor remained in color. The caramel brown carpets and light mustard walls clashed against the black and white decorations that covered the ballroom below. Perhaps guests weren't meant to be up here, which meant it was all the more reason to explore. Casually peeking over his shoulder to see that no one was looking, he gave a light pull on one of the door handles. It did not budge.

A faint rhythm of footsteps came from the other side, so he pressed his ear against the door's scratchy frame. Even in the turmoil of the party, the movements persisted like a beating heart. More and more steps, back and forth.

It must be the hosts!

"Come on," he grunted, now giving a strong heave with each pull.

"What are you doing?" a voice snapped.

Lonnie spun around, hiding his hands behind his back and pressing them to the door. A girl no older than himself blocked his path, her arms crossed over her chest. Black mesh sleeves covered her arms, connecting to an elegant black dress that fell to her knees. Her hair ran up in box braids and curled together in a low bun on the back of her head.

"Just exploring," he said as casually as he could muster.

She lowered her shoulders in a disarming way.

"I would recommend just sticking to the ballroom," she said in a thick English accent that made it almost sound like a warning.

"Thanks, but it's not exactly my first time here." Lonnie tried to awkwardly walk around her.

"I know. That's why I am telling you... Leonard."

Lonnie felt a pit in his stomach at the sound of his name. He stepped closer, encroaching on her space in as threatening a way as he could muster.

"Are you with them?" he spat.

The blue and gray in her eyes bled together to make a light hue that was calming, yet clashed with her sharp pupils. "With *us*, you mean?" she whispered in a smug tone.

Her head turned so slightly that Lonnie almost missed her peeking at a shelf in the corner of the hall. Another small red dot glowed in the shadow.

More cameras! How am I supposed to get anywhere if they are always watching?

"Yes, of course. With us," Lonnie corrected himself, feeling like an idiot for saying the contrary out loud.

"My God, you have quite a lot to learn." She smiled, extending her hand. "My name is Amara Wexler."

"Lonnie Grambell, though it seems you already knew that." He responded self-consciously.

"Oh yes, we are all quite familiar with you."

"We?" he muttered, but then froze as she gestured back toward the stairs.

Ahead, a group clustered together. The closest figure stood with their back to Amara and himself. Lonnie gasped, caught off guard by the person's red, untamed hair.

Hannah?

Amara tapped the person on the shoulder, causing them to excuse themselves from the group of people. Their face had her same constellation of freckles and shimmering green eyes. But as Lonnie's gaze continued down, he found an orange patch of stubble emerging from their jaw, followed by an Adam's apple concealed in their throat. His stomach tightened as the hope dispelled from his chest.

"I believe you two already know each other." Amara beckoned him over.

Lonnie looked at him with dismay. It wasn't her, but Amara was right; he did know who this person was. He knew him quite well.

"Lonnie?" the boy responded, like he was staring at a car wreck. "Hi."

He wore her face... her hair... even her last name.

"Hi, Carter," he spit out.

Hannah's twin brother stood in front of him, his pasty skin accentuating the idea that Lonnie was staring at a ghost. The last he'd seen Carter was when they rescued him from that makeshift dungeon at the gala and dragged him to the front steps.

What happened to him?

The events of the front yard played in his head like an old film. The creature corpses spread out on the red-stained steps, their limbs slowly locking up as the rigor mortis set in. Mrs. Blythorne's bleeding body reached out from the top platform, frozen in this jarring stretch. From the way she lay, it had seemed as though she, like everyone else, was trying to escape the house, but Lonnie had no pity for her. His own skin was stained red from Hannah's blood dripping down his torso.

He remembered seeing in his peripheral vision two black vans pulling down the driveway. Jamie had just helped lay Carter on the grass. He was so skinny, his arms like twigs, and his voice so weak that he could barely speak. Two men had jumped from the first car, snatching him from Jamie's hands and dragging his limp body to the pavement. Lonnie had tried to protest, but another set of men came from the second van and stabbed a syringe into his neck. Carter's sister's corpse was taken next, followed by his own mother, who gave one last look at him before jumping into the first van. After it drove away, Jamie and Lonnie were soon grabbed and tossed into the remaining one.

"You look good," Lonnie added.

It felt like a civil thing to say, but in actuality, it also held some truth. The sickly-looking boy he had rescued almost a year ago had changed. His hair was long and shiny, and his frame had expanded, with light muscles protruding from beneath his suit. Even his face was more defined as the baby fat had diminished from his cheeks.

"Thanks."

The air felt so thick between them that Lonnie was finding it hard to swallow.

"I—" He stopped as Jamie appeared from the crowd, butting into the conversation.

"There you are." Jamie looked like he was going to say something else, but was momentarily stunned by Carter, who now stood beside them.

"What is he doing here?" Jamie asked, as though Carter wasn't present.

"I imagine the same reason you're here," Carter said, reinserting himself into the conversation. "I was invited."

"Were you invited last year?" Jamie added snarkily. "I know I saved your ass, but don't think for a second I forgot what your family tried to do."

Carter's mouth tightened as he stood there shamefully. He let his chin sink, dropping his stare down to Jamie's nose.

"Don't blame Carter. We all know you don't exactly get a choice here," Amara countered.

Is that true?

His fingers grazed the envelope in his pocket, and his spine stiffened.

"I am sorry," Carter blurted out. His eyes were wide, as though even he was shocked by his words. "For what it is worth."

"Not much," Jamie scoffed. His body was shifting back and forth as though he was itching for an exit to materialize. He noticed Amara standing beside him. "Hi, I'm Jamie."

She politely shook his hand. "Amara Wexler."

An awkward silence followed their quick introduction, leaving the four of them standing in a circle.

Lonnie finally let out a fake cough and pushed himself between them. "So I take it you two are quite familiar with this place. Do you know where the new hosts are?"

Amara looked at him like he was mad. "Why do you want to find them?" She stepped back, eyeing him up and down.

"I'm just curious, is all. I wanted to introduce myself."

"I wouldn't," she said. "Best to have yourself as low on their radar as possible."

"Who are they?"

What did she mean by that?

Lonnie's scar started to hurt, drawing him to run his finger-nails over it again and again, until suddenly her hand rested atop his. He looked up, and she gave him this toothy grin that made him feel an awkward warm sensation in his stomach.

"Come on, I want to show you both something."

She guided him down the stairs, with Carter and Jamie following closely behind them. Lonnie knew Jamie must be livid by this duo's pairing, but honestly, he would just have to get over it.

Amara dragged him by the hand, moving confidently across the ballroom, passing through all the people with a refined elegance. Each turn and twist felt seamless, as though she had been traversing these halls her entire life. She was a siren, leading him away from land.

"Where are you taking us?" Lonnie pried.

"Almost there."

They ventured down a hallway, approaching a bookshelf that resided in the middle of the carpet. Amara causally smiled at the passing guests, waiting patiently for them to cross from her line of sight. Then, laying her hand gently under the wooden board of one of the shelves, she slid her finger until it made a light click. With her other hand, she pushed in on the wood, sliding the whole wall back as though on a track. Openings appeared on either side, and she gestured for Lonnie to enter. Jamie and Carter rounded the corner of the hallway just as they entered.

"Hurry up!" she hollered toward them.

They exchanged looks, then broke into a slight sprint until they crossed through the passageway. Once all four of them were inside, she slid the fake wall closed, hiding them within its dark interior.

What fresh hell have I got myself into now?

Chapter 7

The Nowhere Room

Darkness enveloped the room, making Lonnie's neck begin to sweat.

Why did I follow her?

Regret was setting in as he realized he had just accompanied this complete stranger away from the safety of the party. Filled with nerves, he reached his hand back, trying to find the latch to unlock the secret wall door.

Click.

Someone had flipped a switch, causing fluorescent bulbs to flicker on overhead. Lonnie let out a quiet sigh of relief when he noticed the room was some kind of lounge space, and not a medieval torture chamber or a prison cell. Instead, it was rather quaint, with a small wooden coffee table, beige couch, and black recliners. The walls were bare, aside from their strikingly blue wallpaper and one bold white door.

"What is this place?" Lonnie asked, walking cautiously in front of one of the recliners. He rubbed his fingers over it, afraid of what would happen if he were to sit down.

"This... is our secret spot," Amara explained, plopping down onto the couch.

"Amara, me, and... Hannah's." Carter rubbed his neck, avoiding their gaze.

Lonnie flinched at her name.

"What's so special about some office room?" Jamie asked.

"It's private." Amara straightened the pillow beside her.

Muffled party music seeped through the walls, making them shake.

"Not really," Jamie said.

"Not in that way." She laughed. "I mean they can't watch us in here. No cameras."

No cameras.

"How do you know?" Lonnie sat up, alert.

She knocked on the table. "I checked myself."

Why did she not want cameras around?

Lonnie decided not to pry, and instead slid lower in his chair. Jamie was sitting on the other recliner, continuing to make faces at Carter. His nails dug into the armrest, practically holding himself from pouncing.

Please don't pick a fight.

Carter seemed to be ignoring it, putting his full attention into adjusting the forest green tie which had been styled so well with his creme suit. Amara was fidgeting with a ring resting on her forefinger, clearly something on her mind. Just then, she looked up and caught him staring. He darted his attention to somewhere else, but he could feel her gaze linger.

"I know you think you know everything about this place, but believe me, you are playing a whole different game now. You aren't just surviving these trials, you are now a part of it."

"What does that mean?" Jamie asked.

"You are not just a guest... you are a member. Our actions are just as much on display as that boy's will be tonight. Especially yours." She extended her finger accusingly toward Lonnie. "After what you did last year."

"I was just trying to survive. What was I supposed to do?"

"You made a choice, and if my best friend hadn't done what she did, then both of you would not be standing here!" Her voice rose, but she caught herself. "Do you understand?"

Best friend? Does she mean Hannah?

"I'm sorry, I—"

She continued, her tone now tense and sharp. "When you're as wealthy as these people, the only thing you can offer is your loyalty. And if you can't give that, then you're worthless to them."

Lonnie let out a shallow whistle. "Okay, then."

Her brows were unwavering as she spoke. It was as though she had said this phrase a million times before, perhaps to others like Lonnie, or maybe even just to herself.

She's so on edge.

"Great," Jamie added. "Wonderful pep talk."

"Why weren't you here last year?" Lonnie interjected.

"And who says I wasn't?" She cocked her head.

"Well, the fact that you are here now."

Amara laughed wildly. "Yes, I suppose you really did a number on the last party, didn't you? I should count myself lucky that I never received an invitation."

"That's an option?" Jamie threw up his arms in outrage. "You can just not be invited? My God, there are so many rules."

Lonnie's heart fluttered at the idea of never returning here, but it wasn't the circumstances he wanted.

Stick to the plan.

Amara hypnotically spun her ring again. "Oh yes, the higher-up members curate their list very carefully each year. Each person is picked for a specific reason, or not for the same."

"My parents weren't invited last year," Carter added.

"Good for them." Jamie rolled his eyes.

Carter looked like he wanted to say something, but bit his tongue. He dressed in this very collegiate style that conflicted with the evasive attitude he was delivering. Though maybe that was to be expected when he was trapped in a room with the boys who'd killed his sister.

Lonnie rattled his fingers on the wooden coffee table, noticing little marks dug into the side. He leaned in closer, rubbing his fingers over the indents:

A.W.

C.R.

H.R.

The writing was messy. Chips of lead stuck to the holes as though they were dug with a pencil.

"How long have you been coming here?" The question slipped from Lonnie's lips.

"About a decade," Amara said.

A decade.

The word was so defeating. The image of children running through these blood-stained halls made Lonnie want to yack.

"I'm sorry," was all he could manage to say.

"I don't need your pity. It's just one lousy day a year."

"I suppose..." Lonnie traced the writing around the table, now noticing the other side had even more markings cut into it. They were deeper, clearly dug in with something much sharper and refined.

F.L.

_S.M._

_B.G._

Lonnie halted, pressing the palm of his hand into the letters.

_B.G._

Benjamin Grambell?

"Was my brother here?" Lonnie stammered.

Bang.

The memory of a gunshot echoed in his head, giving him goosebumps. That video had been ingrained in his brain ever since his mother showed him the footage.

It's all so barbaric.

Ben was picked for the ritual... just like Lonnie. And he died. But not because he'd failed any trials. Because he'd refused to sacrifice his brother. Ben could have just killed Lonnie when they made him aim the gun at his unconscious body, but he couldn't do it. He was brave, he was strong, and he wasn't a part of this world.

Lonnie rubbed the _B.G._ letters again.

Or maybe he was.

Amara muzzled her lips, but he asked again, this time more stern.

"Benjamin Grambell, did you know him?"

She exhaled, exchanging a glance with Carter.

"Yes, we all did," Carter blurted.

"You _all_." Lonnie's mind spun out. "Wait, so Hannah... She knew my brother this whole time!"

Amara cleared her throat. "Actually, your brother was the one who showed us this room."

My God, the secrets never stop.

The walls of his throat squeezed in, and Lonnie wheezed for

air. He loosened his bow tie, trying to release the tension strangling his throat.

"So, you knew him well then," Lonnie seethed.

"Yes," Carter said.

"And you didn't help him!" Lonnie snarled.

"We were kids," Carter snapped.

"And these other people. F.L. and S.M.? Why didn't they help him?"

Amara carefully knelt to the floor, rolling the edge of her dress to the side. She scratched her nail on their initials, deepening the grooves.

"'Cause they were already dead." She gestured to the walls. "This isn't just our safe room. It's also their lamb pen."

The previous allure of this room was now gone, its walls growing rather claustrophobic.

"Here." She reached into a tiny drawer in the coffee table and pulled out a sharp pencil. "Add your names."

She offered it to Jamie, who looked at her like she was crazy. Lonnie had a similar reaction, but eventually took it, beginning to carve the side of the table.

J.H.

L.G.

He leaned back, but then an idea drew him back to the table. Lifting the pencil, he dug it in again, carving two more letters.

Amara leaned over to see, but grew confused at the added letters.

"Who is R.C.?"

Everyone now peeked, equally as perplexed.

"Roman Capulto," he said proudly. "This year's champion."

She grew flustered. "Why did you do that?"

"He deserves to be remembered. Like everyone else, right?"

Amara opened her mouth to speak, then shut it, leaning back uncomfortably. His name clearly meant more than she was letting on.

Lonnie watched her with curiosity. "Do you know him? What family is he in?"

Carter answered for her. "Never seen him here before, but they add new families all the time. For such an exclusive club, they seem to have a very open-door policy."

"God...you are such a dick," Jamie muttered under his breath.

Lonnie tuned them both out, leaned closer to Amara, who was now staring at the new initials. "You don't know anything about him?"

She finally met his eyes. "I've only heard that he is someone's stepson from a new marriage. That's why he has never been seen here before. Very unlucky family to join into."

"What is through there?" Jamie asked bluntly, pointing to the door in the far corner of the room.

Lonnie was annoyed by the sudden change of subject. They all turned to the white door, silently staring as though a fifth member of the group had appeared.

"Oh, we don't go through there."

He stood up slightly as if to get a better look. "Why?"

"Just nothing good would come from it." She smiled, jumping to her feet. "I think we should probably return to the party. Can't be gone too long."

She's hiding something. I just know it.

With that, she ended the conversation, already making her way to the secret wall door.

The boys followed suit, unsure if this was a choice or just a do as you're told situation.

Amara pressed the wall slightly, peeking out of a crack into the hall. When the coast was clear, she slid the door open, expelling them all back into the chaos of the party.

It was immediately obvious that their presence had not been missed. The guests raged on, their demeanor steadily getting more aggressive and hectic as they continued to drink. Dance partners were juggled from person to person, creating a symphony of choreographed movements. Lonnie couldn't help but search for Roman in the crowd, even though he knew he was long gone.

For just a split second, an urge to cry came over him. He thought of those children hiding in that room. His brother trying so hard to keep those young kids hidden from the carnage of this place. But he wasn't around anymore to protect them.

Nine names. Four dead. Soon to be five.

It wasn't fair.

He wondered if when they carved their names into that table, they realized that one day it would double as their headstone. He sniffled his nose, letting the party drown the spiraling thoughts in his head. A child should never have to fight for their innocence.

I shouldn't have to fight for my innocence.

Amara moved carefully down the hallway as he lingered behind. Jamie walked in tandem beside him, and Lonnie leaned in close and whispered so gently that even the wind wouldn't catch his words.

"We are going to burn this place to the ground."

Jamie looked at him, the corner of his mouth raising ever so slightly. He lifted his hand onto Lonnie's shoulder, pressing down gently, before removing it and walking ahead.

An abrupt clapping suddenly filled the room as the guests ceased their dancing and spread to the outer ring of the ballroom. Amara paved a way through, cutting past guests until they had made their way to the front.

What was going on?

As they reached the neck of the crowd, they found that the audience had built a circle, leaving the center barren, aside from four people. The live music had changed to a quiet acoustic jazz that lightly wafted around the room, no longer blaring from speakers.

"Who are they?" Lonnie whispered to Carter.

Amara let out a trembling breath. "Those are the hosts."

Chapter 8

The Royal Court

The audience circled around the quartet, their eyes yearning for something to quench their attention. Lonnie gazed upon these new hosts, expecting a spectacular entrance similar to the one that Mr. and Mrs. Blythorne had delivered the previous year, though something told Lonnie that this time was different.

The four made an odd pairing, each well over seventy and dressed as though attending different events. The tallest one stuck out like a rose in the grass, even though he tried to conceal himself in the back of the formation. Sweat gathered on his balding head, which he briskly dabbed with a pocket square from his mustard yellow suit. For someone who seemed to be appalled by attention, he chose quite a bold color to wear.

Beside him, a short and broad woman stood with an expression that was completely numb to the crowd. She ran a hand through her thick bobbed hair and stared at her colleagues. Lonnie felt a ping in his chest, as though he recognized her from somewhere.

Who was she?

He turned to Amara for answers, but her attention was elsewhere. If she knew anything, he would have to pry it out of her later.

Oh my God.

Lonnie gasped upon recognizing the third host. The woman had a floor-length gown of glitter and bronze satin. Her hair had been tied into braids, interwoven with ruby studs and topped with what appeared to be a tiara. Though he would expect nothing less from *The Silver Woman*, the beloved Florence Kiltner. Of the four, she appeared to be the most thrilled about being the center of attention. Her arms swept royally through the air, blowing kisses to the crowd just as she had done from the starboard deck in her film, *S.S. Marigold.* The memory of seeing her draped in silver as her boat floated into the harbor, leaving her beloved husband to the lonely edge of the pier, filled his mind. It was the only movie he remembered so vividly before his parents sent him away. He would watch it with his mother on VHS whenever he was sick.

What the hell was she doing here?

Starstruck by her presence, the normal appearance of the final host almost masked him from Lonnie's gaze. A bland-looking man in a baggy wool suit stood to the side of his co-hosts. His brows were bushy, and his eyes shifted back and forth as though he was reciting words in his head. Without missing a beat, Lonnie recognized him as well. Silas Sibil, the bestselling author.

This has got to be a joke.

His adventure series, *The Princes of York*, cluttered Lonnie's mind from all the times he'd buried himself in it while in his dorm room as a boy. He must have looked at that picture on the back cover a hundred times, the author's modest little face staring back at him. The thought of him here both made Lonnie's heart stutter and simultaneously shrivel up and die.

Don't let it be true.

He wanted to hound Amara with more questions, but Silas stepped forward, his face blushing from the ovation. He lifted his hand to quiet the applause and then proceeded.

"Hello, beautiful people," he said with a poise that completely disagreed with his demeanor. "You all look ravishing!"

As he continued to speak, it became obvious that his power came from words. In a few moments, he had taken control of the room. The audience let out another wallop at his compliment and then remained infatuated throughout the remainder of his speech.

"My family and I are honored to be upholding the dear tradition of our departed sister and brother-in-law. Though their exit from this earth was swift and unexpected, we have to remember what they accomplished... and what they built." He rested his arm on Mrs. Kiltner's shoulder, which seemed to surprise even her as she sank slightly under the pressure. "Our father used to say, 'Let the dreamers sleep all night, for the realists will be the ones to take on the day.' My sister Ophelia knew what she wanted, and she was never afraid to take it. And because of that, you, me, us... We are all here together tonight at the first annual Blythorne Memorial Gala. Thank you."

They are all related?

The crowd broke into an uproar, their voices hollering throughout the room. Lonnie saw the man next to him dry a tear from his cheek, which he would have thought ridiculous if he himself didn't also feel the adrenaline coursing through him. It was like he had just heard a warrior's chant on a battlefield.

What just happened?

Lonnie stepped backward, moving deeper into the crowd as the hosts shifted toward a nearby group of patrons. Amara was already pacing away from the circle of people when Lonnie tugged her arm.

"There are four hosts?"

She looked directly through him, lost in a train of thought. "Yes."

Without thinking, more words spilled from his lips. "Wait, who is Ophelia? And why are these people all here?"

She blinked her eyes, returning her attention to him. "Ophelia Blythorne?" She cocked her head in confusion. "What do you mean why are they here? Who else did you expect to take over after she died?"

Ophelia Blythorne?

"Wait, Mrs. Blythorne?" Lonnie whispered, vaguely remembering hearing his father refer to Mr. Blythorne's wife as Ophelia in passing.

She had four siblings...

"This is the first year they have ever attended," Amara noted, leaning in closer. "I heard that Ophelia wanted to lead the society all by herself, and that's why they never came. But I think that's rubbish. *I think* because she was the youngest, she was the only one left to take it over from their father."

"What happened to their father?"

Amara suddenly was quite gossipy, which caught Lonnie off guard. After a quick scan of the room, she continued her whispering, "He died a couple of decades ago, and none of the other siblings have been back since."

"Wait, they haven't been back here in decades?"

"Why would they? They were successful, and the

Blythornes had it under control. But now that they are dead, I guess it was time for a family reunion."

Great. Rich, powerful people who blame me for killing their sister and forcing them to take over her horrendous job.

"And they are really all blood siblings?"

She pointed at the tall one first. "The scrawny one is Sebastian Sibil. He is some kind of mathematician... something to do with computers or statistics, I forget which."

She shifted her gaze to the author. "And that is—"

"Silas Sibil," Lonnie interrupted her. "I must have read his books a hundred times each as a kid."

He pointed at the actress standing beside him. "And that's *his* sister?"

"Exactly."

"But that is Florence Kiltner. They can't be related."

Amara raised her finger. "She's Florence Sibil. Kiltner was a stage name."

"I've loved them both for so long," Lonnie muttered to himself. "How did I never know?"

But they were so successful. They didn't need to be here. They didn't need the money.

Lonnie's gaze shifted to the last woman, who had detached from the group to smoke a cigarette on the terrace. Her face was so familiar, but he still couldn't place it.

"And her?"

"That's Daphne Sibil. She runs the biggest tech company across the northern hemisphere." Seeing Lonnie's blank stare, she continued. "I'd bet money that you have her phone in your pocket right now."

Lonnie pulled out his phone and stared at the back of his case. On it was a black circle logo with a white swirl spiraling to the center and a horizontal line cutting across the bottom third.

"Wait, that's the founder of FiberOps Facilities?"

Lonnie now realized why she looked so familiar. He had watched her tech talk online. She was presenting the latest model of her FOF-Phone at their annual summit.

"I don't understand, though. They just can't be a part of this."

"It can't come as that much of a surprise," Amara pointed out.

"That my childhood heroes and one of the biggest business tycoons in the world are a part of a group that sacrifices people to gods? Yes, I am a bit overwhelmed by it." Lonnie looked at them again across the ballroom, a new twinge of disgust in his eyes. But it brought a new thought to mind.

"You said you have never seen them here before?" he asked.

She paused, scratching the side of her head. "Yeah, the whole time I have been here, they have never attended. They just participate from afar every year like a majority of the high-up members."

Participate from afar?

Lonnie squinted his eyes. "And now they run the place. And these other members were just okay with that? I'd think they would be furious."

Amara got closer to him, and her expression darkened. "What are you trying to do here?"

He smiled innocently, "I'm just trying to catch up, so I don't step on anybody's toes tonight."

"Mm." She lightened her expression, giving him a formal smile. "If you really want to survive the night. I suggest you stop being such a nosy parker."

Who is this girl?

Lonnie shifted his weight to his back leg, putting distance between them. It was only then that he saw her whole face. It was quite beautiful. Beneath her tense exterior, there were faint smile lines and dimples that told a different story. He wondered what her life was like in England, or wherever she called home. How many friends was she hiding this whole other world from?

From the way she carried herself, she seemed quite studious and poised. However, the way she dressed gave Lonnie this impression that she knew exactly who she was, and people always liked that. They yearned for friends like that—stationary people to anchor themselves to.

"Please be careful," she said warmly. "I have to go talk to someone, but I will catch up with you later."

The organized circle of bodies suddenly crumbled away as people returned to swinging their partners around the floor. The empty center was filled in, and the music returned to its normal decibel. Amara phased into the jumble, disappearing beyond flailing arms and lavish dresses.

A cold shiver ran through Lonnie as he noticed he was once again all by himself.

Where was Jamie?

Lonnie paced around in a 360-degree circle until he saw Jamie and Carter talking by the nearby wall. He prepared to engage, half-expecting Jamie to jump at him like a rabid dog, but instead, they were merely talking. At one point, Lonnie could have sworn he even saw Jamie smile, but it could have been his imagination.

What could they possibly be talking about?

He walked over but was intercepted by the faintest whiff of Grand Soir perfume. Lonnie froze.

No.

He peeked his head around and almost missed her with her now brunette hair... her natural hair. His mother stood slightly tucked behind a wall, as he remembered her doing behind those graveyard trees so many years ago. This time, however, she wasn't avoiding him; rather the opposite. She just stood there, watching him intensely.

How long had she been spying on me?

Lonnie's mother looked so much different from a year ago. She was more herself without all the crazy makeup and dyes in her hair. She'd barely even dressed up, though it seemed calculated. Her attire wasn't poor enough to be an eyesore, but also not nice enough to draw attention. She floated along the middle ground, perfectly slipping through the cracks of this party. She wore a light layer of foundation, but otherwise kept it naked, perhaps in hopes of tricking herself in the mirror that she had nothing to hide.

Lonnie did not wish to see her, but a tugging feeling begged him to know what had happened to her after she jumped into that black van.

She'd left me. Again.

Somehow, it hurt more this time, knowing that she'd been given that second chance and made the wrong choice all over again. To his recollection, no one forced her into the van; she climbed in of her own volition. She chose to leave him lying on the front lawn, for reasons he might never understand.

Where did that van take you?

Chapter 9

Old Scars

A year prior.

Lonnie watched as the light of the morning was snuffed out from the back windows of the van. He wanted to peek out, but whatever they had injected into his arm made his limbs go limp. The van came to a sudden stop, followed by some kind of garage opening with a loud rustling of chains.

"Jamie..." Lonnie slurred.

Jamie was sitting upright with his back to the wall. He was propped, facing the back window, but his head drooped to the side.

"What do you see?" Lonnie whispered, but it barely made it from his lips.

Jamie remained silent, holding his ribs where Lonnie had performed chest compressions earlier that night.

Shoot.

It's not like it mattered anyway. They were in no shape to run. They were completely at the mercy of whatever awaited them.

Creak.

The back door opened, and to his surprise, he saw two gurneys positioned on the floor with four men in yellow trauma gowns waiting behind them. They quickly jumped into the van, wrapping their hands around both boys. Their touches felt like clouds, which made him again question what drug they had put in him. Dragged to the edge of the van, they were laid onto the gurneys and wheeled through a cement garage to an old elevator. The scorching light from inside blinded Lonnie, forcing his eyes shut.

He tried to speak, but oxygen masks had been strapped over both their mouths. He wondered if it was to help them breathe or so they couldn't attempt to scream for help.

This is bad.

The elevator opened into a narrow hallway with only a single set of double doors at the end. The gurneys pushed through them, and to Lonnie's surprise, the opposing side was covered in medical equipment and surgical tools. The men positioned his gurney beside a metal slab and raised him on top of it. Meanwhile, Jamie's gurney continued forward, slipping through another set of doors.

No!

Looking to his side, knives and tools rested beside him on a tray, and he found himself squirming on the table.

"Please, don't!" he murmured through the mask.

A woman and a small team behind her, all wearing surgical gowns and gloves, approached. He tried to utter out another cry, but a hissing sound proceeded from beneath his bed and into his mask. The light above him grew brighter as the room turned to haze. The woman's eyes were the last real thing he saw, just green emeralds. But even they too faded to white, and he floated away.

They've killed me. I know it.

As light surrounded him, he waited for that earlier drug numbness to cover him like a blanket, but instead, he felt agony surge through his entire body.

Lonnie's eyes opened with a violent jerk.

This was death?

A beeping sound flickered by his ears, making his teeth grit. He followed the surge of pain that traced down his arm and ended at his bandaged wrist. A wire extended from an IV in his vein, and vital monitors were attached to his bicep and finger.

Wait, I'm alive.

His heart rate grew, increasing the beeping noises on a monitor resting beside his head. Listening closely, he noticed the sound of a second monitor a few feet away. Turning to face it, he saw Jamie nestled in a bed beside his own. His breath was coming out slow and ragged, like an old hound dog.

We're both alive?

"Jamie," Lonnie whispered. He had said his name so many times that day that the word was beginning to feel strange on his tongue.

"Mmmm," Jamie responded.

The doors Jamie had been taken through suddenly reopened, and the doctor with the sharp green eyes entered. In her hand was a small bundle of files, which she looked over once more before grabbing a flint spark lighter from the table. Without hesitation, she clicked the steel bards together, forming a ball of flames that consumed all of the paperwork. She then slid the growing fire into the trashcan, letting it slowly extinguish itself.

What was on those?

"Great, you're both awake." The doctor stared at them.

Jamie's heart monitor beeped faster, announcing that he was conscious.

"Where are we?" Lonnie asked, with as much politeness as he could muster.

Ignoring his question, the doctor approached his monitor and clicked a few buttons. The screen made various sounds, which she followed with similar sounds of approval. By this point, she had moved close enough to him that he could reach out and touch her. A dark thought crossed his mind.

I can't go back to that house. I won't let her take me.

Lonnie wrapped the wire attached to his wrist around his forefingers and straightened it into a weapon. She was a petite woman with her hair tied back in a bun, revealing her exposed neck. It would be so quick and easy.

This is crazy, Lonnie finally admitted to himself.

He released the wire and continued watching her work.

If she was going to kill us, she wouldn't have done all this work to keep us alive.

Unless she was planning something even worse.

The image of those creatures in the Blythorne's basement passed over his eyes, and the idea made his body convulse.

If they try, I'll kill myself.

The thought was dark, but somehow reassuring.

Giving the impression she was satisfied with his vitals, the doctor turned away from Lonnie's bed. As she moved, he spotted a tiny inscription on her coat that read: *Dr. Khan.* Next, she approached Jamie's monitor, read it in a similar fashion, and nodded.

"Well, the good news is that you both are going to be fine!" She grinned.

"Thank you," Jamie responded flatly. His voice sounded so small that Lonnie didn't even recognize it.

"Does that mean we are free to go?" Lonnie asked. His hands gripped the edge of his thin blanket.

"No, not yet." Her grin faded.

I knew it.

"Where are we?" Lonnie found himself asking again.

"You're in a hospital."

"Are my parents here?" Jamie again spoke so softly.

"No, your parents do not know you are here."

Jamie's eye caught Lonnie's as they exchanged a horrified glance.

"Do not worry, you can return back to your house in Rhode Island shortly." She sat on her rolling stool, carefully crossing her legs. "We just need to have a discussion first."

"Okay?" Lonnie glared.

"Some people are quite upset with the damage you two caused today—"

"Quite frankly, we are upset with the circumstances as well," Lonnie snapped.

Jamie's eyes widened. Lonnie himself could not believe he had said something so bold, especially after she made it clear she knows where they live. He bit his tongue, hoping nothing else would slip out.

"Don't interrupt me. You must understand what I am about to say. The *only* reason you're still alive is that you technically followed the rules. And with all the death that has occurred today, they think killing the champions would be in bad taste. But they will be watching and waiting for you to give them a single reason to change their mind... Fall out of line or tell another soul, and they will find out. Understood?"

"Why are you telling us all this?" Lonnie grew flustered.

"I suppose we all have rules to follow, don't we? A car will be by in the morning to take you back home. I suggest you get your story straight on how you got those bruises."

Lonnie peeled back the edge of his bandage and saw a thread stitched over a red bruise on his arm.

How do I explain this?

Chapter 10

Olive Chesterfield

Present day.

Seeing his mother approach him jolted him back to the present.

I can't deal with her right now.

Looking for a way out, he drifted back into the crowd. Bodies fought his every step, but he managed to slip out of the ballroom entirely and pass through an archway to a rather regal living room. This room's clientele appeared much more sophisticated; mostly groups of friends unwinding on the rococo couches and eating an assortment of meats and cheeses. Many of the women's dresses were quite bulky, which inhibited them from properly sitting any deeper than a half-hover. The wall behind them was made of glass, illuminating the room in a faint moonlight mixed with the glistening of the overhead chandelier.

Lonnie stepped over a rather large dress and sank into a seat beside the woman wearing it. He positioned himself with his back to the crowd, hoping his mother would grow weary of searching. He watched the moon set through the giant glass pane.

This is going to be a long night.

The smell of something sweet passed by his nose as a waiter approached him, holding a plate of appetizers in his hand.

"No, thank you." Lonnie motioned for him to leave.

"You must try it. It's quite good," the man responded.

The way he stood there gave Lonnie the impression that he was not going to leave him alone until he took a sample.

"Alright, sure. Thanks." Lonnie looked at the plate of what looked like dried pieces of bread with small black orbs and jam.

He hastily plucked one from the tray, and the man extended a black napkin with his free hand.

"Napkin," he said without any hint of it being optional.

Pushy.

Lonnie took the napkin, immediately noticing a hard texture tucked into the bottom side. The waiter's face eased as though a burden had just lifted off his shoulders, and he gave a light smile and walked away.

What?

Lonnie ate the hors d'oeuvre, which made him gag, and proceeded to shift the napkin in his hands. On the backside, there was a small piece of black cardstock with a faint yellow writing that read:

Please proceed to the coat check.

Ask the attendant for Olive Chesterfield.

The invitation!

Lonnie looked for the waiter, but he had already slipped into the next room. Rereading the note in his hand, he removed himself from the peacefulness of the rest area and stormed the crowd.

I have to find Jamie.

Though he realized that was going to be tricky in this place. He could be a foot away, and it would still be impossible to tell between the swaying spotlights and the countless people.

Besides, what if he is with Carter? I can't have him learning about our plan.

Abandoning the thought, Lonnie made his way to the front foyer in record time. He hated how good he was at navigating this place. A tiny nook was cut out of the wall in the corner of the entrance with a little Dutch door and a petite man tucked behind it. Lonnie recalled seeing the coat check prior, but he supposed he never really paid it much mind. It must have been the most forgettable part of this whole endeavor.

A perfect hiding place for a secret entrance.

A lady and gentleman beelined to the front door after grabbing their coats, putting Lonnie next in line. The man summoned him with a disingenuous manner.

"Hello." Lonnie approached somewhat cautiously.

"Hi, can I see your ticket?" The man held out his hand.

Oh no. A ticket?

Lonnie reached into his pocket, hoping the receipt might appear inside.

That waiter must have forgot to give me it!

"Oh no, I don't have one. I just—"

"Sir, I need your ticket. What was the number?"

Did I misunderstand the directions?

Lonnie pulled out the black card with the yellow writing and raised it. "No, I was told to—"

He quickly stopped himself, tucking it back into his pocket.

Does he know about the secret society?

Lonnie tilted his neck ever so slightly, peering around the room to see if any security cameras were watching him.

"Sir, if you can't give me the ticket or number, then I really can't help you. You will have to wait until the end of the night to pick it up."

"Okay, well, thanks anyway." Lonnie began to walk away.

Slightly sliding the edge of the card from his pocket, he read the words again. ***Olive Chesterfield.***

"Wait, sorry!" Lonnie spun on his heel. "Do you know where I can find Olive Chesterfield?"

The man stared at him with a sharp intensity, his eyes scanning Lonnie with agitation. He groaned. "Just give me a minute."

"Thank you."

Retreating into the coat room, the man left the counter empty, apart from a few loose, torn-up tickets and a dimly lit table lamp.

Lonnie stood there stupidly, tracing the line of his scar.

Who is Olive?

The idea of meeting another stranger was not the most ideal circumstance, but what other choice did he have?

And why do they want to meet me?

"Here you go."

The coat checker had reappeared back in the door frame and was now holding something in his hand. Before Lonnie could ask what it was, the man rested it on the counter, revealing in the faint light a greenish-brown jacket.

"What is this?"

"The Olive Chesterfield coat."

"This is Olive Chesterfield?" Lonnie rubbed his finger over

the fabric. "But I didn't bring—I mean, I thought I needed a ticket?"

"You don't need one for this jacket."

"I see." Lonnie took the jacket off the counter and tucked it under his arm.

"Have a good rest of your night, and I hope you get home safe." The man gestured to the front door and then moved onto helping another woman who had been waiting in line.

Lonnie cracked open the front door, letting the fresh air wash over him.

Were they kicking me out?

He opened the door wider, expecting it to shut in his face, but nothing happened. He took a step onto the porch.

Is this really happening?

He descended the steps, looking for someone to stop him. A few guests were lingering in the courtyard, but none were paying him any mind.

No invitation... So, I just killed Roman for nothing.

Lonnie held the jacket tightly in his grip.

What is this, a souvenir then?

"Chesterfield?" he mumbled.

He ran his hand over the lapel and decided to rest it over his shoulders. It clashed with the gold of his suit, but he felt a yearning to try it on. Pressing his hands through the sleeves, he let it engulf him, feeling the texture against the open areas of his skin.

Wait...what's that?

A small weight drew his hand to the left inner pocket, and something metallic met his finger. Lonnie pulled it out and was taken aback by the rather large antique iron key. His invitation.

But where did it lead to?

Spinning in a circle, he searched for a door to appear, but how would he ever find it? There had to be at least a hundred doors around the property. And there wasn't enough time to search them all. The trials would begin any minute now.

Rubbing his finger nervously over the key, he noticed tiny bumps spaced out on the handle. He raised it up to the light of one of the outdoor spotlights, now noting the tiny writing engraved on it.

Wine Cellar

His eyebrows shot up in surprise. "The wine cellar."

He made his way to the shrubbery that was barricading the front of the house, when he spotted Jamie's car in his peripheral. He stopped to face it, fantasizing about taking it and driving far away from this place. He shook off the idea.

Don't be stupid.

Lonnie inched his way around the perimeter of the property, searching for some kind of cellar door to appear. If he was honest, he didn't really know what he was looking for, but he was hopeful. After walking for a couple of hundred yards, he came upon the edge of the house, which rested on a small hill. Lights from the ground-floor window gave him a small amount of visibility as he descended. Bushes and the forest line blocked most of his steps, but he managed to stay on the path. By the time he looked back at the top of the hill, he realized he must have walked down at least a story or two from the ground level.

This is ridiculous. There is no way it's all the way down here.

Just as he was about to turn back and look elsewhere, he caught a shimmer from a bush resting on the wall of the house. Pushing it to the side, he found a pair of large metal doors set at an angle to the wall. A padlock and chain were tying them together, guarding whatever secret was hidden beneath.

The wine cellar.

Clutching the key in his palm, he inserted it into the pad. It sank in with ease.

"Here we go," Lonnie sighed with relief.

The lock clicked open, dropping the chain to the ground. He peeled back the doors, revealing a dark set of wooden stairs hidden inside. His mouth suddenly grew dry, but he tried to hold his composure.

Don't think about it. Just go in.

He blew out nervous bursts of air as he took his first step down. Each movement further from the outside made his stomach tighten just a little bit more. Gripping the handrail, Lonnie finally reached a cobblestone floor.

It's not too late to turn around.

But he continued forward anyway, moving cautiously into the pitch-black room. Cobwebs hung from the ceiling, each catching on his skin. Eventually, he tossed the Chesterfield onto the floor, overwhelmed by the thought of it covered in spiders.

Lonnie turned on his phone light, spotting a long cord extending down from the ceiling. He pulled it, causing a single row of light bulbs to turn on, revealing the contents of the cellar. The walls and floors were all covered in a cobblestone arrangement. Wooden barrels were spread sporadically along the floor, while bottles of wine and champagne were layered on racks in the center of the room. A thick, earthy smell clung to the floor, while the fruitiness of the wine hung in the air.

At times, he would peek at the bottles and wonder how long they had been there, but he would catch himself and keep searching for the exit. Running his hand along the stone wall, he eventually reached a wooden arched door hidden behind a pile of barrels. A faint light seeped out from under the crack, confirming he was going the right way.

This must be it. He pulled the door handle.

What he saw on the other side was like walking through a bad memory. Below his feet, he tracked dirt onto a rust-red carpet that stretched the length of the hallway. The corridor continued on his left until it bent at a corner, while it widened on his right into a semicircular room with spaced-out doors and a staircase that cut downward at the center.

"Here we are," he mumbled.

Lonnie moved to the staircase, peering down its marble steps and into the shadows below. He wondered if the weird art museum he and Jamie had stumbled upon last year was still down there. Or that tiny surveillance room just beside the base of the stairs.

Maybe they had incriminating footage. Real evidence that I could use.

Not a horrible plan, but he would need to be more inconspicuous. No room for slip-ups or showing his hand.

You are just a normal member... so act normal.

But that was easier said than done. Stepping back from the stairs, he passed over the spot where one of those creatures had pinned his mother to the floor. He could still hear her eerie screech and the shots echoing from Mr. Blythorne's gun as he aimed at the horde of them piling through the hall.

Stop. Stop.

It was too late. The memory of hearing tearing flesh and guests screaming made him stumble backward into the wall. He rubbed his hand over it, trying to ground himself in the present, but it wouldn't work. All he could see was those abominations with their numbered jumpsuits and deformed bodies.

He moved his shoe over the carpet, imagining all that blood soaked into the fibers. They had replaced the whole thing, changing it from its beautiful red velvet to this disgusting river of blood.

Was that why they picked this color? In case more spilled tonight?

He tried to shake the idea from his head.

Don't think about it.

Voices echoed from down the hall, knocking him back to his senses. He wiped his eyes and patted down his suit, now noticing all the dirt and grime that had accumulated from his hike outside. A pair of men in plain black tuxes turned around the hallway corner, both already flushed and quite drunk. They laughed to themselves and moved past Lonnie without a care, entering one of the semicircle's doors. Music and chatter shot out into the hall as they passed through, only disappearing again as one closed the door behind them.

The watch party.

Nervous, Lonnie pulled himself from the safety of the wall and followed them. Gripping the door handle, he muttered a curse, then finally walked in.

Chapter 11

A Little Wager

What the hell?

His jaw dropped at the sight. People were draped over all the furniture, filling in every inch of available space the small room offered. In their hands were variations of martinis, cocktails, and champagne, all of which were full to the rim.

Lonnie walked around the large bar, which took up the entire back half of the room. A congregation of guests had filed in around it, each begging one of the poor bartenders for a refill.

Black lounge chairs and side tables were arranged around the room like a distorted movie theater, all facing a large screen at the front, which was set up on a slightly elevated stage. He ran his hand over one of the few empty leather chairs, slightly overwhelmed by the number of people in the room. The walls still had the same paintings he recalled from when he found this space last summer, the most memorable of which was the old parchment hanging behind a casing of glass, the words forever inked into his mind:

The House Rules

1. A champion must be of kin to the House.

2. A champion must sacrifice their mind, body, and heart.

3. The title of House is granted to all whose lifeblood is wrought.

4. A House ritual must be completed in a third of day.

5. A House champion is not to be limited by youth, sex, or role.

6. The champion must spill the blood of a beloved.

7. The life of a champion may not be taken by their own hand.

8. A fallen champion shall gain the House nought.

9. Once a ritual has started, a body must be claimed before it can finish.

10. Break a rule, face a plague.

Goosebumps ran below his sleeves at the sight of it, and he could have sworn he felt a cold breath caress his neck.

You're in your head.

Other pieces of the room had changed from Lonnie's recollection. The walls had been repainted a dark brown, which reflected the light bulbs and gave a smoky effect to the room. The previous carpet had been swapped out with a new patterned design that mimicked the floor of a casino.

But above all else, the new item that really drew Lonnie's attention was the display on the large television screen in front of the room. This was the area most people were huddled around, each shouting words that ran together, making them impossible to understand. Lonnie pushed his way forward to get a better look, but once he did, he was horrified by what he saw. The screen had been split into some kind of chart with ratioed numbers growing and shrinking in all of the boxes. They read:

	<4HRS	Trial #1	Trial #2	Trial #3
Live	1:29	3:7	1:2	5:8
Drowned	149:1	19:1	83:7	119:6
Stabbed	149:1	19:1	77:13	4:1
Burned	149:1	32:1	83:7	41:1
Crushed	149:1	49:1	81:9	118:7
Fell	149:1	21:4	81:9	31:1
Betting Pool	150M	90M	50M	30M

Were these betting odds? Are they making bets?

His eyes trailed down to the corner of the screen, which had a bright red countdown running. The time displayed was: **05:45:03**

From this, the dots started to click, and Lonnie realized what they were making bets on.

You've got to be kidding.

He curled his hands into fists, letting the nails dig into his palms to keep himself from screaming.

What were these people doing?

"Ten million says he drowns in less than four hours!" a man announced, raising his hand at the screen.

Ten... million?

It was even worse than Lonnie could have imagined. They weren't just performing a sacrifice; they were putting on a show. And Roman was the entertainment.

I had been the entertainment.

Lonnie couldn't help imagining what wagers they had made on him. How many people bet he would suffocate in that silver box or drown in that sewer. He chewed on his tongue, staring at these monsters before him.

I can't believe I ever felt bad about killing these people.

The adrenaline coursing through him begged him to shatter the screen with a glass, but he refrained by tucking his hands in his pockets.

Relax. Don't draw attention.

Lonnie grew anxious about his plan. These people weren't here because they believed in some religion. They *wanted* to justify their horrible actions. They weren't clueless devout followers; they knew exactly what they were doing.

"Tearing this place apart is going to be harder than I thought," Lonnie mumbled.

"Your hand, please," a voice ordered from his left, startling him.

A short, slender man with glasses approached Lonnie from the crowd. Behind him, he pulled a tiny cart with an even tinier bowl resting on top. Inside it sat a thick black liquid.

"Sorry?"

Without hesitation, the man pulled out a thin knife from his satchel and grabbed Lonnie by the hand. Then, with a quick jab, he thrust it into Lonnie's finger.

"Ow!" Lonnie whined. "What the hell?"

The man ignored him and simply held Lonnie's finger over the bowl. Drops of blood fell from his body and married into whatever concoction was inside.

"Thank you." The man exclaimed. He handed Lonnie a tiny cotton ball, then disappeared out into the hallway.

Still in shock, Lonnie held the cotton to his finger and looked around to see if anyone else had seen the violation that had just occurred. Nobody seemed to notice or, better yet, mind.

"Lonnie!" another voice called to him.

Oh gosh, is someone else going to stab me?

He turned, surprised to see Amara waving at him. She rushed through the leather chairs and grabbed his arm, dragging him back to the entrance.

"My God, what took you so long?" she whispered.

Lonnie cocked his head, confused by such a question.

"Um... I had a bit of a complication with the coat check."

"The coat check?" Her smile creased. "What are you talking about?"

"The coat... What do you mean? Did you not have to enter through the wine cellar?"

"No, what? Everyone uses the elevator, silly." She reached into her purse and pulled out a ticket. "The waiters give you a ticket to enter. Why were you in the wine cellar?"

"I must have read the ticket wrong." He let out a fake chuckle.

They gave me another test.

Someone here still doesn't trust me.

Just then, the door opened behind him, clipping the back of his heels. Lonnie jumped forward, surprised at how quiet the room had become. The bodies swarming around the screen had all turned and were now staring in his direction.

What were they looking at?

Spinning around, he found himself face to face with Silas Sibil. He gulped.

"Sorry," Lonnie apologized, stepping to the side.

He had a conflicting sense of awe and disgust for this man, and he didn't know what to make of it. Lonnie felt grotesque at how easily he moved himself out of the way. How little it made him feel. He waited for the man to pass, but Silas stood still, his siblings muttering to themselves in the background under the door frame.

"Hello," Silas said to him.

Lonnie glanced over his shoulder, expecting someone to be behind him, though no one was.

Oh, he's speaking to me.

"Hi," Lonnie responded bluntly.

Lonnie examined Silas closely. His features were much more unique than the author photo on his book jackets gave him credit for. The curves of his cheekbones halted at rose-colored blotches on either side of his face, and his nose curved in such a way that had been unnoticeable in the flatness of the photo. Contrary to his normal demeanor, he had wild eyes.

"You're Lonnie," Mr. Sibil declared without doubt.

"I am... You know who I am?"

Of course, he knows who you are idiot. You killed his sister.

The siblings had now joined Silas, entering into the conversation.

Florence let out a jovial movie star laugh. "He asks how we know him. Darling, everyone here knows you!"

"They do?"

Lonnie didn't know how to act. His childhood heroes were standing in front of him, and any emotion he held just didn't seem appropriate. Should he be starstruck or stab one of them with the wine key sitting on the bar counter?

Was it weird that he wanted to do both?

He withheld a nervous giggle as Florence moved in closer, her perfume touching his nose.

"Quite hard to forget after that show you put on last year."

Sebastian and Daphne did not laugh but raised their brows, bemused by her line. Lonnie's hands began to sweat.

"I thought you would be mad... by what happened."

Their smiles faded slightly but still held. If it was a facade, Lonnie found it hard to tell.

"Well, I've learned in the past that you can't control what happens at these things!" Florence let out a whimsical laugh, then hid her smile.

Daphne cut in, her tone deep and rugged. "It's that idiot husband's fault, really, experimenting on those subjects below his house." She waved her hand, in which she held an unlit cigarette. "That's what you get for stepping on the Gods' toes."

Silas pressed a hand on hers, lowering her swinging arm. Lonnie backstepped, noticing he was now trapped between adoring guests and the siblings on either side.

"Well, I am sorry for your loss either way," Lonnie offered, his pitch rising.

Silas took a step forward and cupped his hand. "Thank you, *Lonnie,* that is very kind of you. I know you probably don't have the fondest memory of her, but she did have her moments."

Lonnie wanted to leave the situation, but found Amara was still standing eagerly beside him, as though waiting to be introduced.

"Oh, sorry, this is my friend Amara—"

"Amara Wexler, pleasure to meet you." She extended her hand jubilantly.

Silas let out a chuckle and shook it, as did the rest of the siblings in various personalized fashions. "I am sorry, Miss Wexler, do you mind if I borrow Lonnie here for a few moments?"

"Yes, absolutely." She slid her hand back and retreated to the bar. "Nice to meet you."

Sebastian whispered something in Silas's ear and then stepped away, his remaining two siblings tagging alongside him to the crowd that was waiting to speak with them.

"How can I help you?" Lonnie asked tentatively.

Silas ignored his question, instead finding his way to an empty leather chair. "Come sit with me." He gestured to a seat beside him.

Lonnie hesitantly did so, sinking into the fabric.

"Last year was your first time coming to this party, correct?"

Lonnie flashed back again to that video his mother had shown him. His unconscious body strapped to that chair as they forced his brother to point the gun at his head.

Then *bang*.

His brother fell to the tile, his brain matter blasted onto the wall.

"You could say that," he lied.

"And how did it feel when you knew what was going on here?"

It's another test.

"I mean, it was shocking to say the least..."

Mr. Sibil leaned in, his hand firmly stroking his chin. "Oh, I imagine!"

"But I think I understand."

"Do you?" Mr. Sibil almost laughed, but remained serious.

"The Aztecs, the ancient Greeks, the Romans... People have sacrificed in the name of gods throughout history. If you have a ritual for unlimited wealth, would it not be wasteful to ignore it?" Lonnie bit his tongue, hoping that his words passed the test, but Silas just stared at him, his eyes squinting.

"What an interesting thought." Mr. Sibil gave a crooked smile.

Change the topic.

"Sorry, can I ask you a question?" Lonnie said.

"Of course."

"What inspired you to write *The Princes of York*?"

Mr. Sibil appeared stunned. He leaned closer, as if to whisper a secret. "You know my books?"

"I love them. Actually, quite a lot." Lonnie fawned, the superfan in him breaking through. He tried to reel it back, to hold onto some sense of composure. "But..."

"There's a but..." Silas's voice rose an octave, a mischievous smile growing on his face.

"It's just... they are about these poor boys living in New York, right? The way you described the way they lived, the fight they went through to survive every day... I guess I just always assumed that you came from a similar background. But *this* place, your family... these traditions. Correct me if I am wrong, but those little princes feel a world away."

Silas's eyes grew animated as the smile grew wider on his face. "Wow, and I thought *I* knew how to read people."

"I'm sorry, I don't mean to be rude."

"No, people should question everything. That is why I was so enthralled when I heard of your performance last year!"

Lonnie almost laughed at the word. He supposed it was a performance. He looked around, noting the people carrying their liquor down to their seats, sitting comfortably as if waiting for a movie to begin. Others continued to make bets, the screen numbers flipping up and down every second.

Without context, you would think everyone was gathered for the horse races. Because that's what the champions were to them, just horses put on a track. And if they didn't perform, then they were put down.

If they want me to perform, then I'll perform all right.

Lonnie put on a smile, attempting to embody his mother. "You should have seen it in person. I was quite a show."

Silas laughed, so Lonnie joined in. Holding the lightness, he continued talking. "How come you guys stopped coming here? Didn't you miss it?"

Silas quit laughing.

Crap.

He just stared again, his bushy eyebrows drooping down low.

Change the subject.

It was too late. Mr. Sibil leaned in, lowering his tone. "When I was a boy, my family lived in a small village in the north of Greece. The Germans had just fled after World War II. I remember seeing my mother smile. I *think* it was the first time I had ever seen her that happy. Little did we expect that this was just the beginning of yet another war. But this time, against ourselves. For the next few years, we escaped from village to village, fleeing the fighting. As my parents raised my new siblings, my sister and I would go out and work."

Lonnie noticed Mr. Sibil's eyes begin to gloss over.

"I left this house and wrote *The Princes of York* because I wanted to remember the me I was back then. The hardworking son." His eyebrows furrowed. "I didn't recognize the boy I had become when I moved here."

His gaze shifted to the crowd, where his sister raised an arm, beckoning him to join a small group of people standing beside her.

"Thank you for the chat, but it looks like I am being summoned."

"Oh, okay." Lonnie felt dazed.

As Mr. Sibil walked through the crowd, a gap formed, allowing Lonnie to briefly spot Jamie lurking by the bar on the far side of the room.

He's still okay. Lonnie eased his shoulders.

"Jamie." He waved as he stood from his seat. Jamie turned slightly, shocked by his presence.

"Hey," he replied.

Lonnie impulsively wrapped his arms around him. "Thank God, you're okay."

Jamie tugged away slightly, reminding him that they still weren't on the best of terms from their fight a few weeks back. Letting go, Lonnie took a measurable step back.

"How did you get here?" Lonnie asked.

Jamie pointed to the red-haired boy who was ordering a drink at the bar. "Carter showed me the elevator."

So everyone got to use the elevator but me.

Lonnie brought his tone to a whisper. "You two seem to be getting along."

Honestly, he was surprised they hadn't killed each other by now. Especially considering Carter's family was the whole reason Jamie was sent to this party in the first place.

Jamie scoffed. "I mean, if his guilty conscience wants to help me survive another night in this house, I would be stupid to say no."

"So... you're just using him?"

"Of course." He looked shocked. "What did you think, we were becoming friends? His family wanted me dead. I'm not stupid."

"Yeah, I suppose."

Carter approached, carrying a glass of whiskey, which silenced their conversation.

"Oh, good, you made it." Carter raised his drink, motioning toward the screen behind them. "Looks like just in time, too."

A burst of white noise came from the screen as the giant wager board switched to static. Everyone halted their conversations and watched with a striking intensity as the screen flipped to black.

"He's waking up," a guest gasped in the front.

Lonnie was confused, but upon closer inspection, he noticed a slight movement in the center of the monitor. A blast of light shot across the screen, before easing into a green-tinted night vision. There, sitting in the center of what appeared to be some kind of hole, sat a muscular boy spread out on a dirt floor.

Roman.

Florence stepped in front of the crowd, raising her martini glass and waving it whimsically in the air. "Ladies and gentlemen, the trials have officially begun."

Chapter 12

Up The Spout

05:30:00... 05:29:59... 05:29:58

The timer in the corner of the screen continued to drop, adding stress onto the already excruciating situation. Lonnie peered at the clock on the wall and saw both hands were tied up at twelve.

Midnight, and the night's only just starting.

Roman was rubbing his forehead as Lonnie remembered himself doing the year prior. The pain and confusion that was written on his face brought back a nauseating feeling. It was an ethereal out-of-body experience to watch someone suffer as you did. Yet, he couldn't find the strength to look away from the screen.

Roman tried to lift himself to his feet, but his torso started to sink, dragging him to the floor.

He is too top heavy to stand.

The numbness from the drug would slowly wear off, but he wouldn't know that. How could he? Roman dug his fingers into the dirt below his feet and managed to crawl over to the nearest wall.

The room was rather claustrophobic, a circular-shaped hole no wider than a couple of feet and no taller than a person. Brick walls lined the perimeter, and the floor was a combination of dirt and water puddles. At the same moment as Lonnie, Roman seemed to notice a sliver of light shining into the room. Shielding his eyes with his hand, he looked up. One of the hidden security cameras followed, revealing a cave-like roof. A crevice no bigger than a foot or two wide cut through the ceiling, letting in a light glow.

"What is that?" Lonnie asked the room, his voice echoing louder than expected.

It was then he noticed how quiet it had become. Peering around, he watched everyone staring intensely at the screen. Every seat had been filled, and those who hadn't found one lingered close behind. Even the line for the bar had vanished, and the bartenders had disappeared from their stations.

Perhaps they aren't supposed to be here for this part.

The liveliness of the room had died. No longer did it feel like a sports game. Instead, it was like everyone was patiently waiting and expecting the arrival of bad news. Lonnie noticed a few guests standing in the corner of the room, their eyes closed and mouths moving ever so slightly.

Were they praying?

Other people clutched the leather of their seats, their gaze locked on the screen. The man who had just bet ten million dollars was sitting attentively, drops of sweat running down his forehead. He held his pocket square between his fingers, dabbing it over his face repeatedly.

They are all terrified.

Turning back to the screen, he found that Roman was still pressed against the wall, though now he was trying to use it to climb to his feet. When he got about halfway up, he slipped and landed on his butt with a loud clunk. Enraged, he slammed his hand into the dirt.

"Whoever you are, you picked the wrong person, man!" He jabbed his finger up at the crevice. "I swear to God, when I find you, I will wring your neck with your own spine!"

Jesus…

The audio blasted out of the speaker like a cannon, making a few people, including Lonnie, jolt.

Roman did not seem like the kind of guy to fall apart at the first sign of panic, but his outburst was rather animated. The man he met briefly at the bar was clearly hiding another side within that surfer boy exterior. Maybe it would be enough to survive the night.

Don't get your hopes up.

Roman tried again to pull himself up the wall, this time really digging his nails into the mortar between the bricks. He got to his feet with a huff and walked his hands along the low ceiling for support. Slowly, he shuffled his body over, his shoes splashing as he stepped into a shallow puddle below the crack.

Guests leaned in, absolutely entranced by the screen. Some didn't blink, while others gasped in surprise. Lonnie despised them all, but he couldn't help watching alongside them.

Surely Roman wouldn't try to climb through that narrow crack.

But again, to his surprise, Roman reached into the cave-like hole and tried to pull himself up. His feet raised a few inches off the ground, followed by a loud yelp as he fell back down. He cupped his palm, which had a light trail of blood dripping from it.

"He cut his hand on the rocks!" a guest shouted, raising her own hand.

The others nodded in agreement.

Roman remained flat, his back resting in the puddle. Facing the ceiling, he caught his breath while the light drifted down over him. He tried to roll to his side, but the movement put a crinkled expression on his face. Trying the other way, he managed to get partially on his side before he huffed and fell onto his back again.

With his uninjured hand, he dug into the pocket he had just rolled over. Drawing his phone out like a sword, he lifted it to his face and let the blue light encompass the room.

"You forgot to take my phone, you idiots!" Roman sang out.

Lonnie scrunched his face in embarrassment.

No... I can't watch this.

The phone reignited a fire inside him. Doing as expected, Roman optimistically dialed a number, and the guests just watched amused as it failed to find service.

"Damn it," Roman yelled.

The crowd broke their silence with a sharp laugh, which made Lonnie want to cry. Snide comments were passed from chair to chair, and it only made him wonder what wretched things they had said about him during his trials.

Disgusting creatures.

Roman's anger turned to despair as he fought back the obvious fear that was creeping over him. He flipped on his camera light, which scorched the night vision camera. The screen quickly flipped to normal, the green changing to multi-color. The light made the room more horrid than the darkness. The muddy dirt floor was reminiscent of bile, and the walls were caked in slime and white mold. But the most disturbing element was, without a doubt, the black plaque that was fitted into the brickwork. It was no larger than a piece of paper, but Lonnie knew what it was. It was his first clue. Roman managed to sit up and crawl over to it. Pulling himself to his knees, he ran his fingers across the words written in white ink.

"Up the spout," he recited.

Plop.

He spun so fast, he almost fell over again. A drop of water had landed in the puddle in the center of the room, sending out a small ripple.

"What?" Roman muttered.

From the crevice above, another drop of water fell, creating another ripple.

Plop.

Roman pulled himself up, taking a few steps closer. Peering up at the hole, he jumped as another drop landed on his cheek. Then another and another. He moved his head back just in time as the drops turned into a steady stream. Water was filling the room at an alarming rate, turning the dirt floor into a pond.

Move.

Lonnie looked at the Sibils, who were seated at a small table closest to the screen. They were perfectly still, aside from Silas casually whispering something in Florence's ear.

What were they thinking right now?

Roman clawed at the wall, the water rising up his shins. Ripping off his blazer and shirt, he revealed a white tank top hidden underneath. He let the clothes go, and they disappeared into the darkness below the water.

"Come on!" he pleaded, trying to pry a stone from the wall.

Roman managed to rip off the plaque, which he then

converted into a makeshift crowbar. Holding his phone between his teeth, he started jamming the plaque into the ceiling, chipping and widening the crack.

Lonnie wanted so badly to cheer for him, but he restrained himself, trying not to give away his stance to the other guests. By the time the water had reached his knees, Roman had widened the entrance to the hole by a few inches. But even that didn't seem like it would be enough for his stocky frame to fit through.

He had to try. He was running out of time.

Suddenly, the ten-million-dollar man squawked to the group, "What's happening with the camera? I can hardly see!"

He was right. The screen was beginning to fog up, making it blur around the edges.

"Oh my, I think the water's hot," one woman chimed.

"I think she's right, look at the steam above his head!" a man added. "He can hardly see."

A final woman in a fascinator and bejeweled scarf looked toward the siblings and smirked. "Florence, was this your idea? You actors and your dramatics!"

Everyone then looked at Florence in unison. She gave a pageant smile and shrugged her shoulders, returning her attention to the show.

Roman swung once more. A chunk of the crevice gave way, forcing a bigger jet of water to flood in. Startled, he dropped the plaque and his phone into the dark below. He cursed, but didn't have time to search for them. Instead, he stripped off his shoes and socks, placing his bare feet against the flooded dirt floor. Regaining his balance, he jumped, catching himself with his hands and feet fully inside the crevice. Water continued to beat down his face, lathering the walls around him.

The screen went static for a second, then returned with an aerial view from a new camera. This one was positioned in a metal air duct, at the base of which a panel had been removed. In its place was the top of the cave-like crevice. Roman could be seen inside, slowly shimmying his way up, though his large body made it rather difficult to move through the jagged edges of the crack. The water level kept rising, pooling fast around his waist.

Lonnie had never felt more useless in his entire life as he watched the poor boy from the safety and comfort of the fancy room. He wanted to help him, but what could he do?

Maybe I can break the water pipes.

It was a hopeful idea, but he knew there wasn't enough time to help. Around Roman, steam rose as water continued smothering his face from above. He shut his eyes, shuffling upward at a steady pace.

"Ouch," Roman grunted, blood dripping from his arm as it scraped against a jagged rock.

He ignored it, pushing onward.

"Just drown already!" a man in the corner of the wager room whined.

Lonnie imagined he must have bet a good sum on him.

I hope you lose.

Roman was nearly a foot from reaching the air duct when he stopped moving.

No. No. Why are you stopping?

Roman jostled his head back and forth, flailing his body as much as possible.

He's stuck!

Lonnie didn't take him as a religious man, but in the moment, he probably was reciting any prayers he could manage to pull from his brain. The water climbed to his chin, soon pressing against his sealed mouth, searching for a way in. A faint sniffle came from beside Lonnie, which made him turn. Next to him, Jamie was quietly shaking. His eyes were glazed over as he looked at Roman drowning on the screen.

He must be in agony.

Jamie's arms held himself in an embrace, most likely imagining himself drowning right alongside Roman. Lonnie wanted to comfort him, but Jamie had already turned away, retreating into the shadow at the back of the room.

What an unbearable pain, to watch yourself die.

The water was now up to Roman's nose, forming tiny bubbles as he fought to breathe. Without air, his body convulsed, violently shaking from beneath the water.

I can't watch this. I cant...

Lonnie looked away, hoping that it would be over quickly. He waited for the audience's inevitable reaction to confirm it. But instead, what he heard next was a deep scream bellowing from the speakers.

He's still alive?

Lonnie peeked at the screen to see Roman's agony-stricken face breaking free of the water. The camera zoomed in, showing a pain and deep focus hidden within his eyes. He continued shimmying upward through the crevice, until finally expelling onto the ductwork tunnel.

How did he manage to get unstuck?

The answer became obvious, as he collapsed flat on the duct, blood gushing from his shoulders. Where once was skin, was now a deep red gash with tiny fragments of flesh barely attached. The rest of his body somehow was even worse. His tank top and pants were ripped, revealing red marks hidden underneath, like a thousand tiny cuts.

He looked horrible, but Lonnie couldn't help silently celebrate the fact that he was still alive. Meanwhile, the rest of the audience had varying reactions. Some cheered, while others booed.

Don't you all want him to win?

He supposed that if some were making ten million on a bet, then they wouldn't really care if Roman failed the trials. As long as no one broke the rules and pissed off the Gods in the process.

But surely everyone didn't feel that way. He remembered the people praying just a few minutes earlier. They clearly took this more seriously than the others. But how far would they go for their beliefs?

Starting a civil war among members... could that be the answer to my problems?

Lonnie put a pin in the idea as the screen switched to another camera, this time revealing the full metal duct. It couldn't have been longer than a few meters, its shape a standard 24" x 24" square. Tiny blue UV lights were spaced out evenly across the ceiling, giving it a faint glow. The bottom inclined up at a slight angle before opening into a vertical duct at the end, where the water was streaming down.

Roman lay on the metal, gasping for air as he spat out leftover water. The cave below was fully submerged, but the water didn't stop. If anything, the pressure only increased, already beginning to layer the bottom of the vent. Clearly exhausted, he began crawling up the incline to get ahead of it.

"Come on," Roman muttered to himself.

A faint yellow light was coming from the vertical duct, which caught Roman's attention. He moved closer, as the water pooled around his crouched knees and elbows. When he reached the end of the vent, he stared up at another square duct above him. Water streamed endlessly from a source he could not see, as well as what appeared to be blinding sunlight.

But it's nighttime.

"This is it," Roman cheered.

He tried to climb, but gave up and instead waited for the water to rise and lift him.

Don't do it.

But he couldn't hear him. Roman waited for the water to fill the horizontal vent, and soon was floating up the vertical spout.

"That's not the exit," Lonnie whispered.

Just as he said it, the footage switched to inside the new duct, revealing something that made the room break into gasps of shock and surprise.

The water neared the top, as Roman resurfaced, hitting his head on something hard.

Thud.

He reached out his hand, utterly shocked to find it met with a metal grate. A group of yellow fluorescent bulbs glowed from higher up in the vent, producing that natural light he had previously been drawn to.

"No!" He punched the metal over and over, holding his legs against the edges of the duct to support himself.

The water level continued rising, once again cutting off his air supply as it reached the grate. With a final breath, he tried to pry on the edge of the metal, but the piping had become too slippery. With no other choice, he sank under.

Lonnie felt the room tense again. As Roman held his breath, the guests did likewise. Energy moved through them as one, each heartbeat synchronized and in chorus.

The hue of the UV lights glowed at the top of the water like a gloating sun. It mocked Roman as he sank into the tunnel. Wasting no time, he beat at the walls, prying at every crack and crevice he could find.

Bubbles escaped his mouth, each rising to the surface. Wedging himself between the walls, with his arms pressed behind him, he kicked at one of the panels, each time with more force, until exhaustion overtook him.

Lonnie glanced at the timer in the corner of the screen.

It had already been a minute!

He couldn't possibly last much longer. Swimming down to the bottom of the vertical duct, there was a panel that was slightly darker than the rest. Using the last of his strength he gave it a measurable kick.

Pop.

A tiny bolt shot out from the frame, sinking to the floor. The edge of the panel parted from the wall, revealing an opening in the siding. Roman's eyes widened. He swam over to the panel, digging his hands into the cracks. Running his hands around it, he moved carefully until, eventually, a second bolt shot out.

Pop.

Roman ripped the remaining metal from the wall, more frantic now. The water started funneling in, tugging at him to follow until he eventually slipped through.

His world flipped on its axis as he passed through a passageway and was pulled down by gravity. He fell, floating in the air a moment before landing inside another duct. This one was at a 45-degree angle, which, combined with the rushing stream, propelled him down like a waterslide.

Roman screamed, but his voice was cut off by the sound of his body slamming against the metal. On the screen, the footage kept changing cameras to keep up with him, but even still, the whole thing was a blur. Darkness came in and out periodically as he slid past UV lights set out every ten feet or so. The sound of heavy breathing filled the speakers as Roman struggled for air between crashing waves.

"Help…" he gurgled, flailing his arms.

Thud.

He went silent.

"Surely, he is dead?" a guest asked.

"Where did he go?" another yelled.

Silence draped the room, leaving a sense of dread in Lonnie's head. The screen blinked to a bright red, which reflected a light pink over the guests' faces. They stared in horror as time increased with no change or update.

The Sibils whispered among themselves, but their lack of alertness started to get to people.

A woman with a fur coat and a tiny fan was the first to stand, her face flustered. "The cameras are broken! What are you going to do about this?"

Another guest stood. "For God's sake, Sibils. Get your House in order!"

More guests stirred in their seats, which forced furrowed brows to the siblings' faces. Some, including the ten-million-dollar man, even began to shout.

"This is foul play. I want my money back, or I'm suing you all into the dirt."

"Me too, I didn't pay for this," a woman hissed.

Lonnie was anxious about Roman, but a smile crept on his face at the thought that the siblings' lack of hosting skills might be the downfall of this place all on its own.

"Silence everyone," one of the siblings ordered, waving his hand. "Stop your whining and look."

It was Sebastian, the tall and rather reserved sibling. This was the first time Lonnie had heard him speak all night. His tone was so much deeper than expected. He stepped away from his siblings' table on the side of the screen and now stood center stage. He looked toward the monitor and pointed.

People's snide comments turned to disgruntled mumbles as they followed his eyeline.

"Who does he think he is, telling me to be quiet?" Lonnie heard a person beside him mutter to a peer, to which they shrugged their shoulders and took a sip of wine.

Everyone's eyes glared at the red screen as it moved. A camera panned out, slowly breaking the image apart pixel by pixel until it showed a bright cherry-colored octagon room. Bright oil lamps and paintings hung from each stretched wall, and a large white and gold chandelier hung from the ceiling.

Clank.

One of the paintings swung outward, and behind it, Roman slid down an exposed duct, crashing into the carpet with a hard thud. A small stream was spit out on top of him, creating a puddle on the carpet. Then, as fast as it opened, the painting shut back against the wallpaper, a magnetic click locking it in place.

Lonnie clutched his heart. *Thank God, he's alive.*

Sebastian knelt below the screen, his hand hovering above three gray circular lamps pressed into the wall. Flicking his index finger on the middle one, a red light filled out the gray.

BEEP

A loud siren blasted from the speakers, shaking the whole room. Lonnie recognized that sound all to clearly.

The first trial was done.

Chapter 13

Intermission

"No!" The ten-million-dollar man kicked his chair, flipping it over. Nearby guests gave him some room as he threw his tantrum. "This is ridiculous. How did he not drown? What is he, a damn fish?" The man grabbed his drink and tossed it across the room, shattering it against the wall.

Other patrons shouted with annoyance as glass landed at their feet.

"I want my money back!"

"You knew the odds." Daphne, the short tech genius sibling, looked up from her drink, giving him a pathetic wag of her finger. "Don't be cheap now."

The man whimpered, now growing red from all the people staring at him. Sulking back to the bar, he grabbed a handle of vodka and stormed out of the room. The screen briefly flipped back to the wager board, which now had a yellow highlight in the box bordering *Trial #1* and *Live*. A few people across the room hollered, while most gave sour looks of disappointment.

"Fear not, friends." Silas Sibil stood from his seat. "The night is far from over, so don't go selling your stocks just yet."

Silas looked back at Roman, who lay still on the carpet. Pointing a remote at the screen, he turned it back to the wager board, erasing Roman as if he was just changing the channel to a new show.

"Let's take a small intermission, shall we?" He raised his glass. "I should see how the party above is carrying on... but please, refill your drinks and get comfortable. Also, bring those bartenders back down here!"

The room raised their glasses with small cheers, followed by everyone moving to the bar or starting to mingle with those beside them. Lonnie watched the crowd through annoyed eyes.

So much for all killing each other.

Bodies milled around him, making the air dry from their joyous exhales and rank hors d'oeuvre breath. Lonnie caught Carter talking to Jamie at the far side of the room, his hand resting on his shoulder. Jamie wiped at his eyes like he had been crying, but they were both smiling.

Lonnie crinkled his brow. *I think I need a moment.*

Barging through the crowd, he pushed his way out the door, only to find the hallway was emptier than he anticipated.

Where is everyone?

Lonnie had imagined maybe a few people would have wandered off, but the sheer emptiness made him want to reach back for the door handle.

No. I don't want to go back. Not yet.

He walked deeper into the hall where he spotted the ten-million-dollar man sitting on the floor. His bottle of vodka was already a third drained, and it showed from his expression.

"Are you okay?" Lonnie asked.

The guy responded, his words slurred, "This place is barbaric."

He's probably not thinking for the same reason I am, but it's a conversation starter, nonetheless.

"I know what you mean." Lonnie stepped closer, casually peering around for a security camera. Better safe than sorry. He lowered his tone. "I can't believe those four get to run this place. I mean... they haven't even been to one of these in years. It should be someone more qualified."

The guy nodded his head drunkenly. "Exactly, that's what I have been saying. If anything, I should have been the host. I've been here a lot more times than they have."

Lonnie crouched down now, trying to act calm and collected. "Why not you, right? I mean... with what happened last year. They clearly need better leaders."

The man stared at him with a dumb expression. "What happened last year? I was not invited."

Oh my gosh nobody told him...

Lonnie concealed a smile. "They didn't tell you?"

"Tell me what?"

"All the guests last year were killed." Lonnie pointed at a door directly across from them. "Right in there."

The ten-million-dollar man's jaw dropped as he shook his head. "You're lying."

"Their experiments escaped. They murdered everyone, including the hosts. That's how they really died." Lonnie leaned closer. "This family doesn't care about us. Or your money. There needs to be a change."

The man stared, still clearly processing all the information he had just received.

I think I overdid it.

"What's your name?" Lonnie stuck out his hand.

"Henrik."

"I'm Leonard. Nice to meet you."

"Likewise." His voice shook.

"It's just something to think about, that's all." Lonnie stood up. "Also, the bartenders are back. I'm sure they could mix that vodka with something if you want."

The guy held up his bottle, growing blush again. "Yeah, I should probably go back in and do that."

He pulled himself to his feet and gave Lonnie one last glance as he returned to the party.

What was that?

Lonnie didn't know what power had just come over him. He had never spoken with such suave confidence in his life, yet Henrik seemed moved by it.

First crack in the dam.

But I need to make more.

Still feeling the adrenaline coursing through him, he looked at a door across the way.

The Ritual Room. He shivered.

Seeing if anyone was watching, he sprinted over and grabbed the chilled handle as the cool air bled out from under the frame.

"What am I doing?"

Just do it.

Without thinking, he pried the door open and snuck inside. The cold phased through him, fusing to every cell in his body. Frost chilled on the back of the door, which made it crack when moved.

The room was exactly as he remembered, minus all the bodies and death. Black tiles covered every surface, making the space look like a nebula with the white bulbs as stars shining from the ceiling. Around the perimeter was an empty gutter that reeked of dry metal. And on the right wall, there was a set of black tile bleachers, big and long enough for a couple of hundred people to sit on.

On the left wall was that disgusting symbol that he had seen on all those envelopes he was sent: a white painted outline of those five gods sewn together at the spine. The two twins at the bottom, each holding knives. *Glory and Honor, the warriors.* The skinny one and the burly one positioned above them. *Penury and Avarice, the giver and the collector.* Finally, the blinded one in the middle. *Donor, the pure.* No matter how many times he saw it, it would always make his stomach tighten.

Beside the left wall was a black table and pillar, atop which a large bowl was filled with that same black goo he had dripped his bloody finger over earlier. Curious, he leaned his face in, immediately disengaged by the rancid smell.

"Ugh, it smells like burnt metal and rotting flesh."

Though Lonnie supposed it wasn't far off, remembering how he'd dripped his blood into it earlier in the night. On the table beside him was a large crate. The exterior was a bold white, which contrasted the room, and made him even more curious.

What could possibly be in there?

The idea of knowing made his heart pound, though he couldn't decide if it was in a good way or bad one. Cautiously stepping over, he unlatched both belts that were holding it down and pried the lid open.

"What the...?"

Hundreds of blood samples filled the inside of test tubes with text inscribed around the glass. Lonnie grabbed a few, raising them to the light.

R. Ramirez

V. Laicroft

Who were these people?

He raised the last one in his hand, putting it up to the light.

R. Rodbloom

Hannah's dad?

"People actually send their blood here?"

I suppose that was what Amara meant by participating from afar...

Taking out his phone, he took a picture of the case, making sure to get as many names legible as possible. Carefully, he placed the vials back exactly how he found them, hoping whoever put them in wouldn't notice they'd been moved.

More evidence.

Now I should really get out of here.

But just as he turned to leave, he noticed the light bounce off something further down the table. Peering just past the container, he spotted a leather-bound book lying flat on the counter.

The grimoire...

His mind told him no, but his body pulled him toward it with little resistance. He flipped open the left cover, finding a large heading of text inserted into the center of the page. Lonnie traced over what he assumed were Greek letters, but found it impossible to read what they said.

Flipping through the pages, he noticed some of the drawings Mr. Blythorne had previously shown him: the story of the five Gods, illustrations of the trials, and diagrams of wealth and power. Beside each, there was more Greek writing, but it was only when he looked closer that he noticed someone had added some pen into the margins.

Was this in English?

Incantation.

Offerings.

The farther he flipped through the book, the more common they became, each one written in bold blue ink, which made him think it must have been sometime recently. Lonnie read them to himself, following arrows that connected them to untranslatable bundles of text.

Pulling his phone out of his pocket, he held it between his fingers. With the camera open, he took pictures of pages one after another; only noticing as he finally closed the app that it read in the top right corner: **No Signal.**

A feeling which felt insultingly repetitive.

Clapping from across the hall caught him by surprise. Slamming the book down, he vacated the room in a rush, first opening the door a crack to make sure the coast was clear and then heading off into the hallway as though he had never left.

"What were you doing in there?" a voice demanded.

Lonnie turned to find a man approaching from down the hall. It was Silas.

Crap.

"I said what were you doing in there?" Silas stood now directly in front of him, his arms crossed in dismay.

"I was looking for the bathroom," Lonnie responded, without meeting his gaze.

Silas gauged him for a moment and then responded sharply. "Down the hall, second door on the right."

"Thank you." Lonnie stammered, walking past.

"And Lonnie..."

"Yes?" He refused to face Silas and expose his guilty eyes.

"If you keep looking for trouble here, you're surely going to find it."

Lonnie bit his tongue, unsure how to respond to such a warning. Instead, he merely nodded and then lowered his head as he walked with dismay to the bathroom.

He knew what I was doing. Why did he let me go?

Maybe it's another test.

He stepped inside and immediately flipped the faucet on, letting the noise shroud the outside voices.

The bathroom was surprisingly basic. A simple white porcelain toilet and sink to match. A little bar of soap sat on the counter and baby blue wallpaper threaded the interior. Lonnie stared at his reflection in the cabinet mirror and poked at the bags under his eyes.

"What a long night."

He splashed the water onto his face, hoping it would melt the glum look from his cheeks. Though when it dried away, he couldn't help thinking it looked worse than before.

Ugly.

The cheers grew louder through the wall, no longer hidden by the sound of rushing water.

"Great, what now?"

Lonnie dried his hands on the towel and reluctantly marched back to the wager room, which in his head, he had decided to rename *the lion's den* to complement *the lamb pen* Amara showed him earlier. He gathered himself in the hall, finding the courage to head back, when another voice appeared behind him.

"Excuse me," Amara sang, as she squeezed past him in the narrow hallway.

Lonnie spotted worry lines between her eyebrows as she went by, which caught his attention.

What is she thinking about?

He turned around, noting her entrance was the exact same path as Mr. Sibils, only minutes prior.

"Where were you at?" he asked, as politely as he could muster.

"I was phoning my parents," she said, refusing to slow her stride toward the watch party door.

Lonnie peeked at his phone, which still read no signal.

She's lying. She's hiding something.

"Wait..." He tried to regain her attention, but she kept going.

He glared at Amara. He hadn't noticed before, but her steps were all so calculated. Each one was raised and elegant enough that one might think she wore heels, when in fact she wore black flats.

She's been playing me this whole time.

Lonnie jogged up beside her, leaning in inconspicuously. "Can I pick your brain?"

"Um, I suppose..." She slowed down, but didn't stop her pacing.

"How many members would you say this place has?" He looped in front, blocking her path. "You know, in all."

"We shouldn't talk about that," she whispered, deflecting the question.

"You have been here many times, as you said, surely you have a rough number."

"I don't know, a few hundred perhaps," she responded, holding a dubious smile. "Why are you asking me this?"

"'Cause I want to know why they aren't all here. It feels like

I'm missing an important detail that no one will tell me. How do they pick who has to come?"

"It's a complicated process."

"Please just be honest for once. I saw the vials, Amara."

Her fake smile dropped, and she grabbed him by the hand. "Lonnie, stop talking." She leaned in. "You shouldn't have gone in there."

"That's how they do it, right?"

"Please just go back inside—"

"The people who don't receive an invitation, send their blood samples instead and the members puts them in the bowl. Then it's like they're here, taking part in the ritual. Right? I keep thinking about what you said earlier, about how the list is curated every year."

"Okay." She grimaced.

"And I am still trying to wrap my head around why you weren't on it. If what you said is true, you've been invited here for the past ten years, so why not the last?"

"I don't know what you are trying to insinuate. The higher up members make the list. It's not up to me." Amara averted her gaze, the pitch of her voice straining with each new word.

"But why just the last one, when you've been forced to come every other time?"

She gave him a light pull, leading him toward the door. "Let's just go back inside. This is not the place for this discussion—"

"No, tell me!"

"Please lower your voice," she squealed. "That one was different, that is all."

"No, I don't think it was. I think you're lying again!"

Lonnie tightened his hand around hers, constricting slowly

like a snake. He was so sick of people keeping secrets from him. Especially people pretending to be his friends. She wouldn't tell him about his brother, or the white door, and now she was lying about this.

No, this needs to end now.

"Tell me what changed last year!"

"Why is it so important?"

"Because my entire life imploded that day, and you conveniently weren't there? I find that impossible to believe. So tell me the truth! Now!"

"Fine, I was there!" she blurted, quickly cupping her mouth.

"What?"

"I was there." She lowered her hand, letting the words slither out of her throat.

"I told you not to lie—"

"I'm not." She stepped closer, her mouth nearly touching his ear. "I saw everything. The creatures, the gunshots... You even brushed by me in the ballroom, though you weren't exactly yourself by then."

Her eyes briefly darted to a security camera that rested above their heads, but Lonnie didn't care. He wasn't going to let her get away until he squeezed every bit of information out of her.

"How are you alive?"

She let out a muffled groan, probably realizing that she was never getting out of this conversation. "I was trying to save Hannah. It was right after you fried the electrical circuit, and I knew I had only a small window before they activated the backup generator. So, I put on my ritual cloak and followed the others into the control room. While they were so focused on recalibrating the circuit, it gave me just enough time to splice the wiring for the cameras... and the cells."

"Wait. You're the reason the creatures got out?"

"I just wanted to help my best friend... though by the time I had escaped the house, I found out it was all for nothing."

A tear crept from her eye, and Lonnie found himself wanting to wipe it from her cheek.

"Well, not completely for nothing. You saved my life."

She glanced at the camera above them again and let out a sniffled laugh. "To be determined." She took a deep breath, pulling herself together. "Well, unless you have any more accusatory things to say, we better go before anyone starts to get suspicious."

"Right," he agreed, rubbing the back of his neck. "Good idea."

Amara pushed open the door, as Lonnie followed behind. He couldn't stop looking at her, this newfound information sitting uncomfortably in his head.

This whole time it was her. She was the one who let out the monsters. She is the only reason I am alive...

The two of them reentered the room to find everyone had retaken their seats. Their absence didn't seem to have caused so much as a thought through the guests' minds.

Carter and Jamie were still hidden in the corner of the room, their arms now flailing with bold gestures. Lonnie waved, but stopped.

Are they arguing?

Jamie tried to walk away, but Carter grabbed him by the shoulder, pulling his ear to his mouth. He whispered something that seemed to put him at ease. Jamie gave an apprehensive nod and then went to the bar.

What the hell?

"Let's go." Amara pulled him toward their friends.

Lonnie snuck another glance at her, growing more curious by the thoughts that fluttered behind her eyes.

Amara Wexler, the girl who saved my life.

But something told him she was much more than that.

Chapter 14

A Roman Tragedy

Clink. Clink. Florence Sibil held up her glass and gently clinked it with a knife.

"Trial number two is underway, everyone," she said. "I hope our friend put his thinking cap on, because this one is gonna be a real brain twister."

The screen flipped from the wager board back to the live feed, revealing Roman pacing within the confines of his new cage. It was an octagon room, filled with eight symmetrical walls, each of which was wrapped in an ugly, red striped wallpaper and had a rather unsettling painting framed in its center. Victorian style furniture had been placed around the space, making it eerily homey, compared to the air duct. There was even a fireplace on one of the walls, with a cute brickwork mantle and a roaring fire within. A mahogany desk resided in the center of the room, with various papers, knick-knacks, and picture frames placed on top of it. In the center of the desk was another black plaque with white text that read:

Beauty is in the Eye of The Beholder.

Odd.

"What are those?" Carter blurted out.

Whispers passed around the room in response to his strange remark.

"What are you talking about?" Amara asked.

"Do you not see it?" He gestured. "Look at the floor."

He was right. There on the ground, sprouting out from under the desk, was a glowing white light. From it, a tiny fume of smoke rose and floated to the ceiling.

Roman caught sight of it as well and crouched on his knees. A noise hummed in the speaker.

Is that static?

Roman reached his hand out, and little sparks bounced from the light toward him.

No, electricity!

Lonnie wanted to warn him, but at the last second, Roman receded.

"Phew," Lonnie exhaled.

Roman grabbed a piece of paper from the desk and let it fall on top of the light, watching as it immediately combusted into flames upon impact. "Oh, crap." He scooted as fast as possible to the edge of the wall.

Without warning, the light spread, extending its reach from under the table. Within seconds, a white, diagonal line had burned through the rug, causing smoke to blister in its wake. Eventually, it reached the corner between two walls, where it started its incline up to the ceiling. Wallpaper burned away, leaving scorch marks on metal panels that were hidden underneath.

That can't be good.

Roman carefully stepped over the live wire and stared up at the paintings on the walls. The one that he had entered through showed an image of a woman resting atop a leaning chair. She held a chalice that was dripping wine down a pile of dirty plates, like a demented, cascading bowl fountain.

On the wall to its left, just above an old leather couch, was a painting of a muscular man wearing lavish fabrics. He lounged on a plush chair, with his back to the frame. He held a tiny mirror through which his eyes glared through, almost like he was watching you from behind his back.

On the wall to the right of the duct entrance was a painting of a disheveled man and his horse. The man rested his arms over his head as he lay on the capsized animal. The sunlight baked his face into a shade of red, and flies fluttered above the horse that lay beneath him.

So strange.

The guests were all fully absorbed in this new room. Many of those who were still standing did intellectual poses as though they were analyzing art at a museum. It was rather captivating, Lonnie couldn't deny. Every painting had a story that was so honest and real. And the design of the octagon room itself revealed how much time and energy the hosts put into these trials.

It would've been pretty amazing, if it weren't so sickening...

On the opposing side of the room, the paintings were no less abnormal. Diagonal from the muscular man with the mirror was a woman with large cheekbones and a beautiful sequined dress. Two unaccompanied hands tied a beautiful ruby necklace around her neck. The girl, however, was distracted, a distasteful grimace furling her lip. She stared out of her frame at the one beside her, a squint of jealousy escaping her eyes.

The painting she watched contained a plump woman who draped her naked body over a couch. A slender man sat beside her, one hand on her torso and the other invisible between her legs. However, her expression gave a clue to where it was concealed.

The last three paintings were on the walls by the fireplace. To the left of it, a man sat on a throne with its legs balanced atop a pile of coins. The man relaxed in the seat, his feet dangling over one armrest and his head drooping across the other. A crown rested on his scalp, covering a single eye and leaving the other examining a diamond necklace he held in his fist.

To the right of the fireplace, the painting depicted a man sitting on an old stump on a tiny hill. Behind him, smoke rose in the air, and in the background, one could faintly make out the rubble and bloodshed that riddled a town. At the base of his mound, injured men reached up to him for aid, but he ignored them. Lonnie looked back at the man on the stump, now noticing small daggers were plunged into his eyes, yet he remained unbothered.

Finally, the last painting was the most concerning. Directly above the mantle of the fireplace was a young man. Out of every orifice of his face, he was screaming, his body and clothes singed and ashen from a fire that consumed the rest of the painting. The tips of his hair were ignited like wax candles, and his skin peeled back like old paint. Yet, he remained in his chair, just staring. His eyes were locked on Roman, who stared back anxiously from the middle of the room.

What is he thinking?

What was everyone thinking? Lonnie snuck another glance toward Silas and his siblings.

Grabbing a chair from beside the desk, Roman carried it to the painting of the girl and her chalice. Standing atop it, he reached up and pried at the frame, trying to reopen it and exit the same way he had arrived. After a few failed attempts, he finally gave up.

"Screw it." Roman threw his hands up in anger.

The white electric line had climbed all the way to the ceiling and had begun burning its way to the chandelier. Bit by bit, charred pieces of felt swung to the floor. Roman looked up just in time to see the lights of the chandelier glow as bright as stars before exploding and shedding glass and metal everywhere. The chandelier crashed down on the desk with a loud burst. The room grew darker, now only illuminated by the oil lamps positioned at the top of each wall.

A loud chuckle came from one of the guests. It was the woman with the fascinator on her head from earlier. Her face was bright red from laughing.

"Now, Florence, this one has to be you. This is far too creative for any of those others to have come up with."

This lady is obsessed with her.

Florence laughed. "Oh, stop, you old hen! I'll never tell."

Ms. Sibil took another sip of her drink and clapped in excitement at the screen. It was surprising that this was the first time she had been back in so long; it appeared that she actually was having a good time, a thought that was quite devastating for Lonnie.

Daphne and Sebastian, on the other hand, looked absolutely miserable, two quiet busybodies who wanted to be in a conference room or a lab, but instead found themselves hosting an all-night party.

The jury was still out on where Silas stood on anything. Lonnie was finding him incredibly hard to read.

"Crap!" Roman cut off Lonnie's train of thought as he tried to push the chandelier off the desk.

A second white line ruptured from underneath, slithering across the floor and making its way up the wall. With urgency, Roman carefully jumped over it and fell at the foot of another painting.

Seemingly intrigued, he stood up, grabbing the framed portrait of the man and his sleeping horse, and trying to rip it off the wall. To his surprise, it came off easily, but there was no ductwork passage hidden behind, only wallpaper. He rested the useless painting back against the wall.

"Come on, where's the exit?" Roman hissed.

He attempted to move to the third painting, but tripped on debris, nearly falling backward onto the live wire. Swiveling out of the way, he slammed into the carpet. His cheek pressed into its scratchy texture.

He huffed, his forehead wrinkling. "I'm going to kill whoever put me in here."

"He's quite spirited!" the lady with the fascinator headwear added, looking around for others to agree.

Roman managed to pull himself together, moving to below the painting of the naked woman. He proceeded to lift her from the wall.

"Damn it," Roman said flatly.

Behind the painting was more wallpaper. Roman placed the painting back on the wall and crossed his arms with frustration. The second wire had traced up the ceiling and connected with the first one where the chandelier had once hung. Right as they touched, electrical noise grew from the walls like that of a Tesla coil, and with it, a third wire sprouted from the floor.

What happens when all eight corners are lit?

Lonnie didn't want to know, but he was sure the rest of the guests were utterly fascinated to find out.

Roman, shocked by the new noise, dove onto the desk, and finished pushing the chandelier onto the floor. Grabbing whatever he could, he then rummaged through the drawers and office supplies. However, most of the items he found were unimportant as far as Lonnie could see; invoices for various party catering items, remnants of opened letters, a blank notepad, a letter opener, and a variety of pens. There was also a small stack of books that he found in the bottom drawer, including a hotel-issued *Gideon* Bible, slightly worn copies of *The Grapes of Wrath* and *Twelve Angry Men*, and finally a thicker-set book with a picture of Big Ben on the front, titled *A History of World Landmarks*.

Roman flipped through each, his fingers running down the margins looking for anything out of the ordinary. The insides of the first couple of books appeared untouched, but as he reached the Bible, he stopped after a few pages. Circled in bold pen on Genesis, chapter four, was:

"If you do what is right, will you not be accepted? But if you do not do what is right, sin is crouching at your door; it desires to have you, but you must rule over it"

In the margin beside it was written in cheap black pen:

Greed

Pride

Gluttony

Sloth

Lust
Envy
Acedia
Wrath

He continued through the book, but found no more inked-in additions. He slammed it shut and tossed it with intensity across the room.

"Useless!" he yelled.

The book slammed against the painting to the right of the fireplace, which caused the picture of the man with daggers for eyes to swivel outward on two hidden hinges. Roman gasped. Behind the painting was a metal hatch with no handle, and below it were two evenly placed keyholes.

It's the exit. It has to be! Lonnie cheered in the solitude of his thoughts.

"Yes! Yes, there we go," Roman chimed, getting a second surge of energy.

Zit.

As he cheered, the third line of electricity reached the formation on the ceiling, causing a sizzling noise and vibration to overtake the room. A fourth wire lit from beneath the desk, hitting one of the table legs and causing it to crack and burn. Under the weight of Roman, it fully snapped, sending the books and documents toppling over the now uneven desk. He managed to keep his balance by grabbing the edge of the surface. Smoke from various papers caught on fire, as well as part of the Bible, which had managed to roll beside a wire, charring the corner into a burnt mess.

"Hurry," Lonnie whispered.

Roman jumped down and ran to the next painting, which was of the girl with the ruby necklace. On his toes, he jumped up and knocked the painting from its hook, letting it fall to the ground with a loud crack. Behind it, a script of text was written into the wallpaper with ink.

Within a Room of Fire

"Erif to mooq O ninltiw?" Roman recited, his eyes squinting with extreme focus. "What does that mean?" He hit his head. "Think!"

He stood farther away, giving another look before moving on and prying the other paintings from the walls. He approached the fireplace, but was taken aback by the roasting fire that was coaxing the edge of the mantle. He stepped in close, trying to reach the bottom of the frame, but singed the fringe of his pants on a hot coal and backed away.

He next went to the painting of a man resting on a pile of money and flipped it from the wall with satisfaction.

"Money, money, give me something good," Roman mumbled.

Beneath it, he saw the same bare wallpaper and was about to move on when he noticed a rectangular swatch cut into the center of where the portrait once stood. He grabbed the corner and ripped, watching as the tiny sliver of fabric came clean off. Behind it, a tiny black safe was hidden within the wall. On it were a set of ten numbers arranged beside a bright green button, a tiny metal handle, and a screen with four green dashes signifying number placeholders.

Roman immediately entered *1, 2, 3, 4*, which copied onto the tiny screen, and then clicked the green button. A red light shone from the face, letting him know he was wrong.

"Damn." He stepped away, nearly tripping on the fourth line, which now appeared to be moving faster than earlier.

"Oh crap!" Roman ran to the next painting as the line made haste up the wall and toward the ceiling. "Crap, crap, crap!"

He jumped the live wire and bounced off the couch, knocking the painting of the muscular man with a hand mirror off the wall.

Crack.

The guests at the watch party all let out a gasp, the loudest of which was from Henrik, the ten-million-dollar man. Lonnie noticed he was standing to the side of the screen. He had traded his handle for a cocktail, but by this point, he already looked like a drunken mess with his shirt unbuttoned and bow tie missing. He was eyeing the siblings' table, and Lonnie wondered if what he said had actually made an impact.

Yes, Henrik. Do something stupid.

Just as it seemed he was going to confront the siblings, an explosive sound came from the screen. Everyone looked as a piece of glass from the picture frame hit the live wire and burst into a million pieces. Roman shielded his face as the fragments launched across the room.

Looking down, Roman shuddered at the sight of his bloody torso. However, he soon relaxed as he patted himself down, only to find no loose shards. Instead, all he noticed was dried blood courtesy of the rocky crevice he had escaped from earlier that night.

"Great..."

Where did the glass come from?

Roman must have wondered the same as he picked up the painting, rubbing his thumb over the paper casing. He then flipped it around, uncovering a large mirror spread over the back. The bottom of which was now broken and jagged. Holding the mirror squarely in front of him, he could see the rest of the room inverted behind him.

"Oh my God," he yelped.

Behind Roman's head, he noticed the squiggly lines of ink on the opposing wall start to form words. Putting the painting side backward, he thrust the frame back onto the hook, sticking it in place with the mirror now out.

"Ow!" Roman screamed.

Grabbing his hand, he noticed a scorched mark around his index finger ring. The fourth line had reached the ceiling, sending volts of electricity ricocheting off the walls, one of which connected with Roman's signet ring. In a rage, he threw it off his finger along with his metal belt buckle and other rings, letting them all slide across the debris-riddled floor.

"What does it say?" He ran his finger in a line across the mirror as though a child learning to read. "Within a... With a room—"

The blinding light from the sparks settled long enough for the full sentence to be seen clearly from across the room.

Within a Room of Fire

"Within a room of fire." Roman's eyes darted around the room. "Within a room of fire... Where?"

There, under the mantle, he spotted the curled flames rattling against the brick.

"The key!" Roman roared.

Balancing his steps over the many new wires, he approached the burnt broken leg of the desk. Taking it in his arm, he jammed it into the fire pit, moving bits of lumber and soot from one end to the other.

"Where is it?" He swiped the contents of the fire onto the carpet. Each swing of the leg shrank the fire, until it was nothing more than a pile of ash and charred wood. Smoke rose from the mess, spreading across the ceiling and making the lines of white look like suspended bolts of lightning in a thundercloud. He sank to his knees, searching through the ash and smearing it thin on the carpet.

"Where is the key?"

Zit.

The fifth line had reached the ceiling, making the room grow brighter as the intensity of the lights increased. The tips of Roman's hair stood on end, drawn to the ceiling.

"How is it not there?" He pathetically raised himself to his feet. "There is no other fire—"

Just as he stood, Roman's eyes landed on the painting of the man on fire; his body illuminated by the flames that ripped at his skin.

"The room on fire..." Roman took a running start and jumped, flicking the painting from the wall.

Clink.

A metallic rattle echoed from the frame as the canvas bounced off the carpet. Roman rummaged on the floor until he found the desk letter opener and then plunged it into the heart of the man. With a cold slice, he pulled the knife down until the chest was ripped in half. Sticking his hand into the cavity, he grinned with success as he pulled out an antique skeleton key.

Good job, Roman. Keep going!

Roman hopped over the new sixth line and stuck the key into the slot beneath the metal door. It fit smoothly, turning with extreme ease. A light churning followed, splitting the metal hatch in two. Both halves were beginning to open, until...

Creak.

The doors came to a hard stop halfway.

"Come on." Roman tried to pry it farther, but it wouldn't budge.

Roman poked at the second lock, rattling his brain.

Shifting his attention to the safe, he scowled. "I need that code."

Below the safe, he propped up the painting. "There has to be something on this, I know it."

The faces of the coins and money in the painting had all been blurred, hiding any potential numbers. However, the crown, on closer inspection, had a black drip of paint layered into the largest ruby. There in faint form was the number: **25**.

"Twenty-five. Yes. Two more numbers."

The room shook again as a seventh line buzzed through what remained of the carpet. Roman lost his balance and toppled to the floor, hitting his head against *A History of World Landmarks*. He grabbed his hurt scalp and glared at the cover of Big Ben. The clock mocked him with its sunlight and fresh air.

"Wait."

His pupils grew as he stared at the face of the clock. His eyes darted it to the room and back again. The little hand pointed its sharp, plump arm down at four, while its long, slender one settled at the eleven.

"4:50. 0450. It has to be."

He typed the code into the safe, waiting nervously as it buffered.

Beep beep.

The safe gave a dismissive error sound, followed by a red screen.

"No, it has to be that! There isn't anything else." Roman gathered the books and laid them down in front of him. "*Twelve Angry Men. The Grapes of Wrath*–Wait, Wrath."

He grabbed the Bible, opening it carefully around the charred corner, to the page with the inscription. "Greed, Pride, Gluttony, Sloth, Lust, Envy, Acedia, and Wrath. Wrath, yes! But what about—wait a minute."

He looked up at the nearest painting: a man sitting on a throne of money. "Greed..."

He moved his finger toward the painting of a woman surrounded by plates and chalices. "Gluttony!"

"The paintings are the sins. Which means wrath must be this one." His finally rested his finger on the painting beneath the fireplace.

Dong.

A neon black line parted from the center of the floor, just missing Roman's outstretched leg.

"Oh, no. Come on, think. Think! 4:50, Twenty-five, Grapes of Wrath, Twelve Angry Men."

He lifted the books in the air, letting the light illuminate their covers. *Twelve Angry Men* resided in his left hand, and *The Grapes of Wrath* in his right.

"4:50," he mouthed, miming the direction of the arrows with the books. "Oh my God!"

He dropped the books, his eyes bulging from his face. "Wrath... twelve... 4:50. The room is a giant clock!"

Throwing the book down, he jumped up onto the lopsided table in the center of the room and raised his arms. Pressing his two pointer fingers together, he ran them out toward the fireplace. "If Wrath is twelve, then four would be at 90-degrees. And fifty would be at 300-degrees."

His fingers split off, with one moving to the painting of greed and the other landing on the one of lust.

"Yes!" He slid down the table, making quick work of the demented ground. The black line had reached the edge of the wall, which brought a humming to the air.

"Where is the number?" Roman mumbled, picking apart every inch of the lustful painting from the female breast to the man's butt.

"Come on!"

Tracing with his finger, he tracked from the folds of the couch to the ones on the man's back and finally landed on a tiny gold bangle that was wrapped around the woman's wrist. In tiny font, written across the outer ring was the number *12.*

He froze with awe. "That's it. 1225."

Roman dove over the table, slamming into the wall. The black line had begun its final path across the ceiling, demolishing big chunks of drywall with every inch it took.

"1225."

At this point, his fingers began to shake to the point where he had to steady his wrist with his other arm.

"1... 2... 2... 5."

Beep.

The screen flashed bright green, unlocking the door handle. Roman dug his hand inside, grabbing the second key, which was a twin to the first.

"Yes!" he squealed.

Lonnie couldn't help but cheer, which made the others turn toward him, but he chose to ignore them.

Come on Roman. You are so close.

With the tail of the key in his fist, Roman ran past the fireplace just as the black wire connected to the others.

"No, wait," Lonnie murmured. "He needs more time."

Zit. Zit. Zit.

A few more seconds. All he needs is a few more seconds.

Dong.

A giant flash of light covered the screen followed by a low whistle—and then finally... *Boom.*

Chapter 15

After Party

"Get a broom!" Silas demanded.

The audience recoiled as glass flew at their feet yet again. The man whose cup had just shattered on the floor looked at the contents of his drink seeping into the rug.

"Here you go." A man in a red suit rushed in with a dustpan.

Aside from those two sentences, no one else dared speak a word. A held breath of air was contained inside everyone's throats as they watched the blank static screen eventually go dark.

He didn't make it... I really thought he was going to make it.

A hand brushed over Lonnie's, spooking him. When he looked over, though, he saw Amara had intertwined their fingers, her face stoic and tight.

"What are you doing?" he muttered, but bit his tongue as a tear rolled down her cheek.

He gripped her hand tighter. It was the only way he could think to comfort her. Her palm was like ice against his, rigid and unyielding.

"Is it over?" Lonnie whispered to her.

Ring.

The dial of someone's phone filled the quietness of the room.

Does somebody have a signal?

Sebastian stood up from his chair, immediately growing taller than Silas, who was standing upright in front of him. Pulling a phone from his ugly mustard jacket, he raised it to his ear.

"Yes?" he spoke softly.

Muffled words came from the other end of the call. The audience leaned in to listen. Half of them were still shaking from the ruckus of the last sixty seconds, while the other half now acted keen to know if they had just lost a large sum of money.

"Thank you." Sebastian covered the speaker. "The flames are out."

"Send someone in, then!" Silas snapped.

Removing his hand, Sebastian leaned toward the phone. "Bring in the camera."

He ended the call and lowered himself into the chair until he was once again hidden behind his brother. The speakers, which had recently been muted, came back to life, while footsteps echoed in the receiver, followed by the clanging of metal.

"Here we go," a voice muttered over the intercom.

The screen lit, showing the legs of a hazmat suit. The man raised the camera, aiming at an octagon-shaped metal box with a ductwork tunnel funneling down from above. The whole room was placed in some kind of subterranean warehouse, with only a few overhead lights to illuminate it. Jostling keys made noise off-screen before a gloved hand extended out toward the wall. The key in his hand matched the one Roman had held so recently. The man shoved it into a series of three keyholes in the metal, each one releasing a puff of air as it flicked up the pins. On the third twist, he located a hidden handle and pried it back to reveal a small opening in the wall. He proceeded to step through.

This is so messed up.

Lonnie still had Amara's hand clasped in his own, which he found to be a little confusing, as tears continued falling from her eyes. This surely wasn't her first time watching one of these trials. Though, as he looked around at the lack of children in the room, he wondered how many they had really let her watch prior.

Carter and Jamie were in the back still, both of their jaws slack from the impact of what they'd just seen on screen. Lonnie wondered if Jamie felt as guilty as he did. Roman's blood was just as much on their hands as anyone else's. But if he was being honest, the fact that Lonnie had failed to save him or stop the ritual hurt above all else.

I can't believe I failed.

The idea of waiting an entire year to try again was too painful to even imagine. He'd tried to convert people, he'd taken evidence, and he'd learned all he needed to know, but it was never going to be enough. How could he possibly take down this place? Surely, he wasn't the first to try, and he probably wouldn't be the last.

I'm such an idiot. What am I doing?

The hazmat man on screen made it inside, revealing the fallout of the octagon room. The once bright red walls had become a shell, every drop of color snuffed out and replaced with the bareness of silver. The camera operator swiveled around the room, showing the gap in the wall where he had just entered. Around his feet were piles of ash and sand, all remnants of the paintings and furniture that had previously resided in the room.

The only pieces left standing were the two hatches hanging from the walls and the brick fireplace. The bricks had been covered in a thick layer of soot and various new cracks. At the entrance to the fireplace, a bigger mound of ash had formed. The operator stopped, his attention provoked by something. Crouching, he brought the lens in close, which revealed a light sparkle from the center of the pile.

What is that?

First pushing it with the tip of his finger, the man then plunged his hand in, letting the cinder sieve around his glove. As he raised his arm and let the last bit slide from his palm, he revealed what he had seen. The man held it toward the camera, spinning it gently between his fingers.

A single signet ring.

Lonnie touched the tip of his right palm, as though a cold compress had suddenly overtaken it. He imagined Roman's handshake again, the cool rings pressing into his skin.

This is all my fault.

"Well... there you have it." Silas pointed at the screen. His face grew flustered, but he distracted himself by chugging down whatever was in his glass. "I guess we should send those two unconscious boys downstairs home, right? Won't be needing them for the third trial after all."

He peeked at a tablet that had been residing on their table. "And Das, congratulations! It seems you are our big winner tonight."

The monitor flipped to the wager board, now reflecting a

red circle roped around the box that read: *83:7.* A yellow high-light covered up the boxes titled: *Trial 2 & Burned.*

A man who must have been named Das stood from his chair in celebration, though he cheered in a surprisingly humble way. He gave a slight wave to the crowd, raised his glass, and then returned to his seat.

How chivalrous for a murderer.

Seeing the wager board on the screen brought life back to people. Some were angry at the sum of money they lost, others were happy with what they won, and most were glad that they'd restrained themselves from gambling entirely. Nobody acted disappointed that the trials had failed.

Heretics.

Lonnie had overestimated this crowd's belief in faith. This wasn't a temple of worship; it was merely a gambling house with ugly green cloaks and distorted horse races. Even the guests who were praying prior had become indifferent to the trials. Once the bartenders had been brought back in and the drinking continued, the party had simply reset. Henrik was back at the bar and apparently over his crusade against the siblings, or perhaps too drunk to remember. The lady in the weird head-wear was at Florence's side, asking her about her favorite parts of being an actress. If one walked in from the street, they might even think this was a normal cocktail party, with no inkling that a murder had just occurred.

"Is that it, then?" Jamie approached from behind, peering over Lonnie's shoulder.

"It couldn't be," Carter muttered. "Look at them."

He was right. At their table, the siblings had gathered, whis-pering something impossible to catch. Daphne, who had appeared bored the entire evening, suddenly was very present.

She raised her hand, cutting her brother off, and began spitting words for what felt like minutes on end.

What was she talking about?

As they spoke, they continually gazed over the parlor. But what started as casually watching suddenly turned into intense searching.

They are looking for someone.

Four pairs of eyes hovered over each guest, the strain in their necks growing as they all rose from their seats.

What do they want?

"There," Daphne mouthed.

The people parted between them as if by magic, creating a direct line from Daphne's outstretched finger to Lonnie's chest.

"No..." Lonnie wheezed.

Daphne whispered something in Silas's ear, and he cracked a smile. His eyes darted to Sebastian, who checked his phone and then returned an ominous thumbs up.

"Why are they looking at us?" Jamie blurted.

"I don't know, but it can't be good," Lonnie said.

"Should we leave?"

"Don't think you would make it very far," Carter added. "Amara, what do we do?"

Amara looked as though she was miles away.

"Ladies and gentlemen." Silas had left his siblings' side and jumped to the front of the stage. "You were promised a champion tonight, and it saddens me to say that one was not provided."

The crowd hushed.

"But we do have a surprise that we think you are going to love."

Low whispers of anticipation filled the floor.

"How about we make this year a bit interesting? What say you to a double ritual?"

Applause erupted, causing the glasses to ring on counters.

"I know, it's very exciting. But who should we pick to be our champion?"

Florence chirped, "I would love to do the honors!"

"Lovely."

Walking past him, she pointed her finger excitedly around the room, which made the crowd's raging cheers cut out instantly. A sense of dread encompassed the guests, as everyone suddenly realized that they were all options for tonight's entertainment. Lonnie almost wanted to laugh at their naivety, but he too knew his name was high on the chopping block.

Please don't pick me.

Florence stepped down from the stage, letting her finger guide her through the crowd. People dodged and turned out of her way, each one as white as ghosts.

"We should run," Lonnie whispered to Jamie.

Though we probably wouldn't make it far.

Silas spoke again from the stage. "Even though this is the first time we've ever performed a double ritual, we decided to stick to tradition. Meaning, since it's the same night, why not *keep it in the family*? And how lucky we are that our departed Roman had a relative in this very room with us tonight."

Florence continued hovering through the crowd, her finger aimed at each person's heart. She walked to the woman with the ugly headpiece and aimed it at her chest. The lady gasped in shock, but Florence soon moved on.

"Not you, old hen." She laughed cruelly.

The lady nearly fainted right then and there.

This is so twisted.

Florence kept creeping closer, the gap between her and Lonnie growing smaller, until finally there she was. Her finger pointed at his chest. But then she spoke.

"Not only just a relative, but a sister at that."

Sister?

Grabbing Lonnie by the shoulder, she slid him out of the way, revealing Amara, who was hiding right behind.

"Miss Amara Wexler... our second champion."

Lonnie's neck vein tightened. He turned to Amara, whose expression looked as though she was lost in a trance. Without saying a word, her shaking hands unclipped her earrings and placed them on a nearby table. Her face was constricted, the edges of her cheeks sunken in.

"Amara, what are they talking about?"

Ms. Sibil gripped her arm, her nails digging around her wrist. Lonnie tried to grab her hand, but it went limp.

"Amara!" His tone seemed to catch her off guard.

"Leave." Her voice cracked.

And with that, her lips sealed as she was dragged the rest of the way to the front. A hidden door on the side of the stage swung open, and the short, slender man with glasses returned. On his cart, he carried the leather-bound grimoire as well as an empty blood bowl slightly smaller than the one from earlier. He stopped in front of Amara, taking her finger in his hand. Drawing a fresh needle from his bag, he reopened the puncture in her skin and let the blood drip into the container.

"Here you go, sir," he muttered, propping the book on a stand so that Silas could read it.

Silas flipped through the pages, muttering words in Greek that Lonnie couldn't understand. He hardly looked up, his focus so determined as he tried to spit out every syllable. Only at the end did he finally glance up, his eyes falling on Amara standing before him.

"Now, get her situated," Silas commanded.

The same two burly men in suits who'd dragged Roman from the dance floor suddenly appeared in the doorway. They each took Amara by an arm.

This can't be happening again.

Lonnie took a step forward, his ears steaming. He opened his mouth to speak, but was stopped by an arm barricading his stomach.

What?

"Don't," Carter mouthed, shaking his head.

Lonnie jerked his chin in outrage, but by the time he had refocused his thoughts, Amara had already been escorted out the door, and the people were cheering. The crowd grew rowdier, as their near-death experience made them start drinking twice as much as they already had been. The noise got so loud, he could barely hear himself think.

Why didn't she fight? Why didn't she scream?

"Why did you stop me?" He spun on Carter.

Carter scowled. "I just saved your life."

"No, you just ended your friend's. Which maybe you're fine with, but I'm not." Lonnie tightened his hands into fists.

"Says the guy who couldn't save my sister." Carter pushed in closer. "Or maybe you just didn't want to save her."

"She made that choice all on her own!"

"And Amara chose to go with them. You can't change anything here. Why can't you get that through your dense skull?"

Jamie pushed in between them, sliding them backward. "You both need to stop."

"Seriously?" Lonnie scoffed. "Earlier, you were praying to take a swing at him; now you're best friends. How does that make sense?"

"My God, calm down," Jamie scolded. "We have clearly entered a game we know nothing about. One that he has been playing since he was a child. So maybe it would be in your best interest to follow his advice. And yes, I trust him."

"Fine, do what you want." Lonnie huffed. "Where will they take her?"

"I don't know," Carter said.

"Listen, if you don't want to help, that's fine, but don't stand in my way and pretend you're—"

"I said I don't know. Like he just said, they've never done two rituals in one night." Carter's stare was unwavering.

Oh my God, he's telling the truth.

"Okay, so what does that mean?"

Carter rolled his eyes. "They are making it up as they go."

Chapter 16

THE SPARE

Amara had always disliked lifts.

It wasn't that she considered herself a claustrophobic person, but there was just something about them that set her on edge. Maybe it was the fact that you were squished next to strangers or that the inside was basically a metal cannon. But she knew those were not the real reasons. If she was truly honest with herself, she didn't go in lifts because of one thing.

You had no control.

"Please don't do this." She turned to face the men in suits, her back to the lift doors.

They stared at her with no remorse, pressing the call button and pushing her inside. Following behind her, they blocked the exit with their broad shoulders. She could just barely see the hallway hidden behind, and with it, the door that led back to the watch party. A part of her thought to try and squeeze her way out, but what good would it really do? She knew, one way or another, this was always going to be the endgame.

Why fight it?

The lift ticked up, floor after floor.

Basement.
First Floor
Second Floor

At the final stop, the doors heaved open with an electronic beep.

"Out you go," one of the men huffed, stepping to the side.

She opened her mouth to reply, but they'd already begun pushing her across the stone flooring. She stumbled over the gap, and by the time she caught her balance, the doors started to shut. She charged at them, trying to hold the ends open with her nails.

Stop, don't give them the satisfaction.

Yet, she continued fighting. A primal instinct to survive kicked in that she wasn't aware existed. The doors grew heavier, fighting to close.

No!

The gap narrowed, forcing her to let go so she wouldn't crush her fingers.

"Ow," Amara groaned, shaking out her hands.

The lift closed, followed by the sound of its departure growing farther away.

"Damn you!" she screamed and kicked the metal door before sinking against its frame.

Her heart clenched as she thought about her brother.

Had he been as afraid as I am now?

She loathed herself for keeping her relationship with Roman a secret from everyone, especially her friends. But she had to; otherwise, everyone would have been watching her like a hawk all night, afraid that she might try to save him.

But now that his trials were over and hers had begun, it all seemed like a waste of time. She had so badly wanted to cheer for him up on that screen. The stress of being a viewer had been like a blade to the heart.

Tears escaped, and she couldn't hold them back. She glanced at the security camera looming overhead, ashamed that they got to see her so weak.

They don't deserve to see you like this.

"You have to get a hold of yourself."

She pictured Roman once more in her head, the full weight of him hitting her heart with an unspeakable agony. Tucking it away, she hid him in the deepest parts of her mind.

I can't think of him right now. I can't be distracted.

She grabbed her face, letting her nerves settle. Slowly, she raised her head and stared at the new arena she'd entered. The lift had spit her out into one of the house's hallways. The walls were lined with rippled yellow wallpaper, featuring a wood-textured wainscoting at the bottom. The ground was dark marble with a patterned wool rug. The hall was so normal that it was almost disarming.

Almost.

She pulled herself to her feet, taking careful steps through her new terrain. The rug shifted under her shoes. If she screamed, would the people at the party downstairs hear?

Is the party even still going?

Though she doubted they would help her even if they did hear.

I'm on my own.

As she walked forward, the distance between her and the lift grew further apart. In front of her, a single door blocked her path, and she had an irksome feeling that was where she had to go.

For the first time all night, her legs shook. She took small steps closer, imagining the horror of what lay on the other side. Over the past nineteen years, she had grown to know about these trials and the sacrifices that followed them. Hell, even her own father had been one of those sacrifices twelve years prior. She remembered staying in London with her mother that year as he went off to the House on his own. He never came back.

It was a quick death, they had told her mother. Amara was in agony at the news, but her mother didn't bat an eye.

"It's how it had to be," she had said.

Amara continued to be invited every year after. At first, she was accompanied by her mother, but then she was forced to attend on her own. She had at least met Hannah and Carter, and they were her only light in this bitter darkness. But still, they couldn't protect each other from watching so many die. Each year, it became a little easier, until she thought she had eventually grown numb to it. But then she lost Hannah.

She tightened her laces, taking the moment to ease her mind. Then she pushed the hallway door open, slipping into pitch black. Looking for a switch, her hand floated in the dark, but she soon found it unnecessary as two glowing lines lit across the floor. A path of light in the shape of a runway cut through the darkness, ending at an open metal door. She walked through cautiously.

Clunk.

The door slammed closed behind her, followed by a loud deadbolt that sliced into the wall. She pushed on it but stumbled backward, bumping her head onto something metal.

"Ow." Pulling her phone from a hidden pocket in her dress, she turned on her torch. Aiming it at a rung ladder that hung from the ceiling, she was shocked to spot a port hatch at the top.

"Of course." She looked around for another exit, but found she was trapped in some kind of tower.

These trials are all so dramatic.

Seeing that she had no other option, she slid her phone back into the dress and pressed her flats onto the first rung. One leg after the other, she climbed to the top. Reaching the hatch, she grunted as she pushed the door up, giving her room to crawl through.

Ambient light shone from above as she emerged into the small, enclosed space. Her feet clicked onto marble tiles as the hatch shut behind her. On top of the lid, there was another infamous black plaque that read: **Claim the Castle.**

"This isn't right." She glared in increasing alarm at her surroundings.

She had emerged from the hatch into some kind of cube-shaped room. Four square walls surrounded her. Each was made of some cheap drywall material, with metal columns and beams reinforcing the corners where they connected. In the center of each wall was an identical metal door that overwhelmed her with options.

Why did they put these up?

The floor was entirely covered in black tiles, but the ceiling was made of thick glass. Through it, she could make out a grander ceiling a couple of dozen feet above, but it was hard to see. Small light bars were set up at the top of each wall, which shimmered over the glass.

The lights are too bright.

Amara took a hard breath. She knew what came next. She had seen every sadistic trap this society had made in the past. Would the room fill with water or gas? Maybe catch on fire? The options were endless, each more terrifying than the last.

She held her unsettled stomach until vengeful rage overtook her fear. Amara was done being a perfect, complacent guest. And she was especially done with having her choices picked by others. She hadn't been able to protect her father or Hannah.

Now there was Roman too.

She wasn't going to let herself go down the same way. She inspected the room, prying on the locked doors and pushing on walls, until she found something tucked away in one of the corners.

No way.

At the edge of one of the walls, there was a mount with hooks bolted in. From them hung a long, narrow sword.

"A rapier?" Amara gasped.

Beside the weapon, another smaller plaque hung from a string. This one read: **For your protection.**

"My protection?" She quickly snatched the blade and wielded it in her right hand, making a thrusting motion. Then, she retreated to the corner, watching the doors in case some animal suddenly came bounding through.

She felt her fingers fold so familiarly to the grooves of the handle. The metal rod inside pressed against her knuckle.

They had planned this for me...

<hr>

One month prior.

"Allez!" a voice chanted from what felt like a mile away.

Amara advanced across the strip, a white figure blocking her path. The world outside the metal matting had faded away, letting darkness seep in all around her.

"Ha!" a figure shouted.

Amara watched as her fencing opponent lunged at her, then she stumbled back in quick succession. Electricity ran through her hands like a current, the blade in her grip becoming an extension of her arm. She raised her wrist, pointing the buttoned tip toward the moving figure.

Focus.

A tension grew in her back leg as she pressed it into the mat. The foot locked around the indent of the floor, kicking off into the air. Taking the epee blade, she thrust it out, swatting away the enemy's sword with a twist of her wrist. She advanced closer, suddenly feeling the weight of her own blade grow light under her opponent's. Her sword deflected as the enemy charged, exposing a canvas-encased chest. In quick defense, Amara parried, feeling her balance slip under her feet. The enemy advanced, forcing Amara into a retreat, her feet barely managing to stay upright. A couple of feet or so away, she managed to build a gap between them, finding the time to solidify her stance.

Focus, Amara.

She imagined the eyes of her opponent taunting her from behind the safety of their meshed mask.

Attack.

She sprang forward, sending a series of jabs toward their torso, causing them to dance on their feet. In desperation, the opposing player thrust their blade out.

Attack now!

She dove forward, stretching her legs apart along the floor. The edge of her sword flickered in the air before pressing into the stomach of her opponent.

"Ha!" she screamed.

Beep

Beep.

What? Two?

She tilted her head and noticed the taunting tip of her opponent's blade resting on her collarbone.

One for one.

Amara's blood boiled, but she bit her tongue.

"All right, that's enough for today, ladies!" The coach blew her whistle.

The edges of the gym came back into focus, and Amara could see her coach standing on the sideline, along with her teammates, who were staring out from the bleachers, their fencing masks resting in their laps.

"Better luck next time, Wexler." The opponent took off her mask, revealing short, black, wavy hair. She undid the cable from the back of her torso and made her way from the mat, leaving Amara alone. On a small table beside her, a scoreboard read: *14:15.*

Amara dropped her epee and shook out her hand. A sharp pain burned inside her wrist, but she tried to ignore it. The rest of her teammates headed toward the gym doors as she unhooked herself from her cable and marched along with them.

"Amara..." Her coach sat on the edge of the bleacher. She was a slender, tall woman with blonde spiked hair.

"I know... that bout was mine." Amara grabbed water from her duffel bag and sprayed it into her mouth.

"Nadia is very talented." She smirked. "But you should have won—"

"I know, Coach!" Amara whined. "You don't have to rub it in."

"Do you know why you should have won?"

"Because I'm faster?"

Her coach stood from the bleachers and made her way to the mats. "No, because she was dragging her back foot like it was full of lead." She grabbed the scoreboard and dropped it into the box hidden below the table. "Which is something you would have noticed if you weren't so in your head. You are very talented, especially for a freshman, but your overthinking is killing you."

Amara flexed her hand, trying to loosen it. "Thank you, Coach."

"Where does your head go to?" Coach closed the lid of the box and stared directly at her.

Amara thought about how she would be attending the gala in a couple weeks. It was all she had been able to think about since she found out her brother would be accompanying her for the first time.

So much can go wrong with him there.

Noticing her coach staring, she shook her head and gave a pained chuckle. "Places I would rather not think about."

"I see." She ceased messing with the equipment. "Are you going back to London for break?"

"Probably not."

"Well, either way, try to rest this summer, yeah? We need you to reset come fall training."

"Yes, Coach."

"And make sure to ice that." Her coach pointed at her hand.

Amara gasped, not even noticing that she had pried her gloves off and was massaging the strain in her tendon. "Will do."

Present day.

They couldn't possibly expect me to use this.

Amara poked the tip of her finger with the end of the blade, watching the blood well up.

It's real.

The metal was cool to the touch, like it had been hidden away, waiting for this moment.

Clack.

A noise echoed on the other end of the thin wall, which forced her into a fencing stance. Seeing nothing appear, she immediately dropped it.

"Aaugh..." She grabbed her arm and rolled out her wrist.

Tick. Tick. Tick.

A ticking that sounded like a metronome began from an overhead speaker, its speed and intensity growing with each passing second. Right after it started, the sound of deadbolts unlocking came from all the doors, alerting her that they had opened. Amara stared in disbelief.

"There are too many options."

She pressed her ear against one of the doors, hoping for anything to give her a sign.

Tick. Tick. Tick.

The noise drowned everything out, making it impossible to think.

"Enough!" she whined.

Amara rubbed the worry line on her forehead, then shifted herself to the center of the room. Lifting her blade over her head, she spun in a circle, choosing a random door before her. The sword was much heavier than her typical blade, but she kept it upright and pointed toward the wall.

"You can do this."

With her free hand, she grabbed the door handle and twisted, revealing an almost identical room to the one she was exiting. The only difference was that there was no porthole in the ground, and the black tiles had changed to all white.

Bam.

The door behind her slammed shut, locking in place and sealing her in.

The ticking came to a hard stop, letting the thoughts regroup in her head long enough for her to hear something moving in the distance.

Thud. Thud. Thud.

Amara leaned against the wall to hear better, but the ticking noise returned as fast as it left.

Tick. Tick. Tick.

Amara grew agitated as the ticking burrowed repetitively into her ears. Of the three new doors offered, she chose the one on the right wall first. It was locked.

"What?" She tried again. "Come on."

The ticking grew louder, ripping at her ears.

She moved to the left door next, only to get the same result. By the time she made it to the last door, which was straight ahead from the one she'd entered through, it felt as though her eardrum was on the cusp of bursting. Still holding her blade, she raised her shoulder, trying to cover one of her ears from the deafening noise.

Click.

The door unlocked on the first try. She smiled with relief, pushing it open. The other side revealed another identical cubed room, this time with black tiles. But just as she stepped a foot through—

Thud.

The frame of the door closed, locking to the wall and knocking her back.

"What?" She pulled at the handle, but it remained deadbolted.

Bam.

Bam.

Bam.

Her fist pounded against the metal over and over until she realized it was the only sound she was hearing.

The ticking stopped again.

In a burst of energy, she circled the room, trying all the doors once more in a panic, before ending back at the same spot on the floor.

"Come on, something has to be open. There must be rules. What are the rules?" She tried the door once more.

Locked.

"No!" Anxious thoughts bombarded her, but she tried to relax. Her fingers grew tighter around the grip of her blade, which made her tendons scream.

Creak.

From outside the room, a distant door echoed on its hinges. She drew back her blade as something approached the other side of the wall.

Stomp.

Stomp.

Footsteps grew, and with them came a horrible stench of death. She gagged but didn't make a sound as the steps stopped just on the other side of the wall. Something was there... waiting. The knob of the door began to jiggle, and Amara prayed for it to hold.

"Please..." she whispered, leaning her head against the wall to listen.

She touched her chest, her heart beating so fast she thought it might burst through her skin and into her hand. She tried to block the fear out, but it was impossible. Her knees were ready to buckle, and all she wanted was someone to wrap their arms around her and say it was going to be okay. But she knew no one was coming.

The intruder sounded quite large as it pushed on the door. After trying the handle, they then banged on the wall, the force knocking Amara to the floor. She silently slid back along the tiles until she reached the opposing wall.

Buzz.

A muffled grunt sounded, then soon passed as the intruder moved away from the wall. Amara dared to press her ear back to its cool facade, but she was frozen with fear. The footsteps eventually receded, followed by the opening of the room that was diagonal to hers.

Pop!

An explosion came from that adjacent room, making her jump. She tried to breathe, but the air caught in her throat as the ticking began again.

"What... what the hell is this place?" she muttered. Her flats pressed against the floor, but she couldn't stand.

Come on, Amara, you have to keep moving.

Shaking, she raised a leg forward, pulling herself from the wall. Her curved reflection bounced off the gleam of her sword.

This is a physical trial.

"They aren't going to let me leave without a fight."

Tick... Tick... Tick.

The metronome grew louder. Wielding her sword, she positioned herself in front of the door the stranger had tried to break through. The stench of it still lingered through the cracks, smelling entirely unnatural.

This thing was not human.

She positioned her stance and grabbed the handle, her blade drawn and ready to strike. Building up her courage, she jumped in place repeatedly, then charged through.

To her surprise, the black tiled room was empty, aside from the revolting smell left behind.

"Where are you?" she muttered.

Tick... Tick... Tick.

She looked at the ceiling, cursing at the blaring alert. Her feet drifted across the floor, never letting the blade drop. Following the growing smell, she turned to her right, eyeing the wall to the room responsible for that large explosion.

There you are.

She rolled out her shoulders and practiced a striking pose, which felt utterly ridiculous given the state she was in.

I can't believe I'm doing this.

She grabbed the door knob.

Clunk.

It didn't budge.

"What the—" she roared. "You wanted a fight! Then let me through, cowards!"

She thrust the blade into the wall beside the door, surprised as it passed cleanly through, leaving a tiny hole. She knelt to peer in, the scent escaping through it and tearing up her eyes.

"Show yourself!"

She could only see the shadow of something lurking around within. The ticking now blared louder than before, giving her vertigo. Knowing she had to move, she punched the wall once in anger, then proceeded to the door parallel to her entrance.

Click.

To her initial joy, it swung open, but she grew defeated as it revealed another identical room, again with a white tile floor. She fell to her knees, driven mad by the ticking. Dropping the blade, she pressed her fingers into her ears.

"Turn it off, please!"

Tick! Tick! Ti—

The sequence ended abruptly. Amara took the moment to breathe, stretching her injured hand on the floor in circular motions. "More white tiles."

Black. White. Black. White.

"Like a checkerboard..." She retreated into the center of the room, picking up her sword from the ground. That's when she caught sight of something etched into the middle white tile. She leaned closer, catching the faintest grey inscription: **c6.**

No, this wasn't checkers. They were playing chess.

Timer clocks... limited moves... locked spaces.

All the pieces were beginning to make sense. Well, all of them except for one.

Who is my opponent?

That's when she heard them. The walls all around her shook as the weight of her opponents leaned against them, screeching with a hollow chorus of moans. She spun in a slow circle, facing each door, unsure which was about to open. The noise surrounded her, coming from all sides.

Breathing down the length of her sword, she listened for them. Specifically for the first one that had the nerve to face her. The doors remained closed, and she didn't dare take a bigger breath than her body required.

"Come on!" she shouted.

Fueled by fear, she let it consume her like a fire. Her legs shifted into her attacking stance. No longer was she a debutante guest who shook hands and hugged strangers. Her back leg stretched, lowering herself into a strategic bend of the knees. Her front foot remained forward, and her heel was like a compressed spring ready to burst.

Plays... and counter plays.

Then, it started. The room diagonal to hers was the first to open. The sound of its swinging hinges resonated like a battle cry.

Thud. Thud. Thud.

The opponent's feet clomped across the floor, making a sharp left turn and heading directly toward the door before her. Amara spoke slowly, trying to refrain from letting her voice shake from fear.

"I am not your champion. Or your pawn. Or your sacrifice." She twisted her back foot, letting the grooves of the tiles hug it tight. "But I will be your end."

The door burst open in front of her, pushing her back with a gust of air. She gritted her teeth and pointed her weapon, aligning it with the chest of the beastly creature that had appeared in her sights.

Time to put on a show.

Chapter 17

The Games Afoot

She was braver than me.

Lonnie watched her undo her earrings as though she was preparing to fight, and yet she stood there and welcomed it.

Why didn't you run?

But even just from their short interaction, he could tell she wasn't the type. She was strong-willed, though he imagined she preferred using her wits over confrontation. Still, she had walked out of the room with a sense of calm and power, and that was admirable.

"I don't mean to pry." A man in black trousers and a floral blue button-up stood from his chair. "Is a second ritual a great idea? I mean, where would it even be held?"

The Sibils ceased their chatting and stared at him from the stage. Florence approached the man, watching him grow flustered in her presence.

"Are you opposed to a second ritual?" she asked, her eyes analyzing his face. Her words were sharp, with each one sinking into his skin.

He gulped. "It's just already late, is all I meant."

She moved closer, grabbing his hand in hers. "It is a bit *late*... don't you think?" She raised his hand, showing off the dried blood on his pinkie.

Lonnie looked at his own finger where the man had pricked him. He supposed the second ritual had already started, and everyone was signed up, whether they liked it or not.

Florence grinned a movie star smile and turned to the rest of the guests. "This party is in better hands now, don't worry. I designed this first room myself."

Silas glared at her, a thought flickering behind his eyes. "What are you talking about? I designed it."

"Oh, brother, I changed it. But don't worry. I think you're really going to like what I did with this one." Her smile dropped. "And I for one am excited to see what this Wexler girl has up her sleeve."

Silas raised his brow, but quickly nodded in approval. "Great."

Florence grabbed the remote from the table and pointed it at the screen. "And as for the location." She clicked a button, revealing a normal-looking hallway with a rug and beige patterned walls. At the end of it, an elevator with *Floor Two* on the dial opened with Amara inside. She exited as the doors slid closed behind her.

She's only a few floors away, and I can't do anything.

Lonnie watched the screen with a growing sickness in his gut. So many months of preparing for this night and planning his moves, only to be bested at every turn. He hadn't put a stop to the trials or saved Roman. And now Amara was going to meet the same fate, and he had no way to find her, let alone save her.

I can't watch this.

He turned away to head into the hall when he caught the screen flipping to another wager board. The numbers had reset to zero. This seemed to perk up the audience as they awoke from their drowsiness and started betting all over again.

"500k!"

"One million!"

Their voices rang out, one after the other.

It's never going to stop. They are never going to stop.

It took everything Lonnie had not to scream. His world turned red as he resisted the urge to cut out these people's tongues so they couldn't utter another number.

What is wrong with you all?

The screen toggled back and forth between the wager board and Amara walking timidly through the hallway. As the visual on the monitor flipped over and over, he imagined the footage from his own trials up there as well. He pictured these people laughing at him which only fueled his anger even more.

That's it. I'm doing something.

A half-baked plan began to form in his brain, and he had made no effort to derail it. Lonnie marched toward the hall door, but was met by Jamie and Carter blocking his path. His rage must have been pretty obvious, because Jamie looked awfully concerned.

"Lonnie." He grabbed his arm. "What are you doing?"

"I can't let them do this to her." He swatted Jamie's hand off and pushed through the door and into the hallway. "I'm going to help."

"Don't be stupid." Carter followed, dragging Lonnie away from the few people still lingering out there.

"Do you know how to get to that hallway?" Lonnie leaned

into Carter, his tone almost begging. "You've been here dozens of times. You have to have seen it before."

"She can take care of herself, trust me." Carter tried to calm him. "You will only make it worse."

"How could I possibly make it worse? They can't hurt me. I have no brother. I have no family. I have no girlfriend. What can they take from me?"

"What about me?" Jamie grew flustered. "What about Harriet?"

"They don't care about us. Don't you see that?" Lonnie said. "They sit in there and laugh as we fight for our lives. They do whatever they want. I mean, what's to stop them from throwing her in here next year, just cause they feel like it?"

"I'm not going to make that bet." Jamie scowled.

"Then stay behind. I'll find Amara on my own."

Carter waved his arms. "You're just going to die alongside her, then who does that help?"

"Well, at least I'll have died trying to do something good, instead of just waiting around here hating myself. Maybe my life isn't worth much, but she helped save it. And after what I did to her brother, the least I can do is try to save hers."

He started to walk away, but was halted by Jamie's hand on his shoulder.

"Let me go." Lonnie tried to shake him off.

Jamie's forehead crinkled as if he was deep in thought. "Wait." He put his hand over his face and groaned deeply before turning to Carter. "Would it even be possible to get to that hallway?"

Lonnie's eyes widened with surprise.

"You can't be serious," Carter replied.

"I can't believe I am saying this, but he is right. We owe her for what we did to her brother."

Carter spat, "You're both crazy."

"So do you know a way or not?" Lonnie repeated.

Carter paused again, as a big-eyed woman gazed at them as she passed by. A grand mink coat draped over her shoulder as though a small animal was nuzzling her ear. Eventually, she cleared their sight, giving them room to talk.

"Yeah, I do. But... I haven't a clue how to get there without anyone noticing."

Lonnie peered at the camera overhead, its lens aimed at them.

What was that?

Attached to the base of the camera was some kind of black box. Wires were threaded through it, each inserting into the back of the lens.

Is that a portable battery?

Can't short-circuit them like last year. *Let's hope they have more important things to watch tonight.*

Lonnie wondered if Amara was putting on a good show. This couldn't have been the night she was expecting, though maybe it was. He couldn't imagine anyone surviving in this house this long without finding solace in the idea that each visit could be your last.

"Can you get to it from the foyer?" Lonnie suggested.

"Yes, but we can't exactly take the elevator. They likely have someone there. Plus, they probably have cameras stuffed into every crevice you can imagine from here to upstairs. We wouldn't get more than a few feet. This whole idea is reckless..."

Lonnie pulled out his phone, reading the time that flickered in a faint blue light glow.

_1:30 am._

"There should be a few stragglers at the party upstairs," Lonnie said. "Not a lot, but hopefully enough to blend in."

"So we are really doing this, then." Carter held his head high, giving one last exasperated look toward Jamie.

Jamie smiled faintly, nudging Carter with his shoulder. "I wouldn't mind giving them a big middle finger."

Carter rolled his eyes, but showed an inkling of a smile.

"Well, now that it's settled, we just need a way upstairs," Lonnie said.

"Wait." Jamie's eyes bulged. "I know."

"You do?" Carter and Lonnie uttered in unison.

"Follow me." Waiting for the last few guests to trickle back inside, he dashed across the hallway and ended up at the Ritual Room.

"What are you—" Lonnie raised his eyebrows, but then a sudden memory came to mind. "Oh, you're a genius."

"I know."

Goosebumps ran over Lonnie's skin as he entered the black tiled walk-in freezer. Carter held his sleeves, his breath coming out as a light mist.

"Why are we here?" Carter complained. "I thought we were staying _under_ the radar."

"We are," Lonnie said.

"I cannot think of a worse place to stay under the radar."

"It's fine, trust me." Jamie walked deeper into the room, passing the front table.

The vat of blood was still perched on top, joined now by the smaller bowl from Amara's ceremony in the other room. The smell of iron wafted up Lonnie's nose as he passed.

So gross.

Carter coughed as he walked by, putting the top of his shirt over his nose. Lonnie squinted his eyes, watching him follow close behind Jamie.

He'd better not betray us.

Jamie approached one of the tile walls in the corner of the room.

"What are you doing?" Carter asked.

"Just trust me." His tongue held between his teeth as he felt around for the hidden lever.

Lonnie watched him, rather shocked that he had forgotten about the secret passage. He tried to remember how Mrs. Blythorne had opened it during the guests' massacre, but everything had happened so fast, it was a blur. He hoped that the Sibils hadn't gotten rid of it this past year.

Click.

Just then, Jamie found the switch, forcing a fake part of the wall to swing open. Inside, dirt and spiderwebs covered an inclined tunnel, leading up to the first floor. The hill was longer than he recalled, the rocky foundation a bit more unstable. Faint lines of light were visible from a hatch located at the top.

"What the hell?" Carter's voice cracked.

"Come on." Lonnie pushed past him and into the tunnel. "We're running out of time."

The boys started climbing behind him, Carter apparently still baffled at the sudden presence of this new passageway. "How did you know?"

Jamie cracked a smile. "Long story. I'll make sure to tell you if we survive."

Carter stammered, "That's not funny."

Their hands pawed at the dirt, picking it up beneath their nails. The wall had slid closed behind them, plunging them into thick darkness. The faint light from the hatch ahead illuminated their exposed skin. Lonnie closed his eyes, hoping it would make this whole endeavor feel a little less real. He thought again about what Carter had said.

Am I making things worse? I barely even know her.

Even as the words passed through his head, he knew they weren't true. Maybe he'd only known Amara for a few hours, but that was all the time he needed to know that she was good. And maybe for the first time, something good would get to leave this wicked hellscape.

Lonnie finally reached the hatch, kicking up a bit of dust that flowed into the other boys' faces, making them gag. As he reached for the handle, a bubble of fear inflated in his chest, immobilizing him.

What if it's locked?

Jamie scooted beside him, planting one foot on the dirt and the other on the hatch frame. Carter pressed his hand against Jamie's back, supporting him from knocking them all back down the mole hill.

"Ready?" Jamie asked.

They both hesitantly nodded back.

Pft.

He pried the latch, letting the air release from the opening. A humid breeze came in from the outside hall.

Oh, thank God.

Lonnie nearly cried from relief. Jamie slipped through first, holding the door open for more light to shine in. The extra glow revealed spiders and worms that were crawling along their clothing. Lonnie gagged, but he swallowed it down. Swatting them off, he tried to put on a brave face.

I hate this house.

Carter was the last to exit, tearing the corner of his sleeve on the metal hinge as he went. "Damn it."

Emerging from the dirt like the living dead, they stood tall, cracking their backs in a big stretch. Jamie patted down Carter, knocking loose various splotches of dirt and webs. Lonnie looked at himself, noticing the beating his suit had taken as well. Patches of fabric had torn along his knees and shoulders.

Great.

"Woooo!" Cheers came from the next room.

They all stiffened, suddenly on alert, but the tension eased as music flooded in from the speakers.

"It can't be..." Lonnie followed the music around the corner of the hall.

Lining the foyer were hundreds of people stomping across the dance floor. Each dancer was pacing evenly with their part-ners, throwing them around the ballroom.

"Why are they still here?" Jamie asked, sounding flabbergasted.

Lonnie tore off his tux jacket and laid it on a chair. "It's a sauna in here."

A good portion of the guests had left, but those who remained had the energy of three apiece. This party had become their playground, and they had no intention of leaving. Drinks spilled across the floor, and so had suits, dresses, and coats. The crowd wore what they pleased, which made the chaos of the boys' ruffled appearances blend right in.

Empty glasses covered the bar from earlier, ranging from lowballs to flutes to martinis. And still, people continued to order more from the bartender. The overhead room lights had been turned off, while spotlights shone a hazy glow through the light smoke drifting from nearby projectors. Even the band had stayed, their movements now much more sporadic and unbridled. Sharp jazz notes shot from their instruments, and their riffing carried the crowd in a dazed formation of movement.

Lonnie almost wanted to stay. Why couldn't this be the party he had been invited to? The joys of the rich without the pains of knowing how they got it. These people might be the luckiest he had ever met. So ignorant of what was happening right beneath their feet.

I hate them.

"Guys." Carter tapped them on the shoulder. "I think they know we left."

Following his gaze, they spotted the two burly men in black suits and ear coms standing across the bar. They were searching the crowd for something, or someone.

"We should move," Lonnie said.

"Calmly," Jamie reminded them.

He scooped up some drinks from a nearby table and handed them out to the others. Carter made staggered steps, walking as if without purpose, disguising their destination at the other end of the stage. Lonnie tried to pretend to dance, blending himself in with the people as best he could. Peeking over his shoulder, he noticed that the burly men had disappeared.

"Phew."

A heaviness left Lonnie's chest, and he continued forward only to be stopped by someone's hand wrapping around the width of his forearm. He gulped, turning to face one of the men, his suit jacket bursting under the force of his muscles. The man was so tall that when Lonnie looked up, all he could see was the inside of the man's nostrils.

"Can we help you?" Lonnie asked rather dismissively.

"Mr. Sibil wants you to return downstairs."

Jamie moved forward, politely undoing the man's grip from Lonnie's arm. "Yes, of course, we just wanted to dance for a bit. You know, while the band was still here. And then we will be right back down—"

"He wants you down now," the man commanded.

"Sure," Jamie gulped. "Lead the way then."

The man gestured back toward the way they came, corralling them like sheep. Lonnie looked at Jamie, who had a blank expression on his face.

What was he thinking?

The music got louder, making the dancers' movements more volatile and sporadic. The man led the boys further from the dance circle, eventually passing through an array of cocktail tables that made obstacles in their path.

We need a plan.

Think of a plan.

Suddenly, in the corner of his eye, he saw Carter stir from the back of the group. Lifting the glass that Jamie had placed in his hand, he raised it over his head like a sledgehammer. The man caught Lonnie's stare, and just as he turned to follow it, Carter slammed it into his head.

"Gah!" the man screamed, his voice muffled under the music.

Jamie slammed into the bodyguard's side, toppling them both over a nearby table. Shocked, Lonnie grabbed his friend by the underarms and pulled him to his feet.

"Go to the bookcase," Carter mouthed.

The bookcase?
The bookcase!
The lamb pen!

Tossing their remaining glasses onto the floor, they pushed through the crowd, letting the swaying people shield them from sight. Lonnie lost his grip on Jamie, but continued forward, following the familiar archway of the hall at the end of the room.

Sweat coated every portion of his being as foreign bodies pressed against his skin. He would have been horrified, but the more he sweated, the easier he found it to slide through the pit of people.

That was until they grabbed for his body. Feeling their slimy palms press onto his chest, he gagged. Dropping to his knees, he crawled through the remainder of the crowd, letting their feet bounce around his exposed hands. Above him, he caught a brief glimpse of the second bodyguard pacing through the crowd with a flashlight. Lonnie nearly got stomped by the weight of his giant foot as he passed by. The bodyguard then reconvened with his friend, who now walked with a weird limp and had a bit of blood flowing down the edge of his temple.

"We need to move faster."

Lonnie pushed the people out of his way, diving through legs and arms like a circus act. Eventually he emerged from the crowd, gasping for air. Looking both ways, he saw no sign of Carter or Jamie.

Maybe they already made it.

He slipped away undetected, into the empty hallway. The lights were dimmed like the rest of the house outside the dance floor. It created an ominous feeling, like the world revolved around that ballroom, and the further you got from it, the less it was real. Carter was waiting for him at the bookcase, the secret passage already propped open.

"Jamie?" He sounded panicked.

"No!" Lonnie panted. "He isn't with you?"

A flustered look crossed Carter's face, his ears growing red, and the sweat glistening down his chin. "We have to go back."

Lonnie nodded.

Carter let go of the passage, letting it slowly begin to close, when a voice projected out of a stream of music.

"Go!" It warned.

Carter and Lonnie exchanged a glance as Jamie appeared around the corner. The shoulder of his sleeve had been ripped, and his hair was coated in sweat.

"Go!" he repeated, swatting his hand at the door.

Lonnie paced backward toward the entrance, slowly closing the distance from him to the open passage. A second after Jamie passed the corner, two thumb-shaped men followed close behind. He sprinted across the carpet, jumping at the shelves displayed in the hall and throwing their contents behind him—paintings, Faberge eggs, and paperweights. He took each and lobbed them back, trying to slow the men down.

"Shut the door!" he screamed.

A painting collided with one of the man's noses forcing him to swat it to the side. But most of the items merely bounced off their overinflated chests and fell to the ground. Carter and Lonnie had made their way inside the passage. With an outstretched arm, they reached for Jamie, as the fingers of the attackers came within inches of his neck.

Just a little closer.

Jamie jumped forward and the boys managed to pull him in just as the wall slammed shut behind them. Carter slid a deadbolt over the back end of the bookcase, then dropped to the ground. His breath came out as wheezes, each one broken with words he tried to spit out.

"Well... I... guess..."

He stopped to inhale, as the bookcase rattled behind him under the hands of the bodyguards. Carter grinned, though he looked nauseated. "Well, I guess there is no going back now."

Chapter 18

Beyond the White Door

Thud. Thud. Thud.

Books crashed onto the floor as the men tossed them from the shelf behind the wall.

"Are you okay?" Lonnie touched Jamie's exposed shoulder.

He moved it tentatively. "Yeah, I'll be fine. Can't say the same for the shirt, though."

"We should keep moving then," Carter butted in. "I don't think that wall will hold them long." He paced across the room to the white door. "This way."

"I thought you said we don't go through there," Jamie said.

"Yeah, we don't, but if you want to get to the hallway on the second floor, this is the fastest way."

"Wait, she's that close?" Lonnie shook his head. "There is no way—"

"Can you just trust me? I've walked through there enough times to know." Carter spit.

"All right."

"Now we are going to have to go one by one, otherwise we won't fit."

"What do you mean?" Jamie asked.

Carter propped open the door, revealing a wooden panel with a handle on it. Lifting it up, he found a tiny wooden box inside, no larger than a cabinet. Ropes hung from the outside, hooked to a pulley system.

"Oh, you have to be kidding."

"I told you we don't go through here anymore." Carter reminded him. "Not since we were kid-sized, at least."

"What am I looking at?" Lonnie frowned.

"It's a dumbwaiter. I think the staff used to use it to deliver breakfast to the rooms upstairs, but now... let's just hope it has a high weight limit."

Lonnie whined. "Great."

The pounding on the wall continued as pieces of drywall chipped from the inside.

"Well, I guess we don't have another option." Lonnie climbed inside. "So please just don't let me get stuck."

"Wouldn't exactly be ideal for me either," Carter said.

"See you in a few." Lonnie pulled the case closed behind him, submerging himself in the darkness, accompanied only by the smell of stale wood. The other boys pulled the rope, lifting the body of the elevator with jerky movements.

Breathe... breathe. Lonnie tried not to hyperventilate.

The box finally stopped after a light heave from the pulley. The bottom of it jolted back and forth, reminding him that he was well above its weight capacity.

"Okay, let's do this." He pried open the cover and tumbled out, landing on a fur rug. It appeared he had ended up in some extravagant bedroom. A large bed with pillars and a canvas cover took up a decent amount of the space. The blankets and sheets were pressed, and a large set of throw pillows accessorized the head.

He stepped toward the mattress, but then was reminded of his task by the sound of pulleys grinding. The box slid down and out of sight, leaving in its place the single rope that was carrying it so delicately.

Lonnie rolled up his shirt sleeves, wrapping his palms around the rope. At first it was light, but it quickly became an anchor dragging him down.

Jamie.

He moved his hands, one after the other, pulling down the rope and watching the dumbwaiter rise a little higher. Each pull, he shook out his free hand, letting the burn loosen from his grip. Finally, the box arrived, delivering Jamie out onto the floor.

"Man, you're heavy."

"Shut up," Jamie huffed, prying himself off the floor.

The pulley spun again, dropping the box back down. The two of them grabbed the rope and began raising Carter.

Creak.

The wire sputtered against the pulley.

"Careful, careful." Lonnie eased his grip.

They stacked their hands, pulling in sync, but the box did not move.

"Pull it!" a voice screamed from below.

They pulled again, this time with more energy, but the box heaved under the pressure and rose barely a millimeter.

Crack.

The sound of wood breaking came from inside the dumbwaiter. Lonnie and Jamie peered down the hole to see the top of the box splintering a few feet away.

"Lift it harder!" Carter screamed.

Lonnie and Jamie did as he commanded and pulled on the rope as hard as they could, until the pulley itself started to give away under the strain.

Crack.

Another wood splinter came from inside the tube, but they were too busy pulling to look.

Crush.

The sound of a loud collision came from inside, and the rope grew lighter.

"Carter!" Jamie cried out.

Still holding the line, they carefully peeked over the edge to see the eyes of the two burly men from outside, now peering through the rubble of what was once the box. Their thick frames stuck halfway through the opening.

"Where is he?" Jamie sputtered nervously.

"Pull me up!" Carter's voice echoed through the shaft.

Looking closer, they saw Carter hanging from the pulley rope, his feet pressed against the wall, halfway between the floors.

"Pull it!" Jamie yelled.

He and Lonnie pulled harder, the rope burning in their hands.

"Just a little further Carter!" Lonnie huffed.

Jamie was stronger and took most of the weight, giving the final pull to get Carter's hand swung over the stoop. He grabbed it, dragging him up, just as the pulley ripped from the ceiling. Losing their support, the two boys stumbled backward, with Carter landing on top of Jamie. They panted heavily, jolting their chests against each other. Jamie rested his hands on Carter's back, holding him delicately in place before letting him roll onto his side. They exchanged a warm glance as they pulled themselves to their feet. Carter flinched at the sight of his knuckles now covered in faint traces of blood and scratches.

"Are you all right?" Lonnie asked.

"Not my favorite moment of the night," Carter replied, regaining his stamina. "But yeah, I'll be fine."

They looked down at the men, who growled back angrily. Jamie took it upon himself to spit down the shaft as he shut the dumbwaiter door in their faces.

"Screw them," he boasted, dusting his hands off.

Lonnie smiled, inspired by this new fire that had been lit in Jamie. Meanwhile Carter went over to a light switch that was hidden beside the wall mirror. He flicked it on, illuminating the bedroom.

"Still as creepy as ever," Carter said, surveying the room.

"You guys really used to go up that thing... like willingly?" Jamie eyed him with genuine shock.

"Well, we fit a lot better back then. Besides, it was worth it to have our own floor, away from everyone." Carter stood in front of a rather large painting on the mantle. "Your brother actually used to lift us up and down that thing." He smiled fondly.

"He did?" Lonnie's tone rose.

"Yeah." Carter's smile dropped. "Feels like such a long time ago now."

Lonnie sank at the reminder of his dead brother. "Right..."

With that, the conversation came to a hard stop. Instead, they stood gazing up at the painting above the mantle. It had a familiarity to it. A family, seven in all, sitting so perfectly spread around a living room. Five small bodies were purposefully posed in the foreground, each showing their personality through minor differences in their outfits. The three girls were placed apart: one wore overalls with her hair in pigtails, the second wore a bun and a flower print dress, and the third, who sat directly in the center, had flowing hair and a red patterned blouse.

The two boys sat between them. The skinnier of the two wore a brown and white button-up checkered shirt; the sleeves were large, drowning his arms. He had a sulky smile drawn on his face, which reminded Lonnie of himself when he looked in the mirror as of late. The final child, who appeared significantly older than the rest, had on a thick wool suit complemented with slicked back hair. He looked just like a shrunken-down version of Silas, with the same smile and eyes.

In the back, an old man rested his hand on the oldest boy. His face was weathered, but his body was still fit with a stocky frame. He did not smile, but he had a shine in his eyes that the painter either added of his own choice or found it impossible to ignore. In the far back, a woman rested on a tall chair. Her hands were set over each other in a fashion that showed modesty and poise. She had a beautiful smile which complemented her young face. Honestly, she didn't look old enough to be the children's mother or the man's wife. But her features wove into the kids like a quilt of her life.

"Is that them?" Lonnie asked.

"Yeah," Carter answered. "This used to be their father's room back when he was alive."

Lonnie paused, staring at the painting a little longer. "What about their mother?"

"I don't know. No one ever talks about her."

Carter unlocked the bedroom door, motioning for them to

follow him out. Jamie followed suit, as Lonnie looked once more at the mausoleum the room had become. He frowned.

This whole place is a graveyard.

He flicked off the light and shut the door behind him. Outside the bedroom, they found themselves exactly where they'd seen Amara on the screen. The large elevator shaft resided to their right, and a slightly propped door was waiting for them on their left.

"Do we have a plan?" Carter asked, reaching for the doorknob.

"Nope," Lonnie replied.

"Of course not," he murmured as he opened the door fully.

The boys entered into some kind of grand ballroom, a few football fields wide, with a ceiling at least thirty feet up. Bright spotlights shone down from the top of the emerald green patterned walls, illuminating some weird contraption in the middle of the room. Lonnie, along with Carter and Jamie, all clutched their ears upon entering, as an obnoxious ticking noise blasted from hidden speakers. Even with blocking out the sound, Lonnie felt his teeth vibrating as it sped up slowly.

Tick... Tick... Tick.

"What the hell is that?" Jamie pointed.

Steel columns were fastened to the floor, supporting a large metal box in the middle of the room. It was positioned halfway to the ceiling, creating a loft-like structure. Below this box, there was a tube-shaped silo that connected it to the floor, and a closed hatch was cut into its side.

What on earth?

The strangest part, however, was what Lonnie saw on the ceiling. It was completely lined with mirrors, which reflected a checkerboard pattern on the structure. Looking closer, Lonnie saw things moving on it that he couldn't fully comprehend.

Are those animals?

An industrial staircase had been built along the side of this odd contraption. At the top, a bridge led to a doorway inside.

"Come on, she must be through there." Lonnie started scaling the stairs.

Tick... Tick... Tick.

The noise ended suddenly.

"Stop." Lonnie blocked them from moving forward.

The eerie silence was followed by the faint opening and closing of doors from within the box.

Thud.

Thud.

As the second door shut, the ticking started again.

Tick... Tick... Tick.

They resumed their climb, reaching the top of the stairs. Lonnie tapped his foot on the metal bridge that separated him from the door. He listened as the ticking grew louder again from the hidden speakers.

It was deafening. Trying to ignore it, he moved toward the box, now seeing it had to be at least ten or so feet tall. Looking up at the ceiling, the reflection of the structure was a bit clearer. From here, he could see that the checkerboard pattern was not a roof, but actually from black and white tiled rooms. The structure had an open top, making its interior visible.

Yet, even as he stared inside, he couldn't comprehend what he was looking at... or better yet what kind of animals he was seeing.

Lonnie tried the door, but was hardly surprised to find it

was locked. "Help me up, I think I can jump inside and open the door."

"Are you sure?" Jamie recoiled.

"Just help me up before I change my mind."

Carter and Jamie staggered under Lonnie's feet, helping raise him up and over the ledge. He eventually kicked his feet over, managing to climb onto the frame. Just like he thought, there was in fact no ceiling to the structure. The whole thing was open to the sky, aside from the wall framing that separated each room into its own individual cube. Black and white tiles checkered the floors, making him positive now that he was looking at some kind of clue.

"But what was the puzzle?"

Thud.

Right then, the whole box shook, causing him to lose his balance.

"Wait, no!" he yelped as he stumbled. Within a split second, he was falling over the wall and into the puzzle board.

So this is how I die.

But Lonnie's scream was cut short as a pain slammed into his forehead and chest.

Dunk.

He crashed flat, his eyes staring down at a sea of black tiles. His arms remained braced for impact with the floor, but he was shocked to find them shifting against an invisible surface above it.

"What the–"

"Are you okay?" Jamie shouted. "What's happening?"

Lonnie pressed his hands down and knocked on the clear glass supporting his body. The screen blocked him from the ten-foot drop below, forming a barrier between them. Standing back up, he looked out at the whole ceiling, now noticing each box covered in a thin, nearly clear glass cover.

"Guys, come up here." He stepped over to the ledge and lowered his hand for someone to grab.

Carter looked at Jamie and then pushed forward. "I am not going last again." He took Lonnie's hand, and Jamie helped him scale the side. Jamie was next. As he ran at the wall, both Lonnie and Carter lowered a hand, using the other to support themselves and pull him up.

"Walk along the corners, we don't know how much weight this glass can hold," Lonnie warned.

The ticking stopped again, cut off by the rushed swinging of a door.

"Something's moving fast," Carter observed.

The whole box was beginning to shake again. They braced themselves until it eased.

"Look." Jamie pointed at the ceiling reflection above them.

A large shape on the other side of the board caught their eyes. They straddled the tiny wooden frame, trying hard to avoid the glass. Lonnie peeked over the edge, noticing stone statues resting in the center of many of the small rooms.

"This can't be..."

He leaned down, pressing his face to the glass. The statues were all white, each a different shape. The one he was looking at now had a long, stretched face. The hair on its head grew down into a mane. "This one has a statue of a horse."

He moved back a couple of spaces, staring at a woman with a marble robe chiseled to her skin and a crown plastered over her stone hair. "And this is a queen."

Carter counted down the rows of boxes. "One, two, three, four... There are sixty-four rooms."

Jamie suddenly dropped to his back and stared at the ceiling. "I think it's a chessboard." He pointed up.

Lonnie copied him, trying to get a better view. Eight rows up, eight rows across. Black... white... black... white, checkered across the floor. He squinted, now getting a clearer look at the animals running around the board. But on closer inspection, he realized they weren't animals at all. What he saw was much worse.

"Oh my gosh," he gasped.

"Are those—" Jamie murmured.

"No... they can't be," Lonnie spat.

They are.

A nervous itch pulled him to his feet, as urgency flooded over him.

"Amara!" he called out.

They heard another door breach from one of the middle squares.

"Come on!" Carter motioned, darting over the wooden edges.

It wasn't until they were standing around the box that they saw it below.

The creature.

Chapter 19

The Jesters

Beneath the glass was something unheard of.

On one half of the room was Amara, wielding a long, slender sword. And on the other side was something Lonnie couldn't comprehend.

At first, he thought it was a man, but that was highly unlikely. At least, he hadn't been a man in a long, long time. His skin was gray and rough like sandpaper. His face was hard and crimson, with a sewn piece of flesh where his mouth should be. The slits of his eyes were black with hints of red. And under his skin, his body pulsated with thick veins that reminded Lonnie of cable wires.

"Is that—" He peered closer.

The hands had battered claws, extending from the fingers like sharpened nails. A black garb covered his body like a prison jumpsuit, with a tiny, undecipherable emblem resting in the corner over where his heart most likely resided. He had to be at least seven feet tall, with legs like tree trunks.

Jamie looked terrified. A large lump moved down his throat

as he swallowed. He grabbed his stomach, where one of those creatures had once grabbed him with their long, bony claws.

"I thought they all died," he whined.

So did I.

Lonnie had seen all of them ooze out onto the front steps of the house. They were dying, he was positive. Mrs. Blythorne had to have shot each of them with enough bullets to take down an elephant. But maybe that wasn't enough.

Was it possible someone had shown up to save them after we were taken away in the black van?

Though observing this monstrosity, *saved* wouldn't be the optimum word choice.

Somehow, he was even less human than before, if that was possible. Behind his eyes, the soul had disappeared, replaced with nothing but chaos. The creature stepped further into the room, backing Amara into a corner, his frame nearly double the size of hers. Lonnie wanted to call her name, but he was afraid it would only distract her.

"Why does she have a sword?" Lonnie stared. "Surely, they can't expect her to…"

"Don't underestimate her," Carter stated proudly.

The ticking noise was replaced with heavy drumming that came in bursts, almost as if someone was chanting. Without warning, he lunged at Amara, and she jumped back, caught off guard. Her blade slid to her hip, and she quickly raised it, using it to build distance between them.

"Ha!" She swatted her sword in a defensive motion.

Woah. Lonnie was impressed.

The tip cut at the edge of the creature's jumpsuit, tearing the sleeve. She dodged his lunge again, moving around the room's perimeter. Every attack he made, she moved gracefully out of the way, her blade slicing over his body.

Could she actually kill him?

The drumming began shaking the floor, this time hard enough that Lonnie had to rest on a knee so as not to get bucked off. Amara seemed agitated by the noise, but the monster moved carelessly.

Did he not hear?

Black bile crept from an open gash on his wrist. Drip by drip, it slathered the floor.

Did he not feel?

Amara was holding her own well, but it was growing obvious that her energy was beginning to fade. The movement of her steps grew slower, and her feet lost their bounce.

"How can we help her?" Carter asked, placing his hand on the glass barrier.

The creature struck again, this time catching Amara's dress on the end of his claw as she spun away. He pulled her to the ground, hitting her back against the floor, and knocking the sword from her grip. She was lying face up, and an expression of shock and fear crossed her face when she saw the boys. Lonnie met her gaze. The world between them grew distant, and it was as though for a second they shared words without meaning to speak.

The widening of her eyes told him, *"What are you doing here?"*

He raised his eyebrows. *"We are here to help you."*

She shook her head. *"No, you shouldn't be here."* But the frustration subsided, replaced with an emotional smile. *"But thank you."*

The monster readied himself to pounce again, drawing

them both out of their daze. His giant bare feet moved across the tiles with heavy tremors. Lonnie watched Amara reach for her sword, which was a few feet away. The creature grew closer, and she stretched her arm as far as it could go.

"Come on!" Lonnie cheered.

She managed to loop her finger around the hilt, pulling the blade to her chest just as he leapt on top of her. She let out a huff of air as his weight dropped on her.

No!

But then he stopped. Amara let out a gut-wrenching scream as the tip of her blade burst from the back of the creature. The boys watched in amazement as she shifted to her side, using the blade to rotate him off her. He lay completely still on the floor. Pressing her foot to his chest, she slid the blade out of what Lonnie could only assume was his heart.

Amara gagged, the black ooze from his body had dripped onto her dress and disappeared against the dark fabric. Drops stuck her face that left stains even after she wiped them off. The blade slid from her grip, clanking against the tile. The drumming from the speakers stopped, letting them know that the battle was over. They all sighed in relief, and Amara took the moment to lay down and catch her breath.

She did it. I can't believe—

Wait, what is that?

Lonnie noticed something on the monster's neck. From beneath the flesh, a green glow started growing brighter.

"Look out!" He pointed.

Amara jumped up at his scream, grabbing her sword in the process. She looked around for the danger and finally noticed the glow. She stepped back, raising her blade to it.

"What the...?"

Placing the tip against it, she pressed in.

Pop.

The creature exploded into piles of ooze and flesh, painting the room black from top to bottom, including poor Amara, who was equally unlucky. She let out a disgusted scream and then tossed her blade across the filthy floor.

"Are you all right?" Lonnie spoke through the glass.

She tried to get the guts off her face but was having trouble finding a clean part of her sleeve to wipe it with.

"No!" she spat. "And what are you doing here?"

"We wanted to help."

"I didn't ask for help!" she retorted. "Now you've put us all in danger."

Carter slapped his hand to his face, "I told you we shouldn't have done this. I told you!"

"Ignore him," Lonnie said. "You're right. You didn't ask for our help, but we are your friends."

Tick... Tick.

The speakers came alive again, replaying that awful ticking noise.

There isn't time for this conversation.

"You're in a chessboard," he told her, pointing at the board's reflection in the mirrored ceiling.

"I know," she responded, as though it were obvious.

But she immediately turned her attention to the body splayed out below her. Kneeling, she pulled at the cloth, drawn by the glisten of some kind of patch. Ripping it off, she held it to the light, illuminating a symbol showing an odd shape.

"It's a pawn," she stated firmly.

"There are more of those things over here," Jamie added, standing a couple of rooms over.

Amara resettled her frazzled hair and looked at the doors in front of her.

Tick... Tick... Tick.

"My turn, I guess." She stepped over the corpse, grabbing her sword.

She stretched out her sleeve and brushed the bile off the edge, making the end shine. Lonnie wanted to gag as the ooze plopped on the floor in a small pile.

"Wait, there is something written on here!" She rubbed her sleeve harder, really getting out the layers of tissue and blood that had clotted around the serrated edge.

"The," she read, leaning closer, "the rook."

The rook? Like the chess piece.

A look of realization crossed her face that told Lonnie that he had clearly missed something. She stared at the doors, making hand gestures with her outstretched arms.

Tick... Tick.

"Of course!" she squealed. "I went forward, but that made the left door become locked. Obviously, it was locked because I am the rook! The rook can only move in straight lines per turn."

"Okay." Lonnie nodded in agreement, though he really didn't know the first thing about chess. "What do you need us to do?"

"Find me a path to the king!"

Lonnie looked up to make sure the others had heard her. They were already scattering along the roof, searching in each box.

"Straight lines only," she added. "It's the only way!"

"Got it," Carter answered.

The ticking was blaring, alerting them that Amara's turn

was about to end. Facing the right wall, she darted to the door, opening it and throwing herself inside just in time.

"Phew," she sighed as the ticking stopped. The doors locked.

Seeing she was safe, Lonnie ventured off toward the bordering rooms, trying to find the best path for her to go. He made it about three rooms down when he heard her scream.

Panic blossomed in his chest, and he ran back just in time to catch a large dark shape standing up from the black floor. Dressed in another black jumpsuit, the monster practically blended into the ground. His head was shielded by a black armor casing, and his body was a gross mess of amphibious skin. The emblem on his black jumpsuit was a white cross.

Amara readied her sword, seemingly waiting for him to strike. But the creature stood still, completely unbothered. Raising her blade to his neck, she aimed at the same green light that had started glowing, shining through a gap in the armor. It grew, extending the vein in his neck by double its size.

"It's going to blow!" Lonnie yelled.

She cowered to the ground as black bile exploded yet again onto the walls and on her. She gagged, spitting out loose bile that had slipped over her shoulder and into her mouth.

"I think I found the king." Carter came running back to the glass above Amara's room, Jamie trailing behind.

"What happened?" Jamie asked.

They were all staring at the pile of ooze, which, until five seconds ago, had been a living body.

Amara moved across the floor, trying not to slip on the bloody mess. Ripping the patch from the creature's crumpled-up uniform, she showed them the cross emblem Lonnie had seen prior. "I... I think the bishop just blew up," she said.

"You must have captured it," Carter observed. "That must be the rules."

Rules.

The way he said it made it sound so normal, like it was a game. None of this should be normal. Lonnie studied Amara, who appeared absolutely traumatized as she tried to scrape the blood and guts from her skin. When it wouldn't come off, she gagged, until eventually hurling on the floor.

Seeing the creatures in front of him was like reliving the horror again for the first time. Especially looking into their lifeless eyes. Lonnie had a vivid memory of them from his own trials, but it was nothing compared to seeing them in person. Maybe his brain had a certain way of numbing the feeling down to something he could stomach, but it wasn't doing that now. What he was seeing was real and horrifying.

Lonnie watched Amara's trembling hands. "Are you okay?" he asked.

"Where's the king?" She ignored him, wringing the junk from her hair.

"It's only a guess," Jamie answered. "But there is only one room that doesn't have a see-through ceiling. That must be it."

"Where is it?" she demanded.

Jamie spun in a circle, counting the rooms with his hand. "One to your right and two up."

She paused for a second, then shouted, "He is at e8 then."

"There is one problem, though."

"What now?" Her voice dropped.

"There is no clear path to get there."

She stared at the pile of flesh. "Well, it's not like I have much of a choice then."

Creak... Creak... Creak.

Three doors opened simultaneously, drawing the boys' attention a few boxes to the left. In the farthest one, a beast stirred. Its frame was at least twice as big as the previous two, its body somehow even more deformed and animalistic. Lonnie found no way to believe this had ever been a man. It was too painful to imagine it as anything more than a thing created from chaos and death. Creeping slowly, it walked along the floor on four legs, rather than two, somehow squeezing its big chest through the tiny door and passing down the hall. Lonnie counted as it moved.

"Two rooms right... one up."

It came to a dead stop in the final box, the ticking overhead starting once again.

Weird.

Carter said, "It's got to be the knight."

Lonnie walked over its box, trying to get a glance at its features. He had never seen anything so foul. The body was covered in patches of hair that ran down its torso, drooping over its face.

Was that its nose?

The edges of its face protruded with large, gnarly teeth dangling from its snout. Its spine was warped, the vertebrae jabbing violently against its skin. It defied nature. It defied science.

Carter pointed at its box and then at Amara's. "One to the right and one down. Why would it move there? It can never reach her. Wait—" He stopped himself, cupping his mouth.

"What?" Lonnie asked.

"To reach the king, she will have to move right into its path. It's the only way."

The ticking came to a stop, ending the opponent's turn. The playing field was set.

"Her turn."

Amara stared at the ceiling. She didn't speak another word, but it was clear she was running the plays in her head.

One way or another, she will have to fight the knight.

Tick... Tick.

Amara took up her sword, massaging the edge of her hand carefully. Then, with a wave of confidence, she opened the door and entered e6.

Lonnie was useless from the rooftop. He wondered if this was no different from being behind a screen. He was merely a spectator at the coliseum, one who watched his friends get thrown to lions and be forced to fight with medieval weapons for others' amusement.

The spotlights in the room grew stronger, shining now only on their half of the board. This was the finale.

Amara had taken her position in e6. The king's space was just two rooms in front of her. She looked at the boys above her and gave them a frightened yet confident nod. Raising her sword, she waited.

The ticking stopped right on cue, as if knowing this choice was final. It was the opponent's turn. Three doors opened for the beast, swiftly and expected. And with them came the sound of gargling animal noises across the corridor.

Here it comes.

Amara stared at the now-opened door, readying her stance. Her choices had become inherently easier in this final second. Fight or die. The beast had crept its way through the first two doors and was now standing directly in front of her. The single hallway built between them was their arena.

May the best player win.

Chapter 20

PLAYS AND COUNTERPLAYS

Amara had only two thoughts racking her mind.

The first was the pain in her hand, which was growing by the second. The weight of the steel might as well have been piercing the flesh that held it, though she tried to ignore it. The second thought had a much tighter grip on her. One that she just couldn't seem to push away.

They came to help me.

She stared at the beast across from her. Its mangled fur and rat nose did frighten her, but she tried not to let the fear show. She didn't dare break eye contact, but she could sense her friends standing overhead. Their shadows cast in the light, reflecting their bodies on the wall. If it was the closest she would get to not being alone, it would have to do.

Why did they come here?

They weren't supposed to be here.

She flinched as the beast moved closer to her. Its talons scratched the floor beneath it, tearing at the tile. Its eyes locked on her, crystallized and sharp.

A predator's eyes.

Fourteen months earlier.

She looked stunning.

Her hair draped over the white lace fabric. The curves of her dimples sank into her face.

"Such a beautiful bride," Auntie Debra fawned.

"Yes," Amara grumbled. She pulled at the stitching of her coral blue dress, an itch of disgust creeping over her skin.

What an ugly color.

She kept her opinion to herself. A maid of honor had only to smile and be supportive.

Just get through the day.

The moonlight held the night frozen like a picture. The only breath of life came from the music that serenaded the happy couple on the dance floor. The groom had his hand placed over the small of the bride's back, leading with his heavy foot. She recovered his steps, making them both look effortless.

Six months.

That didn't seem like enough time for an engagement.

Three months to plan a wedding was even crazier.

Though second marriages had no laws, she supposed. Especially in a situation such as this.

A spring wedding.

The walls of One Whitehall Place were especially festive that night, yet Amara had such a sour taste in her mouth. The irony of him waltzing in a room filled with books and yet lacking any knowledge of the world he had just entered.

The poor groom.

The newly married couple's first dance came to an end, and Amara's mother, the now Ella Capulto, left her husband's side.

Meanwhile, Mr. Vicente Capulto moved to the head table, taking one of the four reserved seats. One for Amara's mother, one for herself as the maid of honor, one for Mr. Capulto, and one for the best man.

He sat down beside a muscular boy giving him a playful grab of the neck. They laughed. Amara watched the boy from across the room, picturing their first interaction earlier that day.

Hello, she'd said to him. Her hand was outstretched.

Hi, my name is Roman. His voice was so gravely, yet light. It had no limitations or fear. But she supposed he didn't know yet what he should be afraid of, now that he was a part of her family.

The wedding was riling up, inside voices drowned out by the DJ hidden behind his tiny booth. A quick look around the room could tell anyone whose party this was. In the heart of London, the crowd reflected just that. Their attitude was posh and reserved. Meanwhile, the few Americans in attendance, stuck out like sore thumbs. Their dancing was volatile and reckless. This was a holiday, a fun trip away from home.

But even they weren't entirely here for the groom. Colleagues were something the couple shared. The pitfall of both teaching at the same university department meant that their friends were one in the same, and since he had no siblings and departed parents, that limited the people standing in his corner.

"Hello, sweetheart." A hand brushed her shoulder.

Amara's mother appeared beside her, a twinkle shining from her whitened teeth.

"Hi mum, are you having a good time?"

Amara caught her in a trance. At first, she thought she was staring in awe at her incredible party. But on closer look, her gaze was locked on the sweetheart table in the corner of the dance floor. Sitting there was Mr. Capulto and Amara's new stepbrother.

"I am." Her mother smiled. "Who doesn't want a bigger family?"

Goosebumps ran up Amara's arms, which she quickly tried to rub away. Her mother's face was calm, always poised and humble. But she couldn't hide those eyes. They were ravenous. They were the eyes of a predator who'd just spotted her prey.

***

Present day.

Above her, a drumming noise began again. The beast drew closer, the smell of its breath ravaging her nose. It was only a body's length away now.

What is it waiting for?

Amara positioned her back foot. How does one spar with an animal? It simply wasn't a technique she'd ever needed to learn.

Would it be murder to kill it? Mercy, perhaps?

There wasn't exactly a choice in it either way, so why waste efforts trying to justify it?

"Focus," she commanded, but her mind drifted again.

They came to help me.

In all her years of withering away at this party, she had never seen anything so insane. And yet, just the thought of it plucked at her heartstrings. She barely knew the two guys, and they had risked everything for her. Now feeling their presence above, it created a newfound drive within her.

I can do this.

The beast pressed its large back through the entry. The doorframe nearly tore from the hinges as the monster jostled its shoulders to fit through the gap.

What would Coach say to do?

Find its weaknesses.

She first noted its small arms and legs, supporting an abnormally large torso.

Its frame.

It's top heavy. If it turns too fast, it will topple and roll.

The nose.

It leads with its nose. It's a guide point that can be obstructed.

What are my weaknesses?

The beast crouched on its back legs and charged.

No time.

It paced the floor, its arms moved synchronously in front of it, while it dragged its body behind. She sidestepped around the room, never averting her gaze.

Not yet.

Not yet.

It pounced.

Now.

Pushing off her left leg, she sprang to her right, raising the blade across her chest and striking the edge of its arm.

"Hut!" she blurted.

The impact sent a pain through her tendon that immediately made her scream. Spinning out of the beast's path, she regrouped and tried to shake out her wrist. She attempted to hold the sword in just her left hand, but it felt wrong. She messed with the stance, hoping it might comply, but her feet couldn't seem to understand this new language. Grunting, she begrudgingly took the sword back into her right hand. It burned, but she wrapped her fingers around the hilt as loosely as possible. The blood from the beast dripped down from the tip and over her knuckles.

It gnawed at the gash on its arm, mixing the liquid into its fur. But after a few seconds, it lost interest, as though it was merely an inconvenience.

Amara winced.

Weakness for me.

I feel pain.

Without missing a beat, it charged again.

This time, it kept its weight on its back legs, leaving room for it to turn its hips more easily. It must have thought she would try the same maneuver again.

Clever.

But Amara was ready for it. She faked her same move, resetting back into her original stance. In anticipation, the beast swiveled its back, swatting its talon-like hand into where it thought she would be. Instead, she dove forward, sinking the blade deep into its shoulder.

"Hah!" she cried out.

She felt triumphant, but it didn't flinch. The beast froze, shocked by her advance. Then, without hesitation, it lifted its arm and smacked her, sending her into the wall.

Her bones shuddered under the weight. The thin wall gave slightly, cracking under the force, luckily taking most of the impact. She bounced on the floor, clutching her ribs.

Creak.

The beast took its stance, preparing to charge again. The blade was embedded in its shoulder, blocking its arm from completely extending onto the ground. However, even limping, it was quite agile.

Get up!

Her insides screamed for her to stay down, but she planted her foot beneath her hip, coiling it up like a spring.

Three seconds.

The beast passed the middle of the room.

Two seconds.

The sound of the clinking sword reached her ear.

One second.

Its hot breath touched her face.

Zero.

She pushed off her leg and slid across the tile, just as it landed where she'd been sitting. Its talons grazed her cheek, barely missing her eye. She reached up and felt the gash, fresh blood leaking onto her hand. The beast, noticing her movement, tried to follow, but its legs gave out under its momentum. One by one, each limb buckled, sending it toppling through the wall.

Crash.

A horse-sized hole had formed in the drywall, with pieces of wood hanging loosely from the remaining frame. Her body shook, trying to make sense of what had happened. The drumming from the invisible speakers became louder, only making her more disoriented.

"Amara, get up!" a voice screamed.

Lonnie's head peeked over the rim of the glass. His face was so red and bright. She nodded her chin, dazed as sweat dripped down her forehead and mixed with the blood on her cheek. She hobbled up, bracing herself on the door.

She went to get back into her fighting stance, then remembered her sword was still lodged in the beast.

Where the wall had broken, something stirred in the rubble. The beast emerged, its nose flapping open, splattering black blood over its swollen eye. It reached for the wall to pull itself up. Its talons sank into the remaining bit of drywall, ripping it to shreds.

"I need a plan."

She stepped back, feeling something sharp crunch beneath her feet. She moved her shoe and found a metal bolt. The tile around it had chipped, revealing crumbled pieces of dust and grout.

She looked up at the ceiling where a tiny crack had formed. Barely a pebble in a windshield, but it was enough. It was an idea.

"Break the glass!" she screamed.

"What?" Carter responded.

"Just do it!"

The monster was struggling with its leg, which had been crushed beneath the metal door. Amara took the chance. Grabbing the bolt, she used it to dig around the lining of the tile.

Above her, she heard light pounding on the glass.

Birds pecking at a window.

Would it even break? She couldn't think like that.

All I can do is dig.

Chapter 21

The King Will See You Now

Thud.

Lonnie pulled his hand from the glass below his feet.

Thud.

Thud.

"Come on!" he shouted.

He repetitively slammed his fist down, but the crack refused to grow. Below him, Amara was digging around some tile as the creature slowly pulled itself back to its feet.

I have to hurry.

"I need something sharp." Lonnie patted down his body. He had nothing useful.

Crap.

"Do either of you have anything sharp?"

Carter and Jamie turned out their pockets.

"Here, try the car keys!" Jamie shouted, tossing them in the air.

"Yes, perfect." Lonnie put the key between his fingers and formed a fist, punching it down into the glass.

Crack.

He braced his other hand on the floor.

Again.

He slammed it down.

Crack.

The ground was growing unsteady beneath his feet. The small crack was growing and spreading to the corners.

"Get off the floor." Carter pulled Jamie back to the metal frame.

Lonnie slammed his fist down once more, the tip of broken glass slicing the ends of his knuckle, while the key plunged down.

Crack.

He felt no resistance after that. The key had sunk all the way through and fallen out the other end. Lonnie held his bleeding hand and turned to the others. He stared at Carter, noticing the light reflecting off his waist.

"Give me your belt," he demanded.

Carter did as he was told. Inching along the beam, he handed Lonnie the leather strap.

"Thank you." Lonnie watched the beast free itself from the rubble. Its oddly formed body moved wearily back into the room with blood-soaked fur.

I have to hurry.

Lonnie wrapped the leather of the belt around his palm. Taking his fist, he plunged it into the hole.

The top of the glass shattered, sending shards into the sky. He blocked his face and slammed his hand down again. The hole grew, forming new fault lines over the ceiling. A shard nicked his chin, drawing blood. He aimed his hand to strike once more, but the entire thing started to shake.

Looking down into the room, he pictured the bodies of

Hannah, Roman, and his brother, all inside. He imagined Hannah with the glass shard in her chest, his brother with his brain matter blown against the wall, and Roman burnt to a crisp.

I failed all of them.

His throat tightened at the images of all the people he'd lost. Amara was sitting beside their imaginary bodies, now holding a tile in her hands. The beast was moving in, ready to give its killing blow.

But I can still save her.

Interlocking his hands, he raised them both over his head and smashed them against the glass. They passed through with ease, leaving that sunken feeling to fester in his chest. The glass exploded, raining down like knives onto the beast and Amara. Lonnie watched the rest of the ceiling give, disappearing below, dragging him with it.

Is this how I go?

He tumbled over the edge, this time with no barrier to catch his fall. The bodies he pictured still lingered in his mind down below. He imagined their arms reaching out to catch him. He closed his eyes, welcoming their embrace. But before he reached them, he found himself suspended mid-air.

What?

He was floating, a sharp pain growing in his neck.

A hand had latched around the ruffles of his collar. Slowly, it pulled him back over the edge, letting another pair of hands pull at his skin, until eventually, he was safe. Lonnie touched his body as if to remind himself it was still in one piece.

Carter and Jamie sat beside him, checking that he was okay. Feeling his own pulse, Lonnie pulled himself together, and returned to the opening in the ceiling.

"Amara!"

Rolling to his side, he peered over the now open ceiling.

Crunch.

Pieces of glass broke under the beast's hands, leaving a trail of blood on the floor. Large shards had burrowed into its spine, paralyzing it from the waist down. Still, it kept moving, using its arms to drag itself toward Amara, who was crouching in the corner of the room. Faint cuts striped her sleeves and legs, but above her head, she held a loose piece of broken tile tightly between her fingers.

She chucked it beside her, letting it shatter. The beast kept crawling, a gentle wheezing coming from its lungs. Amara did not appear worried. Instead, her hand traced the floor, searching for a piece of glass.

She curled her mouth, a venomous look growing in her eyes. As the monster crawled closer, however, her expression shifted. Satisfaction had succumbed to sadness. The beast looked so pathetic now, its body splayed out on the ground.

"Yield," she whispered to it.

It kept moving towards her, as if that was all it was programed to do. In the background, the drumming from the speakers gradually faded.

"Please, die with honor," she practically begged.

They all knew it would not. She raised the large, jagged piece of glass in her left hand and plunged it into the side of its head. Instantly, the body went limp, dropping to the ground without resistance.

Amara sniffled, holding back tears. "You're free."

She wiped tears from her eyes, but did not draw attention to them. She tucked herself against the wall, as a green glow appeared on the beast's neck. Amara wasn't even phased as it burst, lightly caking the room in its guts.

"I'm going down," Lonnie announced, kicking the loose glass from the ridge. He hung himself off the ledge, letting his arms descend into the room.

Thud.

He dropped the rest of the way, letting his feet rejoice at the feeling of solid ground. Amara sat close by, alerted by his loud entrance.

"Are you okay?" he asked, offering his good hand.

She took it, using it to pull herself up. "How could I possibly be okay?"

He didn't answer because he had no answer to give. Instead, he just wrapped his arms around her.

"I'm glad you're alive," he said.

"Me too."

Thud.

Thud.

Carter and Jamie dropped into the room, making it feel especially packed, between the four of them and the carcass lying diagonally across the tile.

"Hey," Carter said.

She smiled, giving him a hug. "Hi, luv. I'm quite surprised to see you here."

"Oh well, you have Lonnie to thank for that. I'm afraid to admit, he was the bravest among us."

"Really?" She smirked. "I don't find myself too surprised."

She pinched Jamie on the arm, and they gave each other an understanding nod.

"Now." She sank her shoe in the back of the monster. "I think it's time we get out of here."

Drawing both hands around the blade's handle, she heaved, ripping it from the muscle it had lodged in.

Tick... Tick... Tick.

Hopefully this would be the last time they had to listen to that horrendous noise.

It was our turn.

Amara kicked some of the rubble from the floor, revealing a faint e6 inscribed in the middle black tile. "Forward two to e8."

The four of them proceeded to the next room, which was identical to the others, as to be expected. Amara led the way, dragging her blade along the floor until reaching the final door.

"What do we think is waiting behind there?" Carter asked.

Amara grabbed the handle with no hesitation. "'I'm not sure. But I know we can handle it."

Upon entering, torches lit around the room, producing an eerie orange hue. The walls weren't normal drywall like the others. Instead, the inside was formed with gray brick, and the ceiling was covered in black rock.

Looks like a dungeon. Or perhaps a throne room.

At the end of the opposing wall was a large gold throne. Its backrest extended almost to the ceiling, and the seat was made of red velvet fabric.

"Woah, look at this." Lonnie pointed.

Sitting upon the chair was the corpse of one of the creatures. Vines and overgrown brush stretched from the back wall, wrapping around his arms and legs. He looked like he had been sitting here for centuries, slowly decaying away. Of all of them, this one appeared the most human with some semblance of a normal face. The rest of his body, however, was as experimented on as the others. He had elongated legs, clawed hands, and a clay plaster layered over patches of his skin. Lonnie tried to get a closer look, moving up beside the throne.

"Look out," Carter shouted.

Startled, Lonnie looked up just in time to see the corpse's hand reach toward him from its resting spot.

"My god, is he still alive?" Lonnie squealed, retreating back to the others.

Amara stood in front of them, raising her sword. It was not until now that Lonnie noticed the strings of hair coming from his head. And atop them was a golden crown with rubies encrusted into the edges.

The king.

The corpse's body suddenly came to life. He stretched his joints, snapping free from the binding weeds. The crown scraped the ceiling as the king reached his full, almost ten-foot stature. His legs were at least double the length of Lonnie's, his torso about the same. In his right hand, he held a scythe so large that it could slice them in half from head to toe in a single swing.

This can't be good.

The king watched them now, waiting for their move. Amara stared him down, moving closer to the throne.

"Amara," Lonnie whispered. "Be careful?"

He reached for her arm to pull her back, but she ignored it. She moved closer, taking enough time for the statue to raise his own blade in the air and wind it behind his head. The weapon scraped the rock ceiling, making a screeching noise.

"Amara..." Lonnie repeated nervously.

The king looked ready to swing, but so did Amara. Standing in her stance, she aimed up her blade. They were in a square off, each waiting for the other to make a move. Finally the creature swung, but Amara was ready. She dove forward, thrusting her blade into his chest with impeccable speed. The scythe froze mid swing, locking in place.

The man glared at her in defeat, releasing the scythe to the floor with a loud clang. A green light appeared on his neck just like the creatures prior.

Did she do it?

Lonnie didn't know how to react. Apart of him thought that was too easy to be the end, yet then he realized that was just the appetizer. There were still two courses or better yet two trials to complete before they were home free. And seeing at how hard the first one shaped out to be, he was not loving their odds.

Tick... Tick. Tick.

An invisible hand grabbed the metronome, pausing it in place.

Finally silence.

Lonnie shielded his face, bracing for the creature to explode like the others. But instead, the green light coursed through his veins, making his entire body glow. A burning stench rose from his skin as the light started melting the flesh from his bones.

Oh my God!

Each of his limbs shriveled up and dropped to the floor, until all that was left was a pile of bones and oozing sludge that reeked like hot trash.

"Checkmate," Amara stated victoriously, dropping her sword.

The boys stood around her awkwardly, unsure how to react. They waited for a sign or exit to appear, but nothing changed.

"What gives, where's the exit?" Jamie asked.

Lonnie examined the room, finding there to only be three

doors; the one they had entered through and ones to either side, leading to rooms d8 and f8.

"I don't know." He pulled on one of the doors, finding it locked. "This couldn't have all been for nothing. There has to be an exit here."

Jamie and Lonnie felt along the walls for another secret passage while Amara and Carter started to examine the throne.

"There is nothing here!" Jamie whined.

"Same here, " Carter responded from the chair.

After a few minutes, Lonnie was feeling like an absolute fool. He had pulled down every torch and pressed in each brick, but nothing happened. That was when he noticed a hidden camera beneath one of the torches.

What if we aren't supposed to escape...

Lonnie stumbled back, now seeing how stupid he was. They had walked themselves right into a cage, and now all the Sibil's had to do was fetch them and execute them for their disloyalty.

What was I thinking? I've killed all of us, I'm such an idiot.

The images of all the things they might do to him fogged his mind: poisoning, burning, or worst of all turning him into one of those things. His friends' voices became muffled, as he drowned in his thoughts.

"I think the chair is bolted to the wall," Carter stated.

"Well, what if there is another way..." Amara's voice trailed off. She jumped onto the chair, feeling around the inside of the armrests.

Lonnie watched her, his heart pounding. She was acting so confident, as though they had already won. Around her, he pictures the dead bodies again. Roman, Hannah, and his brother. They stared at him, accusingly.

I've killed her. I've killed them all.

Crank.

"Woah!" Amara screamed.

Lonnie shook his head, the corpses suddenly disappearing. He spotted the now empty throne, realizing that Amara had disappeared.

"Wait!" Lonnie yelped. "What happened!"

"She—" Carter started.

Beep!

A siren filled the air, making them clutch their ears. The whole structure rumbled.

Pop. Pop.

What is that?

Pop. Pop. Pop.

From across the chessboard, tiny explosions echoed. It wasn't until the fifth one that Lonnie realized what was happening.

They are blowing up the rest of the creatures.

All the pawns, bishops, rooks, and whatever else they had set up inside that board. They didn't need them anymore, he supposed, and they were a liability.

Pop. Pop. Pop.

A part of Lonnie was glad that he didn't have to worry about them running amok again like last year. But still, the pain wasn't lost on him. They died all alone. One after another, an explosion triggering in their necks. They were people at one point; he remembered reading one's file in the hospital ward downstairs. Genetically engineered tests that had gone wrong. People made into weapons.

But how did they get there in the first place?

Were they runaways, patients of last-ditch hospital trials, or past champions?

Everyone has a story, but for all these poor people, he just wished they could have had a better ending.

"We have to go!" Carter barked.

Lonnie shook his head. "Right. You're right."

He jumped up onto the throne, just as he saw Amara had.

But how did she disappear?

He searched the seat and around the cushion until finally finding a little switch tucked into the armrest. He flipped it, hearing a gear churning sound from below. His stomach rose into his chest, and just like that, he was falling.

One trial down.

Chapter 22

Down the Rabbit Hole

The piping Lonnie slid down rubbed against his skin, forming blisters and burns.

He imagined it was the metal slide at the playground by his parents' house. The one he used to go on over and over until his body felt raw and bruised under the midday sun. He wondered if it was still out there. It would only be a few miles from here. Maybe after this was over, he could check.

If there was an after.

Lonnie saw a faint light approaching at the end of the tunnel, its warmth slowly consuming him. He flinched as he passed through, finding himself plopped down from the tube and onto the floor.

Sweet ground.

He rubbed his hand on its surface, grateful to no longer be suspended in the air. Yet his peace was soon interrupted by rumbling from above.

Move.

He rolled to the side just in time to see Jamie and Carter tumble out onto the space where he'd just been sitting. Their bodies were tangled together, limbs intertwined and jabbing into one another.

Jamie let out a muffled cry. "Ow."

Lonnie gave them each a hand, pulling them to their feet.

"Thanks," Carter said.

Where's Amara?

His chest tightened. She hadn't been there when he'd landed.

"Amara!"

"Over here," a far-off voice echoed under the sound of the siren.

His shoulders sank with relief.

Tap.

Something metallic crinkled under his foot. Moving his toe, he found a little metal plaque stuck to the wooden floorboard. It read: ***Don't Let Your Eyes Deceive You.***

"Great, another clue."

The blaring beep finally stopped, letting the thoughts trickle back into his head.

Where are we?

The floorboards continued forward to a series of mirrors, like something seen at the county fair. Each one was angled, reflecting their bodies a hundred times over.

"We look like shit," Carter cut in.

He's right.

Cuts dug into their clothes from the slide and the glass. Blood dried against Lonnie's wrist, giving the appearance that he'd dunked his hand in red paint. Carter held up his pants with the ends of his fingers, which reminded Lonnie that he had left his belt somewhere in the other room.

Oops.

"This way." Amara's reflection appeared on all the surfaces in front of them, gesturing them forward.

They nervously followed, stepping into what appeared to be a long hall of distorted mirrors. Thick wooden pillars sandwiched each one, supporting them up. Lonnie touched the glass, watching his image bounce, the folds of his body rippling against the light. Even the ceiling was covered in reflective tiles.

Did the Sibils get a discount on glass or something?

"So, a house of mirrors?" Carter acknowledged. "That doesn't seem too bad."

"Best not to assume," Amara scolded, appearing from behind a wooden pillar.

Piping within the walls of the room creaked, letting out a slow, methodical hum.

"I don't like this," Lonnie admitted.

"We could break the mirrors." Jamie pretended to sock his reflection.

"They are polycarbonate glass. The only thing that would break is your hand," Amara explained.

"You don't know that," Carter said.

Amara pointed to a chipped end of one of the pillars, revealing the edge of the mirror peeking out. It was an unusual blue tint. "If it was glass, it would be clear, but Polycarbonate always has blue edges."

They all looked at her with perplexed stares.

"Why the hell do you know that?" Carter laughed, which gave way for the rest of them to chuckle.

Even Amara smiled, and she dropped her head. It wasn't a lot, but it was the first thing that had broken everyone's never-ending feeling of dread.

"There's a greenhouse I like to visit inside the biology wing at uni." Her focus drifted somewhere else. "My professor says that they use polycarbonate windows because they are stronger to withstand the weather. Makes it the most beautiful place in a storm."

"Sounds nice," Jamie admitted.

Amara smiled, holding that fond memory on her face. "Yes, I hope I can go there again."

Hiss.

"What was that?" Carter jumped.

A sliver of fog crept in from beneath his feet. It covered the wood and slowly climbed their ankles.

"Move!" Amara yelled.

They only got a few steps in as another, more mechanical sound sprouted from the ceiling and floor. Lonnie yelped as a mirror swung toward him. It pressed into his face, swiveling on some kind of turntable. He was spun with it, briefly spotting his friends being dragged by other mirrors. Eventually, his moving wall came to a hard stop, knocking him back and locking up against its new dance partners. All around him, the walls reconfigured, shifting and forming new pathways. The fog leaked in from beneath the wood floor, distorting his vision.

"Are you guys there?" he screamed.

All his friends were nowhere to be found.

"Yeah," Amara replied, from the other side of a mirror.

"Yes," Carter and Jamie repeated, both sounding far away.

"I can hardly see. Are there any clues by any of you?" Lonnie asked.

The sound of rushing fog continued to leak in.

"Hello?" he called, his voice cracking.

"No," Jamie spoke.

"If anyone finds the exit, shout, and we will try to make our way to you," Amara explained.

"Okay," they all replied.

Lonnie hit his curled hand on the glass.

Damn it.

"How am I alone again?" he groaned.

He took his first step, the fog kicking up and rising to his face.

This is a mental trial.

Think.

He recalled hearing that the best way to escape a house of mirrors was to move slowly and always have your hand on the glass. He took another step, his palm held out beside him.

Dink.

He walked face-first into a mirror, letting out a painful grunt. "Super advice."

Rubbing his nose, he held his other hand out in front to block another collision. The hallways were endless, each section showing copy after copy of himself staring back. It was a vicious loop, slowly burning into his corneas.

"Something isn't right."

A lightheaded feeling rose within him, making him lean against the mirror more for support as he walked. An aroma of pine and dirt filled the air, smelling like a forest. It formed an unexpected taste that lingered on his tongue and in his nose.

Odd.

He caught sight of himself in the mirror, his whole body facing away, revealing the back of his head.

"What the hell?"

He pressed his hand against the glass, surprised to find his fingers touching the soft texture of skin. He recoiled in horror as his doppelganger spun around to face him in the mirror. He pawed at his own face, watching his reflection's skin melt away, the muscles on it peeling from the bone and hanging from the tissues. Lonnie opened his mouth to scream, but nothing came out.

The mirrors shifted again, the wood floors scuffing under the weight of the spinning contraptions. He tried to find an exit, but wasn't fast enough. Three mirrors interlocked around him, trapping him in a tight prism. Wicked versions of his face reflected in each mirror, their eyes frozen and jaws dropped in locked motion.

"Stop. Stop!" He pounded on the glass. "This isn't real!"

Panic seized Lonnie, and he clutched his chest. "Ow." He winced, his hand reaching for his back.

Spinning around, he caught his own hand reaching from the mirror. Then came another, grabbing his leg. It pinched his skin, pulling at him like taffy.

"Let go!" He slapped the hand, but then immediately felt another and another.

His clones in the three mirrors had demonic looks on their faces as they reached for his skin. They covered his torso, pulling him down. Six hands, thirty fingers, all lathered on his stomach, pinching and pulling, trying to tear into him.

He screamed, dropping to the unfinished wood floor. The mist shrouded him, funneling up his nose and making his brain fog.

"This can't be real. They aren't real," he mumbled to himself. He lifted his dress shirt and saw bruises riddled down to his waist. "Or maybe it is."

He felt the wooden floor, letting the splinters lodge into his hand.

This is real. This is real.

He could hear the reflections moaning, as if trying to speak. He plugged his ears in horror as they continued to reach for his back. The walls finally shifted again, and he wasted no time. Pulling himself up, he ran down the first passageway he saw. His copies reached out to him from every mirror he passed. They even started whispering his name in a cruel taunting tone.

"Amara, Jamie, Carter!" he shouted. A cold sweat broke across his neck.

His head buzzed, his legs no longer responding to what he told them to do.

Which way? Which way do I go?

"Amara!" he hollered at the ceiling.

A waft of sweet vanilla hit his nose, catching him off guard.

I know that smell.

In front of him, a streak of yellow ran by. "Wait." He chased after it, winding through the walls.

Finally, he reached a straightaway, and the yellow streak transformed into a woman. Her bleached blonde hair and golden dress reflected in the mirrors, making the whole hall glow bright. She stared at him.

"Mom?" he asked.

No, that couldn't be her.

Her face was drooping as if she were a wax statue that had been left in the heat. She cocked her head, watching him uneasily. Lonnie tried to get closer, causing her to run and slip back into the maze of mirrors.

"Wait!" he called out.

He chased after her, suddenly feeling a sharp pain rushing from his nose. He put his hand up to it, shocked at the blood.

What the...

He tried to move forward, but he'd chased her right into another mirror. His face crinkled against its surface. The pain hit him all at once, delayed but not lessened. He clutched his nose; its cartilage shifted out of place. He tilted his head back, lifting his sleeve to block the dripping.

A tap came from his shoulder, jolting him back to his senses. He spun, shocked to see his mother waiting for him. The sequins of her dress were so shiny and detailed, it couldn't be a dream. Every strand of her hair was flowing and real. And the vanilla perfume she wore was unforgettable.

This wasn't her. Snap out of it.

He had just seen her earlier that night. She had brunette hair and a simple dress on. This woman wasn't his mother. She wasn't real.

Yet, he couldn't look away.

"Mom, what are you doing here?"

A strain overtook his voice like he was a lost little boy finding his mom. She touched the corner of his face, rubbing his cheek. Her hand was warm and inviting, which made Lonnie feel safe. Anxious thoughts came to a simmer as the smoke continued to rise around him, drifting up his nose with each inhale.

"You're okay," a deep tone bellowed from the woman.

It wasn't his mother's voice, but at this point, he was too delirious to care. A sense of comfort had settled within him that he didn't want to lose. She hugged him tighter, wrapping her arms around his spine. He couldn't remember the last time she did this. It was so rigid and fortified, building armor around him.

He returned the hug, letting himself melt into her. Roman, Hannah, his brother... all that death just faded from his mind.

All the pain and suffering became a fleeting thought that he was suddenly unsure why he cared so much about. Tears rolled down his face as he felt for the first time in his life perfect bliss. His tears turned to hard sobbing at the release it gave him.

Is this how normal people feel all the time? Is this what I could have had?

He buried his head into his fake mother's chest and continued to sob. Her grip got tighter, pulling him in close. At first, it was nice, but then the sequins of her dress pressed against his face, and their rough texture hurt him.

"This is too tight," he said.

She didn't stop. Her arms wrapped tighter, her grip readjusting and locking at her elbows.

"Stop!" he demanded.

His back crunched beneath the weight of her arms. They shifted from feeling like warm flesh to instead cold metal bars. His lungs were having trouble filling with air.

"Let me go!" He hit her in the chest.

Ow.

He had punched one of the wooden pillars.

What is happening to me?

"Help!" he yelped.

His reality was slipping. Looking into the mirror, he saw no woman standing beside him, yet he couldn't shake this suffocating feeling. He wiggled his body, trying to loosen himself free from this imaginary force, but it was no use. He let out short bursts of air, each time shifting his weight down, hoping he could free himself.

"Lonnie!" a distorted voice screamed.

Footsteps approached from behind, but he couldn't turn to see. A firm grip intertwined between his fingers, dragging him back. His body separated from his mother's, his vision going dark before coming back to find Jamie standing next to him.

"My... my mother," Lonnie blubbered.

"No one is here," Jamie said.

"No, she was—" He looked around, shocked to see that there was nobody else in the hall. His reflections in the mirrors went back to normal, each now following only the movements he performed.

"I don't understand." Lonnie couldn't hold back the tears waiting to burst from his eyes.

"It's the smoke." Jamie pointed to the thin fog beneath him. "It's causing hallucinations."

Lonnie shook his head, pulling up his shirt to reveal his bruises. "No, I didn't hallucinate this. That's impossible."

Jamie grabbed Lonnie's hand, holding up his fingertips. "Look." Beneath his nails were dry splotches of blood and splinters of wood.

I did this to myself?

"How do I know you're real?" Lonnie shuddered.

Jamie's hand slapped him across the face, knocking him off balance. "Get a grip, would you?" He scowled. "We need to find Carter. And Amara."

Lonnie grabbed his arm. "Wait, how are you not affected?"

The walls spun again, and Jamie pulled him in close just in time for the mirrors to lock, creating a new path around them.

"Who said I'm not?" Jamie looked at him, his pupils practically as big as his eyes. "I'd say my tolerance is just a lot stronger than yours."

"What?" Lonnie squinted his eyes.

"You know." He raised his thumb and pointer finger to his mouth, pretending like he was holding a joint.

"Oh, I see."

"But whatever is in this smoke is strong. So we need to hurry." Jamie took his hand again, leading him through varying twists and turns.

I don't feel real.

Lonnie caught glimpses of himself in the mirror, noticing his busted nose and scratched up cheeks. He parted his lips, but they didn't feel like his own.

I'm not real.

He tried not to let that thought bother him, but he couldn't let it go. Jamie pulled him, but he wasn't there anymore. The smoke in this area was higher, climbing almost to his waist. It was getting harder to remember why he wanted to leave.

Where was I trying to go?

"Jamie?" he whispered.

"Come on, don't stop moving," he responded. His grip was strong. It seemed unbreakable, like a tether between their souls.

When will he finally cut me loose to save himself?

Lonnie shook his head, plagued with images of Jamie drowning last year. He pretended they were playing out on the mirrors around him, each showing frame by frame like an old film. No audio came out, but he could picture the screaming that was leaking from his mouth as water sloshed inside, poisoning his body.

"Jamie," he whispered again.

"What?" Jamie slammed against a dead end, forcing him to slide past Lonnie and go down another path.

"You should leave me. I'm slowing you down."

Jamie hit another wall, slamming his hand against it. "I'm not going to leave you. Are you crazy?"

"But I'm the reason you're up here."

Jamie ignored him, feeling around the wall. "Yes—"

One of the mirrors somehow hadn't locked in place. He pushed it, watching it spin on the turntable and open to a new hallway. He grabbed Lonnie's hand again. "You are the reason I'm here. I could have been drinking downstairs and not risking my life."

"Exactly."

"But instead, you convinced me to be a good person and save someone's life. And maybe it was an incredibly *stupid* idea, but at least I can say I tried to do the right thing. So no, I won't leave you behind. Don't give them that satisfaction."

Lonnie sniffled and then laughed, wiping his eyes. "How did you get so wise all of a sudden?"

"Ah, shut up, you're just high." He smiled, letting out a light chuckle.

Lonnie joined him, laughing louder than expected.

They moved down the new hall, grateful the smoke hadn't built up as much inside.

"Get off me!" someone screamed from a few feet over.

"Let's go!" Jamie pried his arm again.

They maneuvered through the pathway and found Amara sitting keeled over against the wall.

"Amara, what's wrong?" Lonnie swept down next to her.

"He broke my hand," she cried out.

"Who did?" He spun in a circle, arms up, preparing to fight.

She pointed at the mirror in front of her, a pain lingering behind her glossy eyes. Her reflection was looking back, its finger pointing at her. Jamie and Lonnie went to grab her arms to help her up, but she swatted them away. The boys instead grabbed under her shoulders and lifted her to her feet.

"There is nobody here," Jamie explained. "The smoke is messing with your mind."

She shook her head, clearly lost in a trance. She slinked back behind them, still pointing at the mirror with terror in her voice. "No, he broke my hand!"

She displayed her arm, but nothing was wrong.

"Amara, your hand looks fine."

"No, it's burning. The whole thing is on fire, I can't... He crushed it."

Lonnie grabbed her shoulders, holding her close. "Who is he?"

She stared past them at the mirror again. Her face was contorted. "Roman."

"No, he couldn't have attacked you. Roman's dead."

"No, he isn't," she snapped. Tears fell from her face, and she pulled Lonnie in close, burying her head on his chest.

"It's okay," he whispered. "This place is messing with your head."

She gently held her *injured* hand, stroking it with her fingers.

"We need to think of a plan." Lonnie whispered to Jamie. "The visions are only going to get worse."

"First, we need to find Carter," he said. "I'm not leaving him behind." A tension in his voice caught Lonnie by surprise.

"Okay, we will. But we can't help anyone if we don't have a plan."

The rumbling started again, forcing them to squish together. The walls spun around them, pushing against their backs until eventually coming to a halt in a new pattern.

"This isn't a maze, it's a mobius strip," Amara said, pushing the boys away to get some space. "We can't find the exit if it keeps moving."

She rubbed her eyes, seeming more cognizant of her surroundings then she was a minute ago.

"Every time you get the pattern, it twists and reconnects, putting you right back where you started."

"So we have to stop looking at it like a maze," Jamie said. "What then?"

Clusters of smoke rose, hitting the ceiling and funneling toward one corner of the room. "Maybe like a giant vent." She pointed.

The smoke drifted across the mirrored ceiling, a slight suction pulling it toward the right. Amara led the charge, following it, keeping her hand out in front of her. When the walls creaked, she shifted back, tightening their ranks as the mirrors spun around them. They couldn't get lost if they all were together... at least that was the idea, anyway. The ceiling and smoke remained moving above them like a north star. They continued following it, changing their pathway with each rotation of mirrors.

"Carter!" they shouted.

His lack of response had Lonnie worried, but he tried not to think the worst. They all had to stay sharp and focused. Reflections played tricks on Lonnie's mind, every second growing worse.

"Lonnie," a voice prodded.

In his peripheral vision, he saw his brother. The side of his head was blown clean off, dripping brain matter down his face.

You aren't real.

"Lonnie," his brother slurred. "Look what you did to me!"

His body followed him mirror after mirror, haunting him.

When they rounded corners, there were two of him. So close, Lonnie swore he could smell him, like rotting flesh and gun smoke.

"Go away," he whispered.

He eventually did, but only to be replaced by worse memories. Ghosts haunted him like bad dreams, each yelling heinous things in his ears.

Mrs. Blythorne was pointing her gun and screaming that he'd killed her husband. Then his father appeared, saying that if Lonnie had died instead of his brother, they could have been a happy family. There was even Mike, his father's sweet friend, who had helped him escape through the ritual room. Now he was covered in blood, begging Lonnie to save him.

"Don't leave me behind!" he cried out. "Why did you leave me? You are a monster, just like your parents!"

The voices never stopped. Until finally, he heard the one he knew would hurt the most.

"Lonnie..." she teased. Her tangled, auburn hair reflected off the mirrors. "Help me," she whined.

Her voice was so faint, each word fighting its way out. Blood was spouting from the glass shard in her chest. She pried the broken piece of the bottle out and dropped it on the floor. He saw water flooding around his legs like the pond by the school he would often dream about.

Lonnie looked away, but he couldn't hold his tears. "You're not real!" he cried out.

"Why didn't you save me?" she pleaded.

"Stop, please."

The water turned red and pooled below him, wrapping around his calves.

"Lonnie!" Amara shook him. Her voice was so distant. "Lonnie!" she screamed again, this time closer.

His reality crumbled around him, the fake blood water seeping through the floor, revealing the dry wood beneath. He shook his head, finding Amara's hand gripping his arm and squeezing until he could feel his vessels wanting to burst.

"Hey!" she snapped, knocking him to his senses. The mirror reflections returned to normal, his ghosts disappearing with them.

"I'm back," he breathed. "Thank you."

"Carter, where are you?" Jamie yelled again into the void.

"Here!" The response came from down the hall.

"Carter!" he cheered. Jamie ran through the mirrors, and Amara and Lonnie followed. Carter was sitting on the floor, his face covered in scratch marks, as were his arms.

Jamie slunk down and hugged him. "I'm glad you're okay."

"Okay might be a stretch," Carter replied and winced. "I heard your voice." He looked at Jamie, who was evaluating his cuts. Amara came over next, touching the scratches on his face.

"What happened?" she asked.

"I've never seen more spiders before in my life." Carter shuddered. "All over me, crawling into my skin. Please tell me you found a way out?"

Amara explained, "We've been following the smoke, looking for a—"

"There's the vent." Jamie pointed up at a tiny metallic reflection tucked amidst the ceiling mirror tiles.

"Yes!" Lonnie cheered, moving under it.

"Amara, come here. We can boost you up." Jamie raised his arms. "Hurry, before the walls move again."

Frantically, she did as he said, and Jamie lifted her onto the other boys' shoulders.

"Hold still," Jamie barked at them. Lonnie and Carter tried to keep their balance, each equally spreading their feet.

"Almost got it." Amara wiggled her finger under the adhesive, prying off the mirrored tile. Giving it a hard pull, she ripped it clean and dropped it to the floor.

"Look out," she said.

All of them raised a free hand over their heads, but thankfully, it flew to the side, digging into the wood floor.

"Sorry," she apologized.

Just like Jamie had said, beneath the tile, the grate showed its face. Amara swatted the smoke out of the way to get a better view. "No," she whined.

They all wriggled below her, trying to see what she was looking at.

"What's wrong?" Carter asked.

They each snuck peeks, but were disappointed to find that the air vent was no bigger than a mail slot. They lowered Amara down, staring at their failed conquest.

"Damn it!" Jamie kicked the tile, skidding it across the floor.

"Jamie, stop that." Lonnie brushed by him. "Maybe we can use it for something." As he lowered down to pick it up, a faint chanting hummed from below. "Did you hear that?"

They looked at him with confused expressions. "Hear what?"

"Sounded like music."

"You're hallucinating," Jamie said.

"No, really!"

Covering his mouth and nose with his sleeve, he dunked his head below the lingering smoke, pressing his ear against the wooden board. Where the mirror tile had landed, the floor had chipped, forming a tiny hole. Unable to see through it, Lonnie pressed down his ear, hearing music coming from below.

No way.

He listened closer, hearing the faint sound of guests talking and feet tapping on the dance floor. "I think we are right above the ballroom," Lonnie shouted, rising back above the smoke.

"There is no way we are that close." Carter dunked under the smoke next, submerged for what must have been over a minute.

Just as Lonnie was about to grab him, he flung his head up, gasping for clean air. "You're right, I can hear them. Oh my gosh, they are so close, we could scream."

"No, don't scream," Amara rebutted. "They can't help us anyway."

"Then we are right back where we started," Jamie complained.

"Maybe not. If we are right above the dance floor, then that means we are in front of the second-floor staircase," Lonnie pointed out.

"But there is nothing in front of the double stairwell. It's a raised ceiling." Carter moved his hands in the air. "It's just the second-floor ballroom, and this room is over the dance floor."

"Wait, what ballroom?" Amara stopped him.

"The room with the chessboard. We saw the whole room; they had that structure standing on pillars in the center of this big ballroom."

"Not *the one* we used to play in?" Her eyes widened, staring directly at Carter.

He looked at her with a blank expression, then his eyes widened. "Oh, my gosh, it was that one, I didn't even realize."

"If that was the ballroom, then that means that the room next to it would be Mr. Blythorne's old parlor. Remember, with the jar of peppermints he kept on the coffee table?" She sounded excited, a smirk growing on her face.

She took the tile piece from Lonnie's hand and swatted away the smoke, revealing the wood. "It's the same floor!"

"So, you're in the parlor?" Jamie asked. "And I'm in the conservatory with the candlestick. Is there a point?"

"Yes, Jamie, there is. Because besides the peppermints and coffee table, that room had *two* doors. One connected to the ballroom and the other to the hall." She pointed across the room. "And if I remember correctly, the door to the hall should be right there. That"—she jabbed her finger—"is our exit."

Chapter 23

The Last Door on the Left

Amara led the charge, and the boys followed close behind.

First, reach the back wall, then walk across it to the corner of the room.

Lonnie felt confident about this plan Amara had suggested. It would be the easiest way not to get lost again in the maze. But the realization they might actually survive this trial had birthed a new thought into his head.

The next trial was a sacrifice.

Did her brother count? Perhaps that was enough to satisfy them.

He knew it probably wasn't. Nothing was ever that easy.

Lonnie continued moving without saying a word. He rested his hand on Jamie's shoulder and let himself be pulled along by their human chain. The smoke was rising higher, forcing them to breathe through their shirts. The dizziness was getting worse; all of them, even Jamie now, were teetering back and forth as they walked. Lonnie couldn't even imagine what they were hallucinating.

Which loved ones would the Sibils make her choose from to sacrifice?

His first thought was Carter. They'd known each other the longest. Ever since they were kids. They had history; there had to be some love there as well.

Did they need a second person? Did it have to be a choice?

Him or her. Lonnie thought to himself, picturing Mr. Blythorne's scratchy voice echoing from that speaker downstairs.

Amara looked back, briefly catching his eye.

It couldn't be me. We hardly know each other.

Right?

He found himself starting to care for her, but surely the feeling wasn't mutual. She was smarter than to become emotionally attached to anyone in a place like this. Lonnie looked at Carter.

No, I'm positive it will be him. The only question is has he realized it as well?

Was that why he was so nonchalant about helping her in the beginning? So agreeable to watch his longtime friend die? Lonnie was beginning to feel threatened. There was this bomb waiting to explode, and it was becoming increasingly obvious that someone here might not be leaving the Catskills tonight.

If I have a choice, it's Carter.

He grew nauseous at how quickly he had come to that decision. But if there was one thing he knew about a Rodbloom, it was that they put themselves first. Maybe it was time this Grambell did the same.

Would Jamie be on board?

He saw them whisper something to one another. A weird bond was growing between them.

Probably not.

"We are here," Amara said, as she reached the back wall.

"Are you sure?" Carter asked.

Much like the ceiling, in front of them was a wall of mirrors, all flat, covering every inch of the surface. She pushed on it, showing how much more solid it was than all the wood-pillared ones placed around the room. As the rest began to spin again, the back wall stayed perfectly still.

"Positive."

Lonnie refocused his attention, averting his gaze from the two boys.

Survive this trial first, then you can worry about the next.

The rotating mirrors came to a stop, and the closest three all were angled enough for them to squeeze past. Keeping her shoulder along the rightmost wall as they moved, Amara grabbed Carter's hand, and Jamie followed suit with Lonnie's, reconnecting the chain.

They advanced a few feet, keeping a straight path. When a mirror blocked them, they decided to wait until it rotated enough to let them through. Amara would pull them close, pushing Lonnie and Carter together. This displeased him, as he had now concluded, they were enemies. And he wanted to be as far away from him as possible.

Every time the mirrors would swivel, the quartet would advance. They repeated this four more times until they finally reached the corner of the room. The smoke had reached their chins, and each breath was starting to hurt. Oxygen was becoming scarce, though that didn't feel like the most pressing issue.

Lonnie didn't want to rattle them, but his vision was going black around the edges. The hallucinations were getting worse.

Jamie's hand felt like sandpaper and Jello all at the same time. Colors were losing meaning, melting off their backs, revealing black and white shades of gray.

I'm real.

He had to keep reminding himself.

"I'm real!" one of his reflections shouted.

"No, I'm real!" said another.

"Shut up," Lonnie whispered. He shook himself, letting the angst flow from his arms.

You sound crazy.

"Help me pull back this mirror," Amara coughed. "Quickly!"

All four of them sank their hands between the two connecting mirror panels.

"Pull," she said.

They each heaved, planting their feet.

Creak.

The glass moved, pulling from the adhesive backing like stretched gum.

Pop.

It detached, falling to the ground with a slam, yet it didn't break.

What do you know, it is durable.

He'd have to remember that if he ever lived long enough to need a greenhouse or a strong windowed manor... or hell, even a house of mirrors.

She batted the smoke away to reveal the door she had spoken of. It was so well hidden that it almost didn't seem real.

They all see it. You're not imagining it.

They stepped over the fallen mirror and opened the petite wooden door, spitting them out into a normal hallway. They shut it behind them just as another siren blared from inside, letting them know the trial was complete. Now in the hallway, they took in the fresh air by the gulp. The smoke leaked from below the frame, but only a little.

Lonnie already felt his brain beginning to defog. His vision was returning, as were colors. The first one he noticed was the yellow from the overhead lights. They were so warm and beautiful, they might as well have been the sun.

But it wasn't the sun.

There was an outdoor window in the hallway, revealing a beautiful full moon watching them from afar, beyond the tree-line. They were at the same height as some of the smaller trees, the tops so close, they could've jumped on them and shimmied down. Lonnie hated that this didn't sound like the worst idea.

Voices spawned from down the hall as shadows crept in from the corner of the wall.

"We need to hide." Lonnie darted to a nearby door, relieved when the handle gave.

He swung it open, gesturing them inside. Leaving it slightly ajar, he peered out. Footsteps approached, revealing the two burly men in black suits from earlier. One now had a bandage over his head where Carter had smashed a glass.

They stopped in front of the parlor door, momentarily kicking at the smoke leaking out of the bottom. Then they cocked their head, listening to their ear pieces.

"Copy," one of them responded.

They turned and faced Lonnie. His heart fluttered, but they didn't seem to notice him behind the doorframe. Instead, they took one final lap around the hallway and disappeared.

They are leaving?

Confused, yet relieved, Lonnie carefully shut the door.

"They're gone," he whispered.

The others released the tension from their shoulders.

"Did they see you?" Carter asked.

"I don't think so," Lonnie muttered. "I'm not sure. I couldn't tell."

"This is just great," Carter whined. "They are probably waiting for us to come out, save them the energy of busting the door down."

"Okay... well, I'm sorry, this was the best idea I could think of. Did you have a better one?" Lonnie moved farther from the door.

"A better plan for us not to die... yeah, not getting in this mess in the first place."

Just drop it.

Lonnie bit his tongue, resisting the urge to tell him off. He could feel the words gnawing at his gums, itching to escape. "Of course, you would say that!" he finally blurted.

Carter turned around, and even in the faint moonlight illuminating the room, Lonnie could tell he was scowling.

"What is that supposed to mean?" he asked defensively.

"You didn't even want to get involved. Because you realized that if she died before reaching the third trial, then you would be off the chopping block."

"Is that so selfish a thought to have... to not want to die?" He grew quiet. "And if you didn't notice, I helped out regardless, didn't I?"

"Well—"

"Here I am!" Carter shouted. "Risking my life, and you still don't trust me. No, you know what? I'm so sick of you!"

He paced the floor until he was in Lonnie's face, his silhouette shadowed by the moon. He winded up his arm, and Lonnie quickly realized that they were about to brawl.

"You just can't seem to let go of this vendetta you have for me because of something my family did. Do you think that's fair? *You* let my sister die while *I* was chained to a wall, and you have the gall to blame me. Jamie forgave me. Why can't you, huh?"

The adrenaline coursed through Lonnie's blood. It was getting harder to think straight. He wanted to say it was the drug fog talking, but he knew it was him. His hands clenched in rage, and he punched Carter in the face.

"You're right, I don't trust you. I think you're going to turn on us the first chance you get."

Jamie tried to push between them, but dodged a stray hand swung his way. "Stop!" he begged.

Lonnie swung again, this time missing his target. Carter grabbed him by both legs, trying to lift him into the air, but was kneed in the chest.

Carter grunted, letting go. He crawled backward, putting distance between them. "Is that really what you think?" he wheezed.

"I think you're selfish and rude, but most of all, I think the only people your family will ever look out for are themselves."

"Is that what my sister did when she plunged that piece of glass into her chest?" Carter spat.

Lonnie's heart sank; the fuel suddenly extinguished from his fire.

"You know, I saw your parents here year after year. Your mom was always laughing and drinking, and your dad would make bets just like all those psychos down there. Hell, he even helped create those creatures that we just killed.

"But I never blamed you for the things they did. Because we aren't defined by our family. I mean, none of them would be doing something this stupid, that's for sure. But also, they wouldn't do something this brave, either."

Lonnie put down his arms, the anger leaving his body. Instead, a wave of embarrassment and guilt took its place as he caught everyone staring at him like he was a monster.

Perhaps I have become one.

"You're right," he admitted. "We don't have to end up like our parents."

Click.

Amara found a light switch, illuminating the room in a yellow-gold hue. She crossed her arms. "Are you boys done fighting?"

Lonnie could see Carter clearer now under the light. He had a red bruise growing around his eye from the punch. Without answering, they both nodded to one another, informally agreeing to put their differences aside.

Lonnie added, "In all honesty, Carter isn't the only one in danger. I can't imagine any of our fates are looking good if they catch us now."

Jamie said, "Great... So what do we do then? Hide out in here all night?"

"No, they will be back. What we need is a plan to get out of this room undetected." Lonnie glared at the setting moon in the tiny window. "What even is this room?"

"I don't know, it's usually locked." Carter rolled his eyes.

They all swiveled around, taking note of its contents. White sheets covered all the furniture, making it rather grim and morose. Lonnie ripped the cover off where he was sitting, sending dust into the air. Coughing, he swatted it away, finding a raggedy mattress hidden underneath. The four corners had large wooden posts, and a big decaled headboard sat at the far end. The detailing was exceptional, with little carvings of birds.

The others took it upon themselves to remove more sheets, collecting them in a pile at the center of the room. An armoire sat across from the bed, its big arms detailed with similar little sparrows. The inside was covered in cobwebs, the hangers empty, dangling from the wooden rod, forgotten and aged. Only a few pieces of clothing remained. Amara pulled one out, blowing off the dust. It was an old, brown, collared button-up shirt with white stripes. Though as she held it up, it only went to about her lower chest.

It was a kid's shirt.

Jamie pulled a sheet, revealing an antique desk. Atop it rested a typewriter with a few missing keys and a yellowed sheet of paper still stuck in the dial. He pried open a few drawers, pulling out a pile of papers, semi-wrapped in string and packaging.

"Hey, look at this." He set them out on the table.

Amara and Lonnie went over, but Carter remained aloof, searching on the opposite side of the room. A clear tension was still lingering between the two boys, even though they agreed to play nice.

"What are these?" Amara asked.

Some of the words had smudged, forcing her to hold the paper closer to her face. But even far away, Lonnie recognized the lines.

I know these names.

"I've read this before," Lonnie said. "Or a version of it anyway. This is *The Princes of York*."

"Silas's children's books?" Amara asked.

"Silas's what?" Carter responded, his back still turned to them.

"Look." Jamie pointed at the bed. There was a tiny emblem etched into the tail of the frame.

S.S.

"This must've been his old room," Amara added.

"Yes, and this had to be his first draft. The words are different." Lonnie looked back at the first page, taking it from Amara and reading it aloud: "Chapter one, Porter and I were too late. The bus turned around the corner, leaving us huddled under the warmth of the streetlight. It was June 14th. How had it already been a year?"

"A year since what?" Jamie asked.

"Um... well, in the story, the two boys' mother gets very sick, and so they try to go out and get her medicine. But see, the father was a stubborn priest, and he believed that she would heal on her own if they just let her be. The main protagonist, August, argued with him, but he forbade them from going. That night, against his father's wishes, he decides to do it anyway, taking his little brother with him. They returned with the medicine and gave it to her. But by the morning, she had died. Fearing their father would blame them, they left and never looked back."

"That was all in a children's book?" Amara asked. "Rather grim, if you ask me."

"But that's why they were so good." Lonnie couldn't help smiling while he talked about it. "They were gritty, harsh, and real. Like... like when the younger brother gets taken by welfare services. The author didn't try to hide the ugly; he wanted to show it."

"The author being Silas Sibil," Carter said. "The man who

is currently hunting us for sport in his childhood home, whilst hosting a nice cocktail party downstairs. Not exactly a role model."

Lonnie wanted to say something cynical in response, but he couldn't deny Carter was right. "I just don't understand how you can write this"—he flipped through the pages—"and act like that."

Amara touched his shoulder. "Lonnie—"

"No, listen to this." Lonnie counted the sheets, looking for a specific paragraph. "Here... Yesterday was the hardest day so far. The snow continued all through the night, and I wrapped Porter tightly in our sleeping bag. He was getting so tall that his knees bent against my chest to stay covered. But I didn't care. He looked so peaceful. Just seeing him made me think maybe there was some good in this world after all. Even if it was just a speck. He will be so excited to wake up and find that it snowed. I can't wait to show him."

Carter rolled his eyes, continuing to rummage through drawers. "So, he's a good writer. Doesn't make him a good person."

"I suppose it doesn't." Lonnie drooped his head.

After everything Silas had done to him tonight, Lonnie hated that he still wanted to defend him. He knew he wasn't a good person, but to fully believe it would simply crush him. He couldn't comprehend that the person whose book's made his childhood bearable, was a part of the reason his youth was so horrible to begin with.

He sat down at the desk, reopening the top drawer. He pushed the papers deeper inside but felt a resistance blocking their path. He pulled them back out, sinking his hand further in to find a tiny black book. The edges of the cover were worn down, smoothed by touch. The black leather was sanded, and the papers were yellowed with age.

Interesting.

He opened it, flipping to the first page. It was outlines of faces and bodies. Lines teasing details but never finished. He flipped on, now seeing the completion of sketches. Heads were drawn over and over again in faint red ink. Rounded, smooth, hairy, oblong, so many different versions, each so detailed, with expressive eyes and edged jaws. They went on page after page. Some drawn into scenes, others floating by their lonesome.

These are amazing.

He flipped through them, some with ink written in the margins.

Μαμά

It was written above a woman's head with beautiful flowing hair, cherry cheeks, and a chin so tight it could be considered pointed. She held a wrapped cloth in her hands, within it was a tiny infant.

Next to the baby it read: ὠφέλεια

"Ophelia." Lonnie sounded it out, recognizing some of the letters. "Mama and Ophelia."

Lonnie took out his phone and snapped a picture before continuing onward. More drawings appeared with more Greek writing beside them. Each one was so detailed and perfect, until he reached the middle of the book.

"Oh, my," he gasped.

The face stared at him, mouth screaming, skin sagging down its wrinkled cheeks. The eyes were missing, pecked out and thrown away. The next page was the same. Another face, the same expression, but only slightly varied. They went on like this repeatedly, each one a replication of the last, but more twisted and harsh.

Lonnie stopped for a second, looking around the room. Amara was pulling off all the remaining sheets, while Jamie had cozied up next to Carter. They were whispering about something by the closet. Probably about him, Lonnie imagined.

He flipped the next page of the journal, only to find a menacing copy of the statue downstairs. It was revolting, the skin so detailed and stretched. The faces somehow were even more real in this drawing than seeing them finalized in stone. The five Gods screaming for their agony to stop. Lonnie took a picture on his phone, staring at it in awe.

Why would he want to draw this?

After that, he no longer drew faces. Greek writing took up most of the pages, apart from varying diaphragms and symbols of houses and villages. Lonnie couldn't help but be gutted.

Who could let a talent like that just fade away?

He stopped going through the remaining pages. As he let go, gravity cycled through the rest, flipping to the very end where it was completely blank aside from one little line. It was written in English, the ink a slightly newer shade than the rest:

This book belongs to Silas Sibil.

His letters swooped with hard squiggles on the tails. Lonnie stared at them curiously, tracing the letters with his finger. Holding the page open, he pulled out his phone, sifting through the pictures in his gallery. He pulled up a photo, setting it beside the book. His eyes fluttered back and forth.

"Hey, come look at this," he said.

The others hobbled over from various corners of the room.

"I found this notebook in the drawer. Look at the handwriting here." He pointed at it.

"What about it?" Carter asked.

Lonnie zoomed in on his phone, displaying the blue inked annotations from the ritual book downstairs. "It's the exact same."

"So, Mr. Sibil has written in the *divine* book. Not that crazy to believe." Jamie shrugged.

"I don't know, I just feel like I am missing something," Lonnie replied.

"A couple of screws, perhaps," Carter joked.

Jamie slapped him lightly on the shoulder. "Hey."

Lonnie put the book into his pocket and then grabbed his phone. Through the cracked screen, he read the time: ***4:15 am.***

"Jesus, it's already 4:15 in the morning." Lonnie turned to Amara. "You still got what, five hours left till your timer runs out?"

"More or less..." she responded.

"Think we could hide out that long?" Jamie asked.

"Maybe not in here," Carter pointed out the window at the treeline. "But surely out there."

Lonnie nodded in agreement. "Let's get the hell out of this house."

Chapter 24

The Watchtower

The hallway was clear as they crept out.

Could it be this easy?

Where were all the cloaked figures and the burly, black-suited men? They wouldn't let them just walk back down to the party and join the other guests. Or maybe they wanted them to. So many plans were playing through Lonnie's head that he didn't know which to follow and which was setting himself up for failure.

Maybe we should've just stayed in the room.

Too late to go back now.

Amara went first, leading them toward two big double doors at the end of the hall. Lonnie recognized them instantly from earlier in the night. They were the same ones that he had tried to enter through from the ballroom stairs during the party. This was where he'd been intercepted by Amara and Carter on the stairwell.

Weird.

His gut told him that it couldn't have been a coincidence. But at the same time, Amara wouldn't have known the trials were back here. She was just as caught off guard as the rest of them. He looked at her, then shook the weird thought from his head. Carter pressed his ear against the door, giving a small grin that let them know that the party was still alive and well.

These guests are crazy.

Carter and Amara each grabbed a door handle, pulling them back. A symphony of electronic music and clomping feet came rushing up the stairs. Lonnie pulled out his phone to check the time again: **4:21 am.**

"I can't believe they are still here."

"How can they be so oblivious to what's happening?" Jamie pondered.

"We should be thanking them," Lonnie reminded him. "They are the only cover we've got."

But even still, he stared at them in awe.

Where do they get the energy?

Their bodies swayed without a care, robotic almost. Each movement was choreographed, preplaced, and planned. The women at the bar were cheering their drinks, their heads jerking with quick motions. The old men were smoking cigars in the corner of the living room, as if they didn't know there was a cigar lounge just down the hall. The smoke surrounded the area, creating a barrier around them. Was everyone shot up with adrenaline? Perhaps it was just one of those things. When invited to a fancy gala in the New York countryside, you'd best stay until they threw you out.

They paced down the stairs. Lonnie swayed back and forth from rail to rail. No other guests were standing on it, which made them look so exposed. It especially didn't help that they were all covered in gashes and had bloody faces.

Thankfully, the dance floor below the stairs was packed.

There had to be at least a couple of hundred people left to hide amongst. They ran down the steps, making their way to the edge of the dance floor. But as they approached the outer ring of people, Lonnie spotted a tall brunette woman walking to them from the living room.

"I don't think that drug smoke wore off completely," Lonnie muttered to Jamie. "I'm still seeing things."

The woman came closer, moving swiftly around the guests in her way.

"No, I see her too," Jamie replied reluctantly.

"Sweetheart." His mother blocked their path, grabbing Lonnie by the wrists. "I need to talk to you."

"Mom, what are you still doing here?"

He swatted his hands free, pacing a few steps away from her.

"Yeah, now is not the best time, Monica," Jamie sassed. He pushed Lonnie forward, trying to get by her, but she got in Lonnie's face, her breath like rosemary.

"Dear, you can't save her," she blurted. "Just leave. Leave this place while you have the chance."

Lonnie spat, "Get away from me, I have nothing to say to you."

"I know. I'm so, so sorry. But I'm not leaving you this time. Not like before." She tried to wrangle his wrists again, but settled for gently resting her hands on his shoulders. "I have your room all made at the house. You can come back with me. My car is just out front."

He looked her up and down in absolute shock. "What are you talking about? I'm not going anywhere with you."

"Please give me another chance. Family has to stick together."

"You are not my family anymore. That was your choice. And I need to go."

He tried again to move by her. This time, he pushed her back into a drunk couple, knocking them to the floor. He wanted to help them up, but he had to move. Kindness was not for those in a time crunch. "Sorry," he called.

Lonnie found himself between Carter and Jamie in a single-file line. Carter's hand was outstretched behind him, waiting for him to grab it. "Take my hand, so we don't get separated."

He looked at it suspiciously, then remembered what Carter had said upstairs.

"We aren't defined by our families."
Let's hope you are telling the truth.

Lonnie grabbed his hand, the grip tightening around his fingers, pulling him forward through the dance floor. The crowd shifted back and forth, making Lonnie dizzy. He supposed this was the equivalent of a mosh pit for rich people in high fashion. They breached the end of the dance floor, the smell of body odor lingering on their clothes.

"That was wonderful," Lonnie noted sarcastically.

There was so much sweat in his hair, he thought if he dipped his head, he might fill a bucket. The foyer and front door were close now. They could see it just through the arches at the end of the ballroom.

"Walk swiftly," Amara pressed.

Lonnie kept himself from sprinting. He supposed that it would look rather suspicious to see four disheveled kids running through their gala. But in all honesty, nothing about this was normal. These people, especially.

Picking their feet up, one after another, they made quick time to the archway, getting there just in time for the lights to drop. Spotlights cut through the darkness, one illuminating the stage and the other planted right on top of their heads. Blurred shapes in the distance blocked the entryway door. Lonnie cursed under his breath. They had done exactly what their hosts planned.

We're screwed.

"Guests!" a joyful voice announced over the speakers.

Lonnie turned back to the stage, this time seeing Mr. Sibil standing there with a microphone in his hand. His siblings stood around him, forming a perimeter.

"You have all been just wonderful tonight. Truly an inspiration. But I have a request for you now. We have a few guests we would like to honor tonight." He pressed his hands together. "Will you please help me welcome these four young adults up to the stage?"

The crowd all followed the spotlight, clapping synchronously as their stares fell on the boys and Amara. A light hand touched Lonnie from the side, pushing him forward.

"Don't be shy, dear," an older woman urged.

The guests gathered around them, making a tunnel for them to pass through. Their heads tilted as they passed, their smiles piercing, and that obnoxious clapping smacking into their eardrums.

Silas Sibil held out a hand for them to grab and pull themselves up onto the stage. Lonnie ignored the outstretched hand and walked up on his own, but Silas never dropped it, leaving it hanging in the air. Once they had all arranged themselves at the front of the stage, the family stepped forward, intermixing between the four. Each sibling grabbed a person, straddling their arm around theirs as a chaperone would.

More like a captor.

Sibil held his arm around Lonnie, pressing him gently to remind him that he was trapped and was not getting away again. Lonnie gulped, trying to put a fake smile on for the audience. The light was blinding, so much so that the bodies didn't seem to have faces, just white glows for eyes and random noises emitting from where their mouths should be.

"Look at you four! You must have gotten into some trouble tonight with all those cuts and bruises. Did you get into a fight with a cactus?" Mr. Sibil chuckled.

The crowd laughed.

"Jokes aside, it's so important to honor the next generation, don't you think?"

The crowd roared in response.

"These are the people we leave the world to. And why we do what we do, right? So, let's give them thanks... and hope they do their best to return the favor."

The crowd cheered again, whooping and hollering. Silas shared a look with Florence, escorting Amara off the stage. Sebastian and Jamie followed, then Daphne and Carter, and finally Lonnie and Silas. Once they had passed outside the range of guests, their smiles dropped. No more words were shared for the duration of the walk. Florence turned down the hallway by the kitchen, taking off a small key necklace from around her neck. She used it swiftly, unlocking and prying open the entry. Behind it was yet another elevator. This one was tiny and made of glass, no bigger than a closet. Florence ushered them inside, the space quickly getting tighter. As Silas and Lonnie were about to step in, Lonnie felt a hand reach out and block his step.

"We will take the next one," Silas said sternly.

"Silas," Daphne warned, giving Lonnie a nasty look.

"I will see you in a minute."

The two stepped back into the hall, letting the elevator door close without them.

Woosh.

The gears churned, lifting it and whisking the others away.

"Why are they going up?" Lonnie asked.

"You will see, I don't want to ruin the surprise." He smiled.

The elevator took forever. The sound of pulleys continued spinning behind the door, but it just never seemed to arrive. Mr. Sibil was waiting patiently, occasionally peering at his watch.

What is waiting upstairs?

Lonnie glared at him. He was much different than his siblings. Not as bubbly as Florence, or as standoffish as Daphne. Certainly not as shy and matter-of-fact like Sebastian. He was so hard to read, like he could change his personality on a whim.

Lonnie reached into his back pocket, pulling out the small leather-bound book.

"This is yours, right?" He shattered the silence.

Mr. Sibil glanced down, his head jerking back at the sight of it. Without waiting a beat, he snatched it from Lonnie's hands. "My goodness, I haven't seen this in ages. Where did you find it?"

"In your old bedroom," Lonnie replied with more lively tone than he intended.

"My bedroom? I haven't had a room here in ages." He flipped through the book, letting memories waft from the pages like old dust. "Thank you for this, truly."

"You were very good... at drawing," Lonnie stuttered.

Mr. Sibil stopped reminiscing, shutting the book. "Yes, my father used to say that." He slid the book into the lining of his wool jacket, then faced the elevator door. "If you want to run, I won't stop you."

His words were so flat, Lonnie thought he had misheard him. "Sorry?"

"You heard me."

"No." Lonnie fumbled his words. "I won't leave my friends."

"I assumed." Mr Sibil turned to face him. "Because you're brave—"

"I'm not brave," Lonnie interjected.

"No? You poisoned that boy to save your friend's sister. You risked your life to help a girl you met a few hours ago. You've been trying so hard to tear this place apart since the second you walked in here. Sneaking around the ritual room, trying to convince Henrik to start a fight, even doing all that research at your school library."

Lonnie's jaw dropped at this new information presented before him. The House has had their eyes on him all evening. Hell, all school year. He felt like an absolute fool to think they had any real shot at succeeding tonight.

"Would you not call all of that brave?" Mr. Sibil asked politely.

"I'd call it reckless," he stated confidently. "What about sacrificing people, experimenting on them, and betting on them. Would you call that brave?"

The elevator arrived. Mr. Sibil stepped inside, holding it open for Lonnie to follow. He did, watching the door close behind him, as his last chance of escape slipped away. The door locked, and the machine lifted them off the sweet and stable ground. Mr. Sibil looked forward again, avoiding his eyes. From his mouth, Lonnie heard the lightest breeze. The words came out like a whisper.

"No. I'd call it reckless."

They lived in silence for the next minute or so. Lonnie worked his way through his past year, wondering what else Mr. Sibil knew about him. Had they known they were going to help Amara tonight? Was that their plan all along? A weird loophole way to make sure she solved her trials while still complying with the rules? Or maybe they needed her to really care about the boys, so her sacrificing one meant that much more.

Lonnie glared at the man beside him with a new level of fear and respect.

What was going on in his head?

The elevator moved so slow that he'd reckon even the dumbwaiter would be a faster method if it hadn't shattered into pieces. Glimpses of floors passed by; a hallway, a screening room, a study. Each one he counted in his head.

Second floor. Third floor. Fourth floor. Fifth.

How high were they going?

Creak.

The elevator came to a stop at what must have been the top floor.

"After you." Mr. Sibil gestured, holding the glass open.

He was so good at acting genuine, a skill Lonnie didn't imagine that his siblings shared. For a moment, he almost felt a sense of chivalry until he realized he was actually just a prisoner being watched for trying to escape.

Lonnie passed through the frame, the ground once again feeling solid under his feet—or at least, somewhat solid. He walked on brittle wood, its beams bending and quaking under his footsteps.

Death by rotted wood. I don't recall seeing that on the wager board.

The room was cylindrical. The walls were a mix of black brick and glass. A large chandelier hung from the framed ceiling that roped up into the rafters. Empty space filled in between the various beams as the ceiling climbed to the top of a rooftop spire. Very castle-esque, very haunting. Who could picture a better spot to die?

On the far side of the room was a large window overlooking the entire forest. Moonlight mixed with an inkling of sunshine that peeked out from behind the mountain tops.

Lonnie glanced at his phone from his pocket.

5:03.

The time was less assuring than he hoped.

They will want to wrap this up before the sun rises.

He imagined everyone was begging for this night to finally end, though the members' idea of how and Lonnie's surely differed. Lonnie couldn't look away from the window. There was a beauty to it—the glass formed a semi-circle to the ground with lines of metal cut through it, bracing it in place. At the bottom, two glass doors were cut into the frame, propping out to a modest balcony that hung over the side of the house.

The stars were still visible, no longer submerged by the smog of the city; they could breathe, they were free. Lonnie wished to be one of them right now. Instead, he was trapped in some tower.

An observatory?

Seriously.

Surely, they had gotten off on the wrong floor. However, the pieces of the puzzle were slowly coming together. Where the center of the floor should have been was pulled away, revealing a six-story drop that ended on the cobblestone court-yard below. A weak wooden railing surrounded the overlook, with three sections cut out and replaced by tiny chains. For a moment, Lonnie thought the walls around the room were covered with moss, but as they shifted, he realized that they were people in forest green cloaks. Men and women moved around the perimeter, their faces hidden behind slit masks and forest green cowls.

Cowards.

They were afraid to show their faces. Lonnie could sense it. It was in the way they stood, their eagerness to stand farthest away from him. They were disgusted with themselves.

Jamie, Carter, and Amara were on their knees on the right of the overlook. Their hands were shackled behind their backs and locked to a chain on the floor. Silas gestured to a cloaked figure, who shackled and escorted Lonnie over to them. The metal cuffs were cold against his wrists.

The other Sibils stood back by the large glass window, resting on tiny metal chairs and talking among themselves. Carter whispered something in Jamie's ear that made his frazzled eyes seem a little less rattled, though he said nothing in return. Meanwhile, Amara was quietly sitting beside them, her gaze stuck on the moon, watching it coast along the skyline. Her lips moved, but no words came out.

"What are you doing?" he whispered to her.

"Praying," she mumbled.

The cloaked figure finished locking Lonnie's shackle to the floor. But as he walked back to the perimeter of the room, he slipped something discreetly into his palm.

Is that what I think it is?

Fiddling with his fingers, he felt a tiny key in his hands. It took everything Lonnie had not to show any surprise on his face.

Why did they give me this? Was it another test or had one of these members actually grown a spine?

Whatever the reason, he didn't care. He was just grateful someone was giving him a chance.

Lonnie shifted his hip, getting his hands in position. Taking the cut edge, he jabbed at the keyhole, until eventually he heard a light click. He bit his lip as he twisted the key. Not too much, though. Just enough to unlock it, but not to have it fall from his wrists.

Lonnie leaned over, nudging Amara on the shoulder. She did not pay attention, her gaze still following the moon. He did it again, this time swinging his arms around and shoving the key into her hand.

Her eyes widened as the warmed key made contact with her cold hands. She quickly snuffed the emotion, returning her gaze to the window. Meanwhile, Lonnie spotted her hands moving carefully behind her back.

Creak.

Sebastian moved from his chair, scuffing it back on the wood. He coughed, pulling out the book from his satchel and proceeding to display it on a podium. Flipping a few pages in, his finger ran over the words, translating them as fast as he read them.

"The third trial, the sacrifice of soul. An offering that grants us passage from our physical world to yours. We use this soul as our passage and our bond. With this opening, may you grant us your wisdom and gifts upon our lives."

He shut the book, darting his eyes to Amara. She straightened, scooting away from Carter beside her.

Did she give the key to him?

Another cloaked figure moved forward from the perimeter, bending down and unlocking her already half-opened shackles. They thankfully didn't seem to notice as they tossed them onto the floor. Raising her, they approached the siblings who were still sitting in their chairs.

"My dear, it's now your time to choose." Florence stood up and cupped Amara's face.

Cold air seeped in through the glass doors, giving the room a chill that nipped at the flesh hidden beneath holes in Lonnie's clothes. He didn't feel cold, though. His heart was beating fast, bringing a warm glow to his chest.

"She's sacrificed enough!" Lonnie blurted.

"Excuse me?" Ms. Sibil stood, her face contorted.

"She already lost her brother tonight, isn't that enough?"

Ms. Sibil tsked, now relaxing her hands on Amara's shoulders. "It is a tragedy, yes, but that wasn't her sacrifice to make. She must make one for herself."

Amara suddenly broke down, drowning in tears. "You don't have to do this." She got in their faces, refusing to let them ignore her. "You can put your fate in your own hands. You can do something good."

"We do plenty of good," Daphne said. She had just lit a cigarette and was now pointing it with aggravation at the girl. "I am so sick of you entitled children. You all live by this idea that everything is black and white. That isn't how the world works, sweetheart. The gray is where things get done. The gray is sacrificing one person if you know it will help thousands. Get them up, and let's get this over with. I want to go to bed."

Three cloaked figures untethered the boys from the floor, directing them to the overlook. Lonnie held his arms still, hoping the shackles wouldn't fall off in the movement. The cloaked members separated each of them, placing one in front of each of the chain ropes. Lonnie was now face-to-face with the edge, his back to the glass window. The moonlight shrouded him in an ancient glow.

Don't look.

Though his eyes were still drawn to the opening below him. Standing at the precipice, the ground looked much further away. Plants hugged the edges of the courtyard, their blooming flowers urging him to jump. In the center, a small fountain dripped with water, giving the illusion that maybe something would break his fall. Dozens of feet lay between him and freedom. What a cruel tease.

"Spin them around," Daphne directed.

Hands latched onto his shoulders, rotating him from the drop. The back of his knees now pressed onto the chain. His heels dangling over the edge, exposed to the air.

Three seconds. That's how long it would take to hit the ground.

Trees filled his view through the glass window. There were so many of them, it was almost hard to believe. In the distance, two orbs of light passed through the forest, reflecting off branches before disappearing beyond the mountainside. He watched in awe until the realization dawned that it was a car.

The guests are leaving.

It's all coming to an end.

Lonnie tried to find an ounce of peace, but his body couldn't stop shaking. He thought of his mother's car. Why didn't he just get in the stupid car? He could have been at her house, in his childhood bed, like he wanted for so many years.

Why did I stay?

He knew why.

That wasn't my home.

He peeked over his shoulder. Jamie stood just on the other corner of the overlook, his silhouette shining under the chandelier.

He was my home.

Lonnie turned, revealing Carter planted on the other corner of the railing. Amara stood behind him, barely visible in the shadows.

And they were my friends.

Well, mainly Amara, but Carter was starting to grow on him. If they survived the night, maybe he would have the chance to see what made Jamie grow so attached to him.

A cloaked figure pulled Amara toward the overlook. Her face was stained with tears. They walked around the perimeter of the railing, passing each one of the boys, like some perverse grade school game. The guard took her by the shackled hands, holding them out toward the edge. One step forward, that would be all it took to push one of them over the rail.

She and the guard walked around and around, to the point that Lonnie nearly peed himself from nerves. Each time she neared, he leaned back, avoiding the length of her arm. She had begun crying again.

"I won't do this!" she stated, wrestling the guard and trying to move away. He held her in place, pulling her to the edge of the railing.

Florence said, "Just get on with it!"

"I can't!"

"My goodness!" She shuffled over to them.

Florence pushed the guard out of the way, forcing them back into the perimeter line-up. Then, grabbing Amara by her forearms, she dragged her in front of Carter, making him start to squirm.

"Him?" she asked, pushing her slightly forward so her hands touched his chest.

"No..." she cried, barely getting the word out. Her voice sounded so small, and it cracked under the pressure.

"Fine." Ms. Sibil dragged her around the corner.

"Ow!" Amara cried, stumbling from the quick strides.

"Him?" Ms. Sibil held her in front of Jamie. Her hands pushed lightly on his chest, forcing him to lean over the pit. Amara clutched his shirt with her fingers, trying to hold him up.

"Answer me!" Ms. Sibil yelled into her ear.

"No!" she cried out.

"Such dramatics." Ms. Sibil pulled her away.

Jamie began crying, trying desperately to cover it under coughs, but he couldn't.

"Stop, please," Amara begged, trying to resist.

"Florence," Silas announced. "That is enough."

"No, I have had enough!" she hissed. "You have become so soft. Making easy challenges that you know would never satisfy the Gods, so I had to redesign them for you. Now you have the gall to tell me what to do. No! I know what I am doing."

Florence dragged Amara by the wrist, pulling her around until she faced Lonnie. Her hands were directed onto his chest. They were like electric paddles, and all it would take was a single jolt to kill him.

"So him, dear!" Florence scoffed. "You're choosing him then?"

Amara shook her head, too exasperated to speak. Tears streamed down her cheeks, leaking into her mouth.

"*Pleuse, stapp!*" she sobbed out incoherently.

Ms. Sibil moved closer, her breath now touching Lonnie's face. It made him furious. As he watched her torment Amara, the tears still dripping from her eyes, he realized he didn't think he had ever hated a person more.

And for the first time in his life, he could finally do something about it.

Three seconds. That's all it would take to hit the ground.

In an instant, he let the shackles fall from his hands, slipping over the edge.

One.

Two.

Three.

They clanged against the ground below, alerting Florence to what was happening, but it was too late. Lonnie nodded at Amara, pulling his arms forward and shoving her back. He then grabbed Ms. Sibil's bony frame and tossed her over the chain.

She screamed as her silver-gold hair flung into the air. The edge of the railing shattered beneath her weight, ripping the world out from under her. Her voice grew so small as it disappeared below. But then came that definitive sound.

One second.

Two seconds.

Three seconds.

Thud.

Chapter 25

My Sister's Keeper

I can't believe I just did that.

A hand grabbed Lonnie's shirt, dragging him back from the ledge. It was Amara, her brow raised in shock at what had just happened. She pulled him into a hug, her arms still shaking as they wrapped around his back.

Never let go.

Her tight grip was the only thing keeping him from falling apart. Lonnie peered over the edge of the outlook, spotting Florence Sibil's body contorted on the corner of the fountain. Pieces of stone had broken under her weight and scattered over the cobblestone, and the water had turned a shade of red as blood dripped from her body.

I'm a murderer. For real, this time.

He waited for guilt to bubble in his chest, but it never came. If anything, he was content with his actions. She had it coming; they all did. And he was just glad it was him who made the first move.

The room erupted into noise, as everyone flew into a panic.

"No!" Daphne screamed, clutching her heart.

Sebastian looked at the cloaked figures. "Grab them now!"

The dressed-up society members started closing in, and Lonnie came to his senses. "We need to get out of here!"

Jamie and Carter threw their shackles off, which made Daphne stare in disbelief. "How did they get free?" she yelled at her brothers.

Lonnie wondered the same. Where was that cloaked person who had given him the key? There was no time to thank them.

Lonnie and Amara met up with Jamie and Carter, finding themselves trapped on all sides by the fast-approaching cloaked bodies.

"There is nowhere to go!" Jamie noted.

People were everywhere, locking arms and closing in around them. Daphne stood from her chair, wiping at the corner of her cheek. She chewed on the edge of her cigarette in her mouth, pulling a tiny pistol from her purse.

"Forget the rules, I want them all dead!" she declared. She aimed her gun at Lonnie's chest. He shifted his weight to dodge it, but there was no time.

A gunshot went off. Lonnie patted his body, looking for the hole, though the noise ricocheted above him, embedding itself in the rafters.

I'm okay?

"No!" Silas's voice echoed under the shot. Confused, Lonnie looked to see that Mr. Sibil had knocked his elbow under the gun. His sister's arm was raised, pointing the barrel toward the roof.

"You're betraying us *again*!" She glared at him with venomous eyes.

Again? What is she talking about? What is happening?

"Go now," Mr. Sibil commanded them. "There's an exit on the balcony!"

He's helping us?

Lonnie wasted no time. Grabbing his friends, he made a break for the window. But the cloaked figures were blocking the way. They slid to a stop, trying to find an opening, but there was none.

"What do we do?" Carter asked.

Just then, they saw a handful of people trip and fall to the ground in front of them. The chain of bodies broke, making an open path to the window.

"How?" Lonnie questioned. But then he saw that one of the cloaked people had shoved the others down from behind. It was the one who had given him the key, he knew it had to be.

But why?

The cloaked figure suddenly grabbed their cowl, ripping it from their head to reveal bleached blonde hair underneath. Lonnie imagined that the smoke drug must still be in his system, because he couldn't believe what he was seeing.

It can't be.

"Roman?" He stared in surprise, as did everyone else in the room.

"What is that boy still doing alive?" Sebastian yelled in fear, pointing at him. "Kill him now!"

He's alive. This whole time, he was alive.

A thousand thoughts were racing through Lonnie's head, but there was no time to think. Roman ran to the window, propping open the glass door at the base. "Come on!" he demanded, gesturing for them to follow.

Lonnie looked back at the siblings to see Sebastian now

fighting with Silas, giving Daphne enough space to aim the gun again at his head.

"Stupid kids!" she snapped.

Silas screamed in frustration. He shoved his arms forward, knocking Sebastian to the floor. He then tackled Daphne, causing the lit cigarette from her mouth to fall out and onto the old floorboards. A small flame grew, eating away at the decaying wood.

Bang.

The gun went off again, this time shooting through the wood to somewhere down below.

"Take the book!" Silas hollered.

Lonnie looked for it, spotting it on the podium. He tucked it under his arm and ran out onto the balcony.

Daphne bellowed, "Enough of this!"

She elbowed Silas, knocking him off her. Then she raised the gun again, shooting multiple shots without aiming. The bullets all collided with the observatory window. At first, it cracked slowly, the lines spreading out like a spiderweb. But then, eventually, the whole thing came down in a loud explosion. Lonnie and his friends cowered on the balcony as the glass fell down from above. The people inside took cover as shards of glass rained down. Lonnie tried to block himself and his friends with the grimoire, doing his best to shield their faces.

Silas pulled himself up from the floor, positioning himself between Daphne's outstretched gun and the balcony behind him.

"Stop this, please," Silas begged.

Daphne frowned, an angry furrow forming in her brow. "You traitor."

Lonnie couldn't believe his eyes. After playing mind games

all night, this was the moment that Silas Sibil decided to grow a heart.

Why now? What changed?

Lonnie's brain ran in circles, trying to rationalize what he was seeing. It was then he remembered their conversation at the elevator. Seeing him now, shielding them from a loaded gun, two words came to mind.

Brave and reckless.

Did our conversation inspire him that much?

Before Lonnie could finish his thought, he heard a bang. Daphne fired the gun. The bullet tore into Silas's chest. He let out a loud groan and dropped to the floor.

"No!" Lonnie's hand flew to his mouth in shock.

"I am done messing around!" Daphne screamed, helping Sebastian up. "Bring me those kids now."

He's dead. Just like that. She just killed her brother like it was nothing...

All night Silas had acted like an indestructible force and now he was dead. Lonnie felt sick, he recoiled in shock. He looked to the others to see if they had just seen what he had, but they were more distracted by the herd of cloaked people running toward them. He leaned over the balcony edge, seeing the six-story drop and lack of a fire escape.

And now she's going to get the rest of us. What a horrible escape plan.

"Why did he say the balcony?" Lonnie stammered.

And why did he sacrifice himself for me? That was so stupid of him.

"There!" Amara pointed.

On the side of the balcony, vines and roses dangled over a bolted down lattice that descended all the way to the front yard below. The wooden crisscrossed structure hugged the facade of the building forming a makeshift ladder.

"Are you crazy!" Carter asked.

"Do you have a better idea?"

"No time for better ideas," Roman argued, climbing over the railing and beginning his descent down the wall.

Is he real?

Lonnie pinched himself to make sure he wasn't still in that house of mirrors. So many ridiculous thoughts were swirling through his head now.

Roman survived, Mr. Sibil was dead, and now we are about to climb down the side of a tower!

Putting it all together, it sounded absolutely mad, but then again, what part of this night wasn't? Lonnie waited, letting Amara, Jamie, and Carter go first. Seeing them all hanging on the trellis, he then jumped over last, tucking the book in his armpit. The wood frame felt so weak under his hands, like it would crumble with just a slight breeze.

"I don't think this is going to hold!" Lonnie warned.

He tried not to look at the ground below but was forced to watch his feet. One misstep and he would go down, and if he did, the others were getting knocked off with him.

I can't think like that.

He continued moving, ignoring the exhaustion in his arms. He looked up, noticing the cloaked figures standing above him on the ledge.

Would they follow us?

They seemed to be debating the same thought.

"Move!" Daphne's voice boomed.

"Go faster!" Lonnie begged his friends.

The ground was still dozens of yards away; it would take too long to get there. And with Daphne and her gun, they were practically sitting targets. Looking around, Lonnie noticed a window perch on the story directly below.

"Roman, go through that window now!" he shouted in the wind.

Roman tried the window latch, but it was locked.

"It's locked!" Amara yelled up. "There is another one a floor down—"

"There is no time." Lonnie moved his feet faster. "Break it!"

Below him, Lonnie heard glass crack, which gave him a quick whiff of relief. He saw them each pass through one at a time: Roman, then Amara, then Jamie, and finally Carter, until only Lonnie was left hanging from the trellis. The wind picked up, forcing him to move tighter against the wood so he would not fly off. He gripped the crisscrossed gaps, praying the whole thing would not collapse under his weight.

"Lonnie, come on!" Amara reached out her arm from the windowsill.

"Here take this!" he tossed the grimoire down to her.

He regained his control, propping both hands freely on the fence. From everyone's jostled movements, the bolts had become loose, sliding the lattice from the wall. This, combined with the rose thorns hidden in the vines, was making it hard to get a solid grip.

"Let me through, idiots!" Daphne shouted, her voice now directly above him.

He refused to look up, knowing that he would be staring at the muzzle of the gun. Lonnie neared the window, the fencing finally ripping from the wall.

"Lonnie!" Amara shouted.

He let go of the lattice as it broke, diving toward the

window. His hands landed on its tiny protruding ledge. "Help!" he called, his fingers slipping.

Amara and Jamie reached out, grabbed him by the wrists, and pulled him up through the opening. He yelped as a bullet whizzed by, piercing the sill between his feet. He fell over the edge, crawling as far from it as he could until he felt safe enough to rest on the floor.

I'm okay…I'm alive.

Lonnie scooted back until he was leaning against an empty bookcase. Around him, he noted pieces of furniture covered in white sheets and empty shelves lining all the walls.

Great another creepy abandoned room.

He held his chest, trying to steady his heartbeat from the insane acrobatics he had just performed outside. The bullet was so close, only a second sooner and it would have struck him right in the spine. He tried not to imagine it, but even now, he swore he could smell the gun smoke in the room.

Wait a minute.

He sniffed the air, now catching a stronger whiff. He stood up urgently, spinning in a circle and looking for the source. Just then, footsteps scattered in the observatory above, creaking and dropping bits of drywall down onto their heads.

"Do you guys smell something burning?" Lonnie muttered.

Had someone started a fire?

"Up there!" Amara pointed at the ceiling. A tiny flame was quickly growing, eating its way down the wall.

Lonnie suddenly remembered Daphne's cigarette rolling on the old wood floor. He had seen the little flame, but he had expected someone to have put it out.

Clearly not.

"We can't stay here," Roman said, starting to walk away.

Lonnie glared at this man who still felt like an illusion. Roman threw off the rest of his garb, revealing his bloody tank top and dress pants underneath. On his feet, he had some shoes that were clearly the wrong size. He must have swiped a pair from a guest at some point in the evening.

"Woah. Woah!" Jamie pumped his hand. "Are we not going to talk about how you are here right now? We watched you blow up."

"There was an exit in the back of the fireplace."

"*Okay...* How would you even know that was there?"

His lips parted as though he might speak, but he bit his tongue. He held a tight expression, staring cluelessly at Lonnie.

No wait, he isn't looking at me.

Lonnie followed his eyes over his shoulder. He spun around and found Amara standing right behind him.

"What did you do?" Lonnie accused her.

A loud creaking came from the ceiling, letting in a gust of smoke.

"The roof's coming down!" Carter yelled, opening the door. "Move!"

They all darted out as part of the ceiling came crashing down behind them. Fire caught, burning the white sheets, turning them into a stinky shade of blackish brown. It was like sitting in the center of a campfire, watching the marshmallows glob together against the wood.

"Follow me, I know an exit," Roman directed.

He moved to the picture frame at the end of the hall, which depicted a large painted portrait of a man that Lonnie recognized from the family bedroom. It was Mr. Sibil senior. He was poised rather triumphantly in some study with a deer head mounted behind him like a trophy.

Lonnie gave it a dirty look. He knew it was ill to speak poorly of the dead, but every fact he learned about this man made him hate him a little more. Roman grabbed the painting and swung it open, revealing a spiral staircase made of concrete and brick.

This is ridiculous.

"How did you know that was there?" Lonnie jumped in front of him, blocking the exit. "No! None of this is making any sense."

"Lonnie, move out of the way," Amara protested.

"I don't care that the place is coming down. I'm not going anywhere until I get some answers from both of you."

The smoke snuck under the door frame, leaking into the hallway. They all started to cough. But he held his ground, keeping them from exiting.

Amara and Roman exchanged a glance before she turned back to him. "I had a plan, okay?" Amara admitted. "Mr. Sibil and I have... we had a plan."

"Mr. Sibil?" Carter asked.

"Silas," she clarified. "He approached me a couple of months ago at uni."

"What was your plan?"

More smoke spewed in, making them cough harder. Amara tried to fan it away with the book, but was unsuccessful.

"I swear I will tell you the whole story, but we can't stay here. Please."

Lonnie sat with the thought, but as the feeling of smoke built in his lungs, he finally caved, letting them all pass. "Fine."

Amara climbed over the ledge in the wall, beginning her descent down the cobblestone stairs. She turned back to them, a confident look on her face. "Tonight will be the last night we ever have to deal with this rubbish tradition. I promise."

I hope you're right.

He entered through the secret passage, following her down the stairs, the other boys a few feet behind. She took out her phone, shining a faint light on the steps.

"You aren't making any sense. Why would Silas reach out to you?" Lonnie pressed.

Her footsteps were so swift, clacking like tap shoes down the stairwell.

"And why would he want to end his family's lifelong tradition?" Lonnie added.

She continued walking, talking over her shoulder. "Because you inspired him too."

"Me?"

"Silas told me he has hated these trials since they first started. He never believed in them, always thought they were fake and a trick. So much so that he ran away when he was a kid and never came back. All this time, he has wanted to put a stop to them, but never knew how. Until you."

"What did I do?"

"You killed his sister, and for the first time since his dad started this tradition, no one was in charge. He saw a way in and begged his siblings to let him come home and help them continue the ritual."

Jamie added, "Why didn't he just take out his siblings, then no one would be left to run the place?"

She stopped abruptly on the stairs and looked at them all. "If you cut a weed, it will simply grow back. If you really want it gone, you have to rip it up by the root. Or in this case—"

"Destroy it from the inside." Lonnie muttered.

We have both been trying to destroy this place the whole night, and I had no idea.

He cocked his head. "So, what was his plan?"

Her phone beeped. Pulling it close, she pressed a button to illuminate the screen.

5:30.

"8 hours!" she cheered to Roman.

Roman groaned. "Finally."

"I'm sorry." Lonnie pointed out. "Eight hours since what?"

"Since his ritual started. It's just like the trial rules state. Rule number four. A house ritual must be completed in a third of a day. Eight hours."

She's right.

Lonnie pictured the parchment with the ten house rules written on it. At the bottom, it read: **10. Break a rule, face a plague.**

They were trying to show everyone proof that nothing would happen.

"So, all night you have been trying to break a rule," Lonnie blurted. "Force everyone to see that all this is a sham."

That's exactly what I was doing...

Smoke was leaking down the stairwell, forcing them to continue moving. It felt as though they had been descending for ages.

She continued talking. "Roman is actually my stepbrother. His father married my wicked mother last year, unaware that she only wed him so that she could sacrifice them instead of us, if required.

Silas came to my school, told me who he was and that our family had been chosen this year. I didn't want to believe it, but he told me he had an idea that could benefit both of us. We planned out every detail. He designed the trials and told me how to beat them. I then discreetly told Roman everything, and that he would have to pretend to be clueless for the plan to work.

At the right time, Roman would know how to escape through the fireplace, and I would act surprised when I was chosen for a second ritual. Everyone would think Roman was dead, and then, he would come out after his time was up and show them that their trials failed and how nothing happened."

"That plan is mad, Amara!" Lonnie pointed out. "You would have died in your trials if we didn't show up!"

"I know," she said. "The others must have been on to Silas, because my trials were completely different from what we had discussed. I was terrified, but I had to play along and keep stalling."

"You nearly died," Lonnie reiterated.

She stopped again, this time on a tiny landing to the side of the stairwell, revealing a wooden doorway cut into the concrete. "But I didn't." She smiled, putting her hand on his cheek, which made it grow warm. "Because you all decided to be brave."

"More like reckless." Lonnie blushed.

"I'm sorry I couldn't tell you all the plan, I didn't want them to find out."

Carter blurted, "So now that his timer is up, what is the *next* part of the plan?"

Lonnie looked at Amara, and they both grinned. All night they had each been pursuing their own agendas, but in this moment, they were finally on the same page.

Lonnie grabbed the door handle. "We are going to burn this place to the ground."

Chapter 26

The Battle of Troy

A Trojan horse.

In Homer's poem, *The Odyssey*, the Trojan horse was a large wooden statue given to the Trojans as a sign that the Greeks had surrendered and were returning home. Little did the Trojans know that this beautiful gift had a secret inside. Under the shroud of darkness, when everyone had gone to bed, dozens of soldiers emerged from the animal's chest. They laid waste to the city overnight, opening the front gate for their infantry to enter.

The Trojans didn't stand a chance.

Lonnie looked at Amara, who had a newfound shimmer in her eyes. He didn't see mystery anymore when he looked at her, but instead just utter amazement.

A Trojan horse.

That is what she had always been. She snuck into this city and presented herself as a gift, but in reality, she had been destroying it from the inside since the moment he met her.

The Trojan horse was overlooked.

The Trojan horse was given access to the city.

The Trojan horse held a secret.

Lonnie smiled once more at her and exited through the doorway.

The Trojan horse won the war.

Light blinded him from the other side of the door. Sunlight shone in through a large window.

We made it to morning.

The ground was uneasy under his feet, and it was then he realized that he was standing on a metal mezzanine. Around him were dozens of books that had been punched off the shelf they had just entered through. The metal flooring shook under the weight of their five bodies.

"This is the library?" Lonnie asked rather stupidly.

Say what you want about this family, but they really know how to make a secret passage.

The tiny staircase wrapped around the wall, leading to the ground. They shuffled down, gripping the railing. The books baked in the morning light, their exposed spines tearing apart. Amara walked past them, still clutching the grimoire tightly under her arm.

I guess they really only care about one book here.

Roman led them all out into the first-floor hallway, weaving their way back to the ballroom. The sunlight had overtaken every corner of the house, bleeding through it like a thick orange paint. The five of them exited the hall, reentering the now empty ballroom. All the guests must have taken the sunlight as their cue to finally leave. Lonnie could hear their cars driving off one by one outside the building.

Moving across the trashed dance floor, they passed by the large statue centerpiece. It towered over them: five mysterious faces, one ludicrous conjoined body.

Lonnie had grown so sick of seeing this thing, he just

wanted to smash it on the floor. As the others ran ahead, he stopped in front of it. In a fit of rage, he tried to tip it, but it was too heavy. Eventually giving up, he punched it instead, which hurt his hand but felt strangely therapeutic.

Just as he was about to catch up with the others, he noticed something at the base. Where the legs stood, there was a tiny gap in the center. It was a little pocket of space you would miss unless you were looking directly at it. A perfect place to make a book disappear.

"What are you doing?" Amara yelled back, noticing that he had stopped running beside them.

"Give me the book!" He reached his arm out for it.

"What, why?" she complained, though she still handed it to him.

Lonnie held the book over the gap, watching as the proportions fit perfectly. "No matter what happens. We can't let them have this book. Silas told us to take it."

"The house is coming down," Amara stated. "It'll burn."

"Good. It should. Lets just hope it's the only copy."

The gap was just wide enough for the book to slide inside. Lonnie turned it on its side and passed it through the legs, watching it fall down into the slit and disappear inside the statue.

Amara and him broke into a sprint now to catch up to the others. The mess of decorations and confetti that spread over the dance floor was just like he remembered last year. But maybe this time would be different. They had almost all made it to the foyer, then they would be home free, everyone still alive and somewhat well.

We can make it.

His illusion was shattered by a door opening adjacent to the entrance. Daphne and Sebastian emerged, followed by dozens of green cloaked figures, some of which had singe marks on their cowls.

No.

Daphne aimed her gun while Sebastian reached for something inside his satchel.

"Run!" Lonnie had just caught up to his friends, pulling at their hands for them to turn back.

Cloaked guests charged at them. They were primal. In their hands were various weapons—novelty things that they must have found from their venture from the top of the house to here. One had a mace, another a sword. Two held a large net, while a few carried small guns of their own. The Trojans were manning for their last stand.

Lonnie led them back toward the living room beside the dance floor, trying a sliding glass door to the back patio. He had gotten it half open when a bullet grazed his head, nicking his ear and shattering the glass. He covered his head and slipped through the door. Outside, there was a large pool and a guest house. Behind them was a tall forest that surrounded the manor on all sides.

"Go to the trees." Lonnie motioned. He beelined it for the forest, kicking up the flowers planted in his path. He looked over his shoulder to make sure the others were coming, happy to see that all five had successfully made it out of the house. Behind him, he caught quick glances of them bounding over roots and fallen branches. They split among the trees, the paths divulging and scattering them. Sticks cracked behind them, as feet marched in quick succession. Lonnie tried to peek back again without tripping, but all he saw was green. The forest green cloaks camouflaged against the foliage, creating an unsightly image of nature closing in around them. The footsteps spread wider, forming almost an arc.

Crunch. Crunch. Crunch.

Bullets whizzed by, planting themselves in the side of trees. Sweat drenched Lonnie's face as it became increasingly obvious that the *House rules* had gone completely out the window.

The leaves broke underneath his feet as Lonnie took breaths in heavy gulps. He could hear the swinging of a mace behind him. It made a *whooshing* sound, growing slowly closer. The foliage all looked the same and every tree was an exact mirror to the ones prior. He prayed again for the safety of darkness to camouflage him once more, feeling exposed in his white and black clothes against the vibrant flowers and leaves.

Where is everyone?

He looked for a sign that they were okay, but it never came. He was utterly alone.

How quickly these trials had become what it always was: a hunt. The prey tagged in fancy clothes were the game, while the hunters wore their uniforms and chased them down. But they couldn't hide behind stupid rules anymore or simulated trials. This was real.

If they want to kill me, they will have to do it themselves.

Lonnie kept running, his feet mismatched on the sloped hillside. He couldn't stop. He wouldn't, even though his lungs begged him to. Instead, he made big strides through the endless reign of the Catskills. The footsteps continued after him. He couldn't seem to shake them.

Whoosh.

Running rapids were crashing up ahead through the clearing; the roaring water suddenly drowning out the noises of the forest. A flock of birds flew past, startling him with their presence. He ducked, trying to swing around them, distracted.

Whiz.

He didn't hear it until it pierced the flesh of his leg. He hollered, muzzling his mouth with his hand, but it was too late. His voice bounced off the trees, alerting everyone to where he was.

A wooden arrow sliced across the thick of his calf, ripping through muscle and making each step excruciating. He hobbled a few feet, but the pain eventually made him crash to the ground. Lonnie clutched his leg in agony. A bush rustled behind him, revealing a cloaked figure hiding there. In their hand was a crossbow, and they were carefully reloading another arrow into the slot.

The person moved closer, closing the gap between them. They couldn't miss now if they tried.

"Why did you have to ruin everything?" a woman's voice whined from under the hood. "You couldn't have just minded your business like everyone else."

She moved past his leg, kicking it out of spite.

Lonnie winced. "Don't do this, please!" he begged. "Can't you see they are lying to you? We broke the rules and nothing happened. Because the trials aren't real."

"Shut up! You did this to yourself." She raised the crossbow to the cut of her mask, pointing it down to his head. "You're just another selfish brat."

"*I'm* selfish?" Lonnie saw red. Wrapping his hands around the wood shaft of the arrow, he snapped off the arrowhead. Then, with all the force he could muster, he plunged it into her shin, dropping her to the ground.

She yelped, clutching her leg.

Lonnie screamed as well, crawling up on top of her. He pulled the arrowhead out of her leg and drove it back down repeatedly against her chest. She screamed, shaking violently to swing him off. Her mask flung back, landing in the dirt beside her. He did not let up, continuing repeatedly like a primal energy had overtaken his body.

"You think I'm selfish, you sadistic piece of shit? What about you, huh? What about you makes you so much better than me?" He shook her. "Answer me!"

Drops of sweat and blood built on his face as he felt her body go rigid beneath him. He quieted from his rage, now seeing the woman's face, her eyes frozen open and staring up at the canopy.

Blink... please.

He hoped she would, but her eyes did not move again. He vaguely recognized her from the wager room. She was no one important, nobody that really caught his eye. And yet, she was still a person who got sucked into this world and let it twist her mind. He leaned over a log, vomiting onto the ground.

His second murder.

The blood was still warm on his hands, and he had nowhere clean to wipe it. He shuddered at the sight of it, trying to settle his nerves.

"Oh, my God," he cried out. "What did I just do?" He looked back at his leg, the blood pulsating around the shaft still lodged in there.

"Over here," someone shouted from the treeline.

They're coming.

There was no time to fix it. He grabbed a small branch from the ground and used it as a crutch. The water rapids caught his attention. As fast as he could hobble, he made his way over a little hillside and down through the more scattered trees.

Whoosh.

The water was deafening as he emerged into the clearing.

I'm a sitting duck out here.

Breaking the open plain in front of him was a rather large river. It was impossible to get to the other side of the forest without crossing it. He didn't have much time. He debated swimming over, but it was too wide. And he would never make it in his condition. He looked around, suddenly noticing a small pile of boulders hugging the side of the bank.

The water must be freezing.

The rustling continued from the brush behind him, growing closer by the second.

But what choice do I have?

Filling his lungs with air, he dove in. The rushing water stung his face, tugging at him, trying to take him downstream. He held onto the rocks, dunking his head under upon spotting the cloaked people emerging from the forest. His body convulsed from the cold, but he tried to hold still.

Through the whirling surface of the water, he could make out blurred shadows coming closer to the bank. Three green figures waddled near the edge.

Go... move on.

A minute passed, and his lungs were burning. Thoughts were losing themselves to the haze. The arrow shaft in his leg ripped and pulled from the water, tearing at his muscles and skin.

Just a little longer.

His hands were slipping from the rocky edge, so he braced himself tighter with his feet.

Just a little longer…

The yearning for air was growing too strong. He reached for the sky, pressing his palm against the water's surface. Through the blurred reflection, a new person stood over him. Their auburn hair was drenched and wrapped around their head. The girl stuck out a hand, touching his through the thin barrier.

Hannah?

The fingers intertwined with his and lifted him from beneath. He emerged, taking a hefty breath of air and planting himself in the dirt along the bank.

"Are you okay?" Someone stood over him.

He looked up to see a girl. She had pools of water running down her black dress and sleeves.

"Amara?"

"They just ran that way." She tried to pull him from the dirt. "So get up, before they come back—oh, my gosh!"

"Where are the others?"

"What happened to your leg?" she asked, dropping him back down.

"I'm fine." He winced as he flattened against the sand.

"You are not fine. Come here, we need to fix this before anyone else finds us." She curled up next to him, resting on her knees. "Sorry, this is all we've got." She ripped at the stitching of his sleeve, pulling it off. "Is this an arrow?"

"Yes." He winced.

"What happened to the tip?"

Lonnie didn't make eye contact, the memory making him woozy all over again.

"I don't. I—" He got quiet.

"Okay, it's pretty deep in there," she said, not pressing him.

"We should probably leave it in, but with the angle it's at, it's going to do more damage with every step."

She mumbled to herself, thoughts racing behind her eyes. "Okay, I'm going to take it out. Just hold very still." She snapped off the fletching and placed both hands on the remaining wooden shaft. "Sorry in advance."

She pulled it out in one swift movement, yet to Lonnie it felt anything but.

"Ah!" he screamed, blood gushing from the wound.

"Shh. Shh." She slapped her hand over his mouth, muffling his words. She took the sleeve and wrapped it around his thigh. "I need a rod or something to tourniquet it." She looked around, but then stopped as she noticed the arrow shaft between her fingers. "My God, let this horrible day end."

She tucked the stick into the cloth, wrapping it tightly and rotating the wood until Lonnie let out a squeal.

"Why do you all know how to do this?" he asked through gritted teeth, remembering Hannah cauterizing his arm in similar fashion at the last party. "Ow."

"Just hold on, it's almost done..." She squinted her eyes. "There."

The blood ceased flowing, clogging up like an old backed up pipe. She let out a sigh, wrapping the loose ends of the sleeve in to keep the stick from falling.

Lonnie lay flat again, muttering through clenched teeth. "I hate the summer."

She sat beside him, her knees curled up to her chin. "Do you know where anyone is?"

"I don't know. Scattered in the forest, I guess." Lonnie got off his back, steadying himself on his uninjured leg. "Your plan doesn't seem to be working, by the way."

"It's gone a bit off the rails, hasn't it?" She almost laughed, and then broke down, hiding her face.

Lonnie searched the ground for his walking stick, finding it sticking out of the water. He leaned down and grabbed it, using it to boost himself up. "Well, can we save it?"

He smiled at her, giving an empathetic grin. She sniffled and laughed a little. "I have one other idea. We need to make it back to the front yard of the house before all the guests drive off."

"Which way is the front yard?" A sudden realization hit him. He spun around in confusion. "Which way is the house?"

Foliage surrounded them on all sides for what must have been miles. He had been so focused on escaping that he'd completely forgotten about the possibility of getting lost.

"I think we go that way." Amara pointed in the distance where a spew of black smoke leaked from the trees, forming a beacon.

"Yeah, that would do it, I suppose."

Amara wrapped her arm around his back, taking the weight of his leg. They found their rhythm moving left to right, forming a three-legged machine.

We can do this.

His thought was interrupted by a gunshot ricocheting off the nearby rocks.

Jinxed it.

Chapter 27

The Sons of Sibil

"Don't move!" a shaky voice trilled from behind their backs.

Lonnie and Amara dove behind the boulders beside them, waiting for the next bullet to strike.

"Damn it," Lonnie grunted, as his injured leg hit the ground.

Amara peeked her head over the rock, catching a glimpse of their attacker.

"It's Sebastian," she mouthed.

"Come out from behind there," Mr. Sibil commanded. "Now."

"You don't have to do this—" Lonnie started.

"Stand up now!" he shrieked. His voice jumped an octave, seeming to startle even himself. The reserved and put together man from earlier in the night had been replaced by this frazzled and trigger-happy person. He shot another bullet at the rock, which bounced off.

"Listen to me!" Lonnie raised his voice. "These trials are over. Roman is alive, and Amara isn't going to sacrifice anyone. It is done."

Sebastian went silent, which made the two of them even more nervous.

"Please, these trials are hurting everyone," Amara added. "They already killed two of your sisters—"

"No! No. That wretched boy killed my sisters!" He shot another bullet at the rock, making Lonnie flinch.

"You killed your sisters!" Amara stated. "These rituals have clouded your judgment, but it is your fault. Can't you see that? Your family has killed so many other people's sisters and brothers and fathers and mothers. And all this time have you ever stopped and asked yourself why? Your father made this tradition over sixty years ago, and no one has ever questioned it or doubted it since. No one knows if these gods are even real, and yet you continue killing people in their name. For what, Sebastian?

"Your own family betrayed you. Silas has been plotting against you this entire time, that was the only reason he came back at all. And now he is dead, by *your* sister's bullet. Do you still think that you are upholding tradition here?"

Silence filled the air as Amara took a breath from her rant. Then Sebastian chuckled. "Silas was not a noble man. If you think that, then clearly you weren't told the full story."

Lonnie found Amara's hand resting beside him. He grabbed it, squeezing tightly.

"Did he tell you he ran away?" Sebastian hissed. "That the oldest child ran away and left all his siblings behind to fend for themselves? Well, not all the siblings. He promised to take me with him."

"What are you talking about?" Amara responded.

"I'm surprised he didn't tell you as he had no problem putting it all in his stupid books."

Lonnie was suddenly transported back to the feeling of the crisp binding of papers in his hand. He brushed around the corner of the broken string. The packaging torn at the edges, so angrily ripped. He pictured the family painting on the wall. The father. The mother. The children. The boys. Specifically, the tall young boy with the brown and white shirt. He pictured Amara pulling that same shirt out of that dusty old armoire.

It was his room we were in.

S.S.

Sebastian Sibil.

Lonnie leaned on the rock, trying to pull himself up. Amara tugged on his arm. "What are you doing?"

Lonnie ignored her, continuing his ascent and trying his best to ignore the pain shooting up his leg. "You are August and Porter. You two are the Princes of York?"

He could see him now standing a couple feet away. Mr. Sibil held a revolver between both hands, his two feet staggered in an odd form. Maybe this was the first time he'd ever shot a gun, or maybe he didn't really want to hit them at all.

"When you were kids," Lonnie added.

Mr. Sibil twitched, like a bad memory he had done so well to erase was seeding its way back into his head. Dirt had gathered on his arms and face, presumably from falling back somewhere in the brush.

Lonnie stood up taller, walking slowly around the rock.

"Yes," he muttered, still aiming the gun.

"All those stories he wrote... they were all true." Lonnie's reality shattered around him.

"Bits and pieces. Only... bits and pieces."

Lonnie played back what he had said earlier in the night. *They were gritty, and harsh, and real. Like... like when the younger brother gets taken by welfare services. The author didn't try to hide the ugly, he wanted to show it.*

"But he left you, didn't he?" Lonnie almost felt sympathetic. "And your father took you back to the house."

"He said he would come back and get me... get all of us... so I waited for years. But he never did. Then one day, I got that package in the mail. He had sent me a manuscript about me... about *us*. He had turned my life into a children's book. And that was the moment I knew he would never be coming back for me. He made a living off of my pain and suffering and then had the gall to say that we chose to stay in this house. To play these games, as if we had any way out."

Lonnie played more of the book back in his head, connecting fictional stories to real life events. The most important of which being something he had said to Amara.

"Well, in the story, the two boys' mother gets very sick and so they try to go out and get her medicine. But by the next morning, she dies."

"And your mother? What really happened to her?"

Mr. Sibil took a step forward, still aiming the gun. He looked so weary, the weight of it pushing down his hands.

"She volunteered." He looked at the sky.

"Volunteered?"

"One year, the guests said it wasn't fair. One of them yelled, 'Why does your family get to choose who must be sacrificed each year, while you give up nothing. The Gods have held no exceptions. There should be no one above the rules.'" He paused. "That's when another shouted, 'Send in one of your kids, you have so many.'" Sebastian sniffled, a single tear tracing down his muddy face. "She said, 'No, do not touch my children. I will go.' My brother tried to help her escape that night, but she wouldn't leave her kids. She had already made up her mind. She wanted to protect us."

Lonnie couldn't help but feel his own eyes glaze over at the pain in Sebastian's voice. Now when he looked at him, he didn't see a monster, but that small boy in that picture. A survivor of something he never asked to be a part of.

"I'm sorry that all of that happened to you. I really am. But you aren't that little boy anymore. Those people... your father, they are all gone. The only one causing other's torture now is you. Please put an end to this," Lonnie pleaded.

Mr. Sibil glared at him, briefly wiping the underside of his eye with the cuff of his sleeve.

"I'm sorry, too. But we are long past redemption." He aimed the gun.

"No!" Lonnie shouted, shielding himself with his hands.

Mr. Sibil lowered his finger on the trigger when a streak appeared from the edge of the treeline, drawing his eye. Lonnie saw the person over the ridge of his shoulder. A blurred dot, growing closer, its limbs swinging up and down. Without hesitation, Sebastian fired at the incoming target. Lonnie cupped his ears, stunned by how loud the gunshot cracked through the air. If the running blur had been hit by the first round, they didn't show any signs of stopping.

Sebastian aimed the gun again, ready to deliver the killing blow, but it was too late.

The person closed the gap, revealing his rosy cheeks and auburn hair.

"Carter, stop!" Lonnie pleaded.

"What!" Amara reacted. Her body remained hidden from behind the rock, but her shaken voice still managed to cut through the noise of the river. "Carter!" she pleaded.

Another gunshot split the air.

"No!" she screamed hysterically, jumping from her cover.

By the time she could see what was happening, Carter had tackled Sebastian, knocking the smoking gun from his grip. Lifting him by the legs, Carter raised him into the air before losing his grip and tossing him over the riverbank.

Thud.

Mr. Sibil fell onto the shallow rock bed, his head cracking on one of the large, jagged stones. His body went limp, the water from the rushing rapids tearing at him. The current wrapped around his skin and pulled him closer to the edge. First his hands slipped under, then his head, and then eventually his legs.

Breaking from his shock, Lonnie rushed over to help, but it was too late. Sebastian had drifted into the center of the river, rolling like a log as the breath sucked from his lungs, and the water consumed him whole.

The three shared a glance, unable to speak. Carter reached down and picked up the stone that had been soaked in Sebastian's blood, and without saying a word, he tossed it into the water, letting the evidence wash away.

Lonnie approached him, wrapping his arms around him. "You saved my life," he muttered.

"Someone had to," Carter replied cynically.

"I'm sorry for everything I said before."

"I know." Carter took deep, shuddering breaths as he stumbled back from Lonnie.

"Oh my gosh!" Amara squeaked.

Lonnie scanned the terrain for more cloaked people, only eventually spotting the splotch of red bursting from Carter's torso. The red was overtaking the white of his shirt, turning it pink.

"Carter, hey." Lonnie grabbed him by the arms. "Hey! Let me see."

"It's fine," Carter said, though his words were broken and choppy.

Lonnie ripped off Carter's shirt, revealing a sticky mess of red.

This is a lot of blood. Too much blood.

But he tried to stay strong. He had to be brave now.

I have to.

"Put pressure here, while I clean it out," Lonnie directed to Carter. He tried to rest him on the ground but found it impossible to bend his injured leg.

Amara ran up from behind the boulder, swooping in beside them. "Just stop, I can... I'll do it."

He obeyed, hobbling out of the way. Lonnie watched her set him by the river and inspect the wound. The blood dripped down his waist and lower back as she pressed her finger around the wound.

Carter hollered in pain.

"Sorry," Amara whispered.

He grew quiet after that, which made Lonnie more nervous than when he screamed. For as long as he had known him, he'd wanted Carter to stop talking, but now all he yearned for was a single word.

"The bullet went all the way through, but I have nothing clean to dress the wound," she said.

Lonnie looked around, but there was nothing usable, let alone sterile. "We can't stay here long. Surely everyone heard those gunshots. We have to make it back to the house."

"You should go without me," Carter mumbled weakly.

"No, we aren't going to leave you." Amara said. She stared at the smoke in the distance. "One of the guests surely called a fire engine by now. They will have a first-aid kit. They can help us."

"But that has to be at least a mile away," Lonnie pointed out.

Amara gritted her teeth, dragging Carter over to Lonnie. "Here, keep pressure on the entrance and exit wounds until I get back."

"Wait!" Lonnie called. "Don't go, I don't know what I am doing..."

But she was already gone, running into the forest and leaving the boys behind. Lonnie managed to lower himself to the ground, placing his hands around Carter's wounds just as Amara had done.

He looks so weak and small now. This should have been me, not him.

"Why the hell did you take a bullet for me?" Lonnie muttered, a vocal fry in his tone.

Carter wheezed, cracking a sarcastic smile. "I guess I wanted to be brave like you."

"I'm serious. Why would you do that?"

The humor suddenly disappeared from his face as he stared longingly at the river's current. "I thought you would have done the same for me."

Why does everyone think I'm brave?

Lonnie looked up, trying to hold back the dam of tears. "I... I am not brave, I'm just angry and so tired of losing people I care about. And I hate myself, because I don't know if I would have done the same for you. I've despised you all night and you didn't even do anything wrong. But when I look at you, all I can think of is Hannah and how I failed her. And now I see the way Jamie looks at you, and I realize I've lost him too. You should hate me, like he does—"

"Jamie doesn't hate you," Carter whispered.

"What?" Lonnie sniffled, leaning closer.

"He calls you his brother." Carter tilted his head, losing consciousness on the grass. "Earlier he said, 'Trust me, my brother will save us.'"

Why would Jamie lie? He can't promise that.

Carter's eyes shut, which made Lonnie panic. He tapped him repeatedly on the cheek, trying to wake him up.

"Hey, don't sleep. Come on, you're going to be fine, okay? Amara is going to be back any second, and then we will go find Jamie."

"Jamie..." He let out a light chuckle.

"Yes, Jamie! I can tell he is falling for you. I have gotten quite good at spotting the signs and just know you will be so lucky. To be loved by him is the most comforting thing in the world.

"But if you leave now, it will break his heart. And he can't have anything more happen to him. I won't let it. So, you are going to be okay." Lonnie scoured the forest line, dabbing a loose tear from his eye. "Amara!"

At least a minute had passed, and Amara was nowhere to be found. Carter grew more rigid in his arms. He was lighter now, just like his sister had been. Lonnie held Carter's face up, trying to get him to open his eyes.

"Just hold on a little longer, please."

Lonnie began to cry, hot tears dripping down his cheeks

and onto Carter's neck. He looked for Amara again, now fearing the worst.

What if they captured her? What if she was already dead?

He pressed his fingers to Carter's neck, feeling his pulse grow slower.

I have to get him to that first aid kit.

"Come on, Carter, we have to get up now." Lonnie dragged him to his feet, trying to support them both on his one working leg.

Eyeing the smoke in the distance, he took his first step toward it, nearly collapsing back to the ground.

"Hold on." Amara appeared from the nearby brush. "Let me help!"

She ran up beside them, handing a walking branch to Lonnie and taking over at supporting Carter. "What are you doing, you were supposed to wait."

"He was getting worse," Lonnie protested.

Amara pulled out some rather large heart-shaped leaves and pressed them against his wounds. "It's burdock. It's sometimes used for anti-inflammatory treatment, so it shouldn't be toxic to the wound. And... also, it's just the biggest leaf I could find."

"Why do you know that—"

"They have them in the greenhouse at school. I researched all the plants there," she said. "If we layer them, it should be enough to stop the bleeding until we get him to a medic."

Lonnie propped up his makeshift cane, feeling the weight finally drift from his foot to the palm of his hand. The smoke had darkened in the sky, spreading over the blue and turning it into a thick gray.

He nodded at Amara, planting the stick into the hillside. "We'd better get going then."

Chapter 28

Maybe We Could Be Heroes

The forest was a minefield.

Each step they took came with its own challenges; broken roots, gopher holes, and patches of moss. Lonnie had come to the realization that they were all utterly exhausted. So much so that one more fall might be enough to take him down for good.

Amara had found a reserve of energy, or maybe it was simply adrenaline. She carried Carter on her arm, adjusting herself with each step to keep the leaves from slipping off his back. Nobody spoke a word for fear that an enemy could pop out at any second. Cloaked figures passed every so often, their voices preceded by the clomping of dress shoes or flat wedges on the ground. During those stints, the three of them would notch themselves behind a nearby tree until the voice had drifted out below the birds and wind. Then, when the coast was clear, they would take off again.

Lonnie found it harder to spot the smoke as they ventured deeper into the forest, but he kept on pace, continuing forward in the direction he knew.

We have to be close.

He wondered if the fire had spread to the ballroom yet. Had the book been destroyed?

Speaking of that book...

What Sebastian had said made him question everything. If The Princes of York books were real this whole time, what else could be real? Or made up, for that matter?

Somewhere in the distance, Lonnie thought he could hear sirens. Maybe they were close, or maybe they were a mirage his mind had made up because it was the only distraction from the pain burning through his leg.

"Wait, wait." Amara lunged in front of him, dragging Carter under her arm.

He was so distracted, he hadn't even noticed the pack of cloaked people cross in front of them. Their shrouds matched the foliage, only differentiable by the white eye covers on their masks. They spread out as more came from the rear, forming some kind of chain, blocking them from returning to the house.

They are waiting for us to come back.

The three of them hid beneath some overextending leaves, crouching under and using the stalks of grass for cover. Lonnie took this sudden stop to again peer around for the bleached blonde of Roman's hair. He hadn't seen him or Jamie since they'd entered the forest.

I hope they are alright.

"Do you think Jamie and Roman are okay?" he whispered to Amara.

Her voice wavered. "I hope so."

The smell of smoke was stronger in this part of the woods. They must be close. Faint drips of sunlight spurred from between the trees just on the other side of the guards.

"They are blocking our only way out," Lonnie whispered.

Carter groaned, his voice like a low murmur. Amara held up the leaves, which were now soaked in blood.

"I think I can hear the fire trucks. They have to be right there," Lonnie said. "But there's no way we can get through unnoticed, especially not in this condition."

Amara looked at him, a wistful smile growing on her lips.

"What?" Lonnie asked, panic lifting his voice.

She grabbed the edges of his face, her hands cupping his cheeks and pulling him in. Her lips pressed against his own, sending volts of electricity in circuits around his heart. He didn't dare move, in case it was an accident or a lapse of judgment. All he knew was that he didn't want it to end. But sooner than he would have liked, she pulled away.

"Thanks for saving my life." She grabbed his hands and guided them to Carter's torso before standing to her feet.

"Wait, what are you doing?" Lonnie shook his head.

"The fire engines are right there. You can save him."

"No, don't do this please," Lonnie begged. "I don't even know what the new plan is."

"What do you mean?" She smiled. "We've had the same plan all night. Expose the truth and..."

Lonnie looked at the smoke in front of him. "Burn this place to the ground."

"Exactly." She smiled wider, this time with fear lingering in her eyes.

And just like that, she was off. She sprinted through the trees with incredible speed. Lonnie kept his head down, but he could hear the cloaked people shifting into formation.

"There she is!" one yelled.

"Get her," another bellowed.

A huddle of footsteps passed by, meanwhile Lonnie counted under his breath.

"Three... Two... One."

He jumped up from the ground, carrying Carter over his shoulder. Holding the walking stick with the tightest grip he could manage, they stutter-stepped forward. The pain returned to his leg, but he would just have to ignore it. Carter was silent now, but he continued walking, and that was enough for Lonnie to know he was still with him.

Just a little bit farther.

They pushed past the first clearing, hearing firemen talking and shouting from just off in the distance.

"We can make it," Lonnie recited to Carter and himself. "We can make it."

"Stop!" a deep manly voice cut into his chant. A cloaked figure emerged from the clearing, approaching him from behind.

Just ignore him.

"We can make it," he whispered. "We can make it."

The person came closer, breaking into a slight sprint to close the gap between them. "I said stop right there!"

Just ignore him. Keep moving forward.

The man grabbed him by the shoulder, his grip tight. Lonnie could hear the firemen now, just on the other side of the brush. He could see the light from the firetrucks. It was all so close.

He tried to ignore the man and continue forward, but his hand only weighed harder on Lonnie's arm.

"Turn around!" the cloaked figure ordered. "I will not ask you again."

Jamie was right, I can save them. I can save them all, I just need to cross the clearing.

"Turn around or else!" the guy spat.

"No!" Lonnie bellowed, his voice deep and definitive. He spun, swinging the walking stick in his hand so hard that it cracked on the man's temple. The man clutched his head and dropped to the dirt. Lonnie stared at him, watching as the blood leaked from his skull through the thin layering of his hood. Without missing a beat, he continued moving forward, dragging Carter on his arm.

And that makes three... When will this nightmare end?

Lonnie propped himself up with what remained of the walking stick. He looked back at the dead man on the ground, but no guilt came over him like he thought it would. Instead, he was just curious. Who was the man under this mask and what had brought him to this point? What brought any of the guests to this point?

He steadied his voice, returning his attention to the sirens in the distance. "Almost there."

He pushed Carter ahead, letting him slip past the final tree. As they emerged from the forest, they were met with screaming and panic. The remaining guests who had recently left the party were all standing in the front yard, wearing unbuttoned clothes and holding heels between their fingers. Some guests were spread out around the plaza, covered in emergency blankets, with soot on their faces.

Apparently, not everyone had left the house as I previously thought.

Ambulances and fire trucks were positioned across the lawn, while people's cars were pushed to the edge of the trees. A few police cruisers were there too, with officers situated around the perimeter, blocking the guests from trying to return inside for their purses and other miscellaneous items they had left behind.

Lonnie stared in awe at the fire, which had now begun flickering out of the front doors. The top of the building was entirely engulfed in flames, covering everything above the third floor in a wave of smoke and ash.

"My God!" one of the paramedics screamed. "I need a gurney over here."

She ran toward them, waving to her team. Lonnie had forgotten how bad they looked. Blood caked their skin.

"My friend needs help." It was all Lonnie could manage to say.

"You both need our help. Is this your blood?" She pointed at his face. Lonnie grabbed it, feeling the warm ooze stuck to his cheek.

Was it?

He pawed at his face in a panic, before remembering that kiss and Amara pressing her bloody hands to his cheeks.

"No, it's not mine. I... I need to go."

"Hey, no, we need to get you to a hospital." She grabbed his arm.

"No, I have to save my friends. They are in danger."

"Are they still in the building?" Her expression grew more stern.

"No, they have them in the forest. You have to send the police after them."

"Hey, the farther they are from the fire, the safer they'll be."

"Lady, you aren't listening to me. They are going to kill them." Lonnie pulled away and began hobbling toward the police tape.

"Wait!" she shouted. But by the time she called for reinforcements, Lonnie had slipped away, leaving Carter in her care.

He approached the first officer he saw perched along the tape.

"You can't go in there." The man held out a strong hand. The officer had salt and pepper hair and a thick black mustache.

"No..." Lonnie's voice now sounded so tired and raspy. "I need your help. My friends have been kidnapped."

"What are you talking about?" The officer leaned in, noticing the blood on Lonnie's face, body, and hands. "Son, are you okay? What happened to you? We need to get you to the ambulance."

Lonnie must have looked worse than he thought as some of the house guests were now pulling out their phones and recording him from behind the police line. He ignored them, focusing on the officer.

"No, please, sir! My friends and I were kidnapped by the owners of this house, and they still have them. They are going to kill them unless you help me now."

"Son, I think you hit your head. Let me help you get to the ambulance."

Lonnie began spewing out his words. "I swear I'm telling the truth. They are in the forest right now. The kidnappers are wearing green robes with masks and cowls. It is their ceremonial garb or something for when they perform their horrible rituals every year. They worship these gods. The Gods of Grandeur, they call them, that grant unlimited wealth if you sacrifice someone in a certain way, according to their ritual book. They are some kind of cult. Please, you have to believe me, I'm begging you!" Lonnie pointed at the trees.

The man stared at him, the cogs churning behind his eyes.

Lonnie gave him a pleading stare, hoping it might speed along the process.

"You're being serious," the officer finally said.

"Yes, I swear! Please just listen to me. You have to do something now, or they are going to get away with it again."

"Hey, hey, calm down." He rested a hand on Lonnie's shoulder. "It's okay, kid. It's okay. I... I believe you."

"Really?" Lonnie let out a sigh of relief. "Oh thank you. Thank you!"

The man reached for his radio and pulled it to his lips. "I'll call in backup. Just wait here with me, and you can tell them everything when they get here."

"What? No! We need to go out there now. My friends won't be alive by then."

"I'm sorry, there aren't enough of us here to manage the fire and send people on a hunt through the forest for green robed witches..."

Lonnie got in his face. "I knew it. You don't believe me. Of course you don't believe me. Why would you? It all sounds too crazy to be true..."

Those final words cut into Lonnie, stopping him in his tracks. He stepped away, staring at the burning house in front of him. A thought shadowed his mind. Pulling out his now cracked phone, he opened his recent photos. He stared at the drawing Silas had done of Ophelia and their mother. Beside them, he read the small words handwritten in Greek.

Μαμά.

Οφηλία.

He then scrolled to the picture of the grimoire with Greek wording covering the page and tiny English words written in blue ink beside it. He stared closer at the lettering, flipping now between the two photos.

Oh, my God.

He traced the Greek letters in both pictures, finding the same swoops and lines. Just like the annotations. Just like the drawing journal.

It's not just the English that's the same.

"It all sounds too crazy to be true..." he whispered.

All our research... and not a single article or story about these Gods.

His eyes grew wide as he turned to the forest.

I understand now.

"I'm so sorry, sir, but I have to go!" Before he could even process the idea, Lonnie snatched the gun from the police officer's holster and aimed it at him. The man raised his hands defensively as Lonnie slowly backed into the forest.

"Don't do this, son! Just put down the gun!" The officer followed him hesitantly but halted at the edge of the forest.

Seeing the gap grow between them, Lonnie put the gun in his pants and hobbled deeper into the forest.

"Stop!" The officer shouted. He turned on his radio, speaking into the receiver.

"We have a 10-32. A young man seen covered in blood has stolen my gun and escaped into the forest. Requesting backup at the large manor off Oliveria Road."

"This is such a bad idea. What are you doing?" Lonnie mumbled, shaking his head.

His gut told him to keep going. Pain was chewing at the edges, and at this point, all he could think about was that kiss on his lips and the courageous girl who'd given it to him.

I have to find her.

He ventured deeper past the pines until he stumbled upon a circular clearing. There in the center were Amara, Jamie, and Roman, all down on their knees, surrounded by Ms. Sibil and her entourage of green cloaked followers.

They are all still alive!

"Please, stop this!" Lonnie protested, feeling the gun jostle against his back.

They all turned to him, their whispers falling silent. Many followers still held the odd weapons that they had taken from the house. Those with crossbows, spears and other long-range weapons raised them, arms at the ready. Daphne Sibil held her hand, holding their fire.

"I told you to leave!" Amara yelled, but was immediately silenced by one of the guards.

"You should have listened to your friend," Daphne acknowledged.

"But you would have found me eventually, right?" Lonnie added. "In my dorm room or at home. Because you never will leave me alone. *Ever*. This needs to end here."

"I don't understand you kids. It's one day a year. Surely, you can set aside your petty beliefs for one day. Spend the other 364 helping the world for all I care, but why are you so hellbent on ruining something that benefits so many people?"

Lonnie stared in disbelief at the crowd. "Who does this benefit? Can you truly say that anything good has come from any of these trials? Have any of you ever actually gained anything from being here or had any sign that these Gods exist at all? Or do you just tell yourself it's all real, otherwise you killed all those people for nothing?

"Look at yourselves. You are standing in the middle of a

forest, wearing ridiculous outfits, and following a ritual blindly, and you never thought to question it at all?"

He took a breath, turning directly to Daphne. "Do you know why your brother turned on you all tonight, just like he did all those years ago?"

"Because he's a traitor, always has been. Bless my sweet, departed sister, but she was a fool for thinking he had any noble intentions when he asked to return to this family."

Lonnie took a step closer, moving his hand carefully over the grip of the gun behind his back.

"The only traitor in your family was your father. Because he was lying to you from the very beginning. There never were any Gods of Grandeur. He made it all up. The rituals, the rules, the sacrifice. Even the book!"

"Enough of this nonsense!" she hollered. "Kill him."

The people raised their weapons, but whispers had begun to grow among them.

"What are you waiting for?" she yelled.

"Your father saw talent in your brother, didn't he? He was always good at making up stories. And all those drawings he used to sketch in that journal were quite convincing. He saw an imagination that he could take advantage of. Something that he could use to finally give your family power and make others listen to him." Lonnie took out his phone and pointed the screen at her. On it was the picture of Silas's journal, with the design of the statue showing in the center. "He forced your brother to write the book and make up these Gods. Silas didn't want to, but it wasn't a choice, so he did. All this death and destruction placed on the shoulders of a child.

"Did you ever wonder why he had run away? Or why he was so against these trials?"

Ms. Sibil squirmed uneasily under her followers' stares. "Stop!" she shouted.

"You've been living in a fairytale that your dad built. And just because so many people believed it for so long doesn't mean that you have to any longer."

"Enough." She looked at the others surrounding her, seeing them lower their weapons. "If none of you traitors are going to do anything about this boy, then I'll do it myself."

She pulled her gun out from her purse, raising it and taking aim at his head. Lonnie was quick to counter her, pulling his own gun free. The cloaked people panicked. Weapons were raised into the air, and it became obvious that bloodshed was soon to follow.

Lonnie undid the safety and held out his gun, imitating something he'd seen once in a movie. Stepping past his friends on the ground, they scooted behind him and out of the line of fire. He gulped, trying to steady the gun, but it felt so awkward and unfamiliar in his hands.

What have I got myself into?

Lonnie wanted to call a ceasefire, but from the look in Daphne's eyes, it was only going to end one of two ways.

Him or her.

Mr. Blythorne's voice echoed again in his head, like an old recording.

They both steadied their guns, each waiting for the other to make a move. Daphne's hand inched closer to the trigger and Lonnie braced himself for whatever came next.

Him or her. Me or you.

"Stop!" a voice shouted from behind a large tree, cutting through the tension.

Silas Sibil emerged, a hand clutched over his chest. Black soot covering him from head to toe.

"Silas!" Daphne gasped. "You're... alive?"

But how?

"The boy is right. About everything!"

She shifted the gun toward him, taking an aggressive step forward. "I don't believe you. Either of you."

"It's true. All these years, I have lived in shame. Afraid to admit to you all the heinous thing father had me do. I didn't know what I was creating, I thought we were just making stories. But then he started using the books to get things. Money, power, followers. Then we all moved to America, and he did it all again. Convincing more people and getting more power, and by that point, who could I tell? Who would believe a child?"

"Why are you telling me this now?" Daphne hissed. "It's been decades."

He gave Lonnie a nod. "Because it's about time the truth came out. No one else should have to die."

"Well, you are too late! You act like I'm the villain when you are the one that left me behind. I simply did what any good daughter would do, and I listened to my father."

Mr. Sibil moved his hand, revealing a bullet hole in the front of his suit. Reaching into the interior pocket, he pulled out his childhood journal, which now had a bullet buried halfway into its pages. Daphne, along with everyone else, stared in shock at the sight.

The journal saved his life.

"He isn't around anymore. Father was a power-hungry man who used a child's stories to take advantage of weak people." He looked around, his eyes glazing over. "And in the end, his selfishness took our whole family from us. And I won't let it take you, too."

"I'm afraid it already has."

"Then let me help you. This time, I won't leave you behind." He reached out a hand.

She glared at him, her eyes darting from one side of his face to the other as her expression turned hazy. The gun shook in her hand, until finally she lowered it. She reached for his hand, but paused as an eerie creaking sound filled the air. In the distance, the house sputtered as a large crash slammed into the ground.

It's coming down.

A thick huff of smoke shot into the sky from the fresh pile of rubble.

"Look out!" Jamie yelled.

He pointed at the flames that had caught the wind and leapt into the nearby trees. The branches caught in seconds, the fire traveling down the trunk until sparking on the low ground brush. The fire danced around them, intertwining with the leaves and petals. In the ensuing chaos, Lonnie helped his friends up, urging them back slowly so as not to draw attention.

"Come on," he said.

But as they made it to the edge of the clearing, the fire caught up with them, overwhelming the forest and eating away at everything in sight. Within seconds, they were cut off.

"We're trapped." Roman backed away from the fire frantically.

The other guests spun around, looking for a way out of the clearing. Daphne took Silas's hand, appearing so dainty and afraid. It was almost hard to believe that she had just had a gun pointed at Lonnie's head.

The gun.

He raised his pistol, aiming once more at Daphne, though she was far too distracted by the flames to notice.

"Lonnie stop," Amara pleaded, trying to grab the gun from his hands. "She's not worth it. Don't let her change you. Not now."

He held the shot until eventually Daphne caught sight of it, freezing in place. Lonnie savored the shifting of power but eventually let the feeling fade. He turned to Amara and gave her a smug smile and then lowered the barrel down to the dirt.

"I won't let this House change me ever again." His hand slid down the trigger, followed by a sharp crack that split through the air.

Bang.

Chapter 29

It Started with a Spark

The gunshot barely had time to linger, before another sprang from the chamber.

Bang.

Bang.

Bang.

They continued, one after another until all that was left was the faint clicking of metal. But afterward, nobody screamed or cried out in pain. They all simply stared at him, as he continued holding the gun at the ground, letting the explosions of the bullets echo over the crinkling of logs and wood. The wind sizzled with the smell of gunpowder mixing with ash. It smelled like what he imagined hell was like, yet he couldn't help but have a smile on his face.

"What did you just do?" Jamie shouted.

Overhead, Lonnie heard the faint sound of metal blades appear. A police chopper floated above them, a muffled voice chanting from the speaker.

"Put down your weapons!"

Lonnie let the gun slip from his fingers, falling alongside all the casings in the singed grass. In a daze, the cloaked figures followed suit, dropping weapons of almost comedic variety onto the ground.

"Over here!" a man shouted from the forest.

Lonnie saw shadows approaching from behind the wall of fire, followed by a current of water drenching over him. A steady hose stream propelled through the trees, chipping off the edges of their bark and extinguishing the burning rubble. The smoke lowered, giving them a doorway to pass through. Firefighters waited for them on the other side, their yellow suits countering the green of the cloaked figures who had gathered around them.

"This way." The captain gestured, urging them through the opening. People did not hesitate, pushing past them and rushing back toward the safety of the courtyard. Amara and Jamie helped Lonnie up, leveraging his weight off his leg and onto their shoulders. They took careful steps as they ventured through the remaining span of forest.

I don't remember going this far.

Though maybe his adrenaline was just finally starting to wear off. They hobbled over scattered hoses and tangled roots, trying their best to not get knocked down by the surplus of firefighters that were traipsing into the forest.

"There." Jamie pointed with his chin.

Red and blue lights shone in front of them as they returned back to the front yard. More squad cars and fire trucks had appeared in his absence, filling up the driveway. The cops seemed on edge, staring at the people pouring out of the forest. They gestured for the party guests to back up behind them as they faced forward, each holding their hands anxiously over the strap of their holsters.

I know stealing the gun was stupid, but this reaction was overkill.

It wasn't just the officers, though. The remaining guests stared in horror as well, as they held up their phones to record. That's when Lonnie spotted the cloaked figures fanning out from the trees behind him, like cockroaches being snuffed out of the darkness.

In the forest, they were invisible, the colors of their cloaks blending into the wild. But out here, they were all anybody could see. The forest green clashed against the backdrop of the firetrucks and the smoke, really accentuating the insanity of their presence.

"Everyone put your hands up!" The police captain emerged from one of the cruisers, aiming his gun at those in cloaks.

His stern, authoritative face made Lonnie comply. The cloaked figures looked around, unsure what they should do, but when he repeated his order, they complied blindly. They raised their arms, the cuffs of their sleeves falling to reveal bits of their suits and dresses hidden underneath.

Silas and Daphne emerged last from the forest, already raising their hands. An uproar from the guests came as they tried to move over the police tape to get a better shot with the cameras on their phones.

"Hold them back," the police captain hollered to his deputies.

Let them record. Lonnie smiled. *I don't want them to miss a single second.*

The officer Lonnie had spoken to earlier looked baffled at the sight, but he eventually pulled himself together and stepped up to the Sibils, addressing them with authority. "Are you the hosts of this party?"

Mr. Sibil turned to Daphne, who gave him a reluctant nod. He looked content as he stepped forward, still clutching his bruised chest. "Yes, we are."

"You are both under arrest for the torture and kidnapping of multiple young adults under the guise of a religious sanctioned ritual. Please put your hands behind your back."

Two officers cuffed them, motioning them to the backseat of the cruiser as they read them their rights. They complied without any resistance. Maybe this felt like justice to them, or a way of atoning for everything they had done. Lonnie didn't know, and frankly, he didn't really care.

The police had all but rounded up the cloaked figures, forcing them into a tight-knit group where they had to remove their cowls and garbs. It was weird seeing them again as people, when for so long he couldn't think of them as anything but the beasts they acted like.

They now matched the bystanding guests, so much so that it would be so easy to slip into the crowd and pretend they were just as confused as the rest of them.

More gasps came from the spectators who continued to document every moment of this assembly. Lonnie smiled.

Yes. Let the world know. Let everyone know.

The flames consuming the house made a beautiful backdrop to the scene. Windows erupted with broken glass, letting smoke billow out of each nook and cranny. Lonnie had sieged the castle and slain the dragon. And the carnage was the most beautiful thing he had ever seen.

Firefighters continued to spray water over the roof, which only weighed down the burnt wood, sinking it deeper into the center of the building, until the whole thing eventually consumed itself. The foyer was visible from the top of the marble steps. Beams had dropped from the ceiling, decorating the tiles with loose chunks of wood and plaster.

Lonnie never wanted to leave. He could watch it all fall apart, floor by floor, until even the foundation sank down into the caves hidden below. But eventually, the paramedics grabbed him, lifting him onto a gurney and shuttling him back into their van. Several of them worked on his leg, this time holding him down so he was unable to flee. He reached for his friends, but they were dragged to another ambulance, each simultaneously treated for their various injuries.

Lonnie tried to ask what was happening, but they shoved an oxygen mask over his mouth, letting the cool air drift through his lungs. He'd forgotten how it felt to lay down. The soft material under his back and the ease to his uncoiling spine were heaven. With everything else slipping away, he realized how long it had been since he'd slept.

"We need to get him to the hospital." The paramedic's voices was muffled in his ears.

Lonnie couldn't fight the weight that was smothering him. Consciousness was a battle he didn't know if he had any strength left to fight.

"My friends," he managed to slur.

"They will meet you at the hospital," a nice paramedic assured him.

He had honest eyes, and that put Lonnie at ease. He released his grip on the gurney's edges and buried his palms under his legs. They cut him out of his shirt, leaving his chest bare and cold, and then wiped it clean, pushing aside the debris and dried blood.

"Who triaged your leg?"

"Amara," Lonnie said.

"She did an amazing job. She might have just saved it."

"She saved my life." He smiled, his words slurring.

The engine sputtered, vibrating the vehicle with a low purr. Lonnie's vision softened, the edges of the ambulance losing focus. The paramedics continued to work around him, but he remained fixated on the window on the back doors. As the ambulance pulled out of the parking lot and down through the gated bend, Blythorne Manor disappeared into the distance with the flames consuming it, and that wretched book along with it.

We burnt it to the ground.

It was the only thought he could relish as he allowed his eyes to close and let the nightmare wash away.

Chapter 30

Visiting Hours

Beep... Beep.

The jingle of machines was comforting. Like a medley of tunes that reminded him he was safe. The hospital sheets, however, felt like sandpaper against his skin, making him jostle back and forth in his half-dazed state. He knocked it to the floor, revealing the large cast plastered around his leg.

It's better than it looks.

At least that was what he told himself. It was all better than it looked.

Right?

Knock. Knock.

The door to his room rattled, and a doctor entered.

"Hello," she said. "How are we doing this morning?" She walked to the foot of his bed and pulled a clipboard from its sleeve.

"Fine, I guess?" he responded with a tinge of pain.

"Wonderful. Well, you will be happy to know that your surgery was very successful. Your leg is going to make a full recovery."

"Great," he mumbled, still in a daze as he examined his room.

He played with the medical tag wrapped around the narrow diameter of his wrist. He was so exposed in the simpleness of his gown. The air from the air conditioner rivaled the staleness around him, pushing cold air from one corner to the next. The room was so large, he couldn't help but wonder why he had been given it all to himself. Especially when he had a friend to share it with.

Unless he didn't make it.

The doctor must have read the stress on his face. She moved closer. "Don't worry. Your friend's surgery went very well, too."

"It did?" Peace filled him.

"Yes, quite an easy surgery, actually. He should count himself lucky to make it out with only a broken rib and some tissue scarring."

Lonnie almost cried at the news. "Can... can I see him?"

She smiled, her voice so sweet as she said, "Of course. I'll have the orderly bring you a wheelchair."

She went over to his arm, uncoiling the wires from his veins. The monitor beside him beeped frantically until she pressed a button, returning it to its simple hum. She then took one more peek at his chart and finally propped it back into its bib. Lonnie couldn't help smiling. She mirrored his smile and left, her faint voice muffled as she spoke to someone on the other side of the door.

He's alive.

The thought made him giddy.

They were all alive.

He waited for the sinking hole in his chest to remind him to be on guard, but maybe it would never come. He peered out the window at the hospital parking lot. People walked in the sunlight, pushing wheelchairs and gurneys between cars and ambulances. The sign for the hospital marked the entrance from the main street.

No more mysterious doctors or driving through sketchy shipping garages. A black van wasn't waiting to take him home, and it never would be again. He relished in his victory.

"It's over," he quietly whispered.

The words tasted like nectar on his lips. He wanted to kick his feet with glee, but tried to hold some semblance of decorum.

Knock. Knock.

The door slid open once more, followed by a wheelchair and a petite man in mustard-colored scrubs.

"I'll leave this for you here," he said, setting it along the corner of the bed. "Your friend is in room 2205, end of the hall."

"Thank you."

The orderly nodded and then propped the door open as far as it could go with the little stopper he materialized from somewhere along the floor. Lonnie waited impatiently for him to leave, and then immediately lifted himself onto the chair. Unlatching the blockers, he pushed the wheels and sped out the door. The hall was fuller than he expected. Doctors and patients were shifting between rooms and gurneys flooded the floor. Lonnie tucked himself by the front desk as a flock of nurses passed by.

Room 2201. The plaque displayed on the wall beside his bedroom door read proudly.

Only four doors away.

Sliding his fingers over the wheels, he put the chair in

motion. The pearl-colored vinyl squeaked beneath him, making tiny noises the faster he pedaled.

2202.

2203.

2204.

He counted the doors as he passed them. Each was unremarkable and forgotten by the time he reached the next.

There.

He pulled in front of a cracked door, the number **2205** engraved into the sign. From inside, he heard a symphony of voices stack over one another.

"Hey, I didn't say that!" Amara's laugh rang out of the room.

"Yes, you did," Carter followed.

Lonnie eased his way inside, letting his good foot ram the door open for his body to follow. As he entered, he saw Amara and Roman sitting on the bedside chairs at the far side of the room. And on the bed, Carter rested, his body spread out, his head barely visible atop the pile of pillows. But he was there, his eyes alert and watching as Lonnie unsuccessfully navigated his way through the door. The wheel of the chair caught on the door frame as the door tried to shut behind him, lodging it in place.

"You're here!" Amara cheered.

The others rejoiced as well, followed by laughter at Lonnie, who was stuck in the doorway.

"Forget this." He laughed.

He hopped up from his chair, leaning himself onto his good leg and the edge of the bed frame. Standing up tall, he could now see Carter clearly. He had on a gown, but through the side openings it was clear his torso had been tightly wrapped with gauze and bandages. Wires ran from his arms, pumping liquid from a baggie hanging above his head.

But he was okay.

"It's better than it looks," Carter clarified.

Lonnie smiled, resting a hand onto his shoulder.

"The MVP, it seems?" Lonnie chuckled.

Carter cracked a grin, rolling his eyes. "Well, I should hope so. I don't see everyone else going around catching bullets."

With the same arm, he reached up and patted Lonnie's hand. It was simple, and yet it held the weight of the world. Everyone else was sitting close by, their expressions all shifting between admiration and relief.

Amara sat closest to the bedside, her hand wrapped around Carter's. Lonnie locked eyes with her, sharing flirtatious glances back and forth. He was so distracted by her face; it took him way too long to realize that she had changed into a T-shirt and sweats. In fact, both her and Roman had. They were wearing a weird mixture of items from the hospital's gift shop and its lost and found. Amara wore a thin pink shirt with red block letters in the center that read:

Be a hero, save a life. Then, in tinier print, it read: ***Donate blood today!***

Lonnie tried not to laugh, but it wasn't like he wore much better. The wind drifted down his spine and onto his boxer briefs, as the back flaps of his gown rattled from the AC overhead. He gripped it closed with a fist, trying to appear as masculine as possible given the state of things.

Roman sat on the farthest end of the chairs, practically hidden by the shadows of the corner wall. He wore an oversized hospital hoodie, but even with that, his muscles were still visible beneath the surface. He gave Lonnie a slight glare, but then nodded gently. Stretching out his hand, he offered Lonnie an intense handshake that could only be followed by awkward chuckles.

Lonnie teetered on the edge of the bed, trying to hold himself off his leg. His eyes darted around the room, suddenly noticing something was off. "Where's Jamie?"

"I don't know. I think he's—" Amara started.

A clang came from outside the room, which forced all of them to twist their necks.

"What was that?" Carter asked, unable to sit up.

Muffled conversations came from just outside the door, at the nurse's station.

"Where is he?" a voice demanded.

More inaudible words were spoken before the door shot open. They all jumped in shock. Jamie shoved the wheelchair into the room, now standing freely in the doorway. He wore a horrid combination of a borrowed scrub top, sweats, and sliders on his feet. His eyes were bloodshot, and his face was redder than Lonnie had ever seen.

"Jamie?"

"Where's Carter?" he demanded.

Carter lifted his head from the pillows, waving his arm lightly. "I'm right here."

Jamie ran to the bedside, practically pushing Lonnie out of the way. He wrapped his arms around him, making Carter let out a painful grunt, but he didn't ask him to move.

"Oh, my God, I've been being interviewed by the cops for hours," Jamie rambled. "They wouldn't let me go... and then when they said you were shot, I thought you were dead. But you're okay..." He buried his head in his lap. "You're okay."

"Hey." Carter let go of Amara's hand and pressed it over

Jamie's face. "They said I'm going to be fine." He chuckled, then coughed from the pain. "You psycho."

Lonnie stood self-consciously on their side, pulling himself carefully from the edge of the bed and over to the chairs. Carter wiped a tear from Jamie's cheek. He tried to sit up, but his injury held him down, so rather, he grabbed Jamie's scrub top and pulled him in. Their lips pressed gently against one another, making them both blush. Jamie ran his hand through Carter's hair, letting the strands tangle between his fingers.

Lonnie swayed in his chair, trying to look past Roman and catch a glimpse of Amara sitting beside him. Their glances met in passing, making his skin tingle.

If this is a dream, I don't want to wake up.

Knock. Knock.

The nurse was swift to enter, her mouth already moving, as though rehearsing what she was going to say.

"The police want to speak with Leonard Grambell. Is he in the room?"

Everyone looked at Lonnie, which made him squirm. He raised his hand in response. "Yes, that's me."

"Please follow me outside."

His smile dropped as he lifted himself from the chair. He grabbed one of the blankets from the edge of the bed and wrapped it around his open gown flap as he sank into the wheelchair. The nurse turned him around, pulling him backward through the door. The gap between him and his friends grew again, but he tried to remind himself that it wasn't forever. It was temporary. It had to be.

She wheeled him down the hall, turning the corner to find a pair of police officers standing outside an empty conference room.

"Are you Leonard?" One of them motioned at him.

"Yes?"

"We just have a few questions to discuss with you. Is now a good time?"

Lonnie turned to the nurse as though she might have words of wisdom, but she was already slipping away, leaving him abandoned in the center of the waiting area.

"I suppose so..."

"Great, after you, then."

Lonnie wheeled the chair into the meeting room, aligning himself at the far end of the table. A portable camera had been set up on the counter, along with a few tabletop microphones. Lonnie leaned into one, poking it with his finger.

"So, what do you want to know?" he asked.

"We've already got a pretty well-painted picture from the eyewitnesses on the scene and your friends' testimonials. But honestly, we want to know what it was like for you."

"Which part?" Lonnie scoffed.

The second officer leaned into their mic, his voice smooth and tender. "All of it."

"Really?"

The man stood up, approaching the camera propped up in the center of the table. He clicked the side, displaying a red dot on the top of the model. The officer smiled and returned to his seat. "In your own time."

Lonnie tried to find his voice, but suddenly found it hard to form words. The men stared at him, but it wasn't harsh or threatening. They had kind eyes. Lonnie fiddled with the quilting of his blanket, taking the edges in his hands.

He waited for them to grow impatient, but they never

spoke or checked the time. They just sat and waited, occasionally writing down notes on their clipboard.

"I want to say..." Lonnie wrapped himself tighter in the blanket.

They both looked up, pushing their chairs closer to the table as though he was whispering a secret.

"That it all started when I met my ex-girlfriend Hannah, or when my brother saved my life. But that would be a lie. Because the truth is, it didn't start then. It started with a story. One created between a boy and his dad."

Chapter 31

The People We Become at Funerals

One year later.

Lonnie put his nose to the wind, letting it bathe him in the smells of summer.

We're close.

The sun nipped at his arms hanging from the car window, but it was too enjoyable to pull them away.

"How far?" he asked.

"Maps says two and a half miles," Jamie read from his phone. He held the wheel tightly, locking his shoulders in a rigid position.

Is he nervous?

Lonnie laughed, hitting him on the shoulder. "Relax. I thought being stressed out was my thing."

"Shut up." Jamie slapped him back. "Someone here has to be. Cause this is crazy."

"I think it's perfect."

Lonnie reached into his pocket and pulled out a white envelope. The middle folded down the line, and the flap barely had any hold to the adhesive. He pressed it to his chest.

Pine needles drifted into the car as they swerved around the narrow bends.

"Roll up your window," Jamie said.

"Stop," Lonnie replied and laughed. "I like it."

The smell grew stronger the deeper they got into the forest. Everything was saturated with nature and wet wood.

It must have rained.

He hoped that wouldn't deter them from coming.

Mud kicked up under the wheels, splashing the side of Jamie's Lexus. He tried to steady the car, briefly slowing down to check his phone for directions. "Half of these roads aren't even on here. I'm just driving in gray!"

Out the windshield, Lonnie caught sight of an old playground. In the center stood a few play structures, including swings, a fort, and one old metal slide. Lonnie smiled fondly. "It's left up here. I remember."

Jamie whipped it around the dirt path until a light bumping came from beneath the wheels. A cobblestone road was laid out ahead, guiding them through a tunnel of old trees. Most of the branches had been sawed off, letting sunlight drip in through the canopy. They were so welcoming, parting the way as their car bounded past until stopping at an iron gate.

"The code is 5742," Lonnie recited.

Jamie let out a sigh and rolled down his window. He punched the numbers into the box and waited for it to ding. Lonnie counted quietly to himself.

Five...four...three...two...one.

The gate finished opening, and they slid through, not stopping again until their car nestled beside a large ceramic fountain.

"We're here." Jamie pulled the car into park, rolling up both of their windows.

Lonnie flinched as it snapped shut but did not take his eyes off the mansion.

I can't believe I'm back here.

Jittery, Jamie stopped the car and flung himself out the driver's door. He walked around to the trunk and pulled out a duffel bag before knocking on the passenger window. "Hey, I think they are here already."

He pointed to the cars resting beside theirs in the front yard.

"Okay, I'll just be a second." Lonnie tucked the envelope back into his pocket and took a big breath.

Here we go.

Stepping out of the car, he joined Jamie as they bounded up the stone steps. Jamie tried not to walk ahead, but it was obvious he could not hold in his energy. He sank his hands into the linings of his red shorts, ever so often messing with the top button of his white short-sleeve shirt.

They reached the top step and stared at the gargantuan house. It seemed small now after everything. Lonnie knocked on the French doors, not so subtly peering through the glass panels at the marble floors.

Feet clacked along the tile until stopping on the other side of the glass. Lonnie shuffled back just in time as the door swung open.

"Hello, boys!" a woman with brunette hair and a simple yellow sundress cheered. Her thick perfume expelled from the house, but Lonnie now found it somewhat amusing. He stepped forward and let her wrap her arms around him.

"Hi, Mom," he responded contentedly, patting her lightly on the back.

Jamie stepped forward, uncomfortably rubbing the back of his head. "Hi, Monica... er, I mean Mrs. Grambell."

"Please come in." She leaned back and grabbed them both by the wrist, pulling them through the entrance. "Your friends are waiting for you out back."

Lonnie listened to the floors scuff beneath his tennis shoes as he stepped deeper into the foyer of his childhood home.

I really can't believe I'm back here.

He looked at his mother, her face now resembling how he remembered her as a child. The Botox and fillers had been removed, revealing more emotion hidden in every wrinkle. Her skin was lightly burnt from the sun, and her gray hairs had been allowed to grow atop her head.

He grinned at her, and this time there was no pretending. It was genuine.

He thought about all the times she had called him and sent him letters this year. All the times she had asked for forgiveness and invited him to come visit. He'd ignored her for so long, but then a realization finally clicked.

I have to stop being so angry at all the things I've lost and start enjoying what I still have left.

Also, the fact that she finally took ownership of her actions without blaming his father or the trials helped the decision as well. So now, here they were, a small broken family again, like Lonnie had wanted all his life.

"Dang," Jamie blurted. "This is beautiful."

He passed under the diamond chandelier and traipsed his way past the banister staircase. Maroon-colored walls surrounded him, which made Lonnie's heart warm. Above him, he found a painting hanging from the wall. It was a simple picture at the park of him as a toddler alongside a teenage version of his brother. Ben held Lonnie on his shoulders, his arms stretched out into the sky.

When did we take this?

Lonnie had never seen it before. He reached out his hand to where Ben's smile was and then carried the hand to his brother's chest.

It's perfect.

Lonnie aimlessly followed Jamie to the back of the house, briefly catching Hilda, the housekeeper, dusting a bookshelf in the next room. He looked at her warmly, and she grinned back. The folds of her face lapped over each other, forming a medley of beautiful shapes.

"Come on," Jamie said. He held the door propped open long enough for Lonnie to catch up. They both strolled into the yard in tandem, where a figure was resting upon the lawn furniture.

Lonnie coughed. "I know we are so late..."

Amara jumped from the chair, staring in astonishment. "It's about time!" she said.

She ran up to him.

"I'm sorry, we overslept," Lonnie apologized. "And then Jamie got—"

But Amara didn't give him enough time to finish. She pulled him in, wrapping her arms around his neck. Instinctually, he grabbed her waist, drawing her lips to his own. She smelled like rose petals, which normally he hated, but on her, he just wanted to ingrain the smell into his skin. Her hair was down, draped along her back, and her blue blouse sagged so perfectly on her shoulders, revealing the edge of her collarbone.

"You're right on time." She smirked.

Jamie strolled past them, looking rather confused at the second empty chair.

"Are you looking for me?" Carter appeared behind them, carrying a pitcher of lemonade and some cups in his hands. He wore a long linen button-up with blue and white stripes and a pair of khaki pants.

"Maybe." Jamie smiled.

Carter set down the pitcher and glasses on the patio table and crossed his arms. "Maybe?"

"Definitely," Jamie corrected, grabbing him by the hips.

Jamie wrapped his arms as tightly as he could around Carter's back and lifted him into the air.

"Woah!" Carter laughed, trying to untangle his arms, which were trapped between the center of their chests. "How do you have so much energy after that drive?"

"I don't know, I guess I was excited." Jamie lowered him.

Carter smiled and took the opportunity to raise his arms. Setting his hands on Jamie's cheekbones, he held him in place long enough to kiss him. "I missed you," he whispered.

Lonnie wrapped his arm over Amara's shoulders and walked her closer to the other couple. "Are you guys ready for this?"

"Yes." Amara leaned into Lonnie.

Carter pulled a white envelope from his pocket. "Yes."

"Alright then," Lonnie said.

He let go of Amara and made his trek into the Catskill forest surrounding the backyard. The others kept pace, watching as civilization faded farther into the distance.

After a few minutes of walking, they finally came up on a small pond hidden between the trees. Lonnie nearly broke down at the sight of it. Images of his brother and him swimming flooded his mind.

"We are here. Jamie?"

Jamie pulled up the duffel bag and tossed it on the dirt. Lonnie bent down and unzipped it, revealing a pile of shovels. Handing one to each of them, they dug into the ground. Carter and Amara made one hole, and Jamie and Lonnie did the other, until they each were a couple of feet deep.

"They're perfect," Amara said.

"You ready?" Lonnie asked, turning to Carter.

Carter was the first to pull out his envelope. He held it so carefully between both his hands, as if the wind might snatch it from him if he even gave up an inch. He unfolded the top, revealing a photograph inside. Once it was safely secure in his hand, he crumbled up the letter and shoved it into his pocket.

He flipped the photo, revealing Hannah standing behind the podium in her cap and gown.

"Is that from our graduation?" Jamie asked.

"Yeah." Carter shrugged his shoulders. "I know I wasn't there, but it was one of the last pictures I had of her. And she just looked so perfect."

Carter smiled at the photograph of his sister. Kneeling down, he rested it inside the little grave.

"It's a great picture," Amara choked. She rested her hand on Carter's shoulder.

"Hannah was everything," Carter stated. "She was heroic and smart and just... just a fearless girl who lived in a world that she knew she should have been afraid of. But that wasn't her style. No... she was the bravest person I know, and I wouldn't be standing here today if it wasn't for her. Thank you for fighting for me, but it shouldn't have been your battle to fight. We were just kids. We should have just gotten to be kids..."

Carter kissed his fingers and laid them gently against the dirt. "I love you sis. I hope you knew that."

Carter rubbed his eyes, stepping back. He leaned into Jamie, who squeezed the edge of his shoulder.

Amara stepped forward next, resting her palm on the dirt. "Hannah was my light in a hellish place, and honestly, I don't know where she got all that positivity from, because it surely wasn't from hanging out with the two of us..." She let out an awkward snort before sitting beside the grave. "But in all honesty, I miss my girl. And I hate that it took losing her to remind me of who I was and how numb I had become.

"Oh, sweetheart. Wherever you are, I hope you know we kicked their asses for you. And that nobody else will ever have to go through what we went through, ever again."

Jamie stepped forward.

"You sacrificed yourself for me when you didn't have to." Jamie scratched his neck. "I won't ever forget that. And I promise to take care of him. I'll make you proud."

Carter hugged him, burrowing his head into his shoulder.

Lonnie sat beside her grave, taking his own envelope from his pocket. He held it tightly in his hand. "You weren't supposed to end up with me. I know that was never your plan. But I'm so glad you did. You pulled me from an edge I didn't even know I was standing on. And maybe we didn't get the happy ending we wanted, but you changed my life. Or at least you reminded me I had one to live."

"Lonnie," Jamie blurted.

"What?" He wiped his eyes.

Jamie pointed to the trees, where a shadow was lurking.

"Mom?"

Lonnie's mother pulled herself from the shadows. "I'm sorry, I'll go. I just wanted to... I don't know. I apologize."

She began to turn away, but Lonnie stopped her. He revealed the envelope, handing it to her.

"Would you like to open it?"

She beamed. "What is it?"

"Just open it." He extended his arm for her to grab it.

She left the shadows of her hiding place, finding her way out into the sun. Taking the envelope, she unfolded it, revealing another picture inside.

"Oh, my gosh," she said as she teared up.

She grabbed Lonnie and pulled him into a hug. He felt his body stiffen, but to his surprise, it eased. He sank into her arms. "Thank you."

"Would you like to say some words?" Lonnie asked.

"Can I?" she sobbed as she fanned out the picture for everyone to see. It was Ben sitting in front of a bunk bed. His dorm room was decorated so boyishly in the background.

"Did you know I took this picture? It was the day we dropped your brother off at college."

She stared at the clouds, as though they were a projector replaying a memory. "Oh, my gosh, he was so excited. He couldn't wait to get rid of us. But I insisted that we stay the whole day and help him set up his room, which he was not happy about. Well, I guess he was happy that you were there to help him. My gosh, he loved you so much.

"My boys... I took this picture right before we went home. But if I'd known what was going to happen, I would have never left his side. Not for a second. My little baby. I should have run away with both of you when I had the chance, I'm so sorry."

She sank to the dirt and placed the photograph into the grave ever so gently. She reached for Lonnie's hand, and he took it, holding back his own tears.

"I hope you can forgive me someday, sweetheart. But I know what I did. I'll always know what I did."

Lonnie helped her up, now realizing it was his own turn to speak. Approaching his brother's grave, he felt himself transported back to the graveyard all those years ago. This time, though, he didn't feel so small and alone. On the contrary, when he thought of his brother now, a warmth overtook him, bathing his body in bliss.

"Ben had so much love to give. When he died, I was actually afraid that the world wouldn't be able to take it. The loss of it all. For all those years, I couldn't for the life of me figure out where it all went. It couldn't all just have disappeared, yet I could feel it missing. Like a hole in my chest. But now, seeing you all here... I understand. We have to love everyone we have with everything we've got. We can't let it just disappear again. We can't stop moving with them."

He squeezed his mother's hand, letting the tears pour down his face. "They are the best parts of us. And now we have to be the best parts of them." Lonnie dug into the duffel bag and pulled out a pile of red petals.

"Are those roses?" his mother asked.

He smiled and put some of them in each of their hands.

"No, they are red tulips. I know it's customary for roses but—"

"It's perfect," she cried.

Amara leaned forward. "But why tulips?"

He beamed, "Cause tulips symbolize unconditional love. And because I remembered they both liked them."

"I love it," Carter exclaimed.

Everyone bent down and took turns dropping them into the shallow graves. Then grabbing dirt by the handful, they slowly filled the holes back up, until they were practically invisible.

Goodbye Ben.

"The sun is setting," Jamie calmly noted.

The others glanced at the horizon, realizing that the day had slipped away from them.

"Would you all like to stay the night? We have more than enough room," Lonnie's mother offered.

Amara squeezed her shoulder. "Thank you, that would be lovely."

They all started back to the house, with Lonnie bringing up the rear.

He turned back to face the graves one more time, as a swift breeze ran through the forest, blowing the leaves into the air. Lonnie took a deep breath, picturing his brother, as he let the air pass through him.

It was funny, but under the scent of pine and earth, he could have sworn he still smelled the burning timber of that manor lingering in these woods.

He laughed to himself at his imagination. But that's all it was.

Lonnie felt something touch his hand. He looked over to see Amara standing beside him.

"Are you okay?" she asked.

He stared at her, wrapping his fingers around hers. "Couldn't be better."

Because at the end of the day... it was only a house.

Acknowledgments

First off, I want to say thank you to all the fans that read the first book. It is because of dedicated readers like you that we are here today with the sequel. I am so appreciative of all the support and love this series has received online and for those of you that have left reviews and shared it with friends.

To my editor, Mary: Amazing job as always! You always know exactly what to say to boost my spirits, while still finding ways to guide my writing in the direction it needs to go.

To my proof editor, Chelsea: You joined at the final stretch of this book journey, immediately jumping in with thought-provoking notes and comments that elevated the story to a new level.

To my old roommate, Julia: Thank you for being my fencing consultant for all my written fights and swordplay. Without you, I would never have done my character's story justice.

To my friends, Hannah and Jessica: Forever grateful to you both for letting me talk your ears off about this book. It has been such a stressful writing year and I can't even put into words how much our talks and rants helped me through these edits and publication.

To my beta readers: Thanks for trudging through the trenches of my earlier drafts and paving the way so others could enjoy the final product today.

Finally, to my parents: Thank you for continuing to support my author journey. I don't think any of us expected me to be going down this path, but here we are. So, let's see where it leads.